THE

Meet-Cute

PROJECT

RHIANNON RICHARDSON

SIMON & SCHUSTER BFYR

NEW YORK   LONDON   TORONTO   SYDNEY   NEW DELHI

An imprint of Simon & Schuster Children's Publishing Division
1230 Avenue of the Americas, New York, New York 10020

For information about special discounts for bulk purchases, please contact Simon & Schuster Special Sales at 1-866-506-1949 or business@simonandschuster.com.
The Simon & Schuster Speakers Bureau can bring authors to your live event. For more information or to book an event, contact the Simon & Schuster Speakers Bureau at 1-866-248-3049 or visit our website at www.simonspeakers.com.
Interior design by Hilary Zarycky
The text for this book was set in Sabon.
Manufactured in the United States of America
First Edition
2 4 6 8 10 9 7 5 3 1

Library of Congress Cataloging-in-Publication Data
Names: Richardson, Rhiannon, author.
Title: The meet-cute project / Rhiannon Richardson.
Description: First edition. | New York : Simon & Schuster Books for Young Readers, [2020] | Audience: Ages 12 up. | Audience: Grades 7–9. |
Summary: High school junior Mia, who hates romantic comedies, must endure the "meet-cute" encounters her best friends set up to help her find a date for her sister's wedding.
Identifiers: LCCN 2020011287 (print) | LCCN 2020011288 (ebook) | ISBN 9781534473522 (hardcover) | ISBN 9781534473546 (ebook)
Subjects: CYAC: Dating (Social customs)—Fiction. | Weddings—Fiction. | Sisters—Fiction. | Best friends—Fiction. | Friendships—Fiction. | African Americans—Fiction.
Classification: LCC PZ7.1.R53327 Mee 2020 (print) | LCC PZ7.1.R53327 (ebook) | DDC [Fic]—dc23
LC record available at https://lccn.loc.gov/2020011287
LC ebook record available at https://lccn.loc.gov/2020011288

For Brittany Davis,
because every regular day makes the great days greater

CHAPTER ONE

There's a difference between expecting something and wanting something. That's why I always close my eyes when I'm swimming. I close them right after I turn my head and take my last breath. I don't need to see where I'm going. I just know. This gives me an edge over the other swimmers, the ones who reach uncertainly, desperate for their hands to make contact. My opponents search for an ending that I have already found.

As soon as I touch the concrete side, I pop out of the water. My chest heaving, I hit the lap timer on my Apple Watch with a wrinkled fingertip. Not bad. But not great. I lift my goggles, breaking the tight suction around my eyes, and immediately get hit in the face with a tidal wave of overchlorinated pool water.

"Incoming!"

I rub away the water clouding my eyes and watch Harold in the lane next to mine close his final meters. A pale white pinball bumping off the lane dividers, he flings water up with his inefficient backstroke as if he were starring in his own aquatic ballet.

Harold and I met at the beginning of last summer. I got my driver's license and my sister's old car, and I didn't have to wait anymore for Mom or Dad to wake up to drive me to the community pool. Harold and I both came to swim laps when the pool opened first thing in the morning. We bonded when Harold complimented my backstroke and mentioned how he can't stand the younger people who come to the pool just to sit on the benches or float on noodles and talk instead of swim. I told him that I, too, noticed that most people around my age don't actually swim at the community pool, which is why I started coming early. I'm glad that Harold—even without goggles and with his questionable technique—takes swimming as seriously as I do. Now that school and swim team have started, I can only come on weekends. Still, we manage to make the most of it.

"I'm surprised you haven't cracked your head on the wall yet," I say, making both of us laugh.

"Well, I'm sharper than you think," Harold says, still laughing.

"You know you can borrow my goggles," I say for the second time today. I'm so conditioned to swimming in a straight line, it's like second nature to me. Harold, on the other hand, bounces around so much, I'm afraid he might bounce into me one of these days. I always look for his silver hair to figure out what direction he's going.

"I don't need those silly things," he insists.

"Would I be a good friend if I let you repeat whatever it

was that just happened?" I add, gesturing to the water still thrashing back into place.

"We're only friends on land," he says, tapping the side of his head to shake some water out of his ear. "In the water we're competitors."

"*Harold.*"

"Rematch?"

I raise my eyebrows, pretending to be surprised, even though we race almost every day. But I take the hint of competition—Harold's smack talk—as far as I can, and pretend that all of his misguided splashing is an opponent in a swim meet, coming up beside me. The hardest thing about summertime at the South Glenn Community Center is that there aren't meets. Up until a couple of weeks ago, Harold was my only taste of competition. Now he works to keep me on my toes so that I can still prepare for meets outside of swim practices.

"There and back," Harold says, eagerly pointing to the other end of the pool. "Breaststroke. On the count of three. One. Two—"

"Harold, just please wear my goggles. I—"

He sucks in a huge breath. "Three!"

I shake my head.

Even when people have to double up in lanes for laps, no one swims in Harold's lane. I watch his silver hair bobbing up out of the water with each stroke.

When he reaches the other end of the pool and starts swimming back, I reset my lap timer, pull my goggles down over my eyes, and streamline into the breaststroke.

Even after practicing all summer, doing the most to get ahead before swim season started, it's still my weakest stroke. I should probably start going to the gym to strengthen my legs. I slip under the surface and savor the feeling of the water pulling at every hair on my skin. I envision the wall ahead of me, and let the water muffle every sound. I don't think about my day, everything that will begin once I step out of the pool. I don't think about my upcoming math competition or the history paper I still have to outline. I just focus on the water. Every stroke releases another ounce of tension.

I pretend it's last year's championship meet.

Except this time I win.

I pass Harold making his way back down the lane, the water around him looking like a small-scale storm at sea, but I know I still have plenty of time. I focus on my form. Focus on pulling my body through the water, on my breathing.

I reach the end of the lane, tap the wall, and streamline into the next lap.

At the shallow end of the pool, there's a cloud of bubbles. I see a pair of legs beneath the water in Harold's lane, legs that lead to a daisy-print bikini bottom. Instead of kicking off into a stroke, the legs start running. I watch as Daisy Print shifts to the side and then back, and I realize she's trying to dodge Harold, who is blindly swimming right at her.

Her legs buckle, and both of them appear under the water. I suck in a deep breath and push off again. I watch them as I close the space between me and the end of my lane. Daisy Print's hair floats around her like white smoke. Harold struggles to get his footing on the slick tile. He grabs the woman's arm, making her slip again. I push myself to the end of the lane, gasping for air when I finally surface.

"Miss!" I hear Harold say. "Are you all right?"

"I'm fine," she tells him.

"See! I told you that you need goggles!" And to the lady I say, "Maybe you should go sit down?"

"Here," Harold says, springing to action. He lifts the lady out of the water with surprising strength and then hoists himself out too, and escorts her over to a bench.

I try not to focus on how this sixty-something-year-old woman looks amazing in her bikini and how sixty-something-year-old Harold just picked her up like it was nothing. "Are you okay, ma'am?"

"I'm fine, dear, thank you." She smiles at me, but holds out her hand to Harold. "I'm Gladys."

"Hello, Gladys. I'm sorry I bumped into you," Harold says, running his hands over his face to stop the water droplets from getting into his eyes.

"'Bumped' hardly describes what just happened," she says, but kindly, with a forgiving laugh.

"Mia's right. I should get myself a pair of goggles. If I had some, I would have won."

I roll my eyes. "Harold."

"I was in the lead."

"I was letting you win. Like always."

"Actually, I made it to the end of the lane before you, so technically I did beat you," Harold replies. To Gladys, he says, "Mia is a star swimmer. She's here almost every morning swimming with me."

"You're so . . . dedicated!"

I would take it as a compliment if it didn't hit my ears so weirdly.

"It's important to keep practicing," I explain. "If I swim throughout the year instead of only in season, I can always be improving rather than trying to get back to my season level."

Gladys nods absently but leaves her eyes fixed on Harold. I notice the way her hair glistens under the fluorescent lights.

"Please. No apologies necessary. And I'm glad you didn't have goggles on, or we wouldn't have bumped into each other."

My watch vibrates, and I glance down to see it's already seven. Usually Harold and I take a couple of minutes to chat after our last race, but with Gladys sitting between us, I figure I'd waste more time trying to get his attention. I'll just have to share this season's meet schedule with him tomorrow. Harold sits down on the bench next to Gladys with his back to me, and I take my cue to sneak off to the locker room, especially since the air-conditioning is already chilling the water droplets on my skin.

I quickly rinse off in the showers and let the water run through my hair. Once I'm dry, I keep my towel around my neck to catch the rivulets dripping from my bun. My stomach rumbles when I sit down to lace up my shoes. I'll definitely need a big breakfast after all those laps.

I take a moment to check my Sunday to-do list. Unlocked, my phone is bright with a string of missed calls and message notifications. The only person who would harass me this early in the morning is my sister, Samantha. I open our family group chat.

> **MOM:** Peach, can you pick up bagels?
> **SAM:** Mia, where are you?
> **SAM:** WEDDING EMERGENCY!!!

I stop scrolling to shove my towel and swimsuit into my gym bag.

> **DAD:** I would like a blueberry bagel.
> **SAM:** Mia, answer the phone.
> **MOM:** If you have time, there's some clothes at the dry cleaners.
> **DAD:** Make that a blueberry muffin ☺
> **SAM:** MIA, PICK UP THE PHONE.

Sam doesn't specify the emergency, which annoys me. The first couple of times she spammed about an "emergency," it was that the florist didn't have the specific-color tulip she requested for the wedding, or the event room at the bed-and-breakfast to host the reception wasn't big enough to fit all the guests, so her only option was the outdoor garden. Clearly not life-altering incidents that would require me to cut my swim practices short and rush home. So now Sam likes to keep it a secret until we are face-to-face and I have nowhere to hide.

MOM: There's no need for all caps.
SAM: It's an emergency.
SAM: Mia, come home ASAP.

I look up from my phone to watch where I'm going, and find Harold standing on the other side of the lobby.

"Hey." I walk over to him.

He doesn't notice me at first. He's focused on something behind me, but when I turn around to see what, there's nothing there.

"Harold?"

"Oh, Mia." He smiles, looking a little flustered. "Sorry. I didn't see you."

"Are you okay? You didn't hit your head too hard, did you?"

He laughs a little. "No, my head is just fine. Though, I think I will give those goggles a try."

"Harry, there you are," Gladys calls as she emerges from the locker room.

Harry? How do you go from nearly drowning a

woman to "Harry" in less than ten minutes?

She's wearing a pair of jeans and a light coat over an old *Rick and Morty* T-shirt. Her hair is soaking wet, dripping dark circles onto the fabric over her shoulders.

"Are you ready?" she asks Harold, flashing me a quick smile.

"Ready for what?"

"We're going to get coffee."

I didn't know Harold *got coffee*, let alone with random people he met five seconds ago. A few weeks after we met, I asked him if he had a family. We'd already had a routine discussion about Sam's wedding, and I was grateful that he didn't have a lot to say about it. Most people get excited and want to know every detail and talk about how lucky she is, but Harold said, *That's nice. I wish her the best with that.* And we moved on. So, when I extended the courtesy of asking about his family, he said that marriage was not in the cards for him. Romance just wasn't his *thing*.

My phone dings in my pocket, and I glance down to see a new text in the group chat.

SAM: Mia, this is important!

Right. The impending doom of Sam's *emergency*. The bagels. The dry cleaning. I leave Harold and Gladys huddled together in the lobby of the community center and bolt out to my car.

CHAPTER TWO

Sometimes I feel like Sam the Bride is more like Sam the Queen. All of her line items and lists are laws, and anyone who dares question her decisions will lose their head. At first she tried to delegate some responsibility to a wedding planner, but she quickly realized that instead of having to pass her demands through someone who didn't always remember the right color, or the right print tablecloth, or the right scented candles, she could just do most of the work herself and avoid paying someone to make mistakes. So, she became bride and planner combined, which I firmly believe should be added to the various dictionary definitions of the word *dictator*.

Her seating chart is like a map of her kingdom, and all the items on her color-coded lists are the supplies she needs to run it. They say every bride wants to feel like a princess on her wedding day, but Sam took it to the queen level when she decided to micromanage every. Single. Detail. At least the title fits her, because in exactly sixty-three days, my sister, Sam Hubbard, will marry into jam royalty and become Samantha Hubbard Davenport. Her prince is Geoffrey Davenport, the heir of the Davenport family jam business.

From the minute Geoffrey stepped through our front door with a basket full of jam, his glasses spotted with melting snow, and wearing a nervous smile, my whole family has been in love with him. It was Thanksgiving break of Sam's sophomore year in college. Geoffrey told us about his family's jam business and how every decision he made in school was to ensure its success, since he would one day inherit it. I was worried at first. It was clear he was inheriting a fortune. He'd been wearing a Burberry scarf when he'd come inside, and had a gold chain tucked into the collar of his Ralph Lauren sweater. But I watched the way Sam stared at him while he talked about the best season to grow crops for jam. I watched the way he rested his hand on top of hers on the table in between their plates, the way he always looked at her every few seconds even though she'd heard these things before and he was supposed to be telling us. When he offered to clean the dishes, Sam said she would help, and I watched incredulously as they walked into the kitchen together. It takes a lot to get Sam to do chores, let alone chores that involve cleaning up after other people.

They complement each other. To start, they're a vision; Sam with her long curly naps, brown-black eyes, and chestnut skin and Geoffrey with his barber fade, thick-rimmed glasses, and track-star body. Their kids are going to be beautiful, and they'll be brilliant. Geoffrey has a degree in organic chemistry, with a minor in commercial agriculture. Sam is the assistant manager at ArchiTech, a startup that makes simplified software for architects. She was always good with computers and started coding in high school. When she was a freshman in college, she took an architecture class as an elective, and for the rest of the semester it was all she could talk about, until my mom said, *Why don't you double major?*

They met in an agricultural architecture class. Sam was already plotting to do a community planning project for her senior thesis in which she would combine coding and architecture to create a greenhouse that could feed starving communities by relying on solar power. She needed to learn about the importance of air flow and temperature control for growing food in a structure designed specifically for that purpose. Geoffrey was taking the class so that he could learn to build better greenhouses to maintain crops through the winter. Since he already knew a lot about the agricultural side of things, Sam wanted to be his partner for every assignment. And, well, who would say no to Sam?

Sometimes I wish someone would. I wish Geoffrey would say, *No, there isn't a difference between baked or broiled salmon.* Or, *No, we don't have to fly in purple tulips for the wedding, when the florist has lavender already.* Or even, *No, I don't want you moving back into your parents' house to plan* our *wedding.* But he hasn't yet.

I guess that's true love.

I park in front of the house and take a deep breath before grabbing the box of bagels and draping Mom's dry cleaning over my arm, bracing myself for what's inside.

I listen outside the front door. Whenever there's a disaster, Sam is pacing around the house, shouting or crying. I crack the door open just a little to confirm that the house is in fact silent. I lock it as quietly as possible behind me and take my shoes off in the entryway before tiptoeing toward the kitchen, savoring the last bit of silence before the Sam-storm.

"I thought I smelled bagels." Brooke startles me. I figured she would've gone home this morning to, I don't know, live her *own* life. "She's in here," she shouts to wherever Sam is.

I turn around to see Brooke pulling a few mugs out of our cabinet. She sets them down next to Dad's Keurig and focuses on setting up a pitcher of coffee, before acknowledging me.

"Hello, mini-Sam," she says, patting me on the head. "And thanks for breakfast," she adds, peeking inside the box. Without asking, she takes out my apple-cinnamon bagel.

Before I can object, Sam glides into the room and wraps me in a hug.

"Did you get me a poppy seed?" she asks, though she's already looking.

"Of course. If I had known Brooke was still here, I would've gotten her a bagel too," I say, loud enough for her to hear, even though she's already refocused on the coffee.

"Oh no, Mia. Why didn't you say something?" Brooke asks through a mouthful of *my* apple-cinnamon bagel.

"You took her bagel?" Sam asks.

"I didn't know."

"It's fine," I say, feeling satisfied by the blood rushing to Brooke's cheeks.

"Here, have some of Mom's," Sam says, and opens the box.

"Where is she?" I ask, reluctantly taking out the smoked-salmon bagel.

"The garden."

I should've guessed. Since she retired, the community garden is Mom's favorite place.

We settle into a moment of silence, all of us chewing on bagels over the sound of the Keurig brewing coffee. The smell permeates the room, and I know I won't be able to resist.

"So, what's up?" I ask cautiously as I reach for my bear-shaped mug in the cabinet.

"Eating," Brooke says, no longer embarrassed.

"I mean, are you okay?" I ask Sam.

"Yeah," Sam says. "It was more of a minor emergency, and we figured it out anyways."

"What did you figure out? Your texts were cryptic."

Sam sighs before saying, "Kevin isn't coming to the wedding."

Kevin who? Sam stares at me, waiting for a reaction, so I try to remember who he is.

Kevin. *Kevin.* Kevin? . . .

"Geoffrey's college roommate?" I ask.

"You mean *your* groomsman? Your date to the wedding!"

His face flashes through my mind. I met him in passing when we were helping Sam move out of her dorm after graduation.

Kevin Krox—or "Krotch," as those who witnessed him drunkenly pee in one of the campus hallways liked to call him—was Geoffrey's roommate and track teammate and, after living in such close quarters for the most stressful years of their lives, best friend. Other than practices and occasional online gaming, the two barely have anything in common. But they were there for each other when Kevin became Kevin Krotch and when Geoffrey was working up the courage to ask Sam on a date.

"I'm surprised you're not as shocked as I am," Sam says before tossing another torn-off piece of bagel into her mouth.

"Why isn't Kevin coming to the wedding?"

"He got accepted to this literature program at Cambridge, and he starts in November. So, we're happy for him," she says unconvincingly. "But that leaves you without a date, which was a disaster—"

"At first," Brooke cuts in. "But then we found a workable solution."

When no one immediately offers it up, I feel nervous. Sam always drags out bad news. I ask, "What's the solution?"

"You can find your own date," Sam says, beaming.

"What?" I ask, figuring I didn't hear her correctly. I think what she means is, *You don't have to have a date.*

"*You* can find your own date. That way you'll be more comfortable with someone you know. You weren't excited about Kevin from the beginning, so look at this like a good thing. It's an opportunity for you to find someone perfect for you."

"Why can't I just go without a date?" I ask the—in my opinion—obvious question.

"No, Mia, that won't work."

"Why not?" I ask. This isn't the same as Sam asking me to run errands for her so she can sit at home and write in her little color-coded planner all day. This is asking me to go *far* out of my way to do something she and Geoffrey should figure out together.

Sam takes me by the shoulders and looks me dead in the eyes. It makes me uncomfortable, and she knows that. Nevertheless, I'm afraid she's about to shake me like I'm the one being crazy.

"You're not going to my wedding alone. All the photos will be uneven. It would look weird if you walk down the aisle alone and every other bridesmaid is paired up with someone."

"I don't see why I have to find my own date. Isn't there someone else you can use?"

"Well, Geoffrey bumped one of the other groomsmen up to be best man . . . but I guess there's one other option for your date. I just don't think Geoffrey is going to go for it so easily," Sam says, turning her attention back to her bagel.

"Who is it?" I don't know why she didn't just lead with this. Again, making a big deal out of nothing.

"Mia, I just think it would be better if you found someone yourself," she says through a chunk of bagel.

"Sam, I don't want to. I already have enough on my plate with swim practice and math team. We've been over this. I can't add one more thing right now, so if you have a solution, just use it."

"The backup groomsman is Geoffrey's brother," she tells me, picking the crust off her bagel.

My heart stops. "You can't be serious."

Geoffrey's brother, Jasper, is a twelve-year-old throbbing gland of testosterone whose Nintendo Switch is perpetually glued to his hand. At the engagement party he was dressed in a Fendi men's colorblock tracksuit and a pair of Nikes that hadn't been released yet. Whenever one of his relatives spoke to him, he didn't look up to respond. He just mumbled while staring at his precious Nintendo under the table. He is what I was glad Geoffrey turned out not to be: spoiled, brand obsessed, and governed by money. What's worse is that he kept kicking my feet under the table during dinner. I ate quickly so that I could get up and leave the room without it looking weird. It turns out he was trying to play *footsies*! How do I know this? How do I know this middle schooler was flirting with me? Because while his parents were grabbing their coats and Geoffrey and Sam were looking for the keys to their—at the time—new apartment, he mumbled, "Let me get your number."

I looked down at him, sure that I'd misheard whatever had just come out of his mouth.

"What?"

"Your number."

I stared at him, listening to the chime of his game as his little character ran into a bunch of coins.

"Why?"

"You're hot; I'm hot. Fate has brought us together."

"Fate? You mean the fact that we're literally becoming family?" I asked, feeling disgusted at the implied incest.

"It's not like we're related by blood." When he said that, he actually glanced up at me and flashed a smile. I can almost swear I saw a baby tooth.

I cringe at the memory.

I'm not walking down the aisle and posing in pictures with a twelve-year-old, especially not Jasper Davenport. What's worse than going to the wedding alone is going to the wedding with a preteen hitting on you the entire time over the low but eternally annoying sound of his Nintendo dinging every five seconds.

"Plus, isn't he the ring bearer?" I ask, figuring they can't pull him away to be a groomsman when he already has a job.

"Toby could do that instead." That is, Toby the goldendoodle, also known as the senior Mr. Davenport's favorite child.

"Fine," I decide. "I'll find someone."

"Thank you, Mia. I'm glad you're being an adult about this."

She starts to turn back to her bagel, but her comment holds me in place. "Have I not been an adult about other things?"

Without looking at me, she admits, "I just feel like you've been shirking your responsibilities when it comes to helping out with the wedding."

Of course, she would use the word "shirking."

"It's not my wedding," I say in my defense.

"You're right. You're not obligated to do anything. The reason friends and family help someone with a wedding is because they love them. So just do this for me. Do this one thing that I'm asking you to do for me, if it's so hard for you to take responsibility and want to do it for yourself."

I want to explode. I want to remind her of all the things I've done for her. All the errands. The favors. Lending her my twenty-dollar highlighters only for her to use them up and not replace them. Convincing the florist to not give up on her in the midst of her flower "emergency." Buying her facemasks after an all-nighter with her charts and dioramas and color-coded lists. I might not do the heavy lifting, but I certainly haven't sat around doing *nothing*.

But I know none of that is going to matter, because to her I'm the baby sister who only thinks of herself, when in reality she's the big sister who does just that.

"Do I smell a blueberry muffin?" Dad glides into the

kitchen, still wearing his pajamas and silk nightcap.

I back away from Sam and look over toward Dad. I don't want to fight in front of him, especially because I know Sam would just say I'm acting like a child and that Mom and Dad should be doing more to turn me into an adult—whatever the heck that's supposed to mean.

"How are you, Peach?" Dad asks as he pops his muffin into the microwave.

"Great," I mumble on my way out of the kitchen.

CHAPTER THREE

When I was seven, in science class we did a very basic lesson on the concept of dominant and recessive genes. We learned that the dominant ones express themselves and the recessive ones hide until they meet each other and show themselves. We had to go around to our family members and see who had what genes and then determine which ones we had. It turns out, I am all the recessive genes of my family. I have hazel eyes, have hitchhiker's thumb, and can roll my *R*s. My earlobes are detached and my left cheek has a dimple.

Sometime after I did this worksheet, Sam and I had a fight. Either I stole her bracelet or she ate my last Klondike bar. It was something stupid that we blew out of proportion. She was seventeen and I was seven at the time, so she was responsible for babysitting me after school, something both of us thought was stupid. Whenever we fought, I would find my way to the top of the stairs and I would scream down at her, since on the same level she was nearly two feet taller than me. Eventually we would drift away from what we were fighting about and simply start calling each other names or shouting random insults at each other.

At one point in this particular fight, she asked me if I knew what it meant that I had all the recessive genes. She told me that the dominant genes were stronger and that's why they showed up more often. She said the recessive genes were weak, that since I had all the weak genes in our family, that meant *I* was weak. Now I realize that we were just trying to hurt each other and that she didn't mean it. But back then I didn't know any better. For a long time I didn't know any better. She won that fight. I ran up to my room, closed the door, and just stared at myself in the mirror. I stared at all of my recessive traits and wondered if she was right.

I still sometimes think about it—when I'm sitting on the bleachers at school dances while my friends are on the floor either with dates or moving rhythmically with each other in a way that I just can't; when I mouth the words to songs in the car while my friends manage to always sing on key; and when my friend Abigail runs up to her boyfriend at the end of a swim meet and the first thing she does is kiss him.

As I struggle to run argan oil through my tight damp curls, I stare at my eyes and how they look odd against my dark chestnut-colored skin. I think about how gracefully Sam's hair falls, how she never gets pimples, how she never scratches her face in her sleep. I think about how Sam is getting ready to be married to the man of her dreams, and the biggest accomplishment of my life is being one of the best swimmers on a high school team.

My cousin Lucas would just tell me that the recessive

genes are the ones that wait until they've found a worthy host before they show themselves. He'd say that I am the only one in my family worthy of their expression, and for that I am unique. I am special. I try to hold on to that as I get flustered in the middle of my history homework. I try to refocus, and realize that in my annotations on the passage about the War of 1812, I wrote *Joey Delmar* and *Peyton Banks*. When I start writing a list of boys' names in the middle of my English essay, I push my laptop aside and pull out a blank piece of paper. James Palmer. Kyle Richards. Skylar Willoughby. I think of boys I've worked on projects with in class, boys from the clubs I've been in, and even a few of the single guys on swim team. I write the realistic ones in one column, the potential yeses in a middle column, and the far reaches in a third column. Then I go through the list and try to think of who I would actually want to spend an entire evening with, versus who would annoy me as much as Jasper would, and I highlight in different colors.

It isn't until my afternoon alarm goes off that I realize I've wasted my Sunday trying to find a potential date and haven't finished half the homework that's due tomorrow. I haven't even touched the math team practice problems to review before Thursday's competition. In my notepad I write a list of what I still have to do, and decide I'll just have to stay up after movie night to finish.

Every Sunday my friends and I have movie night. The third weekend of the month is always at my house, which means I get to choose what we watch. The new Ted Bundy documentary has been on my mind all week, so I set to work baking sugar cookies and icing them with the various murder weapons he used on his victims. The task helps distract me from Sam's quest.

"Should I be worried?" Mom asks when she looks over my shoulder. Before I answer, she snags a bloody knife and takes a bite.

"It's for movie night."

"And what movie has knives, nooses, saws, and fists? . . . Seems very dark," she says, scrunching up her eyebrows at my icing rendition of Ted Bundy's VW beetle.

"It's the Ted Bundy documentary," I tell her, reaching for the gray icing to finish the tires.

She moves around me and sets her gardening bag down on the other side of the island.

She asks "Don't you want to watch something fun?" above the sound of the water rushing over her soapy hands.

"This is fun. Getting inside the mind of a serial killer." I quickly make another knife cookie before setting the tray aside and cleaning up.

"It sounds creepy. Didn't you guys watch—what was it—*Serendipity* last weekend? Why don't you pick a movie like that?"

Mom peeks into the fridge and pulls out a bowl of green grapes and a bottle of water. She sits down across from me and starts picking the grapes off one by one and tossing them into her mouth.

Her hair is pulled back in a very messy tangled bun. A

few tendrils have fallen and stick to the sweaty sides of her face. There's even a little dirt still on her nose from the community garden, but as she takes a swig of water, I can tell she's not aware of it.

"*Serendipity* is a stupid fictional movie about two people who want the same ugly pair of gloves. A documentary, however, is grounded in reality, and a murder documentary is helpful by teaching us how to not end up like the victims," I explain. "If you know how to identify a predator, you can also know how to avoid them."

Mom shakes her head. "Mia, fictional movies aren't stupid. They help you take your mind *off* the serial killers and predators. They bring light into your life. You already have to be careful out in the real world, so why not escape sometimes?"

"I don't want to take my mind off reality," I challenge. "*Serendipity* is founded on something as ludicrous as people bumping hands in a department store. Give me a movie about real love, realistic romance, and *maybe* I'll think about it."

Mom opens her mouth to say something else, but thankfully the doorbell rings.

"That would be Grace," I say, wiping my hands on a towel before gladly leaving the kitchen.

Since she lives down the street, Grace usually comes over before Sloane and Abby. We usually "taste test" whatever I bake for movie night, and then she helps me put out blankets and cushions in the den.

Grace knows me better than anyone else, maybe even better than Sam and my parents. When I was younger, I used to go to Mom and ask her questions like why some of the boys pulled my plaits or why some girls would hog the swings. She would always have something to say about when Sam was my age, and it got old really fast. Even though Grace, Abby, Sloane, and I all met in second grade, Grace and I were in the same homeroom. Instead of talking to my mom about things, I started telling Grace because she was there more than my other friends. Plus, since she also got her flat twists tugged and sometimes had to choose the slide over the swing, our bond stuck and grew a little stronger. We're closer than I am with my other friends, literally and figuratively. Since she lives around the block, I can walk to her house whenever Sam is driving me crazy. Grace will come to my house any random night of the week to do homework and have an impromptu sleepover.

"So, what's the movie?" she asks as we each pick up an end of the coffee table.

We shuffle to the side to move it out of the center of the room. Then I reach for the comforter that we spread out on the floor to protect the carpet, and Grace starts grabbing the cushions off the couch.

"It's a surprise," I tell her for the third time.

"Okay, but the cookies make it really hard to guess. I feel like I'm shooting in the dark."

"Well, that's good, because if you guessed, then it wouldn't be a surprise."

We fall silent. I try to focus on spreading out the comforter, but my mind drifts back to the list I was working on. More names come to mind. A couple of guys from gym class, athletic types. Maybe I could ask someone from math team, but if he says no, then it might be awkward when we have long after-school prep sessions and competitions together. There's also Benjamin Vasquez, *captain* of the math team. Gosh, if I could go to my sister's wedding with Ben, that would be awesome. We would look amazing in pictures together. Maybe if I ask him sooner rather than later, he'd want to hang out before the wedding. We could actually have a relationship outside of classroom 132, go to some of the fall festivals downtown, and maybe he'd come to some of my swim meets.

"Are you okay?" Grace asks.

"What?"

"You've been messing with the same corner for, like, five minutes," she tells me. She's sitting on the couch, all of the cushions already arranged on the floor.

"I'm fine."

"You don't seem fine." She stares at me for a moment, shaking her head.

Grace leans forward and undoes the buckles on her boots. I watch her, looking down, and notice a new scar on her chin. She was probably climbing a wall at school or found a new tree at the park. I've never understood her obsession with getting to higher ground.

"I wasn't ignoring you," I say, standing up. "I just have a lot on my mind."

"Like what?" she asks, tossing her boots behind the couch.

Being my best friend means she sees right through me when I try to lie.

I still say "Nothing" anyways.

Grace is the kind of person who doesn't stick up for herself, but if one of her friends is in trouble, she makes it her personal mission to save them. If I told her that I needed a date to Sam's wedding, she would probably immediately sacrifice her date. All three of my friends have dates for Sam's wedding. I saw that they confirmed plus-ones on all their RSVPs. Abby is obviously bringing Victor, her boyfriend of two years, and Sloane has been going on and on about the guy she met at music camp. Grace decided to bring one of her cousins since she's still not ready to move on from Shelby.

On my way to the kitchen to grab the cookies and Sprite, the front door opens and Sloane and Abby burst in.

"Mia, have you looked at the field hockey picture I texted you? Please tell me you did." Sloane loses herself to a fit of laughter. "Oh my God, there's this picture of Katherine Veena where she's bodychecking this girl, midjump. Her mouth guard is falling out, and the look on her face—" She can't finish the sentence without doubling over in laughter. I can't help but smile as she pinches the bridge of her nose, breathless.

"I haven't checked my phone since I started getting ready for movie night."

"Sloane, you're not supposed to send yearbook photos to your friends," Grace says. Though she admits, "However, it was very funny."

Abby hangs her coat in the closet by the door while Sloane tosses her shredded jean jacket over by Grace's shoes before pulling the scrunchie out of her hair so that her braided weave can tumble down from the top of her head.

"Are the purple strands a new addition?" I ask as we all find our usual spots.

I sit in the corner between the couch and the chaise extension. Abby sits between Grace and me, and Sloane lies down on her stomach in front of all of us with her feet tucked under the cushion that we use as a table.

"They are." Sloane flashes me a smile over her shoulder as she rolls around until her blanket hugs her like a burrito.

"So, what are we watching?" Abby asks through a mouthful of popcorn. She leans forward to look at the cookies and frowns.

I open Netflix and cue up the Ted Bundy documentary.

"I've been dying to watch this," I tell them, grabbing the car cookie.

"I don't want to watch this," Abby says, setting down the popcorn. She zips her Sherpa jacket and holds it tighter around her.

"Yeah, this is going to give me nightmares," Sloane agrees, rolling over to face us.

"Come on. This is interesting." I look from Sloane to Abby and see that they're not convinced. I look to Grace last, waiting for her to stand by me, but she just shrugs her shoulders.

"Why can't we watch something fun? I don't want to watch a movie about someone who killed a bunch of girls," Abby says.

"It's my weekend to pick, and I think this is going to be really good," I say, even though I can tell it's a losing battle.

"Movie night rules mandate that if no one wants to watch the chosen movie, we can vote on a new one," Sloane says, freeing an arm to hold out her hand for the Roku remote.

I relinquish control, knowing I can't beat all three of them, and watch the TV as she immediately browses the movie section and clicks on the romance genre. How predictable.

"*The Holiday* is back on Netflix. We could watch that," Grace notices.

"I'm fine with that," Sloane says, biting off a piece of a noose cookie.

"Me too," Abby agrees.

I roll my eyes and pull the plate of cookies into my lap. If they don't want to watch the documentary, then they don't deserve the documentary-theme cookies.

Instead of going upstairs to get my laptop, I open my

phone and go into my Google Docs, where I was working on my English essay. I start clicking on the links to my sources until I find exactly where I left off. At least I'll have something to do while my friends hijack my movie night.

"Why are we watching a Christmas movie when Halloween hasn't even happened yet?" I ask.

"It's not a Christmas movie. It's a romantic comedy," Abby says through the collar of her jacket pulled up to the bridge of her nose.

"Do you know how ridiculous this is?" I ask. "They meet 'randomly' through some website where they can stay at each other's houses. They don't know each other. One of them could be a thief or a murderer, and the producer is just welcoming this woman into her home to steal her stuff and lie about her departure date."

"Shhh," Sloane hisses.

"What's with you and murder this weekend?" Grace asks.

"Yeah. Anything you want to confess?" Sloane asks, winking at me.

I ignore her and stare down at the open article on biographical literary criticism on my phone.

Just when I allow myself to think the night can't get any worse, Sam saunters into the den with the stemless wineglass that's been glued to her hand for the past few weeks.

"Aww, you guys still do your little movie nights?" she asks, sitting on the armrest of the couch. Even though Sam has been going between living at her apartment and spending the night here sometimes, this is the first weekend she's stayed over during our movie night.

No one answers her, even when she says, "Oh, I know this movie. It's the one where the girls trade places and they flourish in each other's lives."

I laugh, thinking about the similarities between pre-house-swap Amanda Woods and Sam.

"What?" Sam asks.

"Nothing," I say, not looking up at her.

"Hey, did Mia tell you guys about how she's playing bachelorette?" Sam asks.

Sloane immediately hits pause, and all three of my friends turn to look up at Sam.

"Go mind your business," I tell her before she can say more.

"My wedding is my business," she says, leaning down to poke me between my eyebrows. "She needs a date to my wedding. As of today, her groomsman is no longer attending and she's desperately in need of a suitor. I thought it would be simple, but this morning she practically threw a tantrum about it, and I don't know, maybe you guys can help her out?"

"Literally, leave," I say, staring into her unblinking eyes.

"*Literally*, grow up," she says, mocking me. "Just thought I would help you along in your quest," she lies, standing up. "Enjoy your movie."

Once Sam is out of the room, Sloane rolls all the way over with her arms still tucked inside the burrito. "Well, that explains it."

"Explains what?" I ask.

"Why you're so snarky today," Grace answers.

"I am not snarky."

Sloane looks to Abby, who looks to Grace. They all share a glance, and I can tell they're doing that thing where they talk with their eyes instead of their words. It's something I've never been able to understand, and I hate when they do it in front of me.

"Guys!"

"So, you need a date to the wedding. It's not a big deal," Grace says.

"That's easy for you to say. All of you already have dates. I don't even know who to ask."

"Why can't you go alone?" Sloane asks, wiggling out of her burrito and reaching for a cup of Sprite.

"Because Sam said all of her pictures will be uneven, and *Brooke* convinced her that I could find a date."

"That nasty Brooke, believing in you, thinking you're a hot commodity," Abby kids, though her sarcasm doesn't help.

"Brooke's date is an *outline* in all of Sam's planners. She dates someone new nearly every week. Of course she thinks it's easy to find someone last-minute," I explain, feeling frustrated.

"Well, even if Brooke doesn't count, we still believe in you—" Grace starts saying.

"Please don't say that," I interrupt. "I don't want you guys to have to *believe*. It just goes to show that no one thinks this is going to be easy, and that shows it's not all in my head."

I feel a lump rise in my throat as my mind flashes back to the spring fling last year. We all went bowling after the dance, and at one point I was the only one sitting at our lane. Sloane and her date were playing the arcade game where you ride a motorcycle, and she was sitting on the back with her arms wrapped around his chest, in complete bliss. Abby and Victor had snuck off to "use the restroom." And Grace and Shelby were still together back then. They'd taken an Uber back to Shelby's house, because her parents had been out of town for the weekend. I was sitting alone, dateless, feeling like a sack of weak genes, reminding myself to smile and give a thumbs-up when Abby winked at me as she walked away arm in arm with Victor, and reminding myself to wave at Sloane when she looked for me over her shoulder at the motorcycle.

The feeling comes to me again as I imagine all my friends slow dancing at Sam's wedding. Sam and Geoffrey at the center of it all, my parents dancing somewhere close to them. And me, sitting at a table next to Jasper while he plays his Nintendo and mumbles pickup lines to me.

"We don't think it's going to be hard for you to find a date! Why don't we just help you figure out where to start?" Abby asks, her voice soft as she wraps her arm around my shoulder.

"We didn't mean to make you feel insecure," Sloane says apologetically.

"Sam meant to," I mumble against Abby's shoulder.

No one objects, and I sigh at the realization that it's possible that Sam wants me to fail so that I'll have to pose in all the pictures with Geoffrey's little brother. Instead of her pictures being uneven, they would be comedic, something she can hold over my head for the rest of my life. Then again, comedy isn't really her thing.

"Why don't you ask someone from school?" Sloane asks.

"I don't know. I started making a list, but the more I think about it, the weirder I feel about asking them," I admit.

"Let's see the list before you write anyone off," Grace says, holding out her hand.

I quickly run up to my room and grab the piece of paper I wrote the names on. Back downstairs, I drop the list into Grace's lap before sitting between Sloane and Abby where they've formed a tight circle. They all lean their heads together and read the list.

"No," Abby murmurs.

"Weirdo," Sloane says, pointing to a name.

"Douchebag," Grace whispers.

"Smells bad," Sloane says.

"Not photogenic," Abby adds.

I cover my face with my hands.

"What about Ben Vasquez?" I ask.

"No," all three of them say in unison.

"I veto. You're not spending your sister's wedding

talking about equations with Ben *Vasquez*, who is a butt-head, by the way," Abby decides.

"He's not a butthead," I say, laughing. My heart starts fluttering just thinking about him. "Also, who uses that word anymore?" Abby sticks her tongue out at me. I picture Ben and me holding the math team trophy from last year's championship, how our hands were so close, they nearly touched.

Ben Vasquez is the math team captain, a soccer star, and occasional drama club member—when the semester play is one he wants to be in. Generations of his family have attended Vanderbilt University, and he plans to be no exception.

"If Ben goes with me to my sister's wedding, maybe he'll have a good enough time that we'll hang out more and get to know each other and . . . well . . ."

I imagine what it would be like to have his arms around my waist and to kiss his pillowy lips.

"Just, no," Abby cuts in, drawing me out of my blissful Ben bubble. "Next."

"If not him, then maybe Joey Delmar?" I ask.

"That won't work," Sloane says. "There are murmurings in yearbook about him and Cynthia. I think they hooked up at a party a couple of weeks ago and they low-key want to do it again."

"I think I put Paul Springfield on the list," I say, grasping at straws.

"The slowest swimmer on the team." Abby laughs.

Sloane takes the paper out of Grace's hands and tears it down the middle.

"Hey." I reach for the papers, but Sloane tears them again and again.

"Maybe the answer isn't you asking someone from your classes or a club. Maybe you have to meet someone new," Sloane says.

"Preferably someone hot," Abby adds.

"I've got it." Grace stands up like she's about to give a speech. "You should have a meet-cute." She reaches for the remote and cues up *Hitch*. She starts fast-forwarding and presses play at the scene where Hitch swoops in to save Sara from some random man flirting with her at a club.

I roll my eyes.

"No, Mia, look. If you bump into someone and have a moment with them, it gives you the perfect opportunity to start a conversation and see where it goes," Grace explains.

"Doesn't that defeat the purpose of a meet-cute? If it's planned and on purpose?" I ask, feeling ridiculous that we're even entertaining this idea.

"Well, maybe you just need to give yours a little nudge. Like you see a cute guy walking down the hallway, and you accidentally drop your notebook right in front of him—"

"Or you stumble into his arms and he catches you," Abby cuts in, wrapping her arms around herself theatrically.

"Or maybe you spot a hottie who dropped something and you stop to help *him*," Sloane suggests.

"Either way," Grace continues, "you see a guy, you make an excuse for you two to interact, and whatever happens, happens."

"That kind of stuff doesn't just . . . happen. . . ." As I say it, watching the meet-cute unfold on the TV, I remember Harold bumping into Gladys this morning, the way he hoisted her out of the pool, and how from that moment forward she couldn't take her eyes off him.

"Okay, so—let's say I decide to do this meet-cute thing. Where do I even find the guy? If none of the ones I suggested work?"

"You find someone new in someplace new," Grace says.

"How about you can't meet them at school. You have to meet them out in the world. It'll be more interesting that way," Sloane suggests, carefully dropping the torn-up pieces of my list into the now empty bowl of popcorn.

"No way. I don't want to bump into complete strangers. Any one of them could be *in a relationship*. And what's worse is that none of us would know anything about them. They could be a weirdo or a creep or something."

I can picture it now, me dropping my purse on the sidewalk downtown in front of some gorgeous guy. We both bend down to pick it up. Next thing I know, he suggests we stop into a café to get coffee and he leads me down an alley, and I'd never be seen again. Or we're hanging out at the Art Institute and his girlfriend shows up to throw a slushy in my face.

"We'll pick the targets," Abby suggests.

"We're calling them *targets* now?"

"We each will pick someone that we know, that you don't know. We'll go through social media and figure out the best way for you to 'bump into' them, and then bam— you have a meet-cute with someone who isn't a complete stranger—"

"And they aren't a boring weirdo," Sloane adds.

We fall silent.

"Mia, you're running out of reasons to say no," Grace says, already smiling at the victory.

I admit that she's right. I can't tell if I feel relief or if my stress has just been reallocated to their crazy plot. But even a guy I've never met has to be better than Jasper.

CHAPTER FOUR

I count down the seconds before lunch. Even though Mrs. Eldredge is still lecturing, I pack up my notes and slip my pen back into its case. The second the bell rings, I hop out of my desk and file into the hallway just in time to catch Grace leaving her algebra class.

"So, what have you guys come up with?" I ask as we turn down the hall toward our lockers.

"I don't think I'm supposed to tell you," Grace says sheepishly, stopping to turn her locker combination. "Plus, we've only had one night to come up with names, Mia."

"If I guess who you put on your list, will you tell me if I'm right?"

Grace laughs to herself, which she knows frustrates me. She tells me to hold on a second, so I step a few lockers down and get my lunch before catching up with her to head to the cafeteria.

"Have you guys picked anyone yet?" I ask as I sit down, and then I see Sloane staring at a half-full piece of paper. She has a stick-figure diagram that I can barely make out, except for the hearts floating between two poorly drawn heads.

"I'm still working out the logistics of mine," Abby answers without looking up from her notebook. She's created a folder fort around herself so that no one can see what she's writing.

"Keep yours hidden," I hiss at Sloane when I notice a few people glancing down at our lunch table. "I don't need the whole school to know about this."

"Maybe if they knew, someone would just come up to you and ask to be your date and we wouldn't have to jump through all these hoops," Sloane offers, gathering her braids into a ponytail.

"But then who would get the Starbucks gift card?" Abby asks, biting her lip.

"What Starbucks gift card?" I ask as Grace returns to the table with her tray of pizza, salad, and apple juice. The pizza would be the perfect thing to stress-eat right now.

"Even though we love you and you finding a date and being happy is reward enough," Sloane says sarcastically, "we figured we'd up the stakes for ourselves by including a prize for whoever's meet-cute wins."

"Wins?"

I stare down at my turkey sandwich and glance over at Grace's oily pepperoni pizza. She catches me watching, so I quickly reach over and snatch a piece of pepperoni, figuring she had to know it was going to happen.

"If you go to the wedding with the date I choose, then I get the gift card," Grace explains before erasing a line of writing on her paper.

I look at each of them, wondering what they could be writing. How hard is it to come up with a list, and why would you write a list in paragraph form? Grace turns between a few pages filled out in her blue journal.

"What is that anyways?"

"My plan for your meet-cute," Grace answers, sliding her tray to hide the paper when I try to take a look.

"Why do you have a plan? I thought I was just meeting people that you picked out for me."

"Okay, so we did some deliberating and decided that it should be more guided than just throwing you and someone else together," Grace says.

"We love you, and have full faith in you, but you're not the smoothest when it comes to boys," Sloane adds, stealing one of my Pringles.

As much as I want to defend myself, I know they're right. The last time I tried talking to a guy was at homecoming last year, and we ended up talking about the ethics behind investing in Chick-fil-A, not a very romantic topic—especially if you have differing political views.

"So, what's your plan? Or, your *plans*," I ask, trying to shake away the cringe-worthy image of Grace stomping up the bleachers at homecoming to yank me down, mid-argument with Nate Fischer.

"I'm thinking something along the lines of *Serendipity*," Grace muses with a mouth full of crunchy lettuce. She holds up a finger and drinks some apple juice before continuing. "You remember the meet-cute from *Serendipity*?"

"Refresh me," I say, even though I remember talking about it with my mom.

"We watched it like two weeks ago, dude." Abby bobs up from her fort, frowning. "That was my movie night pick."

"Right, so *remind* me what happened," I say, turning back to Grace.

"Jon and Sara reach for the same glove in Bloomingdale's while holiday shopping. It's the last pair of black cashmere gloves, and in that awkward moment where they both want the same thing, that's their meet-cute."

"You want me to bump hands with someone over a pair of gloves?" I ask, feeling the familiar lump in the pit of my stomach manifesting. "Grace, it's October in Chicago. No one is shopping for gloves! And the wedding is the third week of December. Hopefully I won't still be trying to find a date by the time there's one pair of gloves left to fight over."

I'm trying to imagine myself in a store, shopping for a pair of gloves that I don't need. "How would you even get a guy to shop for a pair of gloves specifically? Like, what are the chances that I'd go into a store thinking, *Serendipity, Serendipity, Serendipity,* and find the boy you're setting me up with in the gloves section?"

Before Grace can answer, Sloane holds up a hand and says, "Enough. We're not doing this."

"Doing what?" Grace and I ask in unison. Abby peeks her head over the top edge of her folder.

"We're not telling you anything else about our meet-cute ideas. You'll have information on a need-to-know basis, okay? I don't need your bad pessimistic mood all up in my meet-cute mojo," Sloane explains. She pushes her reading glasses up onto her forehead and presses her face into her palms.

"When will I have my first meet-cute? Can I at least know that?" I ask, figuring I can rationalize some information out of them. "I'll have to make sure it doesn't overlap with math team or swim practice or—"

"We can keep track of all your stuff. Just try to let us handle this, and when it's time, we'll pass the reins on to you," Sloane tells me as she closes her folder, her paper tucked inside.

Sloane starts eating her ramen, and I can hear Abby crunching on her salad behind her folder-fort. We fall silent, and as I chew on my turkey sandwich—realizing I forgot to put mustard on it this morning when Sam was wasting electricity standing in front of the open fridge figuring out what she was going to eat for breakfast—I try to imagine what meet-cute moments Sloane and Abby may have picked. Sloane is very into the damsel-in-distress movies like *Maid in Manhattan* and *The Wedding Planner*. But Abby really has a thing for the comedy side of the rom-coms. Sometimes I think she barely cares about the romantic plot, only when it overlaps with something funny happening.

We've been having movie nights for years. Up until

now I haven't really given them much thought. It's weird to think that I have this arsenal of information on falling in love but no idea how I'm supposed to use it.

"So, in other news," Abby says, breaking the silence. "Our first meet is next week."

"What day?" Grace asks.

Across the cafeteria I see Ben Vasquez emerge from the lunch line with his tray in hand. He's wearing a blue Camp Cuyahoga T-shirt—definitely from his summer exploits—and a pair of dark moss-green pants. His glasses are tucked into the collar of his shirt, which makes his brown eyes seem bigger somehow.

"MIA!" Grace plucks me in the forehead.

"Ow!" I swat her empty apple juice bottle across the table. "What?"

"Nervous or excited for the meet?" she asks slowly, probably for the millionth time.

Abby turns to look over her shoulder and spots Ben as he's slinging his book bag over the back of a chair.

"Oh," Sloane says, noticing too.

"Please tell me at least one of you has Ben on your list. He's the one guy that was on mine that I actually really would want as a date," I say, remembering how quick they were to shoot him down yesterday.

All three of them share a look. Abby raises her eyebrows, Grace faintly shakes her head, and Sloane frowns. I can already tell they're thinking about arguments against him.

"Guys!"

"Mia, he's awful," Abby states.

"Absolutely awful," Grace agrees.

I look to Sloane, who points to her closed mouth, chewing on a piece of chicken from her soup. Technically she's not saying no.

In biology later, I get distracted thinking about Ben and what it could be like to dance with him at Sam's reception. How cool it would be for him to walk me down the aisle, us holding hands. I turn to Sloane, even though she's actually paying attention to the lecture.

"Why don't *you* pick Ben. I know Grace and Abby won't, but you're more realistic than them." Sloane taps her pencil on the desk for a second, and I add, "And you're prettier."

"Liar," she whisper-laughs. "Brownnoser."

"Come *on*," I plead. "You know how bad I want this. If you pick him, my predisposition to wanting him will help you win the Starbucks gift card. What if you pick someone who I don't even like and you lose? At least this way you know you'll have a chance."

"Yeah, and if I pick someone else, I know you'll have a chance of not being screwed over by Ben flipping Vasquez," she counters.

"It's a possibility that I could get screwed over by anyone that any of the three of you choose," I remind her. "At least if it's with Ben, you wouldn't have only yourself to blame."

"Mia, that just made it sad."

I press on, "You know how important this would be to me. Please promise you'll at least consider it?"

"I promise to think about it, but I don't promise that it'll happen," she says, falling quiet when Mrs. Gruber pauses to adjust her PowerPoint. The slides are almost always out of order. When she starts playing a short clip to review mitosis, Sloane whispers, "I also promise that if you bring it up again after this, it will be an immediate and absolute no!" She adds the last part quickly before I can say anything else. So, I take the crumb that I get and shut my mouth.

Even if this scheme ends up a failure, I'd consider it worthwhile if I get to go on one date—one non-math-related outing—with Ben Vasquez.

CHAPTER FIVE

D efinitely the red velvet," I say with my mouth
full. I chew quickly and lick the vanilla frosting
off my lips before taking a sip of the sparkling
grape juice brought out just for my under-
twenty-one-year-old self. I watch Sam take a sip of her
champagne, swishing it around before swallowing.

"Definitely a good one," she agrees before setting her
slice aside.

"I feel like we don't have to taste any more because this
is the one," I tell her, helping myself to another slice.

Mom laughs, covering her mouth with her napkin.
"Mia, this is only the third cake."

"And it's delicious," I tell her, laughing.

I was happy when Mom reminded me of Sam's cake
tasting at the Butterfly Bed & Breakfast after dinner. Both
Monday and Tuesday have gone by and my friends haven't
given me a single update on their meet-cute plans. As I slip
another forkful of cake into my mouth I think *Here's to
tomorrow* to myself. Honestly, if Sam has more wedding
stuff like this that she needs help with, I will happily oblige.
I don't know why she always wants me to run around

buying more Post-it notes and categorizing the stacks of papers she needs three-hole-punched for her binder, when there are tastings to be had.

The dining room of the B&B has a bit of a rustic-grandma's-house feel to it. The vertical wood paneling ends about halfway up the wall and is met with a floral-print wallpaper that has grown on me since the first time I saw it. The dining room has small circular wood tables that each have their own floral arrangement at the center, with tealight candles and a pastel tablecloth. The fact that each tablecloth is a different color makes the place feel cozy. I could curl up on the huge floral-print couch in the library, especially when the fire is going in the winter, and read for ages.

Right now we're the only ones in the dining room because it's after hours. We're at the green table, per Sam's request. The green table is right by the bay window facing the backyard, where Sam's wedding ceremony and reception will be taking place since the dining room inside the inn is too small for her guests. I remember her going back and forth with the owner, and Mom having to calm her down and work out a compromise where we would order a temperature-controlled tent to be set up outside so that the inn could still be responsible for catering, decorating, and hosting the wedding.

I watch Sam while I chew on more red velvet cake as she stares into the yard, remembering how she used to daydream about having her wedding here when she was my age and I was still in elementary school. I try to imagine what she might be envisioning. The arch at the end of her aisle, decorated with ivy vines and carnations? Or maybe she's envisioning herself on our dad's arm, thinking of what she'll look like in her dress, thinking of what Geoffrey will look like at the end of the aisle. Will he cry?

I imagine what I might look like in my bridesmaid's dress, a flowing wave of forest green standing just a couple of steps behind Sam, a part of one of the biggest moments in her life.

"Peach," Mom says, wiping her mouth after trying the lemon cake with whisked blueberry frosting. I spear a piece with my fork just to make sure it's not better than the red velvet. "I got a letter from the school talking about your National Honor Society application."

"What about it?" I ask, noting how faint the blueberry flavor is.

"They said that you need more volunteer hours to qualify for the president or vice president position."

"I wasn't planning on being the president or vice president," I tell her, even though I can almost swear I told her this before.

"Why not?" Sam asks.

"I have math team and swim practice. Plus, this is my junior year. I'm in three AP classes, so I have to make my grades count. I figure just being in NHS will be enough for college applications. That in conjunction with my extracurriculars and good grades will be fine—sans a presidential status."

Mom considers me for a second, and I can tell that I've got her convinced. I use my fork to sever a huge section of my new slice of double-layer red velvet, and I cautiously guide it to my mouth without it toppling back to the plate. The rich flavor mixed with the silky frosting soothes me—mind, soul, and stomach.

"Wait," Sam says as she finishes her taste of strawberry cake. "I was president. You were president," she says to Mom. "Mia, it's barely any extra work. It's more about title, and yes, right now you would have to stomach some volunteering, but you can do it. I looked at your calendar back home, and you don't have club or practice on Fridays. You could do volunteering once a week somewhere and get enough hours to qualify." She looks at my mom and adds, "It would be worse for her to not try at all than to try and simply not get the position."

I want to lie and say Abby or Grace want to be NHS president so that Mom doesn't make me do it, but I have a mouth full of cake and no room to speak without risking spraying crumbs all over Mom.

"I suppose, if you have Fridays free," Mom says, thinking.

I shake my head, but Mom looks at Sam and tells her, "She could volunteer at the garden! We need some extra help cleaning out the flower beds and refurbishing the greenhouse. And it means we can spend more time together!" She turns back to me as I struggle to swallow my mound of mushy cake. "I feel like I barely see you, with your clubs and swimming and your friends. This can be our thing," she tells me, beaming.

I chug some juice to clear my mouth and stare at Mom and Sam. Before I can say *anything*, Sam rushes to ask, "How can you say no to that?"

Right. How could I?

I shrug my shoulders and smile to keep myself from saying something sarcastic and intentionally mean to Sam.

"Great," Mom says, grasping my hand. "I'll tell the group tomorrow. And don't worry. It's not all a bunch of old ladies like me. There's a boy your age who volunteers most days after school."

"Look at that, a young man." Sam smiles at me over Mom's shoulder. She reaches for her glass of wine and takes a sip to hide her laugh.

I grab my glass of juice and take a sip to hide the fact that I'm silently praying Mom doesn't point out the bit of cake Sam has between her teeth.

"And that's why I need to go to the store and waste money on my own pair of gardening gloves and knee pads," I explain to my friends the next day in study hall. "Why would Sam want me wasting time at a garden when she also wants me looking for a date to *her* wedding?"

"I can go with you after school," Grace says. "I'll swing by your house, and then we can go into town. I know the perfect shop for you to find all your stuff."

"*You* know the perfect shop? I've never seen you garden a day in your life," Sloane says, staring at Grace suspiciously.

"My mom gardens," Grace says in her own defense.

"I was thinking about going to Lowe's," I admit. Since none of my friends have presented me with a meet-cute and now I have the impending doom of volunteering on Friday, I've lost my inspiration for my history paper. I zip my pen case, ready to wallow in some self-pity.

"Lowe's is so overpriced," Grace tells me. "Trust me, you can get *everything* you need from this place."

"Okay," I relent, not caring about where the stuff comes from but about the fact that I need it in the first place. Mom told me that there are gloves and pads at the garden, but they're shared by people, and since the summer just ended, some of the gloves smell like sweat and a lot of the knee pads are stained. Gross.

Sloane shakes her head before returning to her history essay. Abby is once again writing behind her secret folder fort, and I can't tell if she has paid attention to a single word I've said.

I bend over the back of my chair and stare down our aisle of the library. We always pick the table in the back corner by the windows when we have study hall, because most people don't know it's here. You have to wander through the labyrinth of shelves to find it. The first time Sloane found it, she wasn't able to remember how to get back to it, and none of us believed that it actually existed. But then during second semester of freshman year, I was trying to sneak away from my English class to check out a section of the library that our teacher hadn't requested to have materials pulled from. As I was tiptoeing toward the back wall, scanning for newspaper excerpts printed from 1920, I found the spot. I made sure to remember what section of the library it was near, and ever since then we've always tried to get the same study period so that we could meet here.

Through an empty space on the shelf behind me, I see movement. In the silence I try to listen to the shuffling to tell whether they're getting closer or going farther away.

"Someone's about to infiltrate," I whisper.

Everyone looks up, and we watch the bookshelf in silence. I startle when I see someone's eye looking right at us.

"Victor?" Abby hisses from behind her folder.

The figure disappears as Abby stands up. She goes behind the shelf and comes back with her boyfriend, Victor—who's on the boys' swim team.

"Did anyone follow you?" Sloane asks, pointing her pencil at him like she's about to launch it.

He holds his hands up in surrender. "No. I swear."

"You may enter," Sloane declares, looking down at her notes again.

When they both sit down on the other side of the folder, Grace says what I start to think. "Why does he get to be on the other side of the fort?"

"Because he's helping me."

"What exactly is he helping you with?" I ask. I originally thought she was working on meet-cute stuff and that the whole point of the folder was so that no one would see her plan and try to sabotage her chances of the Starbucks gift card. I hope she's not showing *my* meet-cute to her boyfriend.

"None of your business," she tells me, before ducking back behind her folder.

Victor huddles down close to her, which is hard for him since he's six feet tall. Victor and I are two of the three Black people on the swim team. He and I have both heard a lot of jokes about how Black people don't swim. There's another girl named Shannon who joined the team last year. There was an incident in the locker room where some of the senior girls were whispering to each other and someone asked why Shannon didn't just go run track or play basketball. She ended up telling the coach, and those girls were suspended. When I asked her about it, she said that when people say stuff like that, it only makes her want to swim faster. It pushes her to practice harder. Victor and I decided we should definitely stick together—Shannon included—and always speak up for each other in situations like that because I used to feel more intimidated about it when I first joined the team freshman year.

Now that I'm thinking about it, I wonder—if Victor *is* helping Abby with her meet-cute—would Abby be annoyed if I ask her to possibly set me up with someone

Victor knows from the track team. Victor runs track in the spring and he knows a lot of people, so that could widen the pool of possible dates.

After school Grace insists on meeting me at my house before we head to the small, supposedly not overpriced store she refuses to tell me the name of. I'm sitting in an armchair, waiting, when Dad wanders into the den. He doesn't notice me at first. He just walks up to one of the two hundred-gallon tropical fish tanks he has built inside the opposing walls adjacent to the TV and starts his afternoon ritual of feeding the fish. Instead of saying anything, I just watch him. When I was younger, I used to feed the fish with him to avoid doing homework. I would drag out his process by saying hi to all his fish and giving them new names. Then I would ask him about each fish. What kind were they? Why did he put them in this tank instead of the other one? Even though I was always scheming, he never tired of answering my questions and telling me as much as he could about the fish.

I don't know when I stopped following him around for this, but now as I watch him completely engrossed in his collection, I notice the sound of water trickling through the filters. It's relaxing.

He startles when he turns around and finds me. It makes me laugh, the way he reaches for his chest like he's about to have a heart attack.

"Peach," he gasps. "I didn't even know you were home."

He laughs a little before crossing the den to his other tank.

"I got home just a little while ago. I'm about to go out with Grace."

"On a fun adventure?"

"Just to get gardening supplies."

Recognition crosses his face even though he's looking down into his container of fish food instead of at me.

"Your mother told me you're going to join her at the community garden. It sounds like one of Sam's ideas." He arches his eyebrow and glances up at me.

I nod before saying, "She convinced Mom that I should follow in their footsteps of being president of the National Honor Society next year."

"That doesn't sound like a horrible thing," he says in that absentminded way where I can tell he's baiting me for my thoughts.

I figure my last chance at not having to volunteer would be convincing Dad it's a bad idea, so I tell him about all the things I'm doing right now and how they're more important than qualifying for a presidency I don't even want and might not get.

"But," he counters, "next year you might not be doing everything that you're doing now, so maybe it's better to take the preemptive steps so you have the option, should you change your mind."

"I'm still going to be swimming and doing math team for extra credit. And, I don't know, maybe I'll put my name up for swim team captain and then I'll have more responsibilities next year, and even now for this season. I mean, it's not like I wasn't going to join NHS anyways. I just don't want to do extra work for it."

Dad screws the cap onto his fish food and turns on the blue lights for his tanks. Then he comes over to the couch and sits down next to me. When he picks up the remote, I can already tell that our conversation isn't going anywhere. My persuasion has failed again.

"I feel like I'll do better this semester if I don't have to volunteer at the garden," I try one last time.

"Then you can tell your mother and see how she feels about it," he says, patting my hand before turning on the TV. Sometimes I think Sam secretly brainwashes our parents against me. She's the reason why I had to start making my own lunches when I was eleven and why I can never eat dinner up in my room or in front of the TV. And now I have to volunteer at a garden for a club I barely want to be a part of, in addition to having to spend precious time finding a date to her wedding!

Usually Mom and Dad are fine with me choosing my "own path" and setting my own standards. They were on top of Sam when she was my age, always checking her homework and making sure she was ready for tests or field hockey games. Dad would make her run drills in the backyard sometimes, which makes me glad we don't have a pool. However, they aren't the same anymore. I don't think Dad would make me swim laps even if he could do it from one of the patio lounge chairs. It felt like when they retired and were able to stop working, they were also able to stop *working* so hard at parenting. Now it just seems like when Sam comes around, they get a jolt of how they used to be and it rubs off on me and my life.

I watch an episode of *Planet Earth* with Dad until the doorbell rings. I grab my wallet with the money Mom gave me, step out the front door, and begin to close it behind me.

"Wait," Grace says, reaching past me for the door. "Wait, wait."

"What?" I ask, nearly dropping my keys.

She takes me by the shoulders, turns me around, and pushes me back inside. She shouts hello to my dad on our way up the stairs and immediately bolts to my closet without a word.

"Hi. How are you? How have the last thirty minutes since school been? Are you ready to go to the store?" I say, cycling through how our greeting should've gone. "Oh no. We're playing dress-up."

She lays an old pair of coveralls on my bed and pulls out the only flannel I own, from a lumberjack Halloween costume I put together when I was a freshman.

She finally turns to me and says, "Boots," like it's supposed to make sense.

"Boots?"

"Where are your boots? Like, work boots."

"*Work* boots?" I ask. "When have I ever needed *work* boots?"

"Okay, a pair of old sneakers." She starts rooting around on the floor in my closet, and I step in and pull out a pair of white Converse that I used to wear until my feet grew half an inch and the shoes started blistering my pinkie toe.

"Perfect." She puts the shoes on the floor at the foot of my bed in front of the outfit. After taking in the whole ensemble, she tells me to put it on.

"Why?" I ask as I pull off my jeans.

"Because . . . ," she says slowly. "This is what you should wear to the store."

"And that makes sense, how?" I ask as I pull the coverall straps over my shoulders. I put on the flannel and realize it makes a nice light jacket.

I walk up to the mirror on the back of my door and look at myself. "I look like a farm girl."

"Great!" Grace says. "Now we can go."

"Go where? I'm not going out looking like this. This is how I dressed when I was five."

"You look like someone who gardens. Now let's go! We have to get there before—" She stops herself, her eyes wide.

"Before what?" I ask.

"Before they close."

"When do they close?" I ask, figuring I probably have more than enough time to change.

"Soon," she says. "Now, let's go."

"I look ridiculous," I growl.

She smiles and opens my bedroom door. "After you, my lady."

Fifteen minutes later, I'm glancing at the skyline through my car window. With the October chill comes earlier sunsets and cloudier days. I picture the Lowe's downtown. It's three stories inside a tall building that sits on top of an underground parking garage. Now that I'm watching the city disappear behind us as we head deeper into the suburbs, I'm a little thankful that we decided to go to Grace's store instead. With all the thoughts buzzing around in my head the past few days, I'm not really in the mood to surround myself with the crowded busyness of the city.

We pull off the freeway in the next town over and turn down a side street that takes us to a hardware store called The Handyman Can. The building is a small two-story house that probably has an apartment above the store. It's coated in chipping white paint, and the windows have navy-blue shutters that draw your eyes to the OPEN signs hanging in each one. The door is a stunning dark green, a color as deep as evergreen trees, and it has a rusted brass bell hanging above it. The sign over the door could use a new coat of paint, but the weathered-ness of it is definitely fitting for a hardware store.

I cringe at the hinges wailing as Grace opens the door. When she jumps too, I can tell that she's never been to her "perfect store" before. With the door closed, we're trapped inside with the strong aroma of WD-40 and wood finish. There's a small fan humming behind the counter and a boy wearing a faded paint-stained apron that says HANDYMAN HELPER on the front. I note that he's reading an actual newspaper, which my dad doesn't even do anymore.

"Is there anything I can help you find?" he asks, pushing his reading glasses up onto his forehead.

"Yes—"

"No." I cut Grace off, flashing her a glare. She knows I don't like to make workers help me, especially when they're in the middle of doing something. I don't want to be *that* customer. So I say, "We're just looking," before taking off down the nearest aisle. I follow the signs and find knee pads and a sun hat. Mom said that they have plenty of supplies like shovels, rakes, fertilizer, and wheelbarrows. She just said that anything I wouldn't want to share, I should get for myself. So I weave up and down the aisles with Grace tailing me silently, until I find the gloves. I pick a pair of baby-blue ones with radishes all over them. Even though they look a little ridiculous, they're 60 percent off.

"Do you have everything?" she asks, smiling like a psychopath.

I try to think of anything else that I might need. It's hard to focus, with the blister growing on my pinkie toe. As I move farther down the aisle, I have to take a second and stop to try to adjust my shoe. I make Grace hold my stuff while I brace myself against a shelf of seed packets.

"I think so. I can't believe I let you make me wear these shoes. I should've thrown them away forever ago."

"The shoes don't matter. I need you to focus."

I look at her, sure I misheard what she said. But she

stares at me, smiling so wide that her mouth is almost too big for her face.

"Focus on what?"

She steps past me and peers around the end of the shelf. Then she looks at me and says, "On him. He's your first target!"

"Who?" I ask. We both lean toward the end of the shelf, and I see the cashier boy, engrossed in his newspaper.

"His name is Kelvin," she whispers. "He and I went to the same summer camp two summers ago—"

Before she can say more, I cut her off and confirm, "You mean, *drama* camp?"

She nods, and I realize that, of course she would set me up with a drama kid, the same way I'm hoping Abby and Victor will set me up with someone from track team.

"He's not, like, that bad. He's a really good actor, but he's also into other stuff and he's really nice."

"What other stuff is he into?" I ask, leaning forward again to really take a look at him.

Grace rattles off her list of facts. He's on the debate team at his high school. He's also a junior. He's into current events and wants to study politics in college. In addition to drama club he also does culinary club, so Grace figures we could talk about baking. He doesn't play any sports, but he likes to watch basketball. He's not too bad on the eyes either. He's tall. I can tell by his torso. He's sitting on a high stool behind the counter, hunched over his newspaper. He has long arms, and his hair is cut so short that you can see the waves in his fade. I try to picture us standing next to each other. He's cute with glasses, but probably looks even better without. He'd tower over me, but in a nice kind of way, the way my dad towers over my mom. Also, I can tell he spends a lot of time outside because he has a slight tan line where his T-shirt collar dips a little low. Our skin tones are really close. He's just a tiny bit darker than me. Sam would say we complement each other. Or she'd say I should spend time out in the sun so that I can tan and we can match for the photos in her wedding.

"What do I do?" I ask, suddenly feeling nervous. "How do I even have a meet-cute? What do I say?"

"You could've asked him to help you find the stuff instead of being so determined to do it on your own," she admits, hiding a laugh.

"Thanks for telling me that when it was useful," I say, shaking my head.

"But, really, you just walk up, and you can talk about the stuff you found, or ask him what he's reading about in the newspaper," Grace offers.

"Then what?"

"Mia, you have to start somewhere. I can't draft the conversation for you."

"I wish you could," I tell her, even though I know she's right.

Grace hands me back my items, and I take a deep breath. I try to think of things for us to talk about just in case the conversation falls flat. Maybe I can ask if he gardens. I quickly glance around to see if there's anything else I could use as a conversation starter, and I decide on a packet of basil seeds. Hopefully he knows how to grow basil.

"Okay, wish me luck," I say, looking down at my unbuttoned flannel over my washed-out coveralls. I notice the shooting star I drew years ago on the toe of my Converse, to make up for the fact that my mom wouldn't buy me a pair of shoes I thought were cool at the time—with shooting stars and a galaxy on them—and I'm thankful he won't be able to see my feet over the counter.

I remind myself to breathe as I come around the corner of the aisle. He doesn't notice me, so I take the moment of privacy to brush back any of my loose tendrils. I'm thankful that I took the time to fill in my eyebrows this morning and put on mascara. Even though I look like a farm girl, at least I look like a put-together farm girl with nice eyelashes.

"Hey," I say. My voice breaks, and when he looks up, I feel a million butterflies burst from their cocoons inside my stomach. "Hi."

"Did you find what you were looking for?" he asks, putting down his newspaper.

"Yeah," I say, remembering to smile. And breathe. Must not forget to breathe.

"Do you want to buy it?" he asks, looking at my arms.

"Oh," I gush, leaning forward so that everything doesn't tumble onto the counter. "Right. Sorry."

He starts scanning the items, and in the silence I realize

that I'm losing momentum. I look back and scan the aisles until I find Grace, hiding close to the exit. She mouths *Question* to me, and flashes a supportive thumbs-up.

"How do you grow basil?" I ask, the words tumbling out. "Kelvin," I add, when I notice his name tag.

He raises his eyebrows at me and he looks down at the packet of seeds conveniently in his hand. I just smile and wait, admiring the dimple in his left cheek.

"Like, from scratch," I add. "How do you grow it . . . from scratch?" I repeat when I start to hear the sound of my heart beating over the silence stilling the air between us.

He smiles at me and then looks down at the seeds again. He flips the packet over, and for a second I'm afraid that the directions are on the back and I'm looking like a thoughtless idiot to him right now. But he quickly flips the packet back over and scans the front before leaning forward on his elbows on the counter. He holds the packet out between us, and I take the invitation to lean down closer, thankful that I'm wearing a crew-neck T-shirt under my coveralls.

"You start off with some potting soil. Plant a few seeds about a quarter inch below the surface, and water it enough that the soil is constantly damp. I think basil takes a week or two to sprout." He pauses and looks at me. I let him catch my eye, and for a second I feel weightless. I feel incredulous that Grace's plan might actually be working. "After you have a plant, you'll want to water it almost every day. Basil is mostly water." He focuses on the picture of basil on the front of the packet. I look at it too and realize that I don't have potting soil at home.

"Does that help?" he asks, adjusting his glasses as he stands up.

"Yes, thank you."

He smiles at me and returns to scanning my items. Even though it was nice of him to give me an explanation, it wasn't a *moment*. Gladys and Harold were inseparable after they bumped into each other. He put her in danger and saved her. The way they met was memorable; it stands out. I have to make an impression. But how?

I try to think of something else to say. I look at his newspaper and see that he's reading about Gilbert Valley's swim meet last week.

"Oh my gosh," I say without thinking.

"What?" he asks, looking down at the knee pads in his hands.

"No, not you," I say, smiling. I reach for his newspaper and look more closely at the picture in the article. When I see the date, I know for sure. "I was in this swim meet last week."

"You were?" he asks, leaning across the counter to look.

"Yeah. We blew Gilbert out of the water." I had one of my best times for backstroke that day. "I came in first in all my races."

"Do you go to Hayfield?"

"Yes!"

"I feel like I recognize you! I have some friends on the

team and I was at that meet." He stares at me for a moment, pushing his glasses up onto his forehead again. "You were *that* girl. My friends hated you, but in a good way."

"That's cool," I say, blushing a little. "That was a solid meet. And Gilbert isn't *that* bad," I tease.

"You don't have to sugarcoat it," he says, laughing. "You guys smoked us."

"You go to Gilbert, then?"

"Yeah," he admits, taking a moment to scan my gloves. "So, your total comes to twenty-four dollars and sixty cents."

I look down at the screen in front of me and read the prices. "I thought the gloves were sixty percent off?"

Kelvin frowns down at his screen and says, "No, they rung up full price."

"They might have rung up full price, but there's a sign that says they're sixty percent off."

"I don't even think we're having a sale on gloves right now. I know we are in paint," he says, not looking at me. He rubs his chin, still staring down at his screen.

"I can go get the sign if you want," I tell him, turning on my heel.

"I mean, the gloves are just twelve bucks."

"*Just* twelve bucks?" I ask, raising my eyebrows. "Look, I can prove they're on sale."

I take a step back toward the aisle with the gloves, but Kelvin says, "Even if there is a sign, my manager has a lock on the register. I can't change the price."

I open my mouth and close it, realizing it would probably ruin things even more if I asked him to get the manager.

"Sorry about my friend," Grace says, coming over and wrapping her arms around my shoulders. "She's just having an off day."

Kelvin looks between us suspiciously, not sure what to do.

"I don't know if I want to buy the gloves at full price," I say.

"Mia," Grace hisses.

"Grace," I mimic her.

"I'll buy the gloves. Okay?" she says, looking back and forth between us. "No biggie." She pulls her backpack purse off her shoulders, and as her braids fall from behind her neck to form a curtain around her face, I catch Kelvin giving her the once-over.

"Loosen up, guys. The tension in here is so unnecessary," Grace says, flashing Kelvin an apologetic smile.

"Sorry. I mean, if I could change the price myself, I would," he says to her, accepting her debit card.

"I understand. It's no big deal. It's definitely not worth you getting in trouble," Grace tells him.

"That's nice of you," he says, smiling back at her. Even though he smiled at me before, now I notice the way his eyes seem to glisten under the fluorescent lights. I also notice the way the fan is blowing Grace's hair gently back from her face. "Do I know you from somewhere?" he asks.

"I don't know. Do you?" Grace asks coyly.

He hands her *my* bag of stuff and shifts his weight to

one side, leaning against the counter. "I feel like we were in a play together."

"Oh my gosh," Grace says, pretending to be surprised, like the actress she is. "Drama camp, two summers ago?"

"Yes!" His eyes get wide, and for a moment his mouth hangs open. "Oh my gosh, I remember you. Grace?"

"Yes, and you're Kelvin," she says, laughing, pointing to his name tag.

"It's been forever since I've even thought about that play," Kelvin admits.

Grace leans into the counter, my bag around her wrist. "I know. I still can't believe they had us act out a donor's play instead of a real one."

"And it was such trash, too," Kelvin reminisces.

I watch the way their eyes stay locked on each other, how naturally they've both managed to lean to the same side and with each sentence get closer. Elbows on the counter. Chins propped in the palms of their hands. Even though I know Grace is just being conversational, I feel frustrated watching Kelvin. This is what it looks like when a boy is interested. He leans in. He smiles uncontrollably. He laughs.

And here I am, some grumpy old lady haggling over the price of a pair of radish-print gloves. I slip out of the store without either of them noticing and make it as far as my car before the blister on my toe stops me from taking a therapeutic rage walk. What's worse is that I can't drive off, because I'm Grace's ride home.

For a second I stare at my reflection in the window of

my car. This is the face of the least-flirty girl on the planet.

As soon as I get into the driver's seat, I kick off my shoes and text Grace that I'm waiting and ready to leave. I wait a few moments to see if she'll read it immediately, but I have no such luck. No free Starbucks for her, and no date to the wedding for me.

CHAPTER SIX

On Friday after school, I drive home and try to get ahead on a couple of my assignments before it's time to go to the community garden. Mom has her vinyasa yoga class from two thirty to three thirty, so I'm sitting in the kitchen wondering how much daylight we're going to have left when she breezes through the back door, promising to be ready in ten minutes. I tell her to take her time, but she just smiles at me, pouring herself a quick cup of water at the kitchen sink before running upstairs to trade her yoga pants and stretchy long-sleeve top for a flannel and jeans. She and I end up looking alike because instead of the ridiculous coveralls Grace thought were garden-appropriate, I go for an old pair of jeans, my trainers, and a T-shirt. Mom laughs when she comes back through the kitchen, realizing we both have on our hats, with our knee pads in one hand and our gloves tucked into our pockets.

"Ready?" she asks, holding the door open for me.

"As I'll ever be," I tell her, thankful for owning one thick flannel to keep me warm in the fall chill.

I watch our neighborhood pass by outside the car window. We drive by Grace's house, and I see her dad outside mowing the lawn. She told everyone about the meet-cute yesterday, and Sloane admitted she thought Grace was up to something with the gardening gloves. They were able to laugh it off as a funny memory that I'll get to keep, but it wasn't so easy for me to brush away. My first meet-cute was a disaster, to say the least. And I still have mixed feelings about the way Grace was able to casually carry on with Kelvin even though my moment with him had passed.

I try to push away thoughts about yesterday as we drive by the Yin house and I see their daughter sitting in the driveway with some of her friends. I used to give her swim lessons when she was in elementary school and I was still in middle school. Then we pass the community pool and I note all the cars outside, and feel thankful that it's not very busy in the mornings.

It isn't until we cut through town and start passing the arboretum that I realize the community garden has been under my nose this entire time. It's sponsored by our town's nature reserve, and past a patch of tall grass and a large row of apple trees, there's a hidden driveway. There's a small sign attached to a black fence post, and the gates are wide open.

We pull into the gravel parking lot, and there are a few people walking in the direction of a metal arch flanked by patches of sweet alyssum. Through the arch I can see chicken-wire fences and individual plots. From here it looks like one big wire wall. Some people have on hats; a few people carry individual knee pads or foam blocks with handles. And, like Mom said, most people seem to have their own gloves either hanging out of a tote or hanging out of their back pockets. I notice that most of them are like my mom, middle-aged with graying hair and a sense of urgency in their stride.

"I'm so excited for you to meet everyone," Mom tells me when she turns off the car.

"So, this is where you come *every* day?" I ask, getting out of the car.

As we approach the arch, I look in the direction of the greenhouse. It sits at the back of the property, a wooden frame with glass windows. A few windows are broken, and the white paint is peeling off the wood, exposing gray and rot in different spots. Outside the greenhouse entrance are troughs and sections of goldenrod and Russian sage flanking a makeshift walkway that's currently overgrown with grass.

"Inside the greenhouse is where the vegetable garden used to be," Mom explains when she catches me staring. "But there was a tree to the side of the greenhouse, and a few years ago a branch fell off and broke some of the wooden beams in the roof and one of the beams inside the house. It wasn't safe to work in there because at any second it was like the roof might cave in." She watches the greenhouse ahead of us, staring up at it like some monument. "We tried planting vegetables out here, but the animals would just eat them before we could harvest anything. No matter what we tried—cayenne, natural pesticides—they didn't stop."

She goes on about how they were able to raise enough money over the summer from selling flowers in the neighborhood to have the beams repaired so that the greenhouse is safe again. I tune in and out, taking in my surroundings. The air smells like a concoction of things, a floral perfume mixed with wet dirt, fertilizer, and moss. I feel out of place when we approach the rest of the group. There are people already kneeling down, pulling weeds, dirt covering the shins of their jeans. A few more people are wheeling out fragrant manure from the supply shed, and others are digging spots for trees along the perimeter of the garden.

"Beth," a woman says. She leaves her spot near an in-ground trough a few rows away, and makes a beeline for my mom. "Thank goodness you're here." She braces herself with a hand on my mom's shoulder and barely looks at me before pointing in the direction of the greenhouse. There's a boy, probably the youngest person here other than myself, standing on top of a ladder, hammering into one of the frame pieces. "I don't know what we're going to do with that greenhouse. It's atrocious."

"Oh, Gloria. It's not atrocious," Mom says. She squints up at the boy, and then her eyes travel down to the doorway, where the door has been gently set against the side of the house since it's no longer attached at the hinges. "It seems like Gavin has a handle on things. If anything, it's a genuine work in progress now that people can actually go inside."

"He knows about plants. He's not a carpenter," Gloria says, ignoring my mom's silver lining.

"I'm sure it's fine. Plus . . ." Mom turns to me. Gloria notices me for the first time and turns her entire body to face me. "This is my daughter, Mia. She can help with the greenhouse!"

"Does she know anything about building a green-house?" Gloria asks my mom even though she's looking at me.

"Do *you* know anything about building a greenhouse?" Mom challenges.

Somehow this is enough to satisfy Gloria. She adjusts her bucket hat and tightens the drawstring below her chin before taking my mom by the hand and leading her in the direction of a trough.

So, I guess this means I'm helping Gavin.

Upon closer inspection, I see that there are weeds lining the base of the greenhouse along the sides, and vines reaching toward the roof. Inside, sunlight slants through the windows, and rays filter in where the windows either have holes or are completely broken. There are a few faded signs for different veggies, like kale and carrots. For the most part, the inside of the greenhouse is old dry dirt with weeds festering in the different plots where plants used to be.

I figure it'll be easier to start weeding outside, so I find a spot of weeds with tiny white flowers, set down my knee pads, and get to work. I'm actually thankful to have the gloves because they protect my hands from some thorny plants that I find. It's a shame that even though the flowers are kind of cute, they're destroying the other life around them.

I'm not sure how long I'm working before Gavin comes down from the ladder. The metal creaks under his weight as he carefully places his feet on each rung. I use the hem of my flannel to wipe the dirt I feel on my cheek, and turn to Gavin as he approaches me. He's kind of short, but I can tell that he's muscular by the fit of his army-green long-sleeve shirt. He's wearing cargo pants and a pair of work boots that make him look like a mix between a park ranger and someone who spends his time hunting gators. I think his bucket hat, which matches Gloria's, definitely makes him lean more toward gator hunter.

"Hey," I say.

"Hey, um," he starts. He strokes his beard, looking down at the patch of weeds that I've pulled. I look down at my own work and feel a small amount of pride. The dirt that comes up with the roots is darker and richer than the dirt on the surface. Once I get a rake and shovel from the shed, we'll have a patch that we could plant something new in.

"I feel like I've done a lot, but also I've barely accomplished anything," I admit, gazing past the length of the greenhouse.

"I don't think we've met," Gavin says, crouching down next to me.

"I'm Mia, Beth's daughter."

"Beth's daughter," Gavin says, smiling. He looks off in the direction of where our moms are. I glance over too, but I don't see them by the troughs anymore.

"And you're Gloria's son?"

"Grandson," he corrects. "But, Beth's daughter—Mia, I—how do I put this? You're pulling baby's breath."

"What's that?" I ask, reaching for the pile of weeds next to me.

"It's a type of flower. Not actually a weed. And this particular patch that we've been growing on this side of the greenhouse is actually reserved for a wedding," he explains.

"No," I gasp. "No, you're joking. You're just messing with me," I say, even though it sounds more like a question. I watch his face, hopeful as he breaks into a laugh. But he shakes his head.

"I'm not joking." Gavin tries to stop laughing, but can't, which makes me feel even more embarrassed.

"Oh dear," I grumble, trying to hide my face—which is most definitely turning red—from Gavin.

I get up and brush the dirt and baby's breath petals off my jeans. The supply shed is on the other side of the greenhouse, and inside it stinks strongly of mulch. They keep a huge pile in the back of the shed. I gather a small shovel, a rake, and a watering tin, and make my way over to the wheelbarrows. I can just replant the flowers and pretend this never happened, and beg my mom not to bring me back here. Obviously I'm a danger to their whole project, not a helping hand.

"Mia!"

I startle. I turn on my heel and slip on some water. I quickly try to regain my footing, only to step on the handle of a shovel, which slips right out from under me, taking my foot with it. I try to reach for a shelf but find that it's just a piece of wood propped onto nails in the wall, and I flip over a bunch of small pots. I fall backward, helpless, and land in the soft, damp mulch.

"Oh my God," I gasp, horrified. I look at the pieces of broken pots scattered in front of me, and see that my shoes are covered in mulch. I can feel it on the backs of my arms inside the sleeves of my flannel, and along the back of my neck. It's probably in my hair! "Ugh!"

Even though my mind is racing, the sound of Gavin laughing cuts right through all my thoughts.

"What's so funny?" I growl, trying to figure out how to stand up without using the mulch to brace myself.

Gavin crosses the shed and holds out his hand to me. "Come on, that was hilarious. It looked like it could've been right out of Looney Tunes."

Looney Tunes? Who is this guy? Now he doubles over with laughter, and I take the opportunity to throw a handful of mulch at his hair. When he doesn't stop laughing, I grab more and throw it at his stupid shirt.

"The whole point of gardening clothes is getting them dirty," he says when he regains himself. He holds out his hand again, and when I ignore it and try to reach forward to push myself up from the floor, he just grabs my arm and hoists me into the air with a surprising amount of strength.

"Sorry," he says, even though he's joking. He uses his foot to brush aside the pot pieces, and grabs the shovel that I tripped on. "I was just coming to help you replant the baby's breath," he tells me, starting to shovel mulch into one of the wheelbarrows. "I figured if I announced myself we could've avoided . . . that."

"Well, mission *not* accomplished," I say, before mumbling "Thanks" while I get as much of the mulch out of my hair as I can.

He reaches into the pile of mulch for the tools I'd been gathering and hands them to me. Without a word he takes the wheelbarrow by the handles and leads the way back to my desecrated side of the greenhouse. On our way out of the shed, I grab an extra rake and shovel.

"I wasn't laughing at you," he says after a while. "I was laughing at the situation itself."

"You were laughing at me falling into a pile of mulch. Therefore, you were laughing at me," I tell him as he holds out his hand for one of the plants.

"No, I wasn't. Honestly, if the roles were switched, tell me you wouldn't have laughed," he says as he puts the plant into one of the fresh holes.

"I would only laugh because now you deserve it," I tell him, feeling some of my animosity dissipate as I imagine him twirling in a puddle, losing his footing on a shovel, reaching for a false shelf, and falling into mulch. "Although, it would be hilarious if you fell into the mulch face-first."

"That's just cruel," he says, pretending to gasp.

"Honestly, if I fell face-first, you wouldn't have laughed harder?" I mimic him.

"I can neither confirm nor deny what would've happened," he says, holding up his right hand as if to swear.

We work in silence, developing a rhythm between us. I rake the soil and make a hole; he plants the baby's breath and adds mulch to prevent more weeds from growing. Then we repeat. We get through eight more plants before he breaks the silence.

Gavin asks, "So, what are you doing here? Clearly you're not into gardening."

"Volunteer hours," I say. "How about you, Mr. Handyman? Is this, like, a hobby or something?"

"For my grandma, yes. Though, for me, being here wasn't necessarily my choice either," he admits, not looking up from the patch of dirt that he's patting around the roots of a plant.

"Then, why are you here?"

"Punishment," he says. When he doesn't offer more, I take the hint and refocus on the task in front of us.

By the time Mom comes to tell me it's time to leave, the only thing we accomplished is undoing the mess I created.

"Any fun Friday plans?" he asks as we return the supplies to the shed.

"Homework. You?"

"It's Friday. You have all weekend to do your homework," Gavin says. "Do something fun tonight. Promise me?"

"What's it to you?" I ask, laughing a little. "Plus, you didn't answer me. What are *you* doing?"

He pauses, dumping our leftover mulch into the pile. "Um, just some . . ." He mumbles something I can't quite hear.

"Did you say what I think you just said?"

He smiles at me before saying, "Okay, so go do something fun for the both of us while I stay inside and do homework."

"Why can't *you* do something fun for the both of us?" I ask, taking the opportunity to replace the shelf I pulled off the wall.

"Because I'm grounded, and you're not."

"Right. Your punishment," I say, watching for his reaction.

He doesn't say anything. I look across the shed at the indent in the pile of mulch from where I fell. Then I look at him, wiping out the wheelbarrow and replacing it with the others.

"Thank you," I say as sincerely as I can.

He looks over at me and smiles; his whole face lights up. "I didn't think you were going to say it, but look at that."

"And now you ruined it," I say, turning around to leave.

"See you," he calls after me, even though I'm already outside.

CHAPTER SEVEN

S aturday morning, I get up with the sun and head over to the South Glenn Community Center, ready to decompress from my week with some mildly competitive laps against Harold. When I pull into the parking lot at 5:56 a.m., I'm a little surprised that his car isn't already here. Usually he arrives before me, and since he's friends with Clarence, he manages to get inside before the doors are supposed to unlock at six.

When I see Clarence wave from the entrance, I figure my showing up first and beating Harold to the water might be just the edge to start our competitive mood this morning. I quickly change in the locker room and savor the stillness and isolation of having the pool area to myself. It might only last for a couple more minutes, but still, it's rare that I get to inhale the scent of chlorine in near silence. The fans in the ceiling make a low hum as they circulate the air, and the water laps against the edges of the pool, calling to me.

I get in, swim to the other end, and turn over to streamline as far as I can underwater before starting a few hundred meters freestyle. With each stroke I push the hardware store incident further out of my mind and focus on the swim meet next week. But the image of Kelvin's face rises to the surface, the way he smiled at me fading into the way he smiled at Grace. I take a deep breath before sinking back under. I propel myself forward, faster. I focus on the win, and with the water passing over every inch of my skin, I work harder.

On my next push off the wall, I see a familiar set of pale legs covered in bushy white hair under the water in the edge lane. I swim a little faster until another set of legs appears. When the bubbles around the legs dissipate, I make out a pair of lime-green bikini bottoms. Instead of coming up for air, I keep my rhythm and hold my hands out farther as I pull myself toward the end of my lap. It isn't until I open my mouth for air that I realize how out of breath I am.

"That was a minute and forty-nine seconds," Harold tells me, beaming. "You'd better swim like that next week."

"I know," I admit, looking down the lane. I see Gladys come up for air at the other end of the pool. As she gets closer, I realize that her lime-green bikini has flamingos all over it.

"Ready to race?" he asks, pulling his new goggles down over his eyes. I feel a brief moment of pride that he finally took my advice and bought a pair. Even though, deep down, I think it was probably Gladys who got him to do it.

"Yeah," I say, still watching Gladys as she does a small dive forward and disappears under the water. "You and Gladys, huh?"

Harold turns to me, surprised. He pushes his goggles back up onto his forehead and looks from me back down to the end of his lane, where Gladys had been. Finally he says, "Yes." It comes out sounding more like a question than a statement.

"Has she been coming to the pool with you this week?"

"We actually took a couple of days off from swimming," he says. Hearing him say "we" is odd, but also nice. I try to imagine him out at Starbucks for their first date, sitting across from Gladys, talking over steaming cortados. "She was moving in the rest of her things."

"Moving?"

"She moved here from Pittsburgh," Harold tells me. "Gladys's son just graduated from college, and since she's originally from this area, she decided it was time for her to come back home." Harold smiles, obviously pleased by her decision. "I helped her unpack some of her stuff this past week. Her son seems like a great guy."

"Right," I say, noticing that Gladys is more than half-way back to us. "Ready?" I ask.

Harold quickly pulls his goggles back over his eyes. I set the timer on my watch, and we count down from three before pushing off. I realize we didn't agree on what stroke to do. I go for the butterfly since it's the closest chance Harold has at winning, and this way I won't get too far ahead of him and be alone at the end of the lane with Gladys, waiting for him to finish.

When I'm done with my second lap, I find Gladys

lifting Styrofoam weights over her head in the shallow end.

"Hello, dear," she says, smiling. She puts the weights down on the surface of the water and starts stretching with one arm reaching over her head.

"Hey, Gladys," I say, feeling a little awkward.

"Harold is excited for your meet next week," she tells me. "He's been keeping track of your times in this little black book. He really cares."

Even though I already knew this, it makes me smile to hear it. Harold kept track of my lap times throughout the summer and measured my averages to track my steady progression. He predicted that I would be able to continue decreasing my lap times if I continued practicing every day, and he suggested that I'd see a more rapid improvement if I started conditioning outside the pool. I imagine that it's what my dad would do if he was still a hard-ass when it came to high school sports.

Harold makes it back to our end of the lane, and he plants a kiss on Gladys's cheek when she's mid-lift. "Did you want to go over Mia's times right now?" she asks him.

Harold explains to her that our plan is to get together to review my averages on the mornings of the meets, and that today he's going to record some of my lap times so that he can give me the most up-to-date numbers.

We begin, Harold sitting on the edge of the pool. I decide to start with backstroke, and hold on to the wall while Harold readies his stopwatch. He almost always forgets his glasses at home, and without them he has a hard time reading the different buttons. Usually I help him, but Gladys wades over to him to set the lap timer. I watch her help Harold, noticing how their heads tilt together the same way my parents' do when they're trying to discuss something quietly—almost like they're trying to think with one brain. Only, my parents have been together for nearly forty years; Harold and Gladys have been together for about a week.

So, maybe it's not impossible to meet someone and immediately find a natural sense of familiarity with them. Maybe I can even do that by Sam's wedding.

I hold on to my sense of hope much later as I leave the pool to get ready for the Davenports' jam flavor launch.

"I feel like it's not going to be that bad," Abby tells me as we trail behind my parents into the Birch Tree hotel for brunch.

"You haven't seen him in action," I warn her, trying to hide behind the wall of my parents and Sam, keeping my eyes peeled for Geoffrey's younger brother, Jasper.

"This is so exciting," Abby says, distracted. We walk into the dining room of the hotel, which the Davenports have rented out for their Jazzy Jam brunch. Today is the release of their plum jam, the newest flavor in their line. Geoffrey told us that since they used a new method to make the jam smoother, they wanted to incorporate smooth jazz into the theme, really make the flavor memorable and distinct. I had to hold in my urge to laugh.

Geoffrey really puts a lot of thought into every aspect of his jam.

All the tables are pushed together to form one long dining table down the center of the room. On opposite sides of the room, behind where people will be sitting, are two mirrored buffet tables where guests can line up for food. On the dining table is a long ongoing centerpiece littered with fake plums and vines and plum-scented candles spaced throughout. At the ends of the buffet tables are individual small tables set a few inches apart with all the flavors that the Davenports have produced since their founding. Of course the plum flavor is held up on a literal pedestal, with a small card talking about the origin of the flavor, from the conception of the idea to the jam's manifestation in the sealed jar.

"Babe," Geoffrey calls from the end of the buffet line. He pushes his glasses farther up on his nose. I watch as he and Sam share a kiss. They start whispering to each other as Sam centers his necktie, also plum printed, with gold detail leaves.

"This looks amazing," I hear Sam say as she turns to face us again. "I'm so excited."

Abby reaches for a plain bagel and takes the spoon from the open jar of plum jam. As she's spreading it onto her bagel with care, she realizes that no one is talking and all of us are staring at her.

"May I?" she asks.

"Go right ahead," Geoffrey says. "I'm interested to hear

what you think. You'll be the first person outside the focus group to try it. I mean, other than myself and my family, of course."

"I haven't even tried it yet," Sam admits, scouring for a poppy seed bagel.

Abby doesn't finish spreading. She immediately takes a bite and chews voraciously. Geoffrey leans in a little, watching her face as it goes through a range of expressions.

"Sweet, with a tang in the aftertaste. Rich. I'm sensing a little apricot?" Abby asks. Geoffrey nods. "Smooth, on purpose?" He nods again. "Excellent."

"Thank you," Geoffrey says, looking relieved.

"That's why I bring her," I say jokingly, though I know that for Abby this is the number one reason why she'd get up before noon on a Saturday. She loves everything jelly and jam. For her, peanut butter and jelly is more like peanut butter and *jelly*.

"Why don't you rehearse your speech," Sam suggests before taking a bite out of her bagel.

"There's a speech?" Abby asks through a mouthful of bagel.

"Yes," Geoffrey says, smiling. "This is the official launch, after all." He looks down at his notecards and flips through the first two. "That's just the greeting and opening." He skims the third and taps the card with the back of his hand. "This one. 'What makes the plum jam special, perhaps our best flavor yet, is the complex measures we took to make it. You'll note the hints of apricot and subtle but sour green grape flavor underneath that of the prominent plum. We started with our typical jam-making process by taking the pulp and skin from the plum to simmer into a coarser spread. Separately we took the juice from the apricot and the juice from winter-grown grapes and made a jelly.'"

Geoffrey pauses and peers at us over the top edge of his glasses.

Sam's smile immediately widens, and Abby gives Geoffrey a thumbs-up. When he looks to me, I prompt him to go on.

"'Then we mixed the two together. The abnormal smoothness to the spread comes from half of it being a jelly. The winter-grown grapes allow for a slight bite that is augmented when the jam is served chilled. We're hoping to experiment more with winter-grown crops now that my soon-to-be-wife and I are collaborating on greenhouse architecture and the technology to help these fruits survive cold climates.'" Geoffrey blushes when he mentions Sam, and Sam blushes a little too. I try not to gag.

"I think the speech is great," Sam says when he finishes.

"I do too, and I think jelly jam is genius," Abby adds.

I reach down for a bagel and spread some of the jam across a piece. I take a bite and chew as slowly as I can while Geoffrey practically jumps out of the collar of his shirt in anticipation.

"Okay, so, fine, you did a good job," I say, laughing a little.

More people start to arrive, and Geoffrey gets swept up in welcoming guests and buyers. The Davenports have been working on a contract with Whole Foods, and this brunch is the first one they've been invited to since starting negotiations. Geoffrey makes sure to give small introductions to the new flavor while not getting too far into discussion before his speech.

I cling to Abby, thankful that Geoffrey let me know that Jasper and their parents haven't arrived yet. I scan the room from our seat at the table and note that a few of the local newspapers sent reporters to cover the event. Some of Geoffrey's other family members who are involved in the family business are here. His father and grandfather are sitting at the end of the table closest to the podium, representing the generational succession of the company. Abby and I are situated toward the middle of the table. Even though my parents are supposed to sit next to us, the open seat gives me anxiety because I know Jasper could slip in at any moment, and my mom wouldn't think anything of moving down a few seats so that he could sit and chat with us instead of having to make his way down to the far end of the table with the rest of the Davenports.

"Let's walk around," I suggest when the anticipation is too much.

We walk down to the podium and look at how the makeshift stage is decorated. Then we go by the jam table again so that Abby can make her ultimate bagel, where she organizes all her favorite Davenport Delicacies onto one large carb. Then, when I spot Geoffrey's parents, I decide we should step out for some air.

"Again," Abby says, "no idea what the big deal is." She hugs her jean jacket around herself, and I tuck my ears inside my hat.

"I just can't look at him right now."

"He's a little kid. You're a junior in high school. Why are you so worried?" she asks impatiently.

"I'm worried that if I don't find a date, I'm going to have to spend my sister's wedding with him!" I remind her. "Instead of remembering it as this supposed beautiful ceremony and life-changing occasion that Sam keeps describing, the only thing I'll remember is how I had to babysit Jasper all evening."

"Mia," Abby says, taking me by the shoulders and shaking me a little. "I promise on my soul that it's not going to come to that, okay? You'll go with him over my dead body."

"Go with who?" a familiar high-pitched voice asks. "And where are *we* going?" Jasper asks, bumping my hip with his, even though his hip falls slightly below mine.

"*We* aren't going anywhere," I say.

"Except to the wedding," he says, smiling. "I heard about your predicament from your sweet sister just moments ago. I had to come let you know not to fear any longer, because your knight in shining armor is here." Jasper gives a theatrical bow. When he straightens up and bobs his eyebrows, he looks like Franklin from *My Wife and Kids*. Cute, but too young to date, and equally annoying.

"Like I said, *we* aren't going anywhere together," I repeat, bending down to meet his eye.

"I feel like you're just fighting destiny," Jasper says. His Nintendo makes a sound, and he immediately lifts it back up so that it's nearly touching his nose. He starts pressing the buttons. "Just let it happen," he mumbles over the chimes of his game.

I start walking away, but the sounds of static explosions and rapid gunfire follow me across the lobby of the hotel.

"Are you really going to play that during the party?" I ask, stopping outside the banquet hall. I look around and realize that Abby slipped back inside when I wasn't looking, completely shirking her responsibilities.

"I'll turn the volume down," he says, not looking up.

"Why don't you turn it off while your brother is talking, since he worked so hard on his speech?" I ask, waving my hand to try to get Abby's attention.

"Why don't you unbutton the top button of your dress?" Jasper asks.

I barely believe what I hear, until I look back at him and catch him staring at me instead of his Nintendo.

"You wish."

"Oh, I do, very much," he agrees, leaning against the doorway.

I turn to look at the banquet room just in time to catch Abby gliding through the doorway. While Jasper is distracted, she snatches his Nintendo, flashes me a wink, and takes off down one of the hotel hallways.

"What are we playing today?" she asks, and giggles as Jasper tries to jump high enough to get his Nintendo back.

As I watch them, I reimagine the scene, only with Abby in her dress for the wedding and Jasper in whatever expensive designer suit he's convinced his parents to buy. Is this what Sam's reception is going to be like? The thought makes me cringe. Like Abby said, over my dead body am I going to the wedding with Jasper.

CHAPTER EIGHT

At swim practice on Monday, Abby tells Victor about the jam event. She also tells him about Jasper, and I'm relieved when she doesn't mention that he might be my date to the wedding.

"Who are they?" I interrupt when a group of boys I've never seen before comes out of the boys' locker room. "Don't they know we have practice today?"

"Boys' tryouts are coming up," Victor tells me. "We've been doing a lot of recruiting."

Right. After the girls' season starts, boys will bring their recruits to our practices to give them a sense of how the practices are run, and sometimes the boys will even do conditioning when our practices are winding down.

I pull myself over the edge of the pool so that I am sitting with my feet dangling in the water and push my goggles up onto my forehead. "Are any of them actually going to make it?" I ask, letting some of the water out of my swim cap. I hate that it never seals perfectly.

"A few," Victor tells me. He stands to go join the boys in the bleachers, kissing Abby on the cheek first.

The boys' team always has more recruits than the girls'.

It's harder to find new talent over the summer, when school's not in session and half the people you meet at the community pools go to different schools. The boys wait until school starts, and they make announcements, join their table with ours at the activity fair, and use our swim meets as recruiting grounds. It also helps that a good amount of the boy swimmers date the girl swimmers. That definitely increases their numbers. However, there are always fewer boys than girls that actually make the team and stick with it.

Coach blows the whistle and tells us to line up for partner relays. Abby and I go back to our split lane, and she slips into the water, ready to kick us off. She always leaps from the start with fire, getting her lead early so that she can slow down toward the end. I, on the other hand, start off slower—allowing one or two swimmers to get ahead of me before I give my all and push ahead at the end, after my opponents have tired themselves out. When we can do partner relays for drills, we're virtually unbeatable.

"That was awesome," someone says as Abby pulls me out of the pool after our first set of relays.

I take off my goggles and wipe my eyes, to find a boy offering me my towel.

"You're Mia, right?"

"Yes," I say, drying my hand before shaking the one he's holding out to me.

We fall silent, and a familiar awkwardness comes over me.

"This is Ritchie," Victor says. I feel embarrassed that I didn't think to ask.

"Nice to meet you," I tell Ritchie.

"You too," he says, smiling at me.

Coach has us do a butterfly stroke relay and then tells us to pick our weakest stroke to practice for time. The times we set today we have to beat by Wednesday's practice, so that we're in good shape for our meet.

Our junior varsity swimmers get out of the pool and let some of the boys' team have a few lanes for conditioning. Two of them join Abby and me in our lane, and we time them first before taking over and timing each other. During my laps I catch Abby staring at Victor doing stretches a few lanes down instead of at the stopwatch.

I finish and tap the time on my Apple Watch, thankful that I was keeping track on my own, before calling out, "Earth to Abby."

She quickly clicks the timer and reads my time out to me. Three seconds off. I smile and shake my head as I climb out of the pool.

"You're gonna feel sore tomorrow," she tells me.

"Yeah, and what are you gonna feel?" I ask, teasing as I wrap my towel around me.

"Hopefully still full from a well-deserved dinner," she says, laughing.

There's a team dinner at Maria's house tonight, and her mom always goes all out. We review what we think she'll make for us as we walk to the bleachers to watch the boys do their conditioning. She had a pasta night last year. Make-your-own-pizza night the year before, when the boys' team didn't join us. She even made cauliflower crusts for all of us so that we wouldn't carb load before the meet.

Abby's eyes stay fixed on Victor, as he swims and while he keeps time for his partners.

I scan the pool, watching more of the recruits slip into the water as the rest of the girls finish their laps. Ritchie and his partner catch my eye as they start practicing in the lane closest to the bleachers. I'm surprised when he breaks away from the wall with good form. There's confidence and familiarity in his stroke.

"Where'd that guy come from?" I ask, nudging Abby.

As if he heard me, Ritchie turns to the bleachers as he's getting out of the water and waves.

"You mean Ritchie Hutchins?" she asks, waving back. When she turns her attention to me and Ritchie keeps smiling, I realize his smile is for me.

"Yes," I say, looking away. I keep my hands tucked inside my towel and pull it tighter around my shoulders.

"I think he's new, like he transferred schools," she admits.

"So, he's not a freshman?" I ask, watching him crouch on the block, ready to dive over his partner.

"I don't think so," she says, still watching Victor. I watch her eyes flick to Ritchie's lane and follow him as he does a really good breaststroke. "It's obvious he's not new to swimming."

Coach blows the whistle, and everyone gets out of the pool. Before people start toward the locker rooms, she reminds us about the team dinner and says that Maria's mom has invited the boy recruits to attend so that they can see what swim team is about outside the water.

Victor comes up to the bleachers, smiling hugely. "I have intel," he says, looking back and forth between Abby and me.

"What's your intel?" Abby asks.

Victor looks around to make sure no one is within earshot before whispering, "Richie Rich has the hots for you know who."

"You don't have to say 'you know who' when you're talking to 'you know who,'" she tells him.

"Who is 'you know who'?" I ask.

They ignore me.

"What do we know about Richie Rich?" Abby asks Victor. They tilt their heads together, and I feel a little awkward. Nevertheless, I still listen.

"He's been a swimmer for—I think—four years. He transferred from Holloway Charter school because his parents got a divorce. He lives with his dad who owns, like, four Taco Bells. He's really good at *Halo*—"

"Intel we can use?" Abby cuts him off.

Victor pauses before saying, "I believe he's single."

"Richie Rich is single?" Abby asks, jumping up and down. Victor joins her, and they hold hands like two sorority girls before turning to me. "He's single!" Abby repeats.

"Ritchie?"

"Yes!"

I start to ask why we care that Ritchie is single, but Abby shushes me. She and Victor wave someone over, and I turn around to see Ritchie coming out of the boys' locker room.

"Oh, hey," he says, and smiles, not sure at first if we're looking at him or if someone came out of the locker room behind him. He shuffles over to us so as to not slip, before asking, "What's up, guys?"

His hair is still soaking wet and plastered to his forehead. He's wearing a gray-and-red Holloway sweatshirt and a pair of Adidas slides that squeak with each step.

"About to go change for the dinner," Abby tells him.

"Do you have a ride?" Victor asks.

"I don't even have the address," Ritchie admits, glancing toward me.

I smile politely, but feel exposed when he keeps staring.

"Why don't you ride with us?" Victor asks.

"Yes! You can meet us at Mia's house, and we can all drive over together," Abby says, catching me off guard.

"That would be awesome. I mean, if you guys have enough room," Ritchie says, looking from them to me.

"It's not my car," I tell him, but Abby pinches the back of my shoulder, so I add, "But it's cool with me either way."

"Great. Victor will text you Mia's address," Abby says. "We're going to go get dressed and then head over to her place, so let's aim for, like, twenty minutes?" Victor gives her a look, but she glares him down before he can ask why we wouldn't just go straight to the dinner.

I wait until the door closes behind Ritchie before turning to Abby and Victor.

"This is great," Victor sings.

"Good looking out, babe." Abby wraps her arms around Victor, and they sway to some imaginary victory song in their heads.

"Wait, so is this your meet-cute?" I ask.

Victor smiles nervously, not revealing anything. Abby tells him that he should go get changed so we can go get changed, but I know it's because she wants to talk to me alone for a few minutes. She holds the door to the locker room open for me and immediately starts explaining.

"We've been scouting material together, and I figured his perspective could help. I want to do the meet-cute thing, but a lot of guys don't care about bumping hands over a glove or picking up stuff that girls drop on the floor," Abby explains. "I want this to be fun, but I also want it to work."

"Okay," I say, keeping up with her as I turn my shower on.

"Ritchie wasn't a planned meet-cute. Tonight wasn't planned at all. But, I mean, he likes you. It's obvious he likes you, and I think since there's some natural momentum, it can't hurt for us to take advantage of the opportunity and help you see where this goes."

We finish rinsing and head over to our lockers to dry off.

"He seems cool," I say. He's slightly taller than me, definitely able to balance out a wedding photo. But I'm interested to see if he can hold a conversation. "I guess this could work."

We get dressed, leave the locker room, and cut through the school to the student parking lot. I used to find the empty school weird and off-putting, but after so many club meetings and late swim practices, it's become comfortable. I like knowing that the school gets to rest when we're not around.

We are hit with a wall of October chill when we step outside. The air mixes with the exhaust from Victor's 2012 Ford truck idling at the curb.

"Do you want a ride to your car?" Abby asks me.

"No. I'll just see you at my house." As the words leave my mouth, I remember the other weird part about tonight's arrangement and ask why she decided not to head straight to the dinner.

"So that you can change and look cute for your meet-cute," she says, smiling. "See you soon."

I cross the nearly empty parking lot to my car. On the drive home I try to imagine what Ritchie might look like when his hair is dry and combed out of his face. I try to picture him in a tux with a carnation and white rose pinned to his pocket. It's not an atrocious image, but definitely one that might take a little getting used to.

I park behind Sam's car in the driveway and take a moment to look up Ritchie on Instagram. His profile is public so I can see everything he's posted. His page bleeds the red and gray of his Holloway school. They wore uniforms and even had matching school scarves in the wintertime. He definitely would look good in a tux, but he comes off as preppy. I'm more into someone who doesn't wear brands or logos, whose clothes are able to show who they are without representing someone else.

When I walk into the house, I nearly don't hear Sam calling my name from the kitchen. I'm still staring at his profile, scrolling down to a football game from last year. He's posing with a petite brunette from his school. Their sweatshirts match and he has his arm around her waist—not her shoulders. I wonder if this is what he's used to, someone who wears lipstick and heavy eye shadow, whose hair is curled to perfection and long enough that it falls halfway down her back. Even her nails are perfect, painted a deep brown, curled around a Starbucks coffee cup.

"Mia," Sam says, snapping her fingers impatiently.

I look up in time to see her opening her wedding binder.

"Thank goodness you're finally home."

As she takes a deep breath to—no doubt—give me a mouthful of wedding-related problems to solve, I take the opening to say, "I'm here for five minutes. Then I'm going to a team dinner."

"You always have team dinners. You never eat dinner at home anymore."

"You're being dramatic," I tell her.

I start toward the stairs, Sam's flats clicking along the hardwood floor behind me.

"I need you tonight," she says.

I try to close the door to my bedroom behind me, but Sam catches it and follows me inside.

"What about Mom, Dad, or Brooke?" I ask as I start unloading my notebooks onto my desk.

"They're not you. You're my sister," she pleads, sitting on the end of my bed.

"And Mom is your mom and Dad is your dad and Brooke is your best friend. All of them should be more qualified to help you than I am," I say, forcing a comb through my wet tangled chlorinated hair.

I hadn't even thought about what I should do with my hair. Usually we head straight to team dinners from practice. That way we get first pick of the food. My hair is always a mess, and I just put on sweatpants and a sweatshirt. If Ritchie needs a cute dress instead of a sweatshirt, he'd probably prefer fruity-smelling dry hair to this nest.

"Mia, you're not funny," Sam says, an edge in her voice.

"I wasn't trying to be," I snap back.

I turn around to find Sam bent over her binder. Her glasses are sliding down her nose, and she has a dark blue pen uncapped, poised over her paper. The blue pen means she's working on the menu. She starts biting her nail, and I can't take it anymore, so I dare to ask what the problem is.

I sit down next to her and see that she's circled a picture of shrimp on the cocktail menu.

"Geoffrey's cousin is allergic to shellfish. Like, deathly allergic."

"So, you get rid of the shrimp," I tell her, standing up when the doorbell rings.

I bend over and push all my hair up on top of my head.

I gather it into a ponytail and ignore the knots forming as I twist it into a bun.

"Mia, it's not that easy," Sam says as Abby materializes in my doorway.

Abby tosses me a balled-up mass of fabric. I catch it and hide behind my closet door to change.

"What's another popular finger food?" I ask as I peel my swimsuit off.

"Pigs in a blanket?" Abby answers.

"I'm not serving pigs in a blanket at my wedding," Sam hisses.

"What about cheese, grapes, crackers, and tiny cuts of meat?" I ask, pulling at the hem of the dress, surprised it's not longer.

"You mean charcuterie?" Sam asks.

"Yeah," I say slowly, looking down at the deep V neckline dancing on the edge of dangerous. "Hey, Abby?" I ask, stepping out from behind the door so I can look in my mirror. "Are you sure this is my size?"

I stare at my reflection and see Abby and Sam analyzing me in the mirror. Sam's face is how I feel on the inside, confused and slightly horrified.

Abby, on the other hand, is smiling. "It's perfect."

The dress is short enough that I won't be bending down for anything tonight. And the neckline makes me regret calling those light scarfs Sam used to push on me stupid.

"I think it looks nice," Abby says, nudging Sam when she sees me still frowning.

Sam pushes her glasses back up her nose before saying, "I think it looks young. . . . Like, you look like a teenager." The way she says it, I can't tell if that's a good thing, since that's what I am.

"Okay, good," Abby says, grabbing my mini backpack off the floor and tossing it to me.

I fill it with my phone, keys, ChapStick, and a travel-size lotion.

"We have to go. They're waiting," Abby says.

"They?" I ask as we leave my room.

"Victor and Ritchie," Abby clarifies as we run down the stairs.

"Who's Ritchie?" Sam asks, right behind us.

"A new kid on the swim team," I tell her.

"A potential date." Abby tells her the truth.

"Mia, what about my cocktail hour emergency?" Sam asks, stopping us at the front door. Abby waves to Victor from the porch, and the cold October breeze sneaks in and kisses goose bumps onto my bare shoulders, making me realize I forgot to grab a jacket out of my closet. I shiver.

"How about I brainstorm more cold appetizers that fit your Asian-fusion theme and text you the list in the morning, and in the meantime you can Pinterest cocktail hour menus?" I say, trying to find some compromise so Sam won't feel completely abandoned.

"Fine," Sam says, sighing. She sets her binder down, pulls her sweater off, and drapes it over my shoulders. "Have fun," she whispers, looking down at the neckline of the dress again as if to reaffirm that it wasn't a figment of her imagination.

I mouth *Thank you* to her before following Abby down the front walk. Even though the sweater helps with the chill, it does nothing for my legs. Abby is wearing a dark green circle skirt with a cropped black hoodie. She also put her hair up into a bun, but it looks a lot neater than mine.

As we approach Victor's truck, the back door flies open. Ritchie is smiling at me, his wet hair combed back from his face. He traded his wet trunks and Adidas slides for a pair of jeans and New Balance sneakers. He's still wearing his Holloway hoodie, though, which makes me think back to that girl in the football photo.

"What took you so long?" Victor asks, pulling away from the curb the second my door closes.

He immediately busts a U-turn, flinging me back against the door and then throwing me forward into the seat when he straightens out the car. I plant my hands down so that I don't tumble all the way into Ritchie's lap.

"You might want to put your seat belt on," Ritchie whispers to me. His teeth reflect the streetlights in the darkness of the back seat. His smile makes me feel a little less embarrassed.

I take his advice and feel ten times more comfortable knowing I won't get flung all over like a pinball for the rest of the ride.

"He is a bit of a crazy driver," I whisper back, thankful for the heat inside the car.

Ritchie laughs a little, and I can feel him staring at me across the silence between us. As I stare out the window, I try to think of what to say. All I know is that he used to go to a charter school, his parents are divorced, and he plays *Halo*. I guess the only thing we have in common is swimming. I wish Abby had told Victor to pick me up first. At least that would've given me a chance to hear what she was thinking.

"You look nice," Ritchie says quietly, his voice above a whisper.

I catch Victor's eye in the rearview mirror, and he quickly looks away.

"Thank you," I say, reminding myself to smile.

I take the opportunity to really look at him, since he's already staring at me. His olive-tone skin makes me wonder if he has Mediterranean heritage. He has light-brown eyes, and the contrast in them is electrifying. Or maybe it's his unbashful smile with perfect teeth that's electrifying. Or the fact that his eyes and his smile and his entire body are turned toward me.

I wonder how Abby would've planned our meet-cute. Am I supposed to trip into his arms at some point in the night? Do we reach for the same fork at dinner, and that's the first time we touch? Should I fling a piece of chicken at him across the table?

"Ritchie," Abby says, the silence probably making her uncomfortable. "We were trying to figure out how many years you've been swimming."

"I already told you," Victor says. "Four."

"You said you think, not that you know," Abby snaps, before turning to look at us between the seats.

"This will be my fourth year," Ritchie says. "I picked it up at the end of middle school."

"That's cool," Abby says, glancing at me before adding, "Mia's been swimming since she could walk."

"That's impressive. It makes sense, though, since you're really, really good," Ritchie says, making be blush.

The attention makes me nervous, so I tell him that Abby's been swimming just as long as me.

"Yeah, but I'm going for scholarships." She turns to Ritchie as if to have a private conversation. "She's not trying to get a scholarship, and she's been swimming her whole life! And is one of the best on the team!"

"Wait, why not?" Ritchie asks as Victor slows the car to a stop.

I look out the window and see Maria's house. A few people are closing the front door behind them as they duck inside.

"Oh, look," I say, thankful for an excuse to avoid the ever-looming topic of *my future* and *my continuing education*. I feel my stomach grumble and throw open my door, practically cheering, "It's time for dinner."

I stumble away from the truck, forgetting how far off the ground it is. I'm thankful Abby didn't say anything about me wearing Vans. Being able to firmly plant my feet on the ground saves me from falling into the woodchips lining the walkway up to Maria's front door. I turn around to wait for Victor to lock the car and catch up with us. I watch Ritchie check the bottom of his shoe, and I wonder what he would do if I fell into the woodchips. I wonder if he would risk getting a scratch on the sole of his New Balances to hold out his hand, or if chivalry isn't his thing.

I've always liked Maria's house because there's something warm about it. The outside is painted a dark blue that nearly blends in with the night sky and complements the pine trees lining the sides of her yard. The windows are outlined in white paint, and the front door is a deep almost red-looking wood with a gold knocker. There's a porch swing that creaks when it sways, and the red lantern on the floor next to it makes it seem like when you walk up to her house, you're walking up to a cabin in the woods. Especially since it's smaller than most of the houses in her neighborhood.

Immediately inside the front door, a few of our teammates sit at the bottom of the steps, bowls in hand. To the left of the stairwell is a small hallway leading to the dining room and then the kitchen. That's where the fragrant and intoxicating smells are coming from. To the right of the stairs is the living room, where a few of the guys have set up camp. Some have already placed their bowls down to spear some marshmallows by the fire.

I breathe in the spicy scents of garlic, ginger, tomato, samosas, and mint yogurt sauce.

"Indian theme," Abby and I say at the same time as we kick off our shoes next to the mound building by the door.

There are already a few people sitting down at the dining room table. Abby says hello as we squeeze by to the kitchen, and I can't help but notice as a few of the girls do a double take when they notice me wearing a dress. When I hear some of the boys in the kitchen, I quickly button up the sweater Sam loaned me.

"Hello, girls, and Victor," Maria's mom greets us, lifting her wooden spoon out of the huge pot on the stove. "And who is this unfamiliar face?"

"I'm Ritchie," he says, holding out his hand. Mrs. Gurdip swats it away and leans in for a hug.

"Hello, Mrs. Gurdip," I say, accepting my own hug before stepping over to look down at the orange sauce bubbling. "Gosh, this smells amazing."

"It's my famous chicken tikka masala," she says, grabbing a paper bowl and ladling some into it. "Tell me what you think."

I take a plastic spoon from a bag on the counter and gently blow over an orange chunk of chicken before taking a bite. I watch as Abby and Victor hand their bowls to Mrs. Gurdip, and then my eyes meet Ritchie's. Now that we're under the fluorescent kitchen lights, I can see a beauty mark just above his lip. And as his smile widens while I chew on a piece of chicken, I spot a slight, but adorable, snaggletooth.

"This is fantastic," I say, still chewing. "Can I have some more?"

I wait as she adds some to my bowl and points over to a

tray full of samosas. I take a couple and pour myself a cup of Pepsi before going into the dining room.

"This is her best dinner yet," one of the boys is saying.

Everyone nods in agreement, silently chewing.

I catch movement out of the corner of my eye and find Shannon trying to get my attention. She waves me over to her side of the table, and I take a seat next to her. I don't realize how tired I am from practice until I lean back into the cushion and feel my entire body relax.

"What's with the dress?" she asks quietly, blowing over her bowl.

"It was Abby's idea," I say. "She wanted to dress up for Victor, but she didn't want to be the only one who changed after practice."

Abby, Victor, and Ritchie join us, Ritchie sitting between Abby and me. Ritchie tries to make conversation, but we keep falling into silences because while he's talking, I'm chewing, and when I finally finish and ask him a question, he's started chewing. Slowly but surely I find out that he loves Indian food, and there's a restaurant downtown that he and his brothers go to for their birthdays where they make the best samosas he's ever had. In addition to swimming, he does archery and soccer, which I didn't see on his Instagram. He also has a cat named Tac, who I don't remember seeing on his Instagram. I try to imagine him cuddling up to Tac, a chubby three-legged Siamese, and it makes me smile.

"You have a nice smile," he tells me.

"You do too," I say, which makes him smile even harder.

"Do you want my last samosa?" he asks, taking my empty orange-stained bowl out of the way. "And I can get rid of these?"

"Sounds good to me," I say, gladly taking the samosa and dipping it into my mint sauce. "The trash can is in the kitchen."

"He gave you his last samosa," Abby says after he walks away, swooning and leaning across his empty seat. "I think this is going well."

"I mean, we're just getting to know each other," I say, pushing her back toward her seat when she starts making a kissy face at me.

"I think at the rate this is going, we'll be sipping Starbucks during first period in no time," Abby whispers, winking at me.

When Ritchie gets back from the kitchen, the two of us drift into the living room and find a couple of pillows to sit on in front of the couch. I spear a couple of marshmallows and hold them over the fire in the fireplace, glancing at *Seinfeld* on the TV.

"Even when my parents were together, my house was never like this," Ritchie says, quiet enough that only I hear.

"What was it like?"

He scooches his pillow closer to mine before saying, "Empty. Even with my brothers and me, the house always felt underused. We would always go to our friends' houses so that we wouldn't get embarrassed by our parents' fighting.

And when we were home, we usually ate in our rooms, did homework in our rooms . . . I would watch TV on my Mac more than I would downstairs."

"It sounds like you guys were all separate," I say, watching him stare into the flames. The way the yellow light flickers on his face, giving him a sheen of moisture, softens his features. I can make out the peach fuzz on his chin. And in the shadows from the ceiling lights, I can make out his eyelashes and a fleck of dry skin on his nose.

"My brothers and I were still close, but until we moved in with my dad, I guess I didn't realize how much time we were spending apart even though we were in the same place."

"I know this is nothing like parents getting divorced, but my sister moved in with her fiancé, and now whenever she stops by the house, it's like the ghost of our childhood settles over us. Sometimes it feels like she moved back in. She'll stay over late, planning her wedding, and end up sleeping in her room. More and more, she comes back to the house after work and ends up staying for a few days, and then when she leaves again, it just feels cold and empty . . . but I don't notice it until she's gone.

"It was actually kind of funny, because the first time it happened, we ended up going to the November Always diner for Sunday brunch, which we hadn't done since Sam was still in high school."

"I feel that," Ritchie admits.

But—in a way—I feel it for the first time as the words

leave my mouth. Whenever Sam is home, Dad is down-stairs more, and Mom doesn't hole up in their room for her evening reading. She'll hang out in the den, which is where she, Sam, and I used to have our late-night talks. I really miss it when she's gone, because my parents and I automatically go back to orbiting in our own little spheres.

Ritchie and I stare at our marshmallows, pulling them out when mine catches fire and he decides not to test his luck with his. I let the flame go for a moment, watching as the white melts and bubbles into black before I blow it out.

"Let's give our spots to someone who needs them," he suggests, standing up and holding out his hand to me.

I take it and let him lead me through the house that I know better than he does. I look back once as we head down the back hallway. I see Abby sitting on the couch with her legs crossed, Victor holding two sticks with marshmallows over by the fire. Then I turn back and point at a door at the end of the hall when I feel Ritchie hesitate.

Our eyes adjust to the brightness of the garage. I leave the door cracked open behind us and gather the skirt of my dress behind my legs before sitting down next to Ritchie on the steps leading down to Maria's mom's SUV.

"Why don't you want a swim scholarship?" he asks.

I think back to all the times Sam's made fun of my swimming, or criticized how much effort I put into it. I don't want to tell Ritchie that I'm afraid swimming won't be enough. I know that with my times and my individual wins at meets, I should be able to get a pretty good scholarship, but I don't think swimming is what I really want to do for the next four years—at least, it's not what I want to focus on. But, I know if I say that, the next question is going to be, *What do you want to focus on?* And I haven't even begun to scratch the surface of that question.

Instead I say, "Because swimming isn't all that I am." Before he can ask more, I change the subject. "When did you guys move?"

I take a bite out of my marshmallow and savor the smoky flavor as it melts in my mouth.

"The middle of August. We didn't move very far, but we changed school districts," Ritchie says.

"Do you like Hayfield so far?" I ask, remembering his pressed khakis and button-down Holloway uniform.

"I do. I mean, I miss my friends, but I like the new people that I'm meeting."

"That's good," I say through a mouthful of marshmallow.

"I especially like you," he adds, watching me.

"You just met me," I say, laughing. I try to lick the sticky marshmallow off my lips, but it's hard to focus with him staring at me.

"And you seem really cool, and I like you so far."

The butterflies in my stomach make me say, "I like you too."

I stare back at him, watching his eyes watch mine. I see my own reflection, and for a moment I can't believe that he likes what he's seeing. A girl with messy hair, awkwardly clothed in a small dress with a sweater clearly strategically buttoned. And yet he still likes me. So far, that is.

I take a deep breath and look down at the other half of my marshmallow, barely clinging to the spear. I want to say something cool, or at least keep the conversation going, but I'm at a loss for words.

"Don't do that," he whispers, reaching for my chin and turning me to face him again. Only, now his face is a lot closer.

"Do what?" I ask, trying not to be obvious about glancing down at his lips. They're so pink. I lick mine, worried that they're still sticky or chapped.

"Break the moment," he says.

"We were having a moment?" I ask jokingly. But he doesn't laugh. He just leans in a little closer, and I know that with his hand under my chin he can feel my breath catch in my throat.

I try not to breathe too heavy. I try not to think about how I probably have stinky tikka masala breath. I try not to think about how he has stinky tikka masala breath. I try not to think about how us both having the same stinky tikka masala breath would cancel them both out. No, I focus on his face in front of my face. I think back to the movies I've watched with my friends over the years. So, this is how it happens. This is the magical moment, My First Kiss.

When he starts moving in closer, I let my eyes drift close and I hand myself over to—

"Mia!"

The garage door bursts open, knocking me in the back and pushing me forward off the stairs. I stumble, but a hand catches me by the wrist and yanks me the rest of the way into the garage.

"What the—"

Abby claps her hand over my mouth and yanks me down behind Mia's mom's car. She holds a finger up to her mouth, her eyes wide, and I decide I can kill her later.

"Ritchie Christopher Hutchins!" Someone has thrown the garage door open again, and this time it smacks Maria's dad's tool shelf.

"Amanda?"

"Why haven't you been answering my calls?" Amanda asks.

I lean slightly forward and try to glimpse Ritchie on the steps, but I stop short, knowing that we could be seen.

"Amanda, I told you I was doing school stuff tonight," Ritchie explains. I can hear defeat in his voice.

"School stuff, my behind," she snaps. "A house party isn't 'school stuff.'"

"Amanda, does this *seriously* look like a house party? And how did you know I was here? What are you even doing here?"

"I tracked your phone, stupid, and saw that you weren't home doing your 'school stuff,'" she hisses. I hear her kick something, probably the banister. "Crap."

"Don't hurt yourself."

"Shut up! You're unbelievable," Amanda screams. I

hear someone grab the doorknob, and the wind shifts as the door flies. Then someone, probably Ritchie, catches it. Their footsteps pad on the carpet, down the hall and back into the house, leaving Abby and me sitting on the cold concrete floor of the garage.

"What Victor meant by 'I *believe* he's single' is that there's a girl in the picture that—clearly—Ritchie would rather none of us know about," Abby explains, letting out a long-held breath.

"So, he has a girlfriend?" I ask, feeling my heart race. At the same time, a lump rises in my throat.

"Yes, one that clearly knows what she's doing," Abby says, laughing to herself.

I try to laugh, to force myself to find this funny instead of humiliating, but I remember how it felt to have his warm hand cup my chin. I remember how just moments ago we were the only two people on the planet, and I can't stop the stinging in my eyes.

"Mia," Abby says softly. She snakes her arm around my shoulders and pulls me to her.

"He was going to kiss me," I whisper, sniffling.

"I'm sorry," she says. "This isn't what I originally had planned for your meet-cute. I was gearing up for a nice *Notting Hill* moment where someone spilled something on you—or maybe you spilled something on them . . . but after practice, it just seemed like it was happening so naturally between you two—"

"Abby, it's okay, I don't blame you," I interrupt, just

wanting her to stop talking about it. "It's fine."

"But it's not fine. He almost cheated on his girlfriend, and he was going to use *you* to do it."

I can feel her getting fired up. I know that in an alternate universe she would run outside after them and tell Amanda that Ritchie nearly cheated on her, and maybe she would kick Ritchie in the shins for good measure. But we live in the sad reality where once again I'm the one left alone. For once, I started getting the romance, but I ended up on the wrong side of the comedy part. Don't get me wrong, Abby saved me from having my first kiss be a lie . . . but I wish there was a way she could've saved me from the lie without me having to miss out on my first kiss. Without the truth, I had a real moment, what could've been one of the best moments of my life.

CHAPTER NINE

On Thursday morning, Harold and I meet at Heartwood Coffee, a small café two blocks down from the community center, to review my averages. One of the reasons I appreciate Harold's input is because it's a combination of a personal trainer—without having to pay for one—and a toned-down version of what my dad used to be for Sam at her field hockey games. With Harold there's no yelling and no overdone critique the entire ride home when I'm half-asleep and starving after a meet.

I pay for my omelet, oats, and matcha latte and carry my small tray over to a table by the front window. On the day of any competition—swimming or math—I try to keep my meals healthy. No stealing pepperoni off Grace's pizza or sharing candy with Sloane in study hall. This way I'll have more energy and no sugary food or unhealthy carbs to weigh me down.

I'm sprinkling blueberries over my oats when Harold pulls up in front of the café. I watch through the cursive lettering painted on the front window as he races around the front of his car to get the door for Gladys. Typically

I'd be annoyed that he invited her to crash our game-day chat. But when I put swimming aside, I'm kind of rooting for them as an example that meet-cutes can lead to real-life romance, not just the fictional relationships in movies.

"Good morning, Mia," Harold says when they step through the door. I can't tell if his smile is because of the swim meet or because he gets to pull out a chair for Gladys.

When he asks what she wants to order, Gladys insists on getting the coffees so that he and I can get straight to business. Harold gives me the rundown of my most recent averages for freestyle, backstroke, and breaststroke. Since my last meet I've improved each one, but not as much as usual. It doesn't follow with the steady progression he projected. He asks why, but is interrupted when Gladys sets his drink down in front of him. "Thank you, honey," he says, in a way that would usually make me want to gag, but for them it's cute.

"Remember you wanted to tell Mia something about her butterfly stroke?" she says, and points to something in Harold's notebook.

"I can hardly read my own handwriting sometimes," he says, laughing a little as he squints over the top edge of his glasses.

"It says that she swims to the right on butterfly," Gladys reads, her glasses pushed to the tip of her nose.

"Oh, right." Harold touches her arm lightly. "Sometimes you drift to the right a little. Not much, and usually you correct it. I think it's probably an indication that your right side is stronger and that just shows more in your butterfly stroke."

"Noted," I say, figuring during warm-ups I'd better test it and make sure I remember to straighten out.

I take a moment to eat some of my food, watching as Gladys checks her phone and Harold jots something down before taking a sip of his cappuccino.

"So, how is life, dear?" Gladys asks, catching me a little off guard.

"It's okay," I say, though Ritchie's face immediately comes to mind.

"It doesn't seem like it," she says. "Harold has been going on about how excited you usually are on the mornings of these—these, gatherings—"

"They're called swim meets, dear," Harold says.

"Right, excuse me. Swim *meets*," she corrects herself. "Anyways, you don't seem excited. You don't seem like yourself."

I sigh, looking down at the leaf pattern beginning to disintegrate in my latte. At this point what do I have to lose? Maybe Harold and Gladys can give me advice.

"I need to find a date to my sister's wedding," I tell them. I explain how the best man dropped out and my job is to find a suitable groomsman replacement. I tell them about the meet-cute project and how so far it's failing miserably. I add that if I don't find someone, I'll have to go with Jasper, Geoffrey's annoying younger brother—which Gladys finds funny.

"I wasn't supposed to spend my fall semester dealing with *this*," I say, and then pause to take a sip of my latte.

"Hmm." Gladys hums, thinking.

"I think you have nothing to worry about," Harold says decisively. "The fact that you doubt yourself over something as easy as this is preposterous."

Gladys and I stare at him, his mug held in midair. He waves it around like a prop before taking a sip. I want to ask if I heard him correctly and didn't just coincidentally black out.

"It's not *easy* at all," I say, feeling incredulous. "How can you say that?" I want to tell him that he doesn't know what it's like to be in my position, but I stop myself. He was in my position when he thought romance wasn't his speed. He was also in my position however many ages ago when he was a boy in high school, probably just as uncoordinated in romance as he is in the water. He put himself out there with Gladys, and lucky for him, she likes who he is and what he has to offer. And more important, her affection for him is *honest*.

"Because you can do anything," Harold states. It's not the answer I was expecting.

"I can?"

"Mia, you're a good swimmer because you take the time to practice," he explains. "You're a good student because you study. You *prepare*. All *I* know is that Mia Hubbard accomplishes anything she dedicates herself to. You need a date to the wedding? Your plan hasn't worked *so far*? Then prepare better. Plan better. Focus, and you'll find a way." Without missing a beat he says, "Now get your head in the game. I don't want this nonsense taking away from your win."

I smile. Gladys smiles too, and she rests her hand on top of his.

"Harold," I say, curious. "What's your favorite romantic comedy?"

His smile gets even wider. Gladys sets her cup down and watches him, interested to know the answer.

"Good question," he says, chuckling a little. We wait while he thinks for a moment. Recognition flashes across his face, and he says, "*Christmas in Connecticut.*"

"Never heard of it," I admit.

"That's because it's before your time," Gladys tells me, beaming at Harold. "Mine is *White Christmas.*"

"Oh really?" Harold's eyes fix on Gladys, and even with me sitting right here, they share what feels like a private moment. "Well, isn't that something. Now, if you'd please excuse me," Harold says. "I've got to use the restroom."

When Harold disappears past the counter, Gladys leans in a little, forcing me to look up from the blueberry about to roll off my spoon.

"In addition to Harry's sound advice, I just wanted to add a little piece of my own," she explains. "What Harry was saying is that because of who you are, you'll find a way to meet someone. And what I'm saying is that by being yourself, it'll happen naturally."

"I just—I'm not so sure it will." I remember how natural

things were between Ritchie and me, and look at how that turned out.

"It will," Gladys assures me. "What I've learned is that dating is like watching the kettle boil. If you watch it, it'll never get there. But if you look away, it'll boil a lot faster."

"So, you're saying I should stop trying?" I feel my heart speed up as all of my excuses align themselves. I don't have time to just let something happen. If, for my whole life, nothing has clicked into place on its own, what's going to make it happen now?

"No," Gladys says, looking me in the eye. "Try as hard as you have to, but try while being yourself. Don't force anything."

"If the shoe doesn't fit?" I ask, holding back a laugh.

"Bingo." Gladys smiles. "Good luck today. Swim like a fish."

I see Ritchie on my way to calculus. He doesn't notice me at first. He's wearing a blue button-down plaid shirt, a pair of khaki pants, and dark leather Sperrys. The laces are undone and they drag on the floor, which for some reason bugs me.

He has a number two pencil tucked behind his ear and his hair is slick with gel, pushed back from his face. His lips don't look as pink as they did Monday night. And under the harsh white fluorescent lights, he doesn't look as nice. He looks like the guy in his Instagram pictures.

A preppy boy who thinks he can have any girl he wants. Excuse me, any girls.

I scream *Cheater* as loud as I can in my head. Suddenly he shifts his attention and sees me, standing too many steps away from Mr. Jaffrey's classroom. I think about running the rest of the way, ducking into the classroom for safety, but I know that would be obvious. And I would look stupid as the only person running down the hallway.

"Mia." He crosses to my side of the hall, the sunlight coming in from the classroom behind him giving off an angelic glow that he seems to have at the worst moments.

"Ritchie," I say flatly.

He tries to hold my gaze, and I purposefully focus on anything else. I watch as people open and close their lockers, exchange books, and drop papers and pens onto the floor.

"Mia," he says again, quietly. "Look, I'm really sorry about the other night—"

"You should be apologizing to your *girlfriend*," I hiss.

"Mia, it's not like that," he says, leaning closer to me.

I take a step back and look at him. I try to see the same vulnerable boy who was talking about how empty his house felt, but I can't find him anywhere.

"Absolutely not!" Sloane steps in front of me, her heel catching the toe of my shoe. She pushes her shoulders back and stares right into Ritchie's eyes, only she's not captivated by them at all. "Who do you think you are, talking to my girl like that after what *you* did?"

Ritchie frowns and tries to look past Sloane at me, but she steps to the left and blocks his view with her shoulder.

"Move," she says, and by the way she tilts her head, I know she's giving him her disapproving-mom glare. I wish I had a look like that, a look that could quiet people down and make them feel exactly how disappointed you are with them. But since I don't have it, I guess that's what friends like Sloane are for.

"Move along," she says, waving her hand as he finally steps off. Then she turns to me and smiles slyly. "I can't believe Monday night was the best five seconds of your life."

I know she's joking, and I can't help but laugh. "Hey!"

"Five seconds without supervision, and you nearly—"

"Had my first kiss?" I ask, raising my eyebrows.

"Yeah, that," she says, the humor leaving her voice. I can tell she feels bad for me, and instead of waiting for her to come up with something endearing to say, I gesture to Mr. Jaffrey's classroom.

We take our seats at the table in the back of the class. As I follow along with the Taylor series he's having us practice, I remember what Harold said about studying and practicing. I used to hate Taylor series. I actually got a C on the first Taylor series quiz that we had. But I just practiced more and more until I understood it like a system, a constant dependable system with a structured way of solving the problem. I could depend on the structure of the equation as the path to the answer.

I know that love isn't structured or predictable, but it's practicable . . . somehow.

Sloane slips a piece of paper in front of me during the lecture. I quickly grab it and unfold it under the table in my lap.

I have a surprise for you tomorrow after school.

I write underneath *Does it involve food?* and hand it back to her.

She smiles and shakes her head.

She writes, *I promise it's a good surprise, so be happy.* ☺

I force myself to smile, and she draws a heart on the paper before crumpling it up.

By Friday I'm buzzing on the high of winning each of my races. I was able to dive into the water and leave Ritchie and the other night behind me. I swam faster than I have before in backstroke and breaststroke, impressing Coach and playing my part in leading the team to victory. Afterward, Coach told us our times for each race and our relays. I jotted them down in my phone so that I can share them with Harold over the weekend.

By the time I'm closing my notebook at the end of last period, all I can think about is Sloane's surprise. Sloane picks me up at my house after school in her mom's Jeep. When I open the door, I'm blasted with loud barking.

"Gibson, shut up," Sloane coos. "Be a good boy and sit your behind down." She grits her teeth when she says "down," and Gibson listens.

"You brought a small bear?" I ask when I buckle my seat belt. I turn around and pat Gibson on the head, noting the amount of drool staining the back seat.

"Ha ha," Sloane says sarcastically. "Don't insult my golden retriever."

"A big fat golden retriever," I correct her, watching as Gibson's tail wags like a long furry flag. "I feel like your mom is going to kill you."

"She's the one who agreed to dog sit," Sloane tells me before turning off of my street.

She quickly flips through her phone, and Charli XCX starts screaming from the speakers. Gibson stops wagging his tail and lays his head down on the seat. I lean over and turn the volume down low enough that I can ask, "Is Gibson my surprise?"

"No," she says.

When she doesn't offer anything else, I ask, "Where are we going?"

"Somewhere," she says, watching traffic.

"Right," I say, settling into the seat. "I just have to be home—"

"In time for the garden at four, I know," she says, switching lanes and following the signs to downtown. "That gives us a solid hour, so just relax. You'll get information as you need it."

Soon enough we're on the highway, so I figure we might be visiting the Bean. But before we make it to the right exit, Sloane turns off early and takes us into Lincoln Park.

"Are you excited for tomorrow?" Sloane asks, trying to change the topic.

Tomorrow is Nandy's infamous Halloween party. When we were all freshmen, she started hosting it Halloween weekend because her parents would let her stay at home by herself instead of forcing her to go away for a weekend Christian retreat with them. We were all excited to go, until Grace's parents said they didn't feel comfortable about her going to high school parties, like, at all. So we adapted and made up a tradition of wearing our costumes out to dinner and ending the night with a sleepover at Sloane's house. This way Grace's parents would have no reservations about letting her spend the night out, and we could all sneak off to the party together.

"Absolutely," I tell her. "My mom is going to take care of my Princess Leia space buns." Sloane gives me a nod.

But speaking of outfits, I look at Sloane and notice that she's wearing jeans and sneakers, clothes perfect for—oh, I don't know—walking a dog. I, on the other hand, am still wearing my outfit from school. A black A-line skirt, green sweater, and heeled boots. Not ideal for any long-distance walking—or walking in a park.

"Am I dressed right for this surprise?" I ask when she starts slowing down.

"You're dressed perfectly," she says without looking at me.

"Even though I'm not wearing sneakers?"

"Even though you're not wearing sneakers."

"Even though I'm wearing a skirt?"

"Even though you're wearing a skirt."

I sigh, watching the redbrick townhouses passing by outside my window. Sloane parallel parks in front of a set of homes facing a small park area on the edge of Lake Michigan. When she turns off the car, I pull my gaze away from the skyline in the distance and refocus on the *surprise*.

"Are we playing with Gibson in the park?" I ask, getting out. "Because I'm not dressed for mud."

"*We* aren't doing anything," she tells me from across the car as she opens the back door for Gibson.

He immediately pees on the back tire of the car, and then Sloane hands me the leash.

"I've never walked a dog," I tell her, quickly catching the handle before Gibson can yank it out of my hand.

"Just don't let go," she says, leading the way across the street.

"Even though there aren't, like, any dog parks around, a lot of people come here to let their dogs run in the open," Sloane explains. She tells me that we have to keep walking farther into the park because no one wants their dog running right next to the street. I don't mind, because farther into the park brings us closer to the lake, and water always calms me down. We reach a set of stairs and make our way down a small hill to where people are standing, almost forming a fence, watching their dogs play with each other.

Sloane continues, "So, there's this movie called *Must Love Dogs*."

"Okay?"

"And it's about this divorced woman who gets on a dating site to meet men."

"That sounds promising."

Sloane shoots me a glare before continuing. "Anyways, she arranges to meet one of the dudes at a dog park because she's taking care of someone's dog and figures it might be a fun place to hang out."

Gibson's ears perk up, and he starts yanking me forward. I struggle to get my footing, but I figure it's better to follow him instead of tripping and falling on my face. As he pulls with urgency toward his furry friends, we have no choice but to speed up.

Sloane starts talking faster. "And the guy she meets up with doesn't own a dog—even though he said he did—so he has to borrow one, and—well—they fall in love. The end."

"Okay?" I say, not sure what to do when Gibson starts crying and pulling with all his strength.

"Okay, so, welcome to your meet-cute."

"You're being serious?" I ask, managing to wrestle Gibson between my legs. I say "Down" a couple of times, and then I remember to grit my teeth and he finally listens.

"Yes," Sloane says, smiling at the cluster of dogs beginning to notice Gibson's crying. "After I heard about Abby's faux pas—choosing someone without completing a thorough background check, tisk, tisk—I wondered, What would be the best way to rectify her wrong and cheer you up and hopefully accomplish our goal all in one go?" She pauses, waiting for me to answer.

"Me taking a random dog to a park?"

"Has anyone told you you suck at this?" Sloane asks, laughing.

"No one has to tell me what I already know." I smile.

"You're getting your wish," Sloane says, stopping a little ways behind the invisible perimeter the rest of the owners are standing along. She hands me a small container of poop bags and reaches down for Gibson's collar. Then she points off in the distance. I follow her finger and squint, seeing a brown lowrider pit bull trailing behind a boy on the other side of the park.

"Wait," I say, squinting harder. "Wait, Sloane—what?"

Ben Vasquez in all of his fitted-jeans-and-charcoal-gray-bomber-jacket glory, haircut styled to stand perfectly atop his head, with his chiseled features that look good in fluorescent light, sunlight, firelight—probably; I don't know for certain—is walking along the other side of the park.

"No, no," I say, shaking my head. There are so many butterflies in my stomach that I could throw up. Even though we just saw each other yesterday when I stopped by math club to hand in my practice problems before the swim meet, we haven't actually held a conversation—just the two of us talking to each other, not both of us having a group discussion about derivatives of tangent or Maclaurin series—like . . . ever!

"What do you mean, *no?*" Sloane asks. "This is your chance to get the guy you've always wanted. This should be a cakewalk for you."

I turn to her, my mouth hanging open but words only trying to form in my mind. How can she think this is a good idea? I'm inappropriately dressed. My hair is frizzing up from the humidity. I'm—I— "Sloane, we said no one that I already know. And, well, I know Ben Vasquez, so—well—he can't be a meet-cute."

"Mia, you *asked* for this! Haven't you stood in front of your mirror and practiced the once-in-a-lifetime conversation where you woo your prince of Pythagorean theorems with witty repartee? Yes, the man of your dreams is a math nerd and not that nice, in our honest opinions." Sloane pauses to cringe. "However, he is the man of your dreams."

"Of my *dreams*, not reality!"

Sloane closes her eyes and rests her fingers on her temples. She shakes her head and looks down at Gibson, and somehow they seem to have one of those private eye conversations that I never get to be part of.

"You leave me no choice," she says, letting Gibson off his leash before reaching into her pocket.

We watch as Gibson darts over to the other dogs. Then I feel her hand press in between my shoulder blades, and suddenly I'm standing inside the invisible line and all the dogs—every single one of them—has stopped to stare at me.

I look back and see Sloane blowing into a small rod, but there's no sound coming out. The silence is overcome by the thudding of paws on dirt and barking and squealing as I'm bombarded with fur and fluff and licks and paws pressing into my stomach.

"Dog whistle." Sloane smiles at me, giving me a wink.

She quickly puts it away as a few owners run over to get control of their dogs. Without her whistling anymore, most of the dogs are released from the spell. A few take their turns to sniff me before running back over to their owners or the other dogs they were originally playing with.

I watch as Gibson lumbers alongside a Great Dane. They both gallop in this awkward funny way where their back legs don't seem to keep up with the front ones. A few dogs join them, one of them being the pit bull that was walking with Ben. I scan the other side of the park, praying that he's still all the way over there, but I don't see him.

"Mia Hubbard?"

I clip the poop bags to the scrunchie around my wrist and try to discreetly tuck the front of my sweater into my skirt so that I don't look so shapeless. Then I turn around and see said man of my dreams closing the last few steps between my imagination and our shared toes-nearly-touching reality.

"Hey." I try to act surprised, not like I scoped him out the second I got here. "What's up?"

"Not much, just here with Carly." He points to the pit, who is now running with a different group of dogs.

"Nice." My mind blanks and I stare off in the distance

to hide the heat rising in my face. I knew Ben had a dog because he's posted about her on his Instagram a few times. I don't remember seeing her name, and considering the amount of times I check his Instagram feed, I think if he'd mentioned it, I would remember.

"I didn't know you have a dog. I've never seen you here before," he says, looking across the field.

I spot Gibson and point him out. "Yup, that's . . . my . . . Gibson," I say, already wondering how I'm going to explain him away later if Ben ever comes over to my house and sees it spotless, furless, and Gibson-less. I think to maybe correct myself and say I dog sit, but Ben has already moved on.

"How old is he?" Ben asks, watching as Gibson tries to mount the Great Dane. Thankfully she's too tall, but Gibson doesn't stop trying.

"Uh, like, a year old?" I say, not sure if he's supposed to do that. The other dog doesn't seem to mind, but I turn back to Ben to see his reaction.

"He's cute," Ben says, laughing a little. Right. If it's funny that he's humping a dog, then I shouldn't panic, not yet at least.

Ben starts walking, and I fall in step with him. I try not to notice the fact that I'm *walking* with Ben Vasquez. Side by side, both of our hands dangling at our hips, empty. We keep to the edge of the park, having a lot more privacy away from the other owners. He breaks the silence to tell me to watch out for some poop someone didn't pick up. I don't see it at first, and he quickly pulls me out of the way.

When he lets go, my arms still feel the sensation of his hands gripping me.

"Thanks," I say, just about ready to pass out.

We fall silent again, and I look down to make sure I don't step in anything. Ben's wearing his Nike running shoes. He wears the same pair of sneakers every day. Luckily for him, they pretty much go with everything he wears.

I try to think of non-math-related things to talk about. I already know that he finds Taylor series challenging, and graphing logs on his calculator to be oddly satisfying. Like Sloane said, I've definitely given thought to what it might be like to have a real talk with Ben. But in my head it always starts out with, *Gosh, Mia, you're so smart and beautiful. I don't know why it never occurred to me before that you're really cool.* And then I'd say something like, *It's okay, Ben. I mean, I wasn't very forward myself. At least we've made it here now.* "Now" being the moment in which we are sitting side by side on some daydream bench by the beach, waves crashing, the warm sand between our toes. In my dreams he leans in first, and I close the rest of the way, and his lips are everything . . . just, everything.

But now that I'm actually here, I can't remember *all* of the meaningful things I want to know about him. Slowly questions come to me, one at a time.

"Have you decided where you're going to school next year?" I ask.

"Not yet. There's only one place that I want to go, but I'm still waiting to hear back."

"What school is that?"

"Vanderbilt. Everyone on my dad's side of the family has gone there. My older brother graduated from there last year. I want to be next," he says, looking down at me.

I can see that his eyes are hazel with flecks of brown. There's stubble on his chin, making his jawline softer.

"What are you going to study?" I ask.

"I'm torn between pharmacy and psychology," he admits. "Pharmacy would give me a stable job in the future, but I really like psychology and I feel like I'm already so good at reading people."

I want to tell him that he can feel free to read me, but I stop myself.

"Can you start off in classes for both and decide later?"

Ben chuckles, looking away for a moment. I watch as he stops and searches for his dog in the park, before resuming our walk. I spot Gibson easily, peeing on a tree with his best friend, the Great Dane.

"I have to get in first," he finally says.

"Are you worried that you won't?"

"I don't know, honestly."

I want to tell him that he shouldn't have anything to worry about. He's captain of the math team. He comes from a long line of Vanderbilt men, and I feel like a school like that is into that sort of thing. Plus, I know from his Facebook page that he's been doing volunteer work since he was in middle school, going to the synagogue with his mom on weekends to help in the kitchen or to sort clothing donations. I stop myself because I realize listing all of his admirable attributes will either make it obvious that I pay *a lot* of attention to him, or it'll look like I'm trying to impress him.

"When will you know?" I ask, trying to keep the conversation going.

"Early in December."

I try to think of something encouraging but not overly excited to say.

"What about you?" he asks, nudging me with his elbow to get me to look up.

When my eyes meet his, I get that faint feeling again. "What about me?"

"You're a junior. You must have some idea of where you want to go."

He's right. I should already have a sense of where I want to go after high school, what I want to study, and what I might want to do with the rest of my life. But I don't. I've tried giving it some thought, but I keep coming up with nothing. I don't like math. I'm on math team because it's the perfect extra credit to boost my grade and give me extra practice. I figure getting a high score on the AP exam both junior and senior years might save me some gen-ed credits wherever I decide to go—at least, that's what Sam told me. That way, it'll cross one uninteresting topic off my list. Still, I don't like history or science or writing. I'm not an artist, not by a long shot. I've never been able to play an instrument, and even though I've done drama club, I'm not on the path to Broadway by any means. I definitely like the idea of making something, and it would be purposeful if the *something* could help other people.

"I don't know," I say.

"Oh, come on. There must be some school that you like. Some subject that you're into more than others?"

His interest makes me want to be interesting. I wish I could tell him that biology makes me want to study microbiology. Or that I loved environmental science and I want to become a zoologist. But those would be lies.

"I like the idea of Princeton. I visited there when my sister was looking into schools, and I really like the campus. They call themselves the liberal arts Ivy, which sounds promising . . . but I don't think I'm Ivy material."

"Anyone who doesn't think they're Ivy material isn't Ivy material," Ben says, laughing a little. He stares at me, probably reading through all my thoughts, all the times Sam told me I needed to do better in school and grow up and focus. "Believe in yourself as much as the rest of us, Mia."

"Who is 'us'?" I ask curiously.

"Your family, your friends . . . me, even."

"You *even*," I say, teasing even though I'm elated that he said he believes in me.

"I think you have what it takes. You're great in math club. And, I'm not going to lie, when Mr. B. was reviewing report cards to make sure everyone was allowed to participate, I snuck a peek. You're basically a genius."

"I wouldn't call myself a genius," I say, blushing.

"Don't tell anyone, but your GPA is higher than mine."

"You're kidding." I gape at him, feeling the entire surface of my body tingle. He nods and assures me that it's true. *I'm* smarter than Ben *Vasquez*.

"Okay, so maybe I'll apply to Princeton. But I still have no idea what I want to study," I relent.

"You might want to figure that out before you start paying Princeton tuition," he advises as we complete our lap around the park. "Especially because they rarely give out scholarships. If you're going to invest in Princeton, you need to know why."

I spot Sloane leaning against a tree near the entrance to the park. She waves to me and then holds up five fingers. I check my watch and realize I have to leave soon if I want to catch a ride with my mom to the garden.

"Will you let me know *when* you get into Vanderbilt?" I ask.

"Yeah," Ben says, smiling. I catch the slightest red tint in his cheeks and realize that he's blushing. I made Ben Vasquez blush!

"Will you text me?" I ask, hopeful.

"Yeah, sure, but I don't think I have your number," he says, his brow wrinkling. He pulls his phone out of his pocket, and I grab mine.

I unlock it and hand it to him to add his number, and he does the same for me. I create my contact and add a smiley face at the end of my name.

As he's handing his phone back to me, we hear a commotion and turn to see two owners running over to their dogs. The two are so tangled, they look like one dog, rolling around, growling and barking and paws flying.

"That doesn't look good," Ben says, his eyes darting around.

I see Gibson running toward the action and call out to him. When he doesn't look my way, I cup my hands and shout louder, but it doesn't seem to grab his attention. Out of the corner of my eye, I see a small brown dog darting in the direction of the dogs fighting, and Ben sees it too.

"Carly, no!" he shouts.

We both take off running, Ben calling Carly's name over and over. When we're closer, he does three short whistles and snaps his fingers twice. This finally gets Carly to come, walking slowly with her tail between her legs.

Gibson, on the other hand, is jumping over the two dogs fighting, trying to get in between.

"Gibson, come on," I plead, but he doesn't even turn in my direction.

I look back toward the entrance of the park, but I don't see Sloane anywhere.

"What do I do?" I ask Ben while he struggles to keep a grip on Carly's collar.

"What do you mean? Get your dog!"

One of the fighting dogs turns to Gibson, and Gibson starts snarling and baring his teeth.

"Gibson!" I shout.

"Mia, get your dog!" Ben shouts when Gibson starts snapping at the collie that had been under the other dog.

I feel tears prickling in my eyes, and I turn to look back at Ben again. His blushing smile is long gone, and I feel his annoyance pierce through me. He tells Carly to stay and lets go of her. He takes Gibson by the collar and jerks him out of the fight, apologizing to the collie's owner before dragging Gibson over to me.

"Have you never been to a dog park before? How do you not know how to control him? You shouldn't bring him here if you can't control him."

"He's not my dog, okay?" I blurt, holding on to Gibson's collar. He starts pulling in the direction of Carly, and I have to plant my feet and lean in the opposite direction with all my strength to keep him still.

"What?" Ben snaps, pulling Carly back.

I feel so stupid. My nerves make my entire body shake, and I feel my nose start to run as a few tears slip out of my eyes. I can feel the other dog owners staring at us, and I wish Sloane would come step in front of me and pull me out of here, but she's still nowhere.

"He's not my dog," I repeat.

Gibson finally gives in, and I start dragging him out of the park. I hear Ben mumble something under his breath; the word "crazy" hits my ears clearly.

I find Sloane's car when I get back to the parking lot. I throw open the back door and grit my teeth at Gibson, telling him to get in, and he does so immediately.

"I hate this stupid dog. I hate this stupid park. And I hate this stupid plan," I grumble as I buckle my seat belt.

"What—"

"No, we're not talking about it. Just take me home—" My voice breaks and my nerves melt away into full-blown sobs. My embarrassment comes over my body like a blanket around my shoulders, and I let myself sag into the seat. "Please just take me home."

CHAPTER TEN

Y ou're going to be so surprised," Mom tells me later, on the way to the community garden.

"By what?" I ask, still turned away from her, face puffy, looking out the passenger window. On the way home from the dog park, I had to fan my eyes to keep them from getting red. The last thing I need is for Mom to ask me what's wrong.

"Gavin has done so much with the greenhouse. It's amazing what he's been able to accomplish each week." Gavin, like Mom, goes to the garden almost every day, with Gloria. Only, he goes after school and has to work fast in dying daylight. I didn't realize how much there is to do at the garden until Mom started describing the town's vision to me. They're working to refurbish troughs so that they can start growing flowers that they'll sell in the spring. Once the greenhouse is repaired, they'll be able to grow and sell vegetables. And Mom has her own private plot that she pays for to grow specific flowers. She's even started a small lemon tree that she's hoping will hold up.

"What has he done?" I ask, humoring her even though I wish we could just ride in silence for a while.

She goes on to explain how since he started, it's like he's taken on the greenhouse as his own project. She doesn't want to go into specifics because she wants me to be surprised, but she does tell me that it's *neat* that I help him when I can—meaning only on Fridays, instead of fighting to dedicate every bit of my spare time.

"I wonder what he's going to have you do today," she says as we pull into the parking lot.

Same as last week, there are people coming and going from the garden; on their way in, their clothes and hands are clean and ready to work, and on their way out, dirt stains their clothes and skin. They've traded their bucket hats for knit hats since the temperature has been dropping, and all of them share a tired smile with my mom as we head down the rest of the walkway.

"*He's* not going to have *me* do anything," I tell her. "He's not my supervisor."

"Oh, that's not what I meant, Peach," Mom says.

The spot where the gravel turns into grass serves as the threshold between the rest of the world and the garden. When we pass over and the ground softens under our feet, we've officially arrived. Gloria's head snaps around, as if now that we're standing on the grass, we actually exist.

"Thank goodness," she huffs, leaving the worktable she was standing over with a few other volunteers. She comes straight to me and takes me by the shoulder. "Gavin needs an extra set of hands for the next part of the greenhouse, and he's refused to work with any of the other volunteers."

I want to say something snarky like *You're kidding* or *Yeah right*, but Gloria is so intimidating. The bone structure in her face is all hard angles and set lines; her light blue eyes are staring into my soul. I can't look away; all I can do is nod.

"Right over there. He's somewhere inside," she says, pointing at the greenhouse.

I glance at Mom before speed walking over to the greenhouse. I figure regular walking is too slow for Gloria's agenda. Mom just gives me that *I'm sorry but good luck* full-surrender expression that always makes me feel like she's not trying hard enough.

Nevertheless, I figure it can't be that bad working with Gavin again. As I get closer to the greenhouse, I start seeing the changes Mom was telling me about. He reinforced some of the molded parts of the wood frame and repainted it all with a fresh coat of white. The overgrown walkway leading up to the greenhouse is now freshly turned soil. Instead of going inside, I go around the side of the greenhouse to where we worked last week and see that he replanted the rest of the baby's breath with fertilizer, and planted them closer together. At the back of the house he pulled all the weeds and turned all the soil, and did the same along the outside of the opposite edge of the house.

Inside I find him with his back to me crouched over one of the irrigation pipes that used to hang from the ceiling. He hasn't painted the inside of the greenhouse, but he has managed to finish fixing the broken windows. A ray of sunlight slants through the greenhouse, highlighting the sweat beading on the back of his neck and bouncing off the moisture from the oil in his hair.

"What's on the agenda for today?" I ask.

His shoulder blades pinch together and he pitches forward. I hear him mutter a profanity before turning around.

"I honestly wasn't trying to scare you," I say, laughing.

He shakes his head. "You were totally getting revenge, and I'm okay with that."

I hold out a hand and help him stand up. I can feel the dust on his hands. It's dry and soft.

"How can I help?" I ask, gesturing to the pipe.

He steps over the pipe and opens a box on the back wall. "The system for the irrigation still works, and the timers still keep accurate time, but the pipes for the water are just—"

"Old and rusty?" Looking closer, I don't know why he would touch any of the pipes without gloves. "This looks hazardous."

"Yeah, so do you want to help me move them?"

We get to work, carrying pipes with one of us at each end. I'm thankful to have my pair of gloves. We take the pipes out to the dumpster, which is located near the driveway. Then I help Gavin take measurements so that he can ask Gloria about ordering new pipes. We work mostly in silence, only talking when one of us has to pivot or watch out for a hole or rock in the ground.

When we finish with the pipes, we start taking the rest

of the random stuff inside the greenhouse to the dumpster. There are worktables with rotting wood surfaces, rusted watering tins, and old tools that look like they haven't been touched for a very long time. Since we don't have any larger things like rusted troughs or broken chairs, I start picking up what I can carry and hike it up to the dumpster.

Breaking branches and old wood over my knee is satisfying. Throwing a broken plastic lawn chair over the edge of the dumpster is doubly satisfying. It isn't until Gavin mentions it that I realize I was finally getting my mind to drift away from my problems.

"It looks like you're working through some stuff," he says, gesturing to the branch I was breaking over my knee.

"Why can't I just be breaking a branch? Why does there have to be meaning behind it?" I ask.

"Because it's clearly not," he says, laughing. He throws the buckets I carried over into the dumpster.

"How did all of these branches get inside the greenhouse anyway?" I ask.

"There used to be a tree next to it, but that was cut down earlier this year. The tree rotted, and branches started falling through the windows. One storm took out a huge branch that broke one of the structural beams in the roof."

"Who would build a greenhouse under a tree?" I ask, struggling to break a thick branch.

Gavin holds out his hand, and I glare at him, not ready to give up.

"Obviously a very stupid architect," he says, teasing.

"Ha ha. If you're so clever, why don't you snap this one?" I hand him the branch, and he looks at it. Then he drops one side of the branch and stomps the lower end of it, making a clean break. Then he does that again and again until the branch is broken into four small parts.

"Instead of having to use my Hulk-like strength, I figure it's better to make things easier on myself."

I roll my eyes and start walking back to the greenhouse, listening as Gavin runs to catch up with me.

"Are you sure there's nothing on your mind?" he asks, no laughing or teasing in his voice.

"There's always something on my mind. I was just saying not all of my actions are based on—"

"So instead of being defensive, why don't you just talk about it?"

"*Instead of being defensive, why don't you just talk about it?*" I mock, making him smile. But the humor doesn't chase away what's getting at me. Ben's face, his boiling anger, his disbelief as Gibson was fighting with that other dog—all of it comes back to me. And then the look he gave me when I told him Gibson wasn't mine, like I was some crazy freak, some weirdo . . .

"I don't know what I was thinking," I accidentally say out loud.

Inside the greenhouse, Gavin gestures for me to sit on a patch of dirt. I grab my water bottle, and he sits down next to me. In the stillness I look around at the space made by all the debris we managed to clear away.

"There's this guy," I start, looking up from the twig I'm fidgeting with, to see his expression. He's leaning forward, sitting with his elbows on his knees, his chin cupped in his hands. "That I've liked for a while—"

"How long is 'a while'?"

"Since I was a freshman. And I got him to notice me, which was awesome. We talked—like, really talked—for the first time. And just as fast as everything started, I ruined it."

I watch his expression go from curiosity to consideration. He rubs the hairs beginning to curl in his beard, and he squints at something over my head.

"I'm going to need more details than that," he finally says.

"For what?"

"To help you," he says.

"How are you going to help me?"

"I'm going to give you advice, once I know exactly what I'm working with."

"No," I say flatly, standing up. I brush the dirt off the back of my pants and go over to our pile of supplies.

"Come on," he says, standing with me. "I can help you. I'm a guy. I can probably guess what this guy is thinking. I just need to know *how* you ruined things."

"I'm not telling you," I say, handing him a shovel.

He leans the shovel against the wall. So, I hand him the weird soil-turning tool, and he leans that against the wall. I hand him his gloves, and he throws them onto the ground dramatically, trying not to laugh.

"Gavin!"

"Mia!"

My mouth breaks into a smile; his laughter is contagious.

"I borrowed a dog and went to the dog park that he takes his dog to. And let's just say some stuff happened with my dog and another dog, and it came out that I lied about it being my dog."

"You're a horrible, terrible person," he teases. "But really, though. That's not the worst thing in the world."

"You didn't see the way he looked at me. He looked at me like I was some creep."

"Were you being a creep?" he asks, being serious.

"No—well, I mean, I wasn't *trying* to be. But I guess if you look at the situation, it could be construed as *creepy*."

"You," Gavin says, pointing a finger at me, "are a nervous rambler."

"And you," I mimic, pointing a finger at him, "are not helping."

Gavin grabs his shovel and rests his chin on the handle, thinking for a moment. "Honestly, maybe you were being a bit creepy, but it doesn't sound like it was bad enough that he should shun you forever."

"I don't care about him shunning me *forever*. I just need him to not be shunning me right now."

"Why?"

"There's this Halloween party tomorrow, it's the biggest Halloween party every year. I mean, kids from different schools come and everyone is dressed up and my friends and I always have a great time . . . And once me and this guy started hitting it off, I kind of got it into my head that I could ask him to go. And then we'd see each other there and we'd hang out more and talk more and—I don't know," I say, stopping myself from mentioning Sam's wedding.

"I think I know the party you're talking about. Some kids at school were going around inviting people, though I thought it was a joke. It does sound fun though," Gavin says as we walk over to the far side of the greenhouse.

I start stabbing at the topsoil, and he comes in behind me to turn it. We both stop to pull weeds once the ground is loose enough.

"I guess so."

"Well, that's convincing," he teases.

"If you're so into parties, why don't you go in my place?" I snap.

He focuses on the weed in front of him, stalling. I stop what I'm doing to show him that I'm more than happy to wait for an answer.

"Because . . . I think I'm still grounded," he finally says, shrugging his shoulders.

"Right, your mysterious grounding."

"What's mysterious about it?" he asks, stopping to look at me.

"The fact that you won't say why you're grounded."

"You never asked why I'm grounded," he says, smiling.

"Right, and now I feel like a jerk." I sigh, dropping the

weed I'd been tugging at onto the ground. I roll back on my heels and sit down, not caring about the fresh soil that I know is going to leave a stain on my jeans.

"You're not a jerk," he tells me, his tone prompting.

"So, why did you get grounded?"

"It's not going to be that easy." He smiles slyly. "Promise me you won't let this guy get in the way of you having a good time at your party, and then I'll tell you why I'm grounded."

I lean forward and hook my pinky through the one he's holding out. He holds it for a moment when I try to pull away, and I look up from our hands. When our eyes meet, he nods at me and I nod back.

"I stole school lunches for a week straight," he says, returning his attention to the weeds.

"Why?"

"I had my reasons, but telling you why wasn't part of our deal," he says with that same short tone that means I'm not supposed to ask anymore—though, now I wonder if I *am* supposed to ask more.

We go back to pulling weeds, and my thoughts drift to the last time I was grounded. I think it was when I was thirteen and I stayed up all night reading the Hunger Games series because Sloane, Abby, Grace, and I were going to have a slumber party and watch all four movies. Naturally, I didn't wake up on time for school, and when my parents saw that I'd lied about going to bed, they felt they had to do something.

"I'm going as Princess Leia," I say. "My friends wanted me to go as Jasmine because they want to do this Disney princess thing, but I feel like Princess Leia is better than Jasmine."

I glance up and see Gavin smiling to himself, still focusing on the ground in front of him.

"Plus, now that Disney acquired Star Wars, *technically* she is a Disney princess."

Gavin laughs a little, and I try not to let him see me smile.

"So, you like Star Wars?" he asks.

We both stand up to gather our weeds neatly at the center of the tarp we laid down. I grab two corners, he grabs the other two, and we walk toward each other to close the tarp like a sack.

"I used to be obsessed when I was in middle school. I still like it, but I no longer have Star Wars sheets, and I don't use Star Wars posters like wallpaper."

"I think the best part is that I can totally picture you in a girly room with dark-blue-and-black galaxy posters all over your walls."

"Who said my room was girly?"

"Okay, so your room is painted dark blue and you have comic book covers outlining your mirror and *Playboy* magazines under your bed?"

"Oh, so *your* room is painted dark blue and you framed your precious mirror with comic book covers and now I know where you stash your *Playboy*s?"

"Touché." Gavin smiles, winking.

As the sun sets, the temperature drops exponentially. By the time we finish weeding, the outdoor lights have come on and I can see Gavin shivering in his long-sleeve T-shirt. I notice his hands shaking as he goes to turn more soil, and I grab the shovel out of his hand, feeling how chilled the metal pole and handle are.

I start gathering our supplies into a pile. I make my way over to the shed while Gavin takes the tarp to the dumpster. When I look over my shoulder, I see Mom and some of the other volunteers beginning to gather their buckets, shovels, and unused soil into their wheelbarrows to take to the shed. With this party looming on the horizon, and three failed meet-cutes under my belt, something pushes me into the greenhouse and nearly right into Gavin on his way out.

"Oops." I startle, feeling my heart nearly jump out of my chest.

"If you want to scare me, you'll have to keep trying," Gavin says, laughing. He holds me by my shoulders to steady me, which I'm grateful for.

"So, obviously, I'm awkward and not well coordinated," I say, feeling a little shy but reimagining myself walking down the aisle with Jasper. "I need help—"

I look up into Gavin's eyes, willing myself to keep going. Ben is definitely the kind of guy who would laugh about this, but I can tell Gavin isn't. Well, at least I hope he isn't.

"I need help finding a date to my sister's wedding."

Gavin squints his eyes a little and opens his mouth to speak, but nothing comes out.

"I need to find a date to her wedding, and so far I haven't been able to. Like, today was *another* failed attempt at getting a guy to like me and possibly want to be my date. And tomorrow is another really good opportunity for me to try again, but . . . I don't know—I just don't want to mess it up. And, well, you're a guy—so maybe you could—"

"Be your date?" he asks, looking even more confused.

"No! Oh, my gosh, no. I wouldn't make you do that," I say, taking a deep breath. "No. I just need your advice, a guy's perspective."

I laugh a little, trying to pull some air back into my lungs. Okay, I said it. I put it out there and Gavin hasn't doubled over, making light of the situation. He looks at me, staring at me with his brows drawn together, rubbing the short but full beard covering his chin.

"You really are a *nervous rambler*." His lips break into a smile.

"*Okay*," I say, shoving him a little. "I'll try not to talk too much. Noted."

"But seriously," he says, "I don't have a lot of experience picking up guys, so I apologize if my advice isn't *super* helpful. But, as a fellow *guy*, I find that being yourself is the best method."

"At this point I don't think I even know what that means."

Gavin raises his eyebrows. "That sounds like a much deeper problem."

"I mean, everyone keeps saying *Be yourself; give it time*, but that hasn't worked."

"It's not really meant to 'work.' I think the whole point is that when you're yourself, you're not *working* at all. Things just happen."

"And this has been successful for you in the past?" I ask, watching his expression. As funny as he can be, I need to know for real.

"I find that when a girl is herself, I can get an honest sense of whether or not I like her, of whether or not I want to take her on a date and get to know her more, or in your case, of whether or not I could see myself spending a whole wedding with her."

That actually makes sense.

"Okay, then." I take a deep breath and refrain from rubbing my temples, because even though I had gloves on, I can't help but think some mulch might be on my fingers.

"It looks like you did a lot today," Gloria says when we walk over to where she, my mom, and a few other lingering volunteers are still cleaning up. She stands with her hands on her hips, then reaches out one arm to pull Gavin into a hug.

"Yeah, though I don't know why you needed me for all that," I say, retracing our steps through the afternoon. We did do a lot, more than last week for sure.

"There were some heavy things," Gavin says, though I can tell he's thinking back to most of the stuff we carried to the dumpster, and there wasn't anything he wouldn't have been able to drag instead of carry.

"Right," I say.

"I guess you could say I needed the company," he admits without looking at me.

I'm not sure why I don't say anything—maybe because I just opened up more than I ever have in front of a guy—but what I really want to tell him is that I feel the exact same way.

CHAPTER ELEVEN

My phone buzzes with another text in the group chat. Abby and Grace have been hounding me about how my most recent meet-cute went, and since I haven't responded, they've started asking if I'm still coming over before the party. I text back that I'll be at Sloane's on time but that I'm busy and can't talk. Even though I stop replying, I keep an eye on the conversation. Whenever I see Sloane send a message with an update on where she is in getting ready—the last one was a picture of her blue eyeshadow, since she decided to go as Jasmine when I picked Princess Leia—I wonder why she doesn't add a short message explaining what transpired yesterday. But I know it wasn't her fault that my meet-cute with Ben went so bad.

I pick up my phone again and see a notification from Sam in her bridesmaids' group chat. The forty-five-days-until-the-wedding notification is the last thing I need right now. I throw my phone at the pile of laundry beginning to tumble out of my closet, and then I tap the volume button on my computer so that it's loud enough to cover the phone vibrations.

On my laptop, Rusty is about to punch Kate's boyfriend in the face at a party in *Stuck in Love*. After the punch, Kate leaves the party with Rusty and his friend. Rusty drops his friend off first, and Kate isn't ready to go home, so they go back to Rusty's house. When they're alone, when Kate is able to see Rusty as he truly is and Rusty is able to finally be alone with Kate, cue the meet-cute. I grab my notebook and write out a short summary of the scene. I write why the moment worked, and then I try to think of how this might translate into real life. Maybe I could have a meet-cute like this.

So far I've summarized the *Serendipity* meet-cute, the one in *Must Love Dogs*, and the one in *Notting Hill*—since that's what Abby was originally going for with her planned date. This is my fourth sample of evidence, sourced from an article on some of the best meet-cute moments. I'm taking what Harold said to heart, about preparation and practice.

I exit out of the movie and cue up *Four Weddings and a Funeral*. After Gavin told me not to let things with Ben get me down, I realized that this party is a good opportunity for me to plan a meet-cute of my own. I've been so caught up feeling embarrassed about my meet-cutes, looking at them as failures, that I haven't been seeing them as growing opportunities. Swim *practice* is never as good as the meet. In math team we get more questions wrong in our meetings than we do at competition because we all study, practice, and prepare heavily leading up to the big event.

I haven't studied, and maybe if I can consider these past three failures as *practice*, then I can start to make some changes.

By the end of my research, I figure I can go about tonight in a number of ways. I could "trip" over something and stumble into a guy I think is cute and then turn it into a conversation. Or I could accidentally spill a drink, but I think most people would get annoyed and not curious about getting to know me, so that's not a first choice. I could pretend to need help looking for something, even though I've been to Nandy Fagan's house before. I figure that, aside from Ritchie having a girlfriend and ruining everything, us sneaking off to the garage to have a chance to talk was important. We did have a real moment. I felt a connection, and we wouldn't have been staring so deeply into each other's eyes if there were people right there, talking loudly. So maybe I can take that successful piece from my *practice* meet-cute and use it to my advantage.

And then there's option three, which is not watching the kettle and letting the water boil. That's probably going to be the hardest one—since I can't help but overthink—but I figure I have nothing to lose by trying anything, even if that's seemingly nothing.

"You almost ready to head out?" Mom asks from the doorway to my room.

I adjust my belt so that my white gown hangs more like Princess Leia's.

"In a little bit," I tell her, even though I still haven't texted the group chat back.

Mom comes in, and when I hear two sets of feet, I look over my shoulder to see Dad pushing my throw blanket farther onto my bed so he can sit down on the edge. I watch in the mirror as Mom parts my hair down the middle and gently forms two high pigtails. Then she twists a bun and fixes the other to match, both at the perfect height on her first try.

"Thank you," I say, realizing I still have to find my lightsaber.

"You look great, of course," she says, sitting down next to Dad.

I start digging through my closet, ignoring that weird feeling I get whenever my parents come into my room together. They're rarely this formal. Most of the time Mom will just text me if something is going on, even if it's big news like if someone in the family is pregnant. When both of them come into my room, it's usually to tell me bad news, like someone passed away, or the time I had to get most of my hair cut off because I got gum stuck in it from the tunnel on the playground in my elementary school. Right now, though, they don't have the bad news aura about them.

"I think Princess Leia is a great choice," Dad says. "I mean, if you look at some of the things these girls are wearing for Halloween these days." I smile to myself at the last part, remembering the Jasmine costume Sloane showed me from the website she was planning to buy it from. Definitely would've had to cover it up with a sweatshirt on my way out.

"I feel like she does a lot more than some of the other princesses," I say. "Like, Snow White eats an apple and passes out and needs a man to save her. Sleeping Beauty falls asleep and needs a man to save her. And Cinderella is poor and needs a man to save her. But Princess Leia—"

"Is more like you," Mom finishes, beaming at me as I extend my lightsaber. I could've sworn it was cracked, but maybe it was Sam's that cracked. Or maybe I cracked mine and then switched it with Sam's at some point.

"Her plot is complex and interesting," I add before collapsing my lightsaber and sticking it through the notch in my belt.

I push around my pile of laundry until I find my phone. "Okay, I think I'm good to go," I say, seeing that everyone confirmed meeting at six, and it's already 5:40. I put my phone, lip balm, travel lotion, and a sanitary wipe inside my wristlet purse. As I turn to leave my room, I notice my parents are still sitting on my bed. "Was there something you had to tell me?"

They look at each other. Dad's face doesn't give anything away, but I see Mom shrug, and she's doing that thing where she pouts. When she turns back to me, she says, "It's just that it's the first year we aren't driving you to the sleepover. You're all grown up, heading out on your own . . ."

Oh right.

"Do you want to take a picture or something?" I ask, trying to keep myself from laughing.

"No. I want to go back in time to when you were five and dressed like Big Bird from *Sesame Street*," she says, tilting her head to the side.

"But a picture will do," Dad says, standing up.

He motions for me to go downstairs, and they follow me out of my room. I stand in front of Mom's indoor wreath hung on the door, in between two pots with seasonal fake plants. For the fall there are eucalyptus, cotton, and these tan-looking fronds. Wrapped around the pots are long plastic strands of orange and yellow oak leaves.

"Promise me you'll stay my kid forever," Mom says, pretending to be dramatic while Dad steadies his iPhone.

"I promise," I say, smiling. Watching them look at me, seeing the way they stand next to each other and how the air around them seems to bend so that even though they aren't touching, you can just sense how much they love each other and how perfect they are together—it makes me smile harder. It makes me genuinely happy.

The one thing I have always been certain of is my parents being together and loving me, and being ready to take a picture or sign a permission slip, and it has been a fortunate constant in my life. They are who they are individually, in such distinct ways that them being themselves is something you can count on. I get my quiet side from Dad and my questioning side from my mom. I get excited in the same way she gets excited, with uncontrollable smiling and a tendency to create jokes out of joyful situations. I study and focus the same way my dad does, by closing myself into the cave of my room, to think in solitude and to solve my problems without help.

And together, they're a scale perfectly balanced. Acting and thinking. Singing off tune and bobbing their heads to the music. Dancing in the middle of the dance floor and watching from the wall. The energy is comfortable, and while Dad flips the orientation of his phone and I watch him and Mom argue about how to pull up portrait mode, I almost wish that we could rewind to when Sam would've been standing here with me, before she went off to college and moved out of the house, before all the wedding planning began—me dressed as Big Bird and her dressed as Rihanna from the early 2000s. When the most important thing was getting the most PayDays, my favorite candy.

"I have to go," I say after he takes a few more pictures.

"Okay, okay," Dad says, handing his phone to Mom for approval.

I hug them both good-bye and then head to my car. Outside, increasing the distance between me and my annual lie, I feel a weight lifting off my shoulders. Tonight is not going to be another failure!

I park in the street in front of Sloane's house, since Victor's truck is parked in the driveway along with Sloane's parents' car. As I pass Victor's truck and notice Grace's winter coat in the back seat, I feel a little bad for throwing my phone. I could've given her a ride.

"Oh my gosh!" Sloane shouts when she opens the door. Abby and Victor materialize behind her at the kitchen entrance. "You actually make Star Wars look cool."

"Shut up," I kid, laughing a little.

Sloane pulls me into the house, and we all compare costumes.

Abby is Cinderella, though her dress is a lot shorter than I remember it being in the animated version. Sloane is dressed as Jasmine and has traded her usual braided weave for a slick straight one that trails all the way down her back, with blue scrunchies cinching her hair at different spots. Even so, I still spot her purple streak. Grace's Princess Tiana gown is probably the most beautiful. Maybe it's because green is one of my favorite colors or because her gown is truer to form. It touches the floor—which might simply be because she's so short—and it poofs out like a princess gown should. Victor is dressed as Tarzan and has on a padded muscle shirt that is impossible not to laugh at.

"You guys look amazing," I say finally, noticing for the first time how truly unflattering my Princess Leia dress is.

"You do too," Abby assures me.

We pile into Victor's truck, me sitting between Sloane and Grace in the back seat, noticing the way Victor's right hand rests on Abby's leg, their fingers entwined, for most of the ride. While Grace watches the Chicago skyline get farther away, Sloane taps my shoulder to get my attention. She mouths *Sorry*, and I mouth *It's okay*, really meaning it. I know that the way my meet-cute went with Ben is not her fault. She did exactly what I asked her to do, and everyone predicted it wouldn't end well.

I didn't tell my friends that I plan to use tonight as an opportunity to scope out a possible date for the wedding. I want them to have fun and not think about the project. Plus, they've all taken a turn trying to set me up, and I figure it's time I have a go at it myself.

Victor parks the truck, and as Sloane and Grace spill out of the back seat, I take a private deep breath. We turn down Nandy's pumpkin-lined walkway, falling in step with other groups in costumes. I see Charlie Brown, the Mad Hatter, and a can of LaCroix—an unlikely trio.

The moment we step through the door, people notice Grace's dress. It's bright green and sparkly and hard to miss, especially with Nandy's fairy light decorations twinkling in the rhinestones in Grace's crown. I make eye contact with a few people from swim team, and we all migrate in their direction. A few of the boys decided to go as Minions. Shannon dressed up as Beyoncé from *Lemonade*.

Miraculously, without getting separated, we snake our way through the house to the kitchen, where there are bottles of soda, juice, and sparkling water all over the counter. On the kitchen table are bowls filled with candy. I pour myself a cup of Pepsi and help myself to a few gummy worms before grabbing an empty chair in the dining room.

As more people get up from their seats to go dance, Grace, Victor, Abby, and Sloane all manage to get chairs.

Sloane holds up her plastic cup of ginger ale and shouts over the music, "A toast to tradition."

"To Halloween 'dinners' with friends," Abby adds, laughing.

We all toast, and as I look around at my friends, I feel some of the nostalgia Mom mentioned. After next year we won't all be together for Halloween, Grace won't live a short walk away and be able to come over whenever we need each other, and Abby and I won't be racing each other in the pool. And Victor won't be attached to Abby in the way all of us are used to.

Sloane starts telling us about her six-year-old brother and his friends going trick-or-treating. He's dressed as a carrot this year, and his friends' parents coordinated so that one of them is a carrot and another is a jar of peanut butter.

Grace decides to top off her drink, so I follow her back to the kitchen. We have to wait while a Teenage Mutant Ninja Turtle that I recognize from my history class occupies the counter, making what's probably a very sugary but gross-looking concoction. We nibble on candy and watch.

Past the Ninja Turtle, I spot a shiny black dome reflecting the lights hanging from the ceiling in the living room. I follow the figure with my eyes, watching as it moves farther into the house, and just as it falls out of view from the kitchen doorway, I realize it's Darth Vader.

"That's so cool," I say, though Grace is looking down at her phone and probably didn't notice.

She still asks "What?" absentmindedly.

I step away from her, feeling a pull like I'm swimming into a current. Grace still doesn't seem to notice, so I decide to just go to the other side of the kitchen and look across the foyer and see. But curiosity pulls me even farther away, and soon I'm weaving between people dancing. Some are people I recognize from school, a few others I know from swim meets at other schools, but the rest are anonymous because they're wearing masks.

I don't see him. At least I hope it's a him, because if it is, then that means there's a boy at this party who likes Star Wars enough to also dress like a character from it. Someone that maybe without too much effort I could talk to. I scan the room looking for the all black, but I have no luck. People are crammed in, with Nandy's furniture pushed against the walls, and since I'm short, it's like trying to look through a very colorful curtain. A couple bumps into me from behind. At first I think they're caught up in the song, but when I turn around, I realize they're caught up in each other. Or, more accurately, tangled.

When I retreat to the kitchen, I find Grace alone at the drink counter.

"I was wondering where you went," she admits, handing me a clean cup.

"Just wanted to look around, see what everyone else came as," I tell her.

We each pour ourselves a cup of Pepsi before going back into the dining room. We weave through a few clusters of people standing around talking, and as we break into our corner, we find Sloane, Victor, and Abby talking to Darth Vader.

"Oh my gosh, this is her," Sloane says, pulling me to her. "You guys are matching."

"I always tease Mia for being into the original Star Wars, but I guess she's not the only one," Abby says, flashing me a huge smile. "I told her she should go as Rey or maybe a really cute feminine twist on Finn because at least more people would *get* it."

"But then she goes on about the original trilogy and how the original cast are slowly dying out," Sloane chimes in.

They both look at me, and I sense it's my turn to say something. *Be interesting,* I tell myself, nervously looking at Darth Vader. A familiar part of me wants to retreat, to be nervous and stumble over my words and feel shy. Part of me wants to overthink, but as I'm staring at Darth Vader, looking at his helmet and not his actual face, I realize I don't even know who I'm talking to.

"Well, they *are,*" I say, watching Darth's eyes. I think he's smiling. "And anybody who calls themselves a Star Wars fan but can't get original references or recognize the younger versions of the original characters isn't *really* a fan."

Sloane just rolls her eyes, beaming at me, and Grace sips

her drink, looking back and forth between Darth Vader and me like she's sitting on my couch watching a movie.

"I like your helmet," I tell him.

"I like your space buns," he says through the voice distorter. It makes me laugh.

"But you're wearing the wrong lightsaber," I say.

"What?" he asks, looking down at his hand.

"Darth Vader is from the dark side. He's supposed to use red," I say, pulling mine out. I extend the blue baton and knock it against his green one.

"This was all they had left," he admits, laughing a little, which sounds funny through the voice changer.

"Still, very cool costume. You have good taste," I say.

"You too," he says. Then he points his lightsaber at my cup. "Where can I find one of those?"

I offer to take him, and when I turn around, I discover my friends have deserted me. Darth Vader and I squeeze through the dining room to the kitchen and find ourselves alone. With all the empty space around us, it's like the house is no longer vibrating with the music. I watch while he figures out what to drink.

"Are you from Hayfield?" I ask as he pours himself a cup of orange juice.

"No. I go to Massillon."

"That's cool. Are you also the only one of your friends who likes Star Wars?" I ask, leaning back against the counter.

"What makes you ask that?"

"You're alone," I point out. "They abandoned you like mine do whenever I talk about Star Wars or math team."

"Right." He laughs. "I guess you could say that's what happened."

I look past him at the living room. The music changed and now there's a faster beat. It's not a song I recognize, but I like the way it sounds.

"What kind of music do you like?" Darth Vader asks when he catches me bobbing my head.

"Mostly alternative. Some rap as long as the lyrics are good. But, yeah, mostly indie alternative stuff."

"Like who?" he asks, tilting his helmet up just enough that he can bring the Solo cup to his lips. I glimpse his neck and chin and see that he's Black. He also has a well-shaped beard that makes me curious about the rest of his face. I wonder how much hair he's hiding under his mask. Is it a fro, locks, or a barber fade? Part of me doesn't even know what I would want it to be, but the mystery makes me buzz a little.

"I really like Fickle Friends, the Hunna, and Rainbow Kitten Surprise."

"No way!" Darth Vader says, his surprise sounding especially funny through the voice changer. "I love Rainbow Kitten Surprise; they're one of my favorite bands."

"What's your favorite song by them?" I ask, setting my cup down on the counter next to his.

"'First Class.'"

I stop myself from gushing. "First Class" is one of my

favorites by them too. "My favorite is 'It's Called: Freefall.'"

"Another excellent choice," he agrees. "Have you ever seen them in concert?"

"No. I wish," I admit. The sugar from the candy-soda combo starts to hit me, and a song comes on that I recognize. I let my hips sway a little to release some of the energy, and I look back toward the living room and see that more people are dancing than sitting.

"Do you want to dance?" he asks, tilting his shiny helmet in the direction of the living room.

Do I? I'm not very good at dancing, and I usually get insecure and want to sit on the couches or chairs on the outskirts. Abby and Sloane always dance no matter where we are, whether it's a party, a club party for school, or an actual dance. They have no inhibitions and I always envy them. I wish that I could let go.

"Yes," I say, finishing the rest of my soda. I grab a handful of gummy worms and pop a few into my mouth for good measure.

We make our way over to the living room, Darth Vader's cape flowing behind him. When we reach the edge of the room, I spot the purple streak in Sloane's hair, and without thinking, I take Darth Vader's hand and lead him through the swaying and jumping bodies. We get bumped around—I take an elbow to my side, and I accidentally step on someone's foot—but I don't let go. And he doesn't let go of my hand. He interlaces his fingers with mine, and when I get pushed, he catches me. He yanks me back before I can lose my balance completely, and I find myself pressed against him. Even though his shirt is loose and his cape makes it hard to see his shape, I can tell that he's muscular by the way his biceps flex against my arms. As I stare into his mask, making out his eyes through the little holes, I feel like this is our moment. He stares back at me with his brown eyes, looking back and forth between mine—searching.

Without knowing who he is, I have no clue what heading he might fall under. I remember the lists I made the night Sam told me I needed to find a date. All the weirdos; douchebags; and smelly, awkward nerds that my friends said no to. I wonder where I would write him in, but at the same time I don't want to know. I imagine him as someone I don't know, someone I can't categorize. Maybe if his mask didn't cover his mouth, we would kiss right now.

"Come on, move!" Abby shouts behind me, bumping her hip against mine.

Darth Vader lets me go, but still holds my hand and twirls me around. Grace comes up beside me and starts doing her usual shopping cart and sprinkler moves, which always make me laugh. At the chorus of the song everyone screams. We throw our hands into the air, and I find the words to "Tongue Tied" as someone starts throwing rolls of toilet paper all over and people catch them and toss them around. As I look from Victor to Abby to Sloane to Grace to Darth Vader, I feel something unfamiliar. I feel like I haven't been present in a long time. I feel like I'm returning. I feel like I'm returning to something, even with someone totally new in the mix.

I feel like myself.

We keep dancing to the next song and the next. All of us bumping hips and having Darth Vader and Victor take turns twirling us around. I have to stop when I can't catch my breath. Sloane and Abby are still going, and when I scream into Grace's ear, asking if she needs a break, she tells me that she's good and then gives me a wink that I hope Darth Vader doesn't see. Even though I don't want to assume Darth is going to follow me, I feel pleased when I look back over my shoulder and find him right behind me—Victor holding his thumbs up high above everyone's heads farther behind in the living room. We weave up through the people standing on the stairs and make our way along Nandy's upstairs hallway. When I see there isn't a line outside the bathroom, I'm glad. I'd rather hole up in there for a few minutes of peace than have to step out into the late October cold. I hold the door open for Darth. He tilts his head to the side, and I tell him that I'm not using the bathroom, I just want some quiet.

"You're really cool," he says, sitting down on the edge of the tub.

I close the toilet and sit down on top.

"You're not so bad yourself," I say, trying not to blush. He looks funny, dressed in black with Nandy's kitty cat shower curtain as a background.

After jumping up and down, I can feel that my buns

have started to fall. I reach into my hair and pull out the bobby pins, and then I pull out the ponytails and comb through them with my fingers until my hair is down around my shoulders.

"I like your hair like that," he says.

"What does your hair look like?" I ask, leaning forward a little.

"Do you really want to know?"

"Of course. I want to know who the second-coolest person at this party is," I say jokingly, though I really do want him to take off the mask. I'm curious. Is he someone that I've seen before, either around town or at another party, and this mask finally gave him the confidence to make a move? Or maybe we're meeting for the first time and both of us are building from a clean slate. I think, even if we've met before, tonight is like our first-time meeting—our first time getting to know each other for real.

"Can I see your phone?" he asks.

I unlock it and hand it to him and watch as he pulls off his gloves. He types his number into my phone and then creates a contact.

"Really?" I ask, looking down at my new contact: Darth Vader.

"Go on a date with me? Away from all this. And you'll see who I am."

Even though I've been wanting this, it's like I actually didn't think that he could *want* to ask me out. I look down at my phone to hide my face because I feel my cheeks get hot.

I text his number with my name and listen as his phone dings in his pocket.

He doesn't reach for it, just laughs a little.

"You promise you're not a murderer in disguise?" I ask.

"I promise."

"You promise you're in high school and not some creep who snuck in here?" I ask, trying to think of all the ways this could go wrong.

Darth Vader leans forward. He pulls my empty hand into his and looks at me—the only part of him that I see is his eyes. They stare into mine purposefully, pointedly, and I can't look away.

"I promise," he says.

He doesn't look away, and for a moment I have a sense of déjà vu. I feel like this is familiar, and I want to reach out and see if he'll let me take the mask off. But someone pounds on the door and he stands up.

"Anybody in here? Come on!"

Darth Vader throws the door open, and I look over his shoulder and see Nandy dressed as Tinker Bell.

"My parents are, like, five minutes away; you guys have to leave!" she shouts, before moving on to the bedroom next to us.

We run downstairs and dive headfirst into chaos. Almost everyone is leaving through the front door. I see girls looking for their purses, boys waiting for their girlfriends, and people looking for their phones or where they set their keys. As the living room empties, I realize Abby, Sloane, and Grace probably piled into Victor's truck already.

I trust that my friends will be fine with each other, and I take Darth Vader by the hand and lead him to the back of the house. It's less frantic, since most people don't know where the back door leads. The night air chills my skin, but I'm thankful that it wakes me up out of my romantic stupor.

"Can you jump a fence?" I ask breathily as we fall in with a few other kids running to the edge of Nandy's backyard.

"Yes," he says.

There are people dressed as ogres, as Pepsi cans, and as grim reapers. We all help each other by hoisting one another up the fence and then pulling the people below us to the top too. It feels slow as it's happening, but once my feet hit the ground, I wait for Darth to finish helping a bumblebee swing their legs over the fence before he jumps down.

I hear Nandy's mom screaming from the driveway, the slam of her car door not far behind. Through a crack in the fence, I see her dad run around the front of their car, shouting for a boy to stop peeing on the lawn, threatening to call his parents. With Darth Vader's hand in mine, we run, scattering away from the rest of the disguised fugitives. We don't stop running until we reach the November Always diner.

When Sam was still in high school, my family would come here a lot. We'd get breakfast on Sunday mornings, or Dad would get up early to buy us bagels before school.

After Sam went away to college, it didn't feel the same without her. We tried to go every time she came home for break, but then she brought home Geoffrey. They'd get up at six in the morning and do yoga, and then they would drive downtown to a French bistro Geoffrey's mom recommended he take Sam to for a date. It became *their* spot, and our family hangout was obsolete.

Sometimes Abby and I come here after swim meets or I'll stop in for a milkshake. But now that we're pushing through the silver-framed doors, I can't remember the last time I was here. November Always will forever be a favorite of mine because of the retro style. Stepping inside is like stepping through a time portal, a time portal leading to cushiony leather seats and tall milkshake glasses.

We shuffle into a booth and immediately pull out our phones. I imagine Darth Vader doing what I'm doing, trying to see what happened to whomever he came to the party with.

My hands are shaking from the cold as I type and send a few messages to our group chat. No one replies. I try calling Sloane, then Abby, and then Grace. I cycle back twice more, and still no answer. When I see that my battery is down to 14 percent, I realize I can't waste time calling my friends if I expect to find a way home.

"Do you have a ride?" Darth Vader asks, reading my mind. I picture my car still parked in the street in front of Sloane's house. If only she didn't live so far away. If only I had enough battery to order an Uber.

I can feel my heart racing, and I can't tell if I'm out of breath from running or out of breath from the panic.

"I can't reach my friends," I admit, setting my phone down on the table. I cover my face with my hands and focus on the pitch-black darkness. I count in my head and try to control my breathing. It's hard to feel like this isn't the end of the world as I push away the thought of calling my parents.

"What are you going to do?" Darth asks. "I mean, if you need, I can give you a ride."

I weigh my options, knowing I shouldn't test my luck for tonight. Even though Darth has been super nice to me, I still have no idea who he is.

I sigh. "There's really only one thing I can do," I admit, picking up my phone.

On the third ring, a voice comes through the receiver—not sounding at all tired at midnight. "Isn't it past your bedtime?"

"Funny," I say, starting off sarcastic. I stare at Darth across the table, watching his eyes watching me. "Sam, I need you to come pick me up."

CHAPTER TWELVE

Twenty minutes later, I'm shivering outside the November Always diner with Darth Vader. When I see Sam's car turn the corner, I face Darth and ask him if he needs a ride. I'm surprised no one has come to pick him up yet, since he has been texting ever since we escaped the party.

"No, I'm going to walk," he says. I still can't get over his voice distorter, but I keep from laughing.

"It's freezing outside," I say, still hugging myself.

"It's not too bad," he says. I can hear laughter in his voice, and I can see the smile shimmering in his eyes. "I just wanted to make sure you got home okay."

It's hard not to blush, but when Sam shouts behind me, the warm feeling goes away.

"What about your friend?" she asks when I close the passenger door.

I wave to him through the window. "He's all good."

"*He?*" Sam asks, checking her rearview mirror before pulling away from the curb. She glances at me before saying, "I thought you only hung out with girls."

"I have other friends," I say weakly.

"Right, and where are your best ones?"

"I don't know."

"Who was that friend?"

"I don't know," I admit, watching her expression out of the corner of my eye.

I can tell by the way she contorts her face that she wants to parent me right now.

"Then why the heck were you standing outside a diner in the cold in the middle of the night with a boy you don't know? Mia, like, seriously?"

"Seriously, what?"

"I don't get it. You're at your yearly Halloween dinner-sleepover at Sloane's house, and suddenly you're alone at a diner with a boy? A boy dressed like Darth Vader—dressed like *evil*, I might add. Darth Vader was the bad guy."

I want to tell her to cut the crap, but I know I'm not in a position to do so.

"We went to a Halloween party, okay?"

"And did Mom—"

"No, Mom and Dad didn't know about it. They don't know that I went to a party, and quite frankly I would like to keep it that way," I say, trying not to think of how embarrassing it would be for them to find out. I can't even remember the last time I got in trouble for something, and even though they were fine with the idea of me going to the party freshman year, I know that they wouldn't be able to get over the fact that I lied.

While I try to rack my mind for my last punishment,

Sam asks, "So, last year when you went to the Halloween dinner?"

"I feel like I don't have to answer that," I mumble, admiring the blow-up Halloween decorations on someone's front lawn.

"Okay, not going to lie, that's a little badass. Not something I would've expected from you."

I stare at her in her slightly raised driver's seat, her gaze focused on the road in front of her. Not the reaction I was expecting.

"Nevertheless, I think you owe me one." Her voice is too cheery.

"Naturally," I sigh, trying to fold myself into the seat and make myself as small as possible. This is more typical of her.

Sam scratches her scalp and then runs her fingers through her hair. I can tell she straightened it earlier tonight, and I get a waft of the oils. Under usual circumstances the smell would relax me. But right now I'm annoyed at her. She probably washed her hair and did her nails and put on a facemask for one of her self-care nights and lost track of time staying up reading Michelle Obama's autobiography or diving deep into the parenting blogosphere. And here she is, clean and shiny, validated as the Rescuer, my stand-in guardian.

"I'll have to think about what I want to use my one wish for," she muses. "In the meantime, we'll start with you coming to my dress fitting tomorrow. I still have your dress in my closet, so we can bring that, too. You haven't seen the tailor once since buying it."

"The dress fit fine," I huff. "I don't know why I have to put it on over and over to see that it *still* fits."

"Because you might have gained weight or lost weight, and it has to be perfect. Also, because now you owe me and I said this is what we're doing."

"Whatever," I mumble.

She rolls her eyes, hard, and then stares at me for a second before pulling ahead when the light turns green. Whenever she rolls her eyes like that, it's usually because she's close to her edge. I stay silent, knowing that if I even breathe too loud, she'll just talk more to make me feel worse about tonight.

Then again, no matter how bad she makes me feel, it doesn't change the fact that I met someone. On my own! I look out the window to hide my smile, and I try to hold on to this feeling for the next few days.

As obsessive as Sam has been throughout her entire wedding planning process, the one thing that hasn't gone wrong and hasn't caused any stress or doubts is the dress. Naturally, she has a Pinterest account specifically dedicated to weddings, wedding planning, wedding budgets, and anything else that you could put after the word "wedding." When we went into the wedding dress boutique back in the middle of August, Mom, Brooke, and I sat down. They were given glasses of champagne and I was

handed a glass of sparkling grape juice. Sam was away for a while, reviewing her vision board with the clerks, talking to a stylist, and looking at dresses in her fitting room without showing us anything.

I started reading an article on my phone about Jeffrey Dahmer while Mom and Brooke whispered to each other about the lighting in the room and the floral detailing in the wallpaper. I think I was on the section about his third murder when a woman dressed in all black came out from the fitting rooms with a huge smile on her face, tears brimming in her eyes, and her hands clasped as if she were afraid she'd go crazy if she didn't keep them together.

"Are you guys ready?" she asked.

"Yes, out with it," Brooke huffed, before swallowing the last of her third glass of champagne in one gulp.

As if that were her cue, Sam appeared. Even though Sam isn't very tall and is pretty tiny, in this dress she filled the entire doorway. Not like the dress was so big that it couldn't fit through the opening, more like her presence was elevated. It's an off the shoulder long-sleeve dress that has a slight A-line circle type skirt. There's silver beading along the neckline, and it trails down the front of the dress and spirals all over the skirt like a firework. As she moved into the room, it was like the air we were breathing was pure elegance. It was like our minds were cleared out and filled with a calming white space, that space being the creamy white of a wedding dress.

All of her planning. All of her online searching. All of

her frustrations and color coding and highlighting and hair pulling—everything she had been doing came together in this moment. We were in a world that consisted solely of a three-way mirror that captured every angle of the Dress.

"My gosh," Mom gasped, clutching her chest. She too fell into tears. She stood up, went to Sam, and held her face in her hands and said, "My Samantha, when did you become so grown-up? It's like yesterday you wouldn't let go of my hand when I was dropping you off at preschool, and now . . . Oh my."

Brooke said she didn't get how Sam could walk into a store and the first dress she puts on is the One. Maybe, even though Brooke is Sam's best friend, she doesn't know Sam *that* well. Because I know everything that built up to this moment. I know that Sam picked this store because she did the research. I know she picked this dress because she figured out the best fit for her body type, what kind of detailing would complement her curves if she wanted something more fitted versus loose. I know that because of who she is, she was able to nail this one on the first try.

And yes, that first moment when we saw her in the Dress was magical and beautiful and blah, blah, blah. But now, after however many times she's come to the tailor to try it on, the scene is old. I've been to two of her fittings since she started alterations. At the last one, when she stood, admiring herself in the mirror, her trying *Veil? No veil? Veil?* is what did me in.

So, my lack of enthusiasm should be understandable as

Sam pulls up to the stoplight with a huge unnecessary grin on her face.

"This is exciting," she says, leaning up to peek at herself in her rearview mirror. She rubs her lips together to try to spread out some of the tinted lip balm she just put on, before settling back down. When the light turns green, we pull out of the parking garage under Sam's apartment building downtown. Even though her apartment has a view of Lake Michigan, once we're on the ground, all we can see are buildings, pedestrians, and more buildings.

"What's exciting about waking up at seven a.m. on a Sunday when we didn't even get to sleep until one in the morning? What, exactly, is *exciting* about that?" I grumble. At first I had my arms crossed over my chest because of the cold, but now I have them crossed to make myself smaller, to try to pull myself into a tiny ball that can disappear and not have to try on this dress.

"Us spending some quality time together, doing girl things."

"Girl things?" I ask, glancing down at the untouched caramel macchiato Sam got me from the Starbucks in the lobby of her building.

"Yes. I feel like we haven't had sister time in forever. And now we can drink our coffee, put on our dresses, and maybe get a manicure after."

"What if I have things to do today?" I ask, looking at her.

"Do you?"

"That wasn't my question," I tell her, annoyed that she would just up and decide that we are spending a day together without asking. Without even fathoming that with school, swim team, math team, and my wild goose chase to find a date to her own freaking wedding, I might have more important things to do than go put on a dress because she wants to play dress-up.

"Why do you have to be like that?" she asks.

"Like what?"

"Negative? Like, always trying to start something."

"I'm not trying to start anything," I say defensively. "I was asking a question."

"A rude question. You and I both know you don't have anything to do that's going to take up your *entire* Sunday. You do homework, swim, stare at the wall and be a boring little twerp, eat, sleep, and repeat."

"Sometimes I can't stand you," I mumble, wishing I hadn't called her last night.

"Sometimes I can't believe we're related."

"That's dramatic," I scoff, turning to look out the window.

"Oh, is it?" Sam asks, whipping her car into a parking space. It happens so fast that I nearly smack my head against the window.

Before she even shifts the car into park, I throw my door open and get out. "Let's just get this over with," I say before slamming the door shut and leaving her.

When I step into the store, I feel weird. A wedding dress

boutique isn't usually a place where angry people go. It's supposed to be a happy place where you can dream.

So when I sit down on the cushiony bench outside the fitting room we're directed to, I feel more out of place than usual. Sam is chic and sparkly, glossy heels and intricate updos. I'm dark colors and matte finish, hair either in a bun or out and wild. The tailor's assistant is in the back, ready to help Sam zip up when she gives the say-so. I notice the tailor looking down, and I follow his gaze to realize he's scrunching up his brow at my old pair of moss-green Vans. I look at his loafers, so shiny that they reflect the white lights around the three-way mirror. He's very *Sex and the City,* and I'm *Love Jones.*

"Why are you sitting?" Sam asks when she emerges in her gown. She carries the front of the dress so that she can step up onto the platform without tripping over her hem. When she lets it go, the skirt nearly falls to the floor, hanging on her frame—predictably—like it did the last time she tried it on. Without waiting for my answer, she instructs the tailor that he should measure for the hemline to be just above her toes because she doesn't want to trip during the ceremony. She says the sleeves have to be taken in because since she's been working on wedding planning more than working out, her arms have shrunk ever so slightly in a way that she notices more than any of us do.

When she finishes running down her list, she realizes I'm still sitting.

"Go try on your dress."

"I don't even know where you put it." I purposefully stormed out of the car without it, figuring if it was out of sight, it might fall out of mind as well.

"In your fitting room."

"I have a fitting room?" I ask, standing up and stretching. It's still earlier than I would wake up on a Sunday after being out past midnight, so my body comes out of the stretch and begs me to curl back into the fetal position.

"Yes," she hisses, gathering her dress right out of the tailor's hands. "Through there." She points toward where she came from. "Across from mine." She's standing in front of me, gritting her teeth, and staring into my eyes the way Mom would look at her when she'd do something wrong, like accidentally put a metal mug in the microwave or forget her keys. It was a look that made her clip her keys to her backpack and shove all the metal travel mugs into their own cabinet.

I stare back for a moment, wondering if she really is that fed up with me or if she *thinks* this is the only way she can get me into that stupid room. By talking to me like I'm her child or one of her employees. Not her sister. I step around her and the assistant standing off to the side with that awkward *I probably wasn't supposed to see that* look on her face.

Sam, true to form, decided to be traditional. Some of her friends from college had weddings where all the bridesmaids could pick their own dress, regardless of style or color. Another friend just said all the dresses had to be the same color. Sam, however, wants all the dresses exactly the same. She likes the uniformity, the consistency. It's one of those preferences that reminds us we are in fact related.

So, all seven of the bridesmaids, including myself, are wearing deep green dresses. It was Stamica's idea. Stamica and Sam were in a web design class, and she even helped Sam design the ArchiTech website. So, naturally, she's been working with Sam on "designing" her wedding. The winter wonderland theme was her idea, along with the dark green dresses that represent evergreens.

The bridesmaids' dresses are floor length, A-line circle-skirt princess dresses. They're off the shoulder, with ruffled bands that hang around our upper arms; the body of the dress starts off tight around the waist, then flows out. Even though the dress flows and cups our shoulders, it's still very plain. There's no intricate stitching or beading. The fabric does all the work, with a million tides and ripples dangling by our ankles.

When I step out of my dressing room, I can hear Sam wrestling around in hers. Instead of waiting, I just head out to the three-panel mirror. I step up onto the platform and look at myself. I turn my hips and watch as the rest of the dress follows, delayed like a ripple. The neckline dips in the middle, but modestly.

"Wow."

I startle. I didn't even hear the tailor come up behind me.

"Sorry." He blushes. I turn back to the mirror, and we meet each other's eyes.

"Like I told her, it still fits perfectly fine," I mumble, ready to step off the platform.

But Sam comes out of her dressing room and stares at me from the doorway in silence. I think of the way Mom looked at her when Sam tried on her dress. I think of how Stamica and Brooke strutted around the fitting room like models at their fittings because they were so pleased with their dresses, how Sam gushed over them and directed the tailor on what touch-ups had to be done. I just stood off to the side and watched.

"It still fits," I say again, my voice quiet.

She nods in agreement, looking me up and down. "It's beautiful." She says it like she's admitting defeat. I was right, that I haven't changed. Somehow I feel like this disappoints her. I take her reaction as my cue to go put my clothes back on, and I squeeze past her into the fitting room.

CHAPTER THIRTEEN

During the weekdays that I spend not going to the garden after school, Gavin manages to redo the irrigation system inside the greenhouse and set up a few wooden troughs with fresh soil. And on Friday, when Gloria runs up to my mom and says Gavin "needs" me to help him with painting the rest of the wooden beams on the inside, I'm thankful that he won't let Gloria have me work on something else. Otherwise, I wouldn't be able to report back to him about the Halloween party and get his advice about tomorrow night.

"So, everything went well?" he says when I finish a rant-like recap of the night. He reaches down for the can of paint.

He decided that the inside of the greenhouse will be green, to blend in with the plants. I'm in charge of staining the troughs, so whenever he has to move to a new spot, I have to stop and hand all of his supplies to him on the ladder.

"Everything went great, and we've been texting for the past week," I say, handing him the cloth that fell out of his pocket. "I mean, someone who likes Star Wars and listens to Rainbow Kitten Surprise . . . That's, like, impossible to find."

He shoves the cloth back into his pocket so that half

of it is hanging out, for when he gets paint on his fingers. Then he leans against the ladder. He looks down at me, smiling.

"Not impossible because you like both those things. Plus, don't get me wrong, I don't get the hype about Star Wars, but I can vibe with some RKS."

"What?" I gush. "No way. How have we not talked about this? They're one of my favorite bands." Finding other people my age who like RKS has proven nearly as difficult as finding a leprechaun.

"Because you never asked," he says, using a mock accusatory tone.

"You didn't ask either," I remind him, laughing.

"Touché," Gavin says, shrugging and dripping some paint from his brush onto the ground. "But you still don't know who he is?" he asks, though a smile creeps across his face, and I can tell he's finding this amusing.

"I know, it's crazy," I admit, kneeling down next to my half-finished trough. "But this might be—" I stop myself from saying *my one chance,* because I don't want to start putting all my eggs in one basket.

"It's not that crazy," he says. In the dead air between us, I can hear the sound of his brushstrokes against the old beams. He didn't want to sand them down because he likes how it ages the inside, keeps some character in the place.

"Then, what is it?" I ask, noting the leading tone in his voice.

"Honestly, it's a little romantic."

I turn around, expecting him to be looking down at me, ready to laugh. But his back is turned and he's focused, serious.

"Like a masquerade," he says absentmindedly, his hand trailing high above his head. I watch the way he moves slowly, allowing the paint to make contact so that there aren't rushed streaks. Then he slowly pulls the brush away so that the stroke fades out evenly. Then he dips the brush into the paint, reaches back up, and traces his stroke backward. The way he moves so carefully is mesmerizing.

"Like a masquerade," I repeat, seeing how the words feel in my mouth, how the thought feels in my head.

"Chances are, it's someone you know. I can't imagine a stranger being that bold," he says, turning around. "Plus, now he knows who you are."

"Yeah, but it could still be a stranger who just, like—" I look down, feeling self-conscious.

"Who saw you across the room and thought you were *so* pretty that he just had to talk to you?" Now he starts teasing.

I grab some dirt from the trough and throw it at him, which only makes him laugh.

"Again, another possibility. Slim, but not impossible," he says, shrugging his shoulders before turning back to his beams.

"Anyways," I continue, circling back to the whole point of telling him in the first place. "We've been talking all week, and we set a date for tomorrow night."

I wait until he says "Okay?" to know that he's listening.

"I forgot that my sister Sam's bridal shower is tomorrow."

"Yikes." He sets the brush down and turns around on the ladder. He leans against it and crosses his arm, shaking his head down at me. "Now, that's a pickle."

"I really can't tell if you're being serious or sarcastic," I tell him, wiping my hands on my jeans.

He looks down at the ground for a moment, one hand on his hip and the other rubbing his chin. "What if you reschedule?"

"I don't want to reschedule" shoots out of my mouth before I can think. Gavin stares at me, surprised. "I just, I am not going to reschedule this. I need it to happen tomorrow." Now that it's November, the clock feels like it's ticking a lot faster. There won't be any more parties like the Halloween one until the New Year. I'd have to go back to the drawing board of setting up meet-cutes instead of following Gloria's sound advice to just *let it happen*.

"Then . . . bring him?" Gavin replies.

"What?"

"Bring him to the bridal shower?" he asks, raising his eyebrows. I didn't know his voice could rise to such a high pitch, but both of us stare at each other, thinking about it.

"No," I decide. "Sam will just get on me about it. She already shared her thoughts about Darth Vader being a symbol of evil, and me being stupid for feeling attracted to him."

"Why not talk to Sam about it?"

"Just no," I say, sighing.

"Why not just ask the guy for a rain check and see what happens? He might be understanding, go to the shower, and then you guys can still reschedule your date."

"Well, wouldn't that just be perfect," I hiss. "Thank you for figuring everything out for me."

"Hey," Gavin says, his brows coming together. "I'm just trying to help."

"Well, you're not doing a very good job."

"Fine. Then mess everything up." He turns around, kicking up some dust with his foot, and climbs back up the ladder.

The tension charges the air between us and makes it hard to concentrate. I know I shouldn't have snapped at him, but he doesn't understand.

We work in silence for a little bit. I can tell my mind is racing when I snap out of my thoughts and look down to see uneven streaks in my wood stain.

"Gavin," I say. It comes out quietly, but I see his head turn slightly toward me. "I didn't mean to snap at you. I'm just stressed. I don't know how to please everyone, and I don't know what to do to help myself."

"What do *you* want to do? Throw morals and what you think is right to the wind and ask yourself, if there was nothing riding on anything, what would you want to do? The date, or your sister's bridal shower?"

I want to say both, but I know I can't. I know the right answer is Sam's shower because she's my sister and she's only getting married once. But this date would be for the sake of *her* wedding anyways. So, I feel like if I miss her shower, she might be mad at first, but she'd be fine with it in the end because I will have gotten a date to balance out her precious photos.

"The date," I say. "I think the date is the best option."

Even as I make the decision, I still feel conflicted.

I don't officially decide anything until I'm in the shower Saturday night. What am I getting ready for? Am I showering before my date or showering before my sister's party? How would Darth react if I back out now? Do I really want to risk losing him altogether, not just for tonight? After I dry off, I look in the bathroom mirror and will myself to decide. I will myself to choose between what I should do and what I want to do.

"Mia, you're taking forever. You'd better not use all the hot water," Sam shouts on the other side of the door. I know that with the fan on in the bathroom, it's hard to tell if I'm still in the shower or not, so I don't say anything. I just stare at my foggy reflection.

"Mia, I have to get ready. Come on," she says, trying the doorknob.

"You could've been ready if you were at your *own* apartment, getting ready in your *own* bathroom!" I shout back. Even though I grew up with her in the house, it feels extra crowded and unfamiliar whenever she spends the night now. She's been crowding me ever since Halloween.

"No," she says, knocking on the door. "Because then I

would have had to drive all the way over here, which is a waste of precious time. It's faster to just get ready here and then go downstairs."

She jumps when I throw the door open. "Or you could've gotten ready at home in your own bathroom without having to wait for me, and you could dedicate more of that *precious* time to helping Mom with decorations," I say, tightening my towel around my chest. I move past her and head down the hallway to my room.

If I'm slowing her down that much, then maybe I have a chance at going on my date and making it back before the end of the bridal shower. I mean, she still has to wash up, do her hair, and press her outfit. Mom and I haven't finished putting up all the decorations, and I know Sam was supposed to bring supplies to make goodie bags for the guests. If I leave, maybe I can eat really fast during the date, make a good impression, and then come back home before Sam starts opening gifts.

I sit on the edge of my bed and take my phone off the charger. My heart flutters when I see a text from Darth.

DARTH VADER: Looking forward to tonight
ME: Me too :)
DARTH VADER: We still on for 6:30?

I check the time and see I have about twenty minutes to get ready before I'd have to leave to make it to the diner on time.

ME: I'm still getting ready. Should get there maybe 5 minutes late

DARTH VADER: Can't wait ;)

With my thumbs hovering over the keyboard, I hear Gavin's voice in my head telling me to *just ask*. From texting, I can't really tell a whole lot about the kind of person Darth is. He's nice, definitely more on the sweet side, as opposed to the dark side. And I saw that he's a gentleman when he waited for me to get a ride home. Over the course of the week, I found out he likes plants, so we've been talking about the greenhouse and the community garden a lot. He says he's never been but that maybe we could go together. He hasn't given me any hints as to who he is, but he did tell me that he's not a complete stranger. That made me feel a little better. I'm more excited to finally see him, to put a face to our conversations about history class being boring and biology being confusing and his grandma burning the green beans on Wednesday and my mom not realizing she left a trail of hot cocoa from the kitchen to the stairs last night. I remember when he lifted his mask to take a drink and I was able to confirm that he is Black. His skin is darker than mine but not very dark. It's more like a coffee color with one cream instead of two.

The time to ask if he would've wanted to come to the shower has definitely passed. Changing plans at the last minute would be bad, probably be a big red flag. I know it is for me. Plus, what if he wouldn't want to reschedule? Or what if he meets my family and thinks we're all a little out of pocket? I hadn't even thought of that! I can't be the weirdo who introduces someone to their family on the first date!

I smile down at the screen, feeling heat radiating through me. So this is the best decision for us. Date first, shower later.

ME: Me either

I put on a pair of brown tights with my turmeric-yellow miniskirt and an olive-green cropped sweatshirt. I look between a pair of heeled booties and my black Vans, and decide the Vans make the most sense. What if I have to park far from the entrance?

I let my hair down out of its braids. I dried it with a hot air brush this morning and combed more oil through it, so instead of being a tangled mess, it's just wavy and thick. After I put on my makeup, I take one last look in the mirror before putting my phone into my purse and walking over to my window.

The sound of the bathroom door creaking raises the hairs on the back of my neck, and I stand frozen in front of my open window as I listen to the floor creak. I hold still until I hear Sam pass my closed door and shut the door to her bedroom, and then I step out of my window one leg at a time and shut the window behind me.

It's cold outside, enough that I can see my breath in front of my face. I traded my coat for a jean jacket so that I'd look more like a high school girl than the Michelin Man. As I make my way to the edge of the roof, I can hear the music that Mom is playing in the living room. I had to help her start decorating this afternoon for Sam's party. She's really taking the winter wonderland theme to heart. We had to cut out snowflakes to hang from the ceiling. And we used green scrapbook paper to make a bunch of Christmas trees to hide all over the living room as part of a game. Each tree has a fact about Sam and Geoffrey's relationship on it.

Thankfully, directly below my room is part of the kitchen that doesn't have any windows. I toss my purse down first and look over the edge to try to gauge the best way for me to jump off. Which turns out to be for me to sit down on the edge of the roof, praying I don't get any stains on my skirt. I look over the black tips of my Vans and envision my feet on the ground below.

I start counting down from three in my head and then realize that three isn't enough, so I start over from ten. At six, I think I hear a knock at the door in my bedroom, though from out here it could also be in my parents' room. I snap my neck around to look, wondering if maybe I should've locked my door.

When my door doesn't fling open, and my cover isn't blown, I lean forward. A shingle loosens beneath my hip. All too fast, it slides, shifting my body just enough that I lose my balance and feel gravity pulling me as if we'd been playing tug-of-war and I just now gave up.

Needless to say, it hurts when I land in the bushes. I roll

off the bushes involuntarily, my body seeking solid ground without my control. Grass never felt so soft, and I've never been so thankful for my parents' not expanding the deck behind the den.

When I roll over, I feel the cold fabric of my purse. I pull it to me and push myself up off the ground, not wanting to waste any time. I stick close to the house, hiding under windows as I make my way around to the front. I pull twigs out of my hair as I bolt across the lawn, praying Mom or Dad aren't looking out the living room window right this second. For once, Sam's parking in my spot in the driveway proves to be a good thing because all the way down in the street, my parents won't be able to tell if my car is still here or not.

My heart doesn't stop racing until I'm in my car turning at the end of our street, and know there's no way they'll be able to find me for the next few hours. Even though my heart slows, my body buzzes all over. I can't believe I'm doing this! Sneaking out to meet a guy that I really like, a guy that's actually into me. I keep trying to stop smiling but I can't.

I park behind November Always and look at my phone. Darth hasn't said anything since earlier, so I send him a quick text letting him know that I'm here, before getting out of the car. The daunting thing about not knowing him is that I don't know who I'm looking for. Any of these cars could be his, and as I push through the door of the diner, I scan all the booths and barstools, wondering if anyone is him.

Surprisingly, the diner isn't super packed. When you

first walk in, there's a clear path that runs the length of the diner. To the left is the sit-down counter, with a stainless-steel rim that juts out above the royal-blue cushioned barstools. The counter stops short of an emergency exit at the back. On the right side are old train seats that were converted into raised booths. The seats are gray with a royal-blue-and-purple confetti pattern that is fun but also not too much. There's a weird calming energy that comes over me whenever I come here. Even on Halloween, I felt better once we arrived. And in the past, when I came here with my family, there was just always something nice about Sam and me sitting across from our parents, talking over waffles and pancakes dusted with powdered sugar.

It smells of syrup and coffee, and I wave to the waitress behind the counter and point to an open booth. She waves me on, and I step up into the seat, thankful that I can look out the window while I wait. I check my phone again and see that Darth hasn't replied.

"Can I start you off with something to drink?" asks a guy not much older than me wearing a royal-blue paper hat with his diner uniform.

"Coke?" I say, realizing I should wait until Darth gets here before I order a milkshake. I wonder if he's been to this diner before or if Halloween was his first time.

"One Coke coming up," the waiter says, smiling and adjusting his glasses.

I check my phone again when the waiter leaves, and slide it onto the table when I see that Darth still hasn't replied. I remind myself that I could've easily ended up running late, had anything about tonight gone differently. If Sam got into the shower before me. If she came into my room after her shower to go over last-minute plans that I would've had to pretend I cared about . . .

When the waiter returns with my glass bottle, I close my eyes and take a long sip through the straw, savoring the way the bubbles burn sweetly in the back of my throat. When I open my eyes, I startle.

"Mia?"

"Ben?" I say, staring at the last person I expected to see.

"What's up?" he asks, leaning against my table.

"Nothing, just waiting for a friend," I say, watching him. I remind myself that Darth Vader is Black, and Ben is Hispanic, his skin tone significantly lighter. The thought that Darth could be him is nice but unrealistic.

"Mind if I join you while you wait?" he asks, helping himself to the bench across from me.

He waves the waiter back over and says, "I would like two milkshakes. One chocolate and one—" He pauses to look at me.

"You don't have to get me anything," I tell him, leaning forward to sip my cola again.

"We're celebrating. I got an A on my senior thesis paper!"

"Oh my gosh!" I say, louder than I intended. I blush a little and say, quieter, "Congrats! That's so exciting."

"I know. Don't get me wrong. I still have to nail the

presentation portion at the end of the semester, but it's nice to know I'm over one of the hurdles. But, yeah, what kind of milkshake do you want? My treat."

"Chocolate," I say, smiling to myself about how we have the same favorite flavor. I watch him as he looks to the waiter. Does this mean the dog park is officially behind us?

"Two chocolate milkshakes," the waiter says, tipping his hat to us.

"When did you get the grade?" I ask, glancing down at my phone.

"Today," he says, unzipping his jacket. "Earlier this afternoon Mr. Zeigler posted them online. I told my parents and I told some friends, but I wanted to come here and have a milkshake. I told myself that if I got an A, I would celebrate with a milkshake."

"You definitely deserve one," I tell him, leaning back. I admire him as he sits across from me. This is how things were originally supposed to go. We were supposed to end up here together. Thinking about that reminds me of how I thought I'd ruined any chance of him being my date to the wedding.

"You do too," he says, recapturing my attention. I look up from my striped straw sitting in my half-finished cola.

"For what?"

"For solving that triple polynomial equation this week. You, me, and Michelle are the only ones who got it right." He watches me for a moment before adding, "Plus, I imagine that kidnapping random people's dogs to take them to the dog park is an exhausting venture." He smiles slyly.

"I'm sorry about that," I blurt. "I mean, pretending that it was my dog. I don't know why I did that."

"Was that your first time going to a dog park?" he asks.

"Was it that obvious?" I ask, resting my elbows on the table and covering my face with my hands.

"A little," he says.

We pause when the waiter comes back. I notice that his name tag reads MARSHALL B., and I thank him before he walks away. He offers to get me another Coke, and I accept.

"Sloane was dog sitting and brought me to the park and asked me to—take over," I say, trying not to lie without admitting the full truth.

"Ahhh," Ben says, leaning down to take a sip of his shake. He licks the chocolate 'stache on his lip before adding, "So she left a dog in the care of someone who had no idea what they were doing. It sounds like you're the victim here."

He raises his eyebrows, and even though he's joking, I can tell he's being serious enough, so I don't feel as embarrassed.

"I had no idea what I was doing," I admit, leaning toward my straw and taking my first sip of the milkshake.

"Me yelling at you probably didn't make things better," Ben says, and I can hear the apology in his voice.

"Your being there helped," I say, feeling my face get hot.

He smiles at me, and I reflexively look down so that he

can't see how much it affects me. I tap the home button on my phone and see that there still isn't a text from Darth. But there are a few missed calls from Mom and five texts from Dad.

"Where's your friend?" Ben asks.

I tell him that I don't know, and glance around the diner. People from a few of the tables have left since I arrived, and a couple more people have showed up at the counter. But no one looks like they're looking for me.

I catch movement out of the corner of my eye and watch the entrance to the diner. I can see that someone is coming, but through the glass covered with the November Always logo, it's hard to discern if it might be Darth Vader. It's not until the person steps completely inside that I realize another familiar face has arrived.

"Gavin!" I call out, waving.

He looks around and quickly finds me leaning out of the booth. He waves and walks over, then stops short when he sees Ben sitting across from me.

"What are you doing here?" I ask.

"Getting some food. What are you doing here?" he asks quickly, eyeing Ben before looking back at me.

"I'm waiting for someone, and then we ran into each other," I say, pointing to Ben.

"Hi. I'm Ben," he says, smiling and holding out a hand for Gavin to shake.

Gavin takes his hand and shakes it absentmindedly, looking around the diner.

"I'm Gavin," he says, even though he's facing away from Ben and looking over toward the counter.

"Is this not *the* friend?" Ben tries to whisper, but I can tell Gavin hears him.

"No," I say back. "This is Gavin. We've been working at the community garden together."

"That's cool. How has it been?"

"It's going well. We've been remodeling the greenhouse. It's kind of our special project," I say.

I turn to look at Gavin and see him looking down at his foot, braced against the step up into the booth.

"Gavin, this is *Ben*, who I told you about," I say, tilting my head in Ben's direction and widening my eyes at Gavin.

"*The* Ben?" he asks, looking at Ben more closely.

"*The* Ben?" Ben asks, curious.

"I told him about what happened at the dog park," I say. "I was so embarrassed."

"Even though you had no reason to be," Gavin adds quickly.

"Well, it's all behind us now," Ben says before taking another sip of his milkshake. He looks at mine and asks if I want another. Then, before I can answer, he asks if Gavin would like one.

"No," Gavin says, looking toward the counter again. "I'm just getting takeout for me and my girlfriend. I can't stay."

"I didn't know you had a girlfriend," I say, watching Gavin, wishing he would look at me. "And I thought you were still grounded."

"You never asked, and that ended a *while* ago," he grumbles, low enough that I don't think Ben heard. "But, yeah," he says more loudly. "I'm just gonna wait for my food and get out of here." Then to me he adds, "It was nice seeing you," before walking over to the counter.

I watch as he walks up to the edge and starts talking to the waitress. Our waiter emerges from the kitchen with my Coke, and I turn back to Ben, feeling a little weird.

"So," Ben says.

I check my phone and see that Darth still hasn't texted me back. I text him again asking where he is, and if he's still coming, but part of me feels like I'm being stood up. Another part of me fights to ignore the stone settling in my stomach as I tap decline on a call coming in from Mom.

"Are you guys ready to order?" Marshall asks as he pulls my empty Coke from in front of me and sets down the new one.

Ben raises his eyebrows. "I could eat," he says, shrugging his jacket off his shoulders.

"Me too," I say, happy that if I'm going to get stood up on my first real date, at least I'm spending the time with my high school crush.

CHAPTER FOURTEEN

Over a burger and a tuna melt, Ben and I talk about math team, and about swimming and soccer, and then we circle around to his dog, Carly. I wonder if this is what Gladys meant when she said not to watch the kettle, to just let it boil. I don't have to think when I'm talking to Ben; we just move from one topic to the next without even realizing.

"Isn't your sister getting married?" he asks as he reaches across the table to dip one of his fries into my puddle of ketchup.

"She is, in December."

"That's soon," he observes, raising his eyebrows.

"Oh, I know. She knows. Everyone knows," I say, laughing a little. "I still can't believe it."

"Are you excited?" Ben asks.

I sip my Coke, taking a moment to think. "Of course I'm excited. It's just that so many things are changing all at once, you know?" Just being at November Always gives me an eerie feeling that the past is farther behind me than I thought. Sam used to do my hair and ask me fifty questions about the boys in my grade to figure out if I liked anyone—not that she knew any of them. Sometimes she'd tell me about the parties she went to in college, and I'd give her two French braids before she went to sleep. Now when she's home, one of us is almost always slamming our door because the other took too long in the bathroom, or she's asking me to do something for her but is never willing to return a favor as small as bringing me a glass of water from downstairs.

"I definitely understand that," he says. "But change is good sometimes."

"I know," I say, looking down at the crumbs on my plate. "Soon she'll be married, and hopefully she'll go back to living in her apartment full-time instead of spending the night at our house so much."

Ben smiles. "I'm sensing some tension?"

"Like, even though we grew up in the same house, after she left for college and moved out, I got used to having the house to myself. My parents keep to themselves; I keep to myself. Half the time it's like no one else is home. But now Sam has basically moved back in, and she showers when I want to shower. She eats my apples and drinks my fresh pressed juices and uses all my creamer!"

"She sounds like a sister," Ben teases.

"How would you know anything about that?" I ask. "You probably suffer from only-child syndrome since your brother moved out so long ago."

"Not really. My cousins are always around, and my aunts and uncles treat me like I'm their kid whenever they're over."

I try to imagine Ben in his big family. I wonder if his cousins are older or younger, if he's more like a big brother or the younger brother. I don't ask, though. I just keep watching him while he watches me.

"When is the wedding?" he asks.

"December twenty-second."

"A true winter wedding," he says, musing.

"Definitely. Sam is going all out on the decorations, and the tablecloths, and the centerpieces; she even tried to look up weather patterns for December nineteenth through the twenty-second for the past five years so that she could predict whether it might snow or not."

As I list details, I see Ben's eyes widen, so I keep going. "The cake is going to be decorated with snowflakes so that it looks like it's snowing over a forest. And the reception is going to have a range of seasonal cocktails for everyone to try."

"Really?"

"Yeah, and she's marrying Geoffrey Davenport, from the Davenport jam business. So, they're going to incorporate their jams into the dessert menu. There's going to be a sampling of tarts."

"That sounds cool," Ben admits.

We fall silent. He sips his milkshake, and I lean in to finish my cola. Music plays softly from the jukebox, and I notice the words for the first time. It's "Devil Like Me" by Rainbow Kitten Surprise. I nod my head gently to the beat and watch Ben sipping his milkshake, and something stirs inside me.

"Ben?"

He raises his eyebrows.

"I actually need a date to my sister's wedding," I say, cracking my knuckles under the table nervously. "And, I was wondering if—if you're not busy on the twenty-second—if you would want to go?"

Without hesitation Ben says, "That would be great! It's been so long since I've been to a wedding."

"Really?" I ask, feeling like I must be dreaming.

"Yeah, Mia, I'd really like that."

After dinner, Ben walks me to my car. I take him in, dressed in his usual jeans and button-down. He has on a gray bomber jacket that matches the silver moon. We don't kiss good-bye; I just tell him that I'll give him more wedding info in school. Alone inside my car, I feel excited about the idea of us being in school and talking about something other than math team. He's more than just my captain; he's my date!

My cloud-nine feeling dwindles only a little when I check my phone and see a total of eleven missed calls from Mom, with six voice mails, and eight texts from Dad in our family group chat. I am surprised that Sam hasn't reached out. She's probably been rushing around, though I can imagine her stepping into the kitchen with Mom every five seconds to see if I replied. I know they'll be mad at first, but Sam should stick up for me when I tell her I was able to find a date to her wedding.

I text our group chat that I'm on my way home and peel out of the diner parking lot with urgency. I figure I shouldn't prolong my reckoning. The best way to deal with it is like a Band-Aid, tear off the comfort of tonight for the ugly scab that is what I left behind at home.

When my phone starts ringing, my inclination is to ignore it, but when I glance down, I see Grace's name.

"What's up?" I ask.

"Your mom called to ask where you were."

"And?"

"I told her you were here, but she asked to speak to you and I said you were in the bathroom, but then she said she'd wait for you to get out."

"Crap," I say. "Thanks for trying at least."

"Where are you anyways?" I hear the sound of her bed creaking. I can imagine her rolling onto her back and lying upside down.

"I just left November Always. I'm headed home."

"Why were you at the diner?" she asks. Her voice sounds like it's coming through her teeth. She's probably chewing on a Twizzler.

"I had a date with someone."

Nothing.

"Hello?"

"You had a *date*?" she asks, her bed creaking, probably as she rolls back onto her stomach.

"I *did*," I say. "And whoever it was stood me up, and then Ben Vasquez appeared, and it turned into a DATE

WITH BEN VASQUEZ!" I say, feeling my heart race as I relive the moment when Ben took off his jacket and decided to stay for dinner with me.

"What! WHAT! Oh my gosh! MIA. This is—I can't. Wait, who was the date originally with?" she asks as I pull up near my house. I have to park in front of the neighbor's house because there are a few guests parked outside mine.

"I can tell you about it in study hall. It's a long story," I say, turning off my car and leaning across the passenger seat to peer over at my house.

"A name isn't a long story."

"Darth Vader," I say, sorry that the lights are still on in the living room.

"What?"

"I have to go. Thanks for trying to cover for me; I appreciate it," I say, spotting Sam's shadow moving around in her room.

"Okay, I expect a ten-page written report on this date," she says, laughing a little.

"In your dreams," I say, mainly because there's a chance Mom or Dad might kill me and I won't even make it to study hall.

I listen to the sound of the dead grass crunching under my feet as I cross the lawn, and I pause at the front door to look back at the moon. It's the same moon that was in the sky when Ben agreed to go to my sister's wedding with me. The same moon that was outside when I fell off the roof thinking I was finally taking control of the meet-cute project and meeting Darth Vader. Hopefully, by the time that moon gives way to the sun, everything I'm dreading will have ended too.

I twist the knob on the front door as slowly as I can, trying not to let the metal of the latch and doorjamb scrape together. I slide the door open, tiptoe into the house, and close the door as slowly and gently as I can behind me. When I turn around and don't see anyone waiting in the kitchen doorway or standing at the edge of the den, a glimmer of hope enters my heart. As nice as it would be to tiptoe up to my room, I know that it's nearly impossible and it might make things even worse if I come home and avoid the bridal shower altogether.

After taking a few deep breaths, I cross the entryway and head toward the kitchen. Mom and my Aunt Frances are standing at the kitchen island over a half-eaten cake.

"Mia, my darling," Aunt Frances sings when she notices me in the doorway. She crosses the room like she's floating on air, and closes the space between us with a bear hug.

"Hello, Auntie," I say, my face squished against her chest.

She stands back and holds me at arm's length. "Tsk, tsk, darling. You missed a party."

She stares into my eyes, and I can see in her pupils that she can see right through me.

"I'm sorry," I tell her. "How was it? Where is Sam?"

"Sam went upstairs a while ago, after she handed out the gift bags," Mom says, reminding me of her presence.

"And I'm on my way out," says Aunt Frances. "I think your father was just showing your uncle James his fish."

Aunt Frances gives me one more smile and a kiss on the forehead before moving past me toward the den. I listen as she finds my dad and uncle James. When I hear a few other voices, I realize my dad must have taken it upon himself to entertain after Sam went upstairs while Mom started cleaning.

I start gathering paper plates from the dining room and bring them to the trash can in the kitchen. It isn't until I hear Dad say good-bye and the front door closes that the air settles in the house and leaves me alone with my parents and the unavoidable truth.

"Where were you?" Mom asks when Dad joins us in the kitchen.

"At the November Always diner. I went out to dinner," I say.

"Why? When? I didn't even see you on your way out," Mom says.

"I left around six," I say, resisting the urge to sit down. I know that any sign of me relaxing when I'm supposed to be in trouble might upset her.

"I don't understand. Why would you go out to dinner when your sister's bridal shower was tonight?" she asks.

"I had something I had to do," I say, biting my lip.

"At a diner?" Dad asks, raising his eyebrows.

"Tell them what you were doing," Sam says, startling me from the kitchen doorway. She has on her robe and slippers, and she looks like a cloud with its arms crossed. I can tell she re-oiled her hair, because it glistens under the lights. She takes a few steps into the kitchen and leans against the counter.

"I was having dinner at a diner," I say, wishing she would just go home.

"With who?" Sam snaps.

"What do you mean, with who?"

"I mean exactly what I asked. Who did you have dinner with? Because I have my guesses."

"What?" Mom asks, looking between us.

"With a friend," I say, glaring at Sam.

"What's *his* name," she asks.

"You went out with a boy?" Dad asks. "You snuck out to meet up with a boy? Without asking?"

"I had a date! Is that so hard to believe?"

"What boy, Mia!" Sam raises her voice.

"A friend of mine that you don't know," I say, trying to keep my composure.

"It's a friend that *you* don't know either, isn't it?"

"I was trying to find a date to your wedding, Sam, like *you* asked me to."

"I didn't ask you to lie to Mom and Dad and go to a party and meet some random guy you don't even know," she says, her voice strangely calm.

A weird feeling settles over me. She doesn't have her usual fire, the way she sometimes enters conversations, ready to argue. Instead, I see something else in her eyes. Sadness. Disappointment, maybe.

"Mia?" Dad asks, pulling my attention back to him and Mom.

"We didn't go to Halloween dinner this year," I say, hoping Sam won't blow the rest of my lie. "We went to a party, and I met someone and we were supposed to go on a date tonight. It was before Sam's bridal shower started, and it was only supposed to overlap a little. I miscalculated, okay? And, I'm sorry."

"Why didn't you just tell us?" Mom asks. "I mean, you can talk to us. We wouldn't have said you couldn't go—"

"Seriously?" Sam laughs incredulously. "You would've still let her go? On the night of my bridal shower?"

"Well, maybe if we let her go, we could've set boundaries. We could've said, *Be back by this time or you can't go*," Mom explains.

"Yeah, or you could've said, *No. Tonight is about your sister. Reschedule the date with a complete stranger*," Sam quips.

When her voice breaks, both of my parents' heads snap to her.

"Honey," Dad says, moving toward her.

"Don't come near me," she whispers, wiping tears away before they can fall. "If this were me, I'd be grounded for a month or something. But with her you guys barely do anything. It's, *Oh, Mia, don't do that again* or *Oh, Peach, be your own person*. Well, to hell with that."

"Sam," Mom gasps.

"No, Mom. It's like after you both retired, you and Dad

got lazy and you barely try with her. She gets away with anything. I mean, she *snuck out* tonight—"

"And we—her parents—will deal with it," Dad says before turning to me and saying, "Go upstairs."

"No," Sam says. "You don't just get to—"

"Sam," Dad cuts her off, holding up his hand. She looks at him like she's shocked he would silence her. "I think you should go home to Geoffrey."

Her eyes widen. She opens her mouth as if to say something more, but then closes it.

Sam turns and leaves the room. I wait until I hear her door close quietly before grabbing my purse off the counter and following. The hurt on Sam's face when she said I should've chosen her over the date fills my mind. Part of me thought I was doing her a favor, but at the same time there's another part of me that knew it wasn't completely true. I also wanted this for myself.

I can hear Sam on the other side of our wall shuffling around. I picture her angrily grabbing clothes out of her closet and snatching her toiletries off the dresser and throwing them into the overnight bag she's been carting back and forth. The noise, thinking about tonight, feeling my guilt, begins to drive me crazy, so I go take a shower.

After clearing my head under the steady stream of water, I realize that the events of tonight still aren't over when I can hear voices in my parents' room.

"You can't seriously let her get away with this," I hear Sam hiss.

"She won't get away with anything, but you don't get to decide how these things are handled. You're her *sister*, her *equal* when it comes to us. And sometimes it seems like you forget that," Mom says sternly.

"She put herself in danger; she should be grounded. She should have rules and structure," Sam presses.

"Why?" Mom cuts in, laughing, but it sounds fake, incredulous. "Mia is a great daughter, Sam. You know this too. "

"She's acting out. She's exhibiting all the signs of a child acting out."

"By what, not helping you with your wedding? It wasn't right for her to have missed your bridal shower, but this is the first instance when Mia's done something like this," Dad says, his voice surprising me. I didn't think Sam would go back into this conversation with both of them.

"It's not like her to just . . . to—to abandon me," she says, her voice deflating.

"I'm sure she's not abandoning you. If anything, you're in a stage of your life when *you're* leaving *her*," Mom says, her voice gentle. "But I don't think anyone is abandoning anybody, if I'm being honest."

"Of course you would say that. Of course neither of you would see that something is wrong," Sam says, the edge coming back to her tone.

"What's that supposed to mean?" Dad asks.

"That she runs around doing whatever she wants. You barely pay any attention to her, which isn't how I remember you guys to be. You woke me up in the morning, made me eat breakfast, took me to school, checked my homework, made sure I cleaned my uniform for field hockey, made sure I returned my books to the library. And with her? She just goes out. She snuck *out* tonight! On *your* watch!"

"Sam, that's not fair—" Mom starts to say.

"I read parenting blogs so that I can do what—for some reason—you guys no longer do. For her! So that she can be better, so that she can stand on her own two feet and not be left to fall flat."

"That's enough," Dad says calmly, but sternly. I feel on edge for Sam. I wonder how she's feeling right now, if she's mad or—more likely—if her confidence is waning. I wonder if she feels like a sixteen-year-old again.

"You will not disrespect us in our own house," Dad continues. "You will not tell us that we are failing as parents, especially considering all the work and effort and love that we have put in to see you this far. You and Mia aren't the same person. I can't even believe—" He stops himself. The air stills again, and for a moment I'm unable to picture them standing or sitting in my parents' room, all facing each other. Without the sound, the tension, it's hard to ground anything. But then Dad says, "I think that's enough for tonight," and when I hear the floor creak as someone turns to leave their room, I close the bathroom door.

When I hear Sam's door close, I hurry up and tiptoe

back to my room. I press my ear against the wall behind my bed, and I think I can hear her crying. When her feet pound past my door, I wait, and after the final sound of the front door slamming behind her—Mom's Christmas bells jangling violently for a moment—I release the breath I didn't realize I was holding.

Without her in the house, the air stills, the same way it did when we took Sam to college. I remember that on that first night, the quiet sounded quieter, the stillness felt stiller. In the absence of Sam, of her liveliness and her energy, there is a true emptiness that has become foreign to me over the past few months. It's hard to fall asleep to the feeling.

CHAPTER FIFTEEN

Eventually Dad came to my room, and even though I pretended to be asleep, he could tell that I was awake. He didn't ask me to sit up or anything, just said, "You're grounded until I say otherwise." He's happy that I found a date, because he knows how much I don't like Jasper, even though no one else talks about it. But he said there can't be any more funny business. His words, not mine. He described Sam's wedding as a tightly coiled thread that is starting to come undone from one end. Not the wedding itself, but things around the wedding. Like, one of Geoffrey's cousins had a baby, and Sam forgot about the date they set to go meet her at the hospital. And Toby, the Davenports' goldendoodle, had to have surgery because the vet found a tumor. And the senior Mr. Davenport has been bent out of shape about a great-aunt on the guest list. Dad says it's all been adding pressure to Sam's life, and now our family is beginning to feel a side effect of that pressure.

So I'm grounded as a precaution. No more "acting out," as Sam called it. The parameters *until he says otherwise* are that I can go to school, I can go to math club and swim practice, and then I have to come home. I can volunteer on Fridays and swim weekend mornings at the community pool. I can help Sam with the wedding if I should suddenly choose to do so, but other than that I am confined to the house.

Which will make it really hard, arguably impossible, to spend time with Ben. I try to sort my thoughts and explain everything on Monday in study hall.

"I think there's still a way to make this work," Abby says, twirling a piece of hair around her mechanical pencil.

"I'm still stuck on who Darth Vader is. Like, maybe I can ask Nandy if she knew of anyone coming to her party who was going to dress like him. I mean, there are plenty of people we know who like Star Wars, but I'm pretty sure the only people I can think of were dressed as something else at the party." Sloane taps her mechanical pencil against her brow, the wheels turning in her brain.

"At this point I don't even care about Darth Vader anymore," I say, leaning forward and resting my head on my forearms. "Ben and I need to be spending more time together, not less. Especially if there's any hope of us talking about topics outside of math team and the wedding."

"I still can't believe you did all this without telling any of us," Grace cuts in.

"It just happened," I tell her, dropping my pencil into the center of my open calculus textbook.

"It did not 'just' happen," she says, laughing a little incredulously. "You met this guy last week! You've been talking to him and planning a date and hid it from us, and I want to know why."

Neither Sloane nor Abby jumps to my defense. Instead they wait for an answer.

"I didn't tell you guys because I wanted to try to do this on my own. What we had been doing before wasn't working—"

"What *we* had been doing?" Grace asks, raising her eyebrows. "You mean *we*," she corrects, gesturing to herself, Sloane, and Abby. "We have been trying our best to help you, and in return you cut us out of the plan that we came up with *together* and put yourself in possible danger— Like, I'm really mad because you could've gotten hurt."

"Grace, come on—"

"No, don't 'come on,'" she hisses. "You don't know this guy; none of us know this guy."

"Yeah, and the guys that you all know turned out to be really crappy. The guy you picked started flirting with you, Grace!"

"That's not my fault!" she says, leaning forward.

"It was your fault when I had to wait in the car for twenty minutes while you yapped it up with your drama camp pal—that's when it became your fault!"

"If you didn't want our help, then why did you ask?"

"I didn't, Grace. Sam did!"

Grace leans back in her chair with an eerie smile on her face. It slips into a laugh, but not a forgiving one.

"Guys," Sloane tries to cut in, but her voice is too quiet and Grace doesn't pay attention.

"Are you really going to blame Sam for all of your problems? Again?"

"I do not—"

"'Sam embarrassed me by saying I need a date to the wedding,'" Grace begins in a mocking tone. "'Sam made me do volunteer work because she's brainwashed my parents. Sam ruined my life by moving back home to plan the wedding. Sam ate my bagel. Sam drank my juice. Sam used my pens. Sam did this. Sam did that. I have no autonomy in my own life because I *let* Sam push me around and control everything.' I mean, Mia, really, it's getting annoying and pathetic."

Sloane's jaw drops, and she and Abby stare at Grace in utter silence. My brain blanks and tears sting the edges of my eyes.

"If I'm so pathetic, and so horrible to be around, then . . ." I stop myself from saying it because I know I don't mean it. I know that I don't want to push her away.

But it's not hard to guess where my words were going. Grace closes her folder, even with the papers not being tucked into the pockets, grabs her purse off the back of her chair, and disappears into the shelves of books surrounding our study hall table.

I press my face into my hands, dreading the thought of Abby and Sloane getting up to follow her. When they don't, I peek through my fingers and find them glancing from their papers to each other and then to me.

"I do need your help. I just—I thought that, since I

hadn't been having luck so far, I should try at least." I try to think back about what I thought I was accomplishing by cutting my friends out, but with my heart racing and a lump rising in my throat, I can hardly remember what my rationale was.

After a long silence, Abby is the first to finally speak. "I just want to put this out there. I don't like Ben. He's selfish and self-obsessed, and you deserve someone who will worship the ground you walk on. This whole plan was for you to find a date to the wedding, not a boyfriend. I'll help you find time to plan for the wedding with Ben before you have to go home and stuff, but I won't help you guys be together."

She looks to Sloane, who says, "Mia, I think you really need to consider how you want to play this, because I'm not mad at you, but Grace has a point. This is something we were supposed to do together, and the second you cut us out, you *did* put yourself in danger when no one knew where you were. Not only did you lie to your family, but you lied to us, and that's not cool at all. . . . It's not who you are. . . ."

Abby nods in agreement, and then looks down at her folder. Sloane starts stacking her books on top of each other. I don't say anything because I know it's best to just let her walk away to get air, instead of pressing more buttons. So that leaves me with Abby.

I look down, waiting for her to get up, or to say more stuff about Ben, but she just rips a piece of paper out of her notebook and pushes her folder and binder aside. I look over and see that she's writing every day of the week, and then my Monday through Thursday math club and swim schedule. She pulls out a red pen and starts drawing lines in between things.

"Mondays and Wednesdays after your last class, maybe try to talk to him a little at his locker. Tuesdays and Thursdays, since you see him in math club, I can cover for you for, like, the first ten or fifteen minutes of practice if you want to try to have a quick conversation with him after math club before swim practice. Maybe he could come to some practices and then you can talk for a little bit after. Then on Fridays tell your mom you're staying for an hour after school to work in the library. Say you have a research paper due or something. If she needs proof that you're with one of us actually doing work, let me know and I'll stay."

She stops, her pen hovering over Friday after school. I can feel the table shake a little as she bounces her leg, which means she's thinking.

I expect her to say that what I did was messed up, or that I need to apologize to Grace, or that she's worried about me too, but she just adds, "And then hopefully after Thanksgiving you'll be ungrounded and you won't need to—you know . . ."

She pushes the paper over to me and then takes out her headphones. I look back down at my math homework. All the numbers and equations blend together as my eyes blur with tears.

CHAPTER SIXTEEN

try to follow Abby's advised schedule. Ben and I talk at his locker after school. I find out the measurements for his tux, and I tell him more details about the color scheme for the wedding and how evergreen is going to be everywhere. I try to get him to open up about other things, like how Carly has been doing or if he's feeling confident about his upcoming senior thesis presentation. But he never seems interested in talking about much, other than math team and the wedding.

On Thursday it's a little harder to focus during math team practice. Now I have this thing that no one else on the math team has with him, this secret project that we're working on. Just us. While he reviews derivatives, I imagine him in a tux with a deep-green bow tie and a red carnation attached to his pocket. I imagine us dancing at the reception, staring into each other's eyes, and him maybe seeing me as more than a junior that he's known from math team, but as someone he could take to prom in the spring.

When Friday comes around and he has plans after school and can't stay at the library, I'm disappointed. But

Abby and Victor made plans to stay, and I decide to join them instead of going back to prison right away.

"No Ben?" Abby asks, looking up from her planner.

"Not today," I say, slipping into the empty seat across from her.

I start pulling books out of my bag, and after I get set up, Abby sighs. It's the kind of sigh where I can tell she's not actually sighing but she's trying to get my attention or trying to get Victor to ask her what's on her mind. So I take the bait and look up at her.

"Have you talked to Grace at all?" is her question.

"No," I say.

"Are you going to?" she asks.

"Eventually," I say. "I just don't think it's the right time."

"Will you talk to her before the wedding? . . . Like, is she still invited?"

"Of course she's still invited," I say. The thought of uninviting her or of anything wedding related happening without the three of them there has never crossed my mind. Plus, Sam would probably lose it if I took away Grace and her plus-one, ruining the feng shui of her seating chart just one month before the big day.

"Okay," Abby says, smiling to herself. She folds one leg over the other and scooches her chair into the table, satisfied.

When Mom and I pull into the community garden, I'm excited in spite of the cold. When Gavin walked in at

November Always, I was a girl in the process of being stood up, still dateless to her sister's wedding. Now so much has changed.

It becomes apparent that change has occurred both in my life and in our little greenhouse. All the troughs are in place and finished. There are four total, arranged in two rows on the left side of the house. On the right side the soil is turned and there are rows of tilled earth, and the last row on the right is planted with small trees wrapped in burlap sacks. I can smell fresh water and fertilizer in the air, and by the moist dirt on the pair of gloves thrown onto the back table, I can tell Gavin is somewhere close by.

The weather has gotten a lot colder since I first started. I'm wearing an insulated flannel under my coat in case I want to take my coat off but am too cold to just wear a long-sleeve shirt, and inside my Vans I have on wool socks. I trade my mittens for my pair of gardening gloves and head over to the supply shed to get an extra shovel and rake, in case Gavin wants me to do more work on the troughs. I pile some mulch into a wheelbarrow and set a few small pots on top, figuring they might give us something to do with the table at the back of the greenhouse.

After a minute or two of waiting, I head out the back door, propped open with a cinder block, and take a lap around the greenhouse in case Gavin dared to go up on the ladder without a flashlight. It's already dark outside. As I come around the front of the greenhouse, I finally see him walking over from the dumpster. He doesn't notice me at first, but when he gets closer and glances up, I can almost swear he tenses before putting his head down.

"Hey!" I say, beaming as I remember that Gavin *did* meet Ben at the diner.

Without saying anything, Gavin holds out a tote bag to me. I take it without looking to see what's inside and trail behind him back into the greenhouse. The grass crunches under our shoes, creating a white noise in the silence between us.

"Do you remember that guy I was with at the diner?" I ask, following Gavin as he places his tote bag on the table at the back of the greenhouse. He pushes my pots to the far corner before picking up his gloves.

"Darth Vader?" he asks, raising his eyebrows even though he's focused on the inside of his bag and not looking at me.

I turn to my bag and pull it open. There are baby leafy plants inside.

"No, the guy I was with was Ben. Remember, I introduced you. He's the one I've liked for, like, ever?"

"Yes," he mumbles.

We start unloading the plants from our bags.

"Well, he agreed to go to my sister's wedding with me!"

I expect a smile or for him to at least look at me, but he just focuses on turning all his plants so that their labels face forward.

"I thought you were going on a date with Darth

Vader," Gavin says, and he stops fidgeting with the leaves. "Didn't you embarrass yourself in front of the other guy and you were excited about going on a date with someone new?"

"Yeah, I was, until he stood me up. I was lucky that Ben showed up, or I would've felt humiliated."

"What do you mean, you got stood up?" he asks, his tone getting less abrasive.

"I mean I was waiting at the diner that we agreed to meet at, and he never showed up," I say, trying to keep my insecurity at bay. Instead of allowing myself to mope about the fact that Darth stood me up, it's been easier to just focus on moving forward with Ben.

"How are you sure he never showed up if you don't even know what he looks like?" Gavin asks.

"Maybe because no one came up to me. He saw me at the party, so it's not like he was there and couldn't find me," I remind him. "Plus, I'm not even talking about him right now. I'm talking about Ben and how he agreed to go to the wedding with me, and I'm really hoping that it turns into something more. Like, even if we don't end up dating, maybe he'll decide to ask me to prom."

"Maybe," Gavin agrees, though I can tell he's not enthusiastic, not like he was last week.

"Yeah," I go on. "It's been hard, though, because now I'm grounded. It's funny how when I first started here, you were grounded, and now I'm grounded."

"It's not that funny," Gavin says, gathering all the kale

plants and carrying them over two at a time to one of the troughs.

"You're right; it sucks, to be honest. I finally have a date to Sam's wedding, and I really want to spend time with him, talk to him, and get to know more about him. But I can't. And ironically, it's all because of Sam, because she had it out for me."

"I don't think she had it out for you," Gavin mumbles.

"Why are you so grumpy?" I ask, organizing the rest of the plants so that they're grouped by type.

"You easily could've avoided getting grounded," he says. "You could've stayed home, gone to your sister's shower thing, and been fine. Don't act like you went to that diner for her. Don't pretend like this is funny or that you're the victim, when you did and controlled everything that happened on Saturday night."

"Where is this coming from?" I ask, dropping the collard plants into another trough. The garden is the last place I thought I'd be blindsided by another Mia-the-self-saboteur intervention.

"I don't know. Maybe because you're not the only one going through stuff. Maybe because we always talk about you."

"We can talk about you," I say, surprised. "I wasn't trying to hog the mic or anything. You just haven't offered up any information about yourself."

"That's because not everything is about me," he snaps.

"So, what is it, then? We never talk about you, or not

everything is about you? I'm not a mind reader."

Gavin doesn't say anything; he just stands there looking down at the trough across from mine.

"What? Did something happen with your girlfriend?" I ask, remembering that he mentioned her at the diner. "Did you guys break up or something? And me talking about Ben—" It makes sense now.

Gavin curls his fists and then lets his fingers spread out again. I see his breath in front of his face as he exhales the brisk November air.

"Gavin, we can definitely talk about it. I mean, had I known you even had a girlfriend, I would've asked you about her. I would've tried to help you."

"Mia, I don't need your help," he says, laughing sarcastically. "Please, you just started talking to a guy who you thought didn't even like you. And it sounds like the only reason he's interested in you beyond math team is because he wants a free gourmet dinner, not because he suddenly cares."

"Hey!" I snap.

"What? It's true. You've liked him for how long? And after all this time, the second you start talking about your sister's wedding, suddenly he's interested. Doesn't that sound at all suspicious?"

"What's wrong with you?" I feel protective of the small spark that Ben and I finally have. I feel protective of my one good meet-cute. No matter what my friends say about Ben, no matter about Gavin's sucky attitude, I finally found something that works, and I'm not about to let Gavin's negativity take it away from me. "What, are you not able to be happy for me because there's trouble in paradise?"

"Whatever, Mia." Gavin smirks, shaking his head. "Just don't come crying to me when this superficial non-romance comes back to bite you."

"And don't come crying to me the next time you need someone to keep you from falling off a ladder," I bark, before throwing one of the brussels sprout plants onto the ground. I kick it against the closest trough, turn around, and leave the greenhouse. I throw my gloves down somewhere in the grass on my way to find where my mom is working. As I walk, I count the hours I've spent at this stupid garden and figure I have enough for the National Honor Society and there's no sense in me coming back. It's hard to see, since there are generator lights shining only where people are working and not on the spaces of grass in between.

When I find her, I tell her we have to leave.

"We just got here," Mom says.

"You and Gavin have to plant the winter vegetables," Gloria says, looking slightly on edge, as always.

"Mom, we have to leave," I say again, because I know if I try to say anything else, if I slip into any of the emotions rushing through me, I might cry in front of all my mom's friends.

"Mia," Mom says, like I'm some impatient ridiculous child. And maybe I am. Maybe I'm all the things everyone has told me that I am. But even so, I'm not someone who wants to keep standing here.

"Mom," I say, my voice breaking. "Can I have the keys, then?"

This gets her attention and she looks up at me, squinting from the glare of the floodlight behind me.

"Okay, then," she says, looking down at the work in front of her and gathering the tools she took from the shed. "Let me just put these away and we can go. Okay? Everything is going to be all right. We can leave right now."

CHAPTER SEVENTEEN

The week before Thanksgiving break is the last wave of midterms before finals in December. Trying to use my virtually nonexistent spare time to see Ben and also focusing on the cell reproductive process and the minute details of the Civil War have made it impossible to find the right words to say to Grace. She gave me one week of the silent treatment, and was then able to acknowledge me at lunch throughout this week. But Sloane, Abby, Grace, and I all had our heads down to focus during the times we'd usually spend talking to each other. It's like we silently agreed to put the meet-cute tension on hold to offer each other flash cards or help each other find that one very important section in our textbooks that could help finish a paper. By the time school let out on Friday, Grace was already gone and so was my opportunity to apologize in person.

For as long as I can remember, Grace has always come over for Thanksgiving dessert. Both Grace's family and mine are used to hosting our respective Thanksgiving dinners. The first year that we went to the Davenports was so weird because Grace wasn't able to just walk over to my house for dessert. But, thankfully, the Davenports prefer when we host. Geoffrey's parents use the small size of our house as an excuse to not invite their entire family for the holiday. I didn't mind at first because hosting the Davenports meant that I could go back to having Grace come over, and Sam and I could start decorating the Christmas tree at the end of the night. We used to stay up until early in the morning talking about the ornaments that we'd gotten on family vacations or from friends.

Now, as I'm watching Sam in the foyer greeting our relatives at the door, with a smile permanently plastered to her face, I feel how far from our old tradition we are. Not only do I miss Grace, but Sam has barely talked to me since the bridal shower. Before, her going home and sleeping at her own apartment full-time would've been a win. But since I know the reasons why she packed up and left her room here at the house, her going home feels more like a loss.

Dinner is basically a lot of small talk, me tuning out the sound of Jasper's games from across the table, and a lot of my older relatives mistaking me for a senior instead of a junior and asking me what colleges I applied to. I decide to go light on the mashed potatoes and stuffing this year because my second-to-last meet of the season is next week, and the Thanksgiving slump tends to last for a few days. I can't afford to lose the headway I've gained.

My aunt June, Dad's younger sister, sticks me with her baby when she sees me sitting on the couch with "not enough to do." Babies make me more uneasy than dogs, so

I end up frozen in place. Last Easter, Marcel kept grabbing at my boobs because he thinks all boobs have his milk. When I—of course—couldn't deliver, he started crying, and suddenly everyone was laughing at me, telling me that babies cry, it's no big deal, hold him like this, tilt his head like this, let him drool on your shoulder like this.

So, as much as I want to hop up and run away when Jasper makes eye contact with me from the doorway of the living room, I have no choice but to make sure Marcel's head remains in the crook of my arm, and I sink as far into our leather couch as I can.

"There's something about maternal Mia that just doesn't add up," Jasper says, flashing me a smile.

In one motion he turns on his heel, whips his Nintendo out of his back pocket, and lands on the cushion next to me with a game already open. I wonder how long he's ever gone without staring at that thing. I don't ask, though, because engaging is the last thing I want to do.

"Sam told me that you found a date to the wedding," Jasper says, gunshots *pew, pew, pewing* from his game.

"Did she now?" I say, deadpan.

"Yeah. I'm happy, though. I was dreading having to tell you that the Jasp-man is taken. Didn't want to have to break your heart."

"The Jasp-man?" It's impossible not to laugh. I try not to let my shoulders shake, though, for Marcel's sake.

"It has a nice ring to it," he says, even though it comes out more like a question.

So I give him an honest answer. "No, it doesn't."

We fall silent. I think maybe Jasper didn't hear me, or that maybe he decided to ignore me. The high-pitched noises from his game clash with the low rumble and crackle of the fire. I'm surprised that the loud popping noises that come from the wood every so often don't make Marcel stir, but I don't question it.

I watch the flames dance, and then I look up at the stockings Mom already hung from the mantel. She took care of pulling out the decorations this year, so the tree is already decorated—none of the memories discussed and relived. Above the fireplace is an outdated family portrait in which I'm posed on my mother's lap with a straight face. I don't look on the verge of crying, but I don't look happy, either. Usually the picture makes me laugh and we all joke about how I was serious even back then. But something about that doesn't seem funny anymore. The way my mouth is a flat line and my eyes seem spaced out while I'm staring into the camera, it looks like little me is trying to stare into my current-day soul. It creeps me out and I tear my eyes away, looking in the direction of the dining room instead. I wish Aunt June would come back for her baby, but she's laughing at something my granddad said, with her back to me, no end to my torment in sight.

There's a decrescendo in the music in Jasper's game that catches my attention. He sighs before looking up from his game with a wistful smile on his face, like losing is some old favorite pastime of his.

"Yup, the Jasp-man has landed himself a lady."

"I can't take you seriously if you're going to talk about yourself in the third person."

"Fine," he says, rolling his eyes. "I met a girl at school, okay?"

"Okay?"

He stares down at his Nintendo, looking at the screen telling him he lost and offering him a rematch or to start a new game.

When he doesn't hit one of the buttons, I ask, "So, what's she like?"

He nods before saying, "Basically a younger, nicer version of you but with braces."

"Of course," I say, pinching the bridge of my nose. "Of. Course."

"She was actually really nice to me when Toby had to get his surgery. I was scared because Mom had said we might have to put him down if things didn't go well, and this girl was the only person I knew who'd had to go through that, putting their dog to sleep." Jasper looks away. Even though his Nintendo is in his hands, I can tell he's not looking at the screen so much as he's reimagining some of his conversations with this new girl.

There have been a few times when Ben and I have been up late, texting back and forth about nothing important. I wanted to talk to him about Sam, about how I've been feeling like maybe I really messed up. But whenever I try to bring up anything other than the wedding or math team, he always steers the conversation back to himself. Before, I would tell myself it's okay, since I *do* want to know more about him. But now, hearing that Jasper has even found a girl who cares, who's willing to listen when he needs someone, I begin to question *what* exactly Ben and I have.

"Look at it this way: now both of us have dates to the wedding," Jasper adds when I don't say anything.

I stand up from the couch, trying to slowly and gently adjust my grip on Marcel.

"What?" Jasper asks, almost whining.

"Nothing," I say, trying not to laugh. "It's cool that you met someone. I'm glad."

I shuffle off toward the kitchen, careful not to step on the parts of the floor that creak, so that Marcel won't wake up.

In the kitchen I shift Marcel so that I'm holding his tiny body in one arm and am able to use my free hand to sneak a little bit of stuffing into a small dessert bowl. I figure I've earned a little cheat on my strict swim diet, and I take my bowl over to the far corner of the kitchen, away from the living room and dining room.

I'm thankful to find Marcel's portable bouncer hidden on the other side of the island. I put the bouncer on the table, gently lay him inside, and turn the dial to the gentle rocking setting before pulling the tinfoil back on some of the already sliced pies. I take a picture of the half-eaten cherry-and-pecan pie, and I Snapchat a picture to Grace. I draw eyes in the uneaten half and draw a frown in the other half.

I'm surprised when she opens it immediately. She responds with a video of her baby cousin Cambree hooking his fingers at the corners of his mouth and stretching out his lips so that they look like they're about to crack.

I take a picture of another pie and draw a face and stick-figure arms reaching out for a hug. Before I send it, I add a white flag in one of the hands, with a question mark in a thought bubble. Sometimes stick figure drawings can do a lot more than words.

She responds: If I accept your surrender, does that mean I can come over and eat pie?

I reply: Yes, please with a huge smile on my face.

By the time she is cracking open my front door, Marcel is back with his mom and I have two plates with slivers from four different pies, all topped with dollops of whipped cream. I pour hot apple cider into two mugs and drop in cinnamon sticks, pleased that we're not skipping our tradition.

"Thank goodness," she gushes, her face red from the cold. She shrugs her coat off and drapes it over one of the breakfast barstools before grabbing her plate and mug and moving ahead of me toward the stairs.

The sound of everyone chatting gets quieter as we ascend, and with my bedroom door shut behind me, I feel the first bit of peace I've felt all week. I tell her I'm sorry and that she's right about it not being smart, me going on that date with Darth Vader. She tells me I wasn't crazy and that she's sorry for flirting with that guy during my first meet-cute. I jokingly tease her and say, "Oh, so you *were* flirting?" We laugh about it and fall silent. I take a bite of sweet potato pie and pretend that it's the only thing in the world that matters right now. Grace spears a piece of my pie, and I reach over and slice off an edge of her pumpkin. She taps her fork against mine while we chew, her eyes bright and smiling. I'm glad that while things feel upside down right now, at least this hasn't changed.

CHAPTER EIGHTEEN

Every year on the day after Thanksgiving, Sam and I get up in the early afternoon and head out to the Pie & Leftovers Festival. It's a community thing for the people from our neighborhood and the other small towns surrounding us. There was one year when someone wanted the festival to be a big thing, like the kind of gathering you'd see posters about downtown. But no one else wanted it to be that way. Since Mom's gardening friends make up a good majority of the people who actually bring the pies and leftovers, she was able to influence the decision by saying there wouldn't be any food if the festival was publicized. And, well, let's say a lot of our neighborhood likes the shared leftovers more than they like popularity.

On the day of the festival, Mom always gets up early, goes through the leftovers in the fridge, and sets out disposable tin containers of the things we can contribute. Some people bake new pies specifically for the event, but we never do. Mom says a real Thanksgiving pie is made on Thanksgiving for Thanksgiving, and *that's that*.

This year, in a futile attempt to get Sam and me to make

up, Mom says that even though I'm grounded, I'm still allowed to go to the festival as long as I stay with Sam. I can tell Sam is pleased, so I rationalize to Mom that since Sam can bring Geoffrey, I should be allowed to invite Sloane. Ever since Geoffrey started going with us, I've always avoided being a third wheel by inviting my friends. And now that's the last thing I want to be, especially since Sam and I aren't even getting along. When Mom asks Sam if she could just spend the day with me, Sam plays the *Geoffrey and I are one now* card. Still, she's annoyed when Mom relents and says I can invite Sloane.

And by "invite" I mean "beg." I even tell Sloane that Grace and I made up over pie last night, and it's only fair that Sloane give me the opportunity to make up with her, too. So she pulls up and parallel parks a few cars behind us along the street lining Pinecrest Park. We trail a few steps behind Sam and Geoffrey, and Sloane helps me carry the tins of mac and cheese and string bean casserole. I can feel the warmth from the reheated dish through my mittens.

Pinecrest Park is an open field bordered by four different streets. But it's shaped less like a square and more like a curvy trapezoid. There are a few apple trees spread out, and some picnic tables around each one, and toward the center of the park is a man-made pond with a bridge that kind of zigzags over it through some of the overgrown cattails.

To the left of the park entrance, a number of tents have been set up, with tables where people can drop off their leftovers and huddle in front of generator-powered heaters.

There are plates and plastic utensils, and because the festival is so small, it's treated like one big unsupervised potluck. At the north side of the park are more heated tents where the pie competition is held. There's pie eating, pie tasting, a pie raffle to win pies, pies for sale, and pie throwing. Sloane loads up on sweet potato casserole and collard greens before we start walking over to the pies. Some people bring picnic blankets, and various bands spread out through the park to play live music until they get too cold and decide it's time for pie.

The pie eating competition is usually the most crowded attraction. We have to weave through the crowd to find a spot where we'll be able to see. Sloane gets shouldered and nearly drops her plate right into the damp grass, but catches it just in time. When we emerge, I'm surprised to find a familiar-looking slightly-hunched-over back, with hands shoved down in the same worn and washed-out pair of black jeans.

I want to say his name, but I stop myself. I remember how judgy and mean he was a couple of weeks ago, and decide my best bet is to ignore Gavin. But that becomes impossible when Gloria, who I didn't at first recognize standing next to him, starts scanning the crowd. Her eyes almost immediately land on me.

"Mia! Dear, what a nice surprise. I almost didn't recognize you out of your flannel and old jeans."

She closes the space between us and wraps me in a hug like it's completely normal, like this is how we've been greeting each other every Friday for the past couple of months.

"I almost didn't recognize you either," I tell her. Gloria has traded her bucket hat for a wool beanie, and her tense frown for a soft easygoing face. She's smiling, which I don't think I've seen her do before. She looks at Sloane, and then her eyes rest on Sam, probably registering the resemblance.

"This is my sister, Sam," I say.

"Oh my goodness." Gloria beams, a harsh contrast to her usual furrowed brow and edgy tone. "You're glowing, dear," she tells Sam. Gloria takes Sam's hands in hers and looks her up and down, unabashedly taking in how well put together Sam's dark-washed jeans, navy-blue-and-white bird-print blouse, and chestnut-brown boots look.

"Sam, this is one of Mom's gardening friends," I say.

"My name is Gloria," she says, gushing like she's meeting a celebrity.

Sam's shoulders scrunch up to her ears, and her smile nearly takes over the entire bottom half of her face. She's weird about being touched by people she doesn't know. Even though Gloria's attention could easily be pulled away from anyone and anything by my bringing up the community garden, I don't say anything. I just watch Sam make incredibly uncomfortable long and silent eye contact with Gloria.

"Your mother has told me so much about you. Congratulations, my dear. I wish you a long and happy marriage." Gloria looks over at Geoffrey, like she's noticing him for the first time. She says, "You're so lucky," before dropping Sam's hands. "Mr. Turner and I also had a winter wedding. There's something magical about the wintertime, and I wanted my anniversary to fall right in the middle, like an extra holiday."

Gloria starts talking about her own wedding, and I realize that Gavin never talked about his granddad. Gavin mentioned to me once that Gloria has been taking care of him since he was a baby, and he made it clear that his parents have never really been in the picture. But I feel kind of stupid and selfish, having never asked about Gloria's husband. Right now doesn't seem like the right time, so I try to half listen to what Gloria shares with us, watching as Sloane starts kicking at something on the ground. I look at Gavin's shoes. They're different from the beat-up sneakers and work boots that he alternates between at the garden. They're a pair of clean classic Vans, which isn't something I would expect from him. I wonder if he has more Vans, like me, if he has limited-edition prints or cool colors. . . .

When I look up and catch his eye, I flash him a smile. Making up with Grace took a huge weight off my shoulders, so maybe making up with him can help me out too. But Gavin quickly looks down, almost as uncomfortable as Sam is.

"And this is my grandson, Gavin," Gloria says, turning and lightly touching Gavin on his arm.

"Nice to meet you," Sam says, still smiling like a serial killer.

"You too," Gavin says, forcing a quick smile before pretending to notice something on the other side of the park, over Sam's shoulder.

"We really must be going," Sam lies, looping her arm through Geoffrey's. "And we wouldn't want to hold you up from the famous pie eating contest." At the mention of it, Sloane and I look over at the same time and see a man with blackberry juice all over the bottom half of his face. It's amusing and gross simultaneously.

"Oh, well, you must stop by the garden soon—maybe in the spring when we've finished with the renovations," Gloria says.

"That sounds great." I can tell Sam is thinking that an ensured five months of not having to do this awkward exchange again is perfect. "Have a great rest of your weekend."

With that, she turns, using her looped arm to pull at Geoffrey, who had been distracted by the pie eating contest. I smile and say good-bye to Gloria before following Sam, with Sloane trailing a few steps behind me.

"So, that's Gavin," she says, throwing her plate away in a trash can.

"Yeah," I say, leading us toward the pie tasting booth.

"You don't talk about him very much," she says like she's just realizing it.

"There's not much to say."

"How about, *He's hot?*" Sloane asks, incredulous. She turns to look over her shoulder to see if he's still in view.

I pay for both of us to taste all the pies, and watch as the woman on the other side of the table starts cutting slivers from the eight pies up for judging.

"He has a girlfriend," I tell her. The combination of

"Gavin" and "hot" hadn't really crossed my mind before. He's Gavin the gardener who suddenly turned grumpy, the Gavin of Gs. His face comes back to mind, and I instantly remember him looking down at me from the ladder the day he was painting the inside of the greenhouse; the way he leaned his weight to one hip, how he took care with his brushstrokes and moved slowly, tenderly. I try to push the image out of my mind because it doesn't matter now anyways.

"I would be disappointed if he didn't," she says, her tone musing.

"What's it to you?"

The woman hands us our plates and shows us the ballot box at the end of the table, for when we've finished tasting. When she pushes her brown locks out of her face, I notice her delicate gold wedding ring with a tiny rose-tinted diamond. Something about it makes my stomach twist.

Sloane and I start walking over to the stone benches in front of the pond. On our way there I see Sam and Geoffrey farther down. Geoffrey is trying to skip rocks, and Sam keeps pushing the gravel around with her foot to look for stones he can throw.

"Because," Sloane starts saying through a mouthful of pie. "If he was single, I would have to beat you up for not taking him for yourself." She chews some more, and looks out at the pond. As an afterthought she says, "I mean, we could've been done with the meet-cute thing, like, ages ago."

CHAPTER NINETEEN

My parents give me permission to meet Harold at his job on Tuesday after swim practice, to review my lap times before the meet tomorrow. He's been working longer hours setting up an exhibit at the Art Institute of Chicago and hasn't been getting up early to swim. He leads me through the construction site that is the south hall gallery. It's the first time we've gotten together in a while without Gladys. I find myself missing her a little, wondering what she might be up to. Harold's oversize dark gray sweater makes him look more like a grandpa who sits in a leather armchair and reads books than an athletic old grump. Excuse me—grump *with a girlfriend*.

One day, I figured out that he worked at the Art Institute when we ran into each other on our way out of the locker rooms and I saw an Art Institute employee badge clipped to the front pocket of his button-down shirt. Beyond that, he never talked about it much. Then again, he doesn't talk about himself in general.

He gestures to the observation bench in a room that's been partially set up for the exhibit he's managing. When

I sit, he hands me a pudding cup and sets down his own pudding cup and notebook before reaching up and stretching his back. We are facing a Buddhist tapestry depicting the seven realms of heaven and the seven realms of hell. There's a circle at the center of the Buddha, resembling the earth realm.

"I don't know why it's taken me so long to come here," I admit, peeling back the lid on my pudding.

Harold sits down next to me and pulls his plastic spoon from behind his ear. "I appreciate you driving out here. It's just, with this being our most highly anticipated exhibit of the season, they want all hands on deck."

I glance around the room. The tapestry is one of the few things that have been set up already. There are workers on the other side of the gallery still unpacking paintings and sketches and moving sculptures in.

"Well, thank you for taking the time," I tell him. "And for the pudding."

"Of course," he says, smiling down at his own pudding. "This is the best part of the day."

We fall silent, slipping our spoons into the smooth chocolate pockets. It reminds me of middle school. Chocolate pudding was something my mom used to pack in my lunch every day. Then one day my doctor told her that there were healthier sweets that she could be packing, stuff that wasn't so "artificial." Suddenly the pudding was just on Fridays, and then when I started swimming for school, I stopped eating it all together.

Harold takes his notebook from the bench and holds it in his lap, keeping it open with his pudding cup. He uses his finger to go from line to line, looking for the latest recordings. His spoon hangs out of his mouth. We go over my best and worst times since my last meet. Then he reviews the times for this past week and my averages. He prefers to base his assumptions for upcoming meets on my averages.

I don't notice when he's finished going over the numbers until he says, "I would say that the adrenaline of the meet should help you improve on these times, but you seem a little deflated."

He's right that my mind isn't completely in my usual competitive space. Even though thoughts about swimming, practices, drills, and times are floating around in my head, none of them are the thought that's holding.

"How did it, like, happen for you and Gladys?"

Harold raises his eyebrows, more amused than surprised. From the smile in his eyes, I can tell that I'm touching on his favorite topic, but simultaneously he might have known this was coming.

He looks away from me to the tapestry before us, thinking.

"Well, as young as I like to think I am, the truth is, I'm alone and—well—old. I used to go to the pool in the evenings, after I got off work, but then they moved me to a later shift and it made more sense to go in the mornings, and it was like fate put me into a position.

"I used to think I didn't want to be bothered. Before Gladys, you were the only person at the pool that I talked to. When I noticed you always at the pool, always on time, always in the water swimming, I also noticed that you didn't talk to anyone. You ignored everything around you, and I guess I was afraid you'd end up like me. In a way, it made me realize that I *did* feel like something was missing."

When he doesn't continue, I ask, "So, what does that have to do with Gladys?"

Harold turns his notebook over in his hands for a moment before looking at me. "How could I hope for you to take a chance, branch out, and socialize if I didn't want that for myself?" The question comes out sounding like it's more for him than for me.

I remember when Harold started showing up in the mornings. He would swim in the outer lane and splash all around, and one time I heard some of the other morning swimmers talking about him. They called him an old man, said he was wasting space in the pool. I wanted to tell those guys, at least Harold was *in* the pool, while they were sitting on a bench eternally adjusting their swim caps, putting their goggles off and on. But now that I'm thinking about it, Harold approached me. I thought I was doing him the service, but what really happened is, he saw me, he leaned on the lane divider one day when I happened to be taking a short break in between laps, and he asked if I swam for a team.

"Gladys was me allowing myself to see more than what I thought I needed to see. I had my job, my art, my house, and my swimming. I paid my bills, put food on the table . . . And for a while I thought that was enough, but it didn't *feel* like enough."

"Like, something was missing?" I ask, recognizing a familiar feeling within myself.

Ever since middle school, I've worked so hard to convince myself that I never needed to date. I needed good grades, good friends, good lap times, and good club involvement. But maybe I've been trying to busy myself so that I wouldn't even have time to try for more.

"Is there trouble in paradise?" Harold asks, scraping the inside of his pudding cup.

"No," I say, even though it feels like there is, in more ways than one.

CHAPTER TWENTY

On Wednesday morning before school, Abby and I knock on the south entrance doors and wait for our teammates to let us in. It's tradition that for the last home meet of the season, the boys' team decorates the girls' lockers and then someone from the boys' team will lead us from the south entrance once they've finished setting up—that way we don't get any sneak peeks. Then, at the end of the boys' season, we decorate theirs. Everyone spends the morning speculating about who might be in charge of the decorations and what they might do. Some guys go all out and make locker-size posters with our names on them and photos from the season. Victor always picks Abby, and he does her locker in a Christmas theme, since it's her favorite holiday, and brings her one of every flavor of Dunkin' Donuts Munchkins available. Depending on when the last meet falls, there's usually pumpkin, blueberry, and maybe a Christmas one already.

Even though we have our man on the inside, Victor never gives us hints as to who my decorator is. Last year it was Braylon Myers. I was a sophomore; he was a senior.

How we got paired is beyond me, but I felt very lucky. He decorated my locker to look like a swimming pool and did a cutout of me in a swimsuit made from striped scrapbook paper, and the lanes next to the one I was in said YOU WILL DO GREAT. He made it like a poster so I was able to just peel it off my locker at the end of the day, and I kept it hung up in my room for a few months.

But Braylon graduated and I haven't spent much time thinking about who I would even want it to be this year. The reason it's a big deal is because some of the guys do request to decorate for specific girls, and when that happens, they usually make it known, to see if the girl likes them back. In a perfect world I would ask Ben to decorate my locker. Last night we stayed up texting, going over the list of things he's going to need for college. I scrolled through the Bed Bath & Beyond website on my phone, looking for links to a bedspread that wasn't too simple but not trying too hard. I could barely keep my eyes open, I was so bored. I did find some that *I* liked, but I figure there's a good chance there will be new prints out when it's my turn to choose.

"Ladies, ladies, ladies," Chris Stone sings as he comes around the hallway corner to where we've been waiting. "Please follow me, and feel free to split off from the group as we pass your respective hallways, and hopefully you are satisfied with this year's decorations."

We start following him. Some of the freshman girls cluster together and start giggling. I can't make out exactly what they're saying, but it sounds like one of them is hoping Chris did her locker.

"Also," he says, turning around and running his hands through his bowl-shaped haircut. "I bet you guys will do amazing. You've worked hard, and I hope you have a great last home meet."

We all say "Thank you," nearly in unison, and as we do, I notice a teacher jump at his desk in one of the classrooms. The freshman hallway comes first, then the senior, then the sophomore, and finally—all the way at the other end of the school, because it's not enough that junior year is the hardest year of high school, so the administration needed to make things harder for us—the junior hallway.

Abby and I are practically holding on to each other when we turn the corner, both of us curious to see who my decorator is. Needless to say, I'm floored when I see Ritchie standing next to my locker, a few lockers in front of Victor. Both of them are holding Dunkin' Donuts bags, which probably means Ritchie asked Victor for help.

"Hey," he says, casual, as he hands me the pink-and-orange bag.

I take it and stare at my garden-themed locker.

"What is this?" I ask, my eyes trailing the rose petal border of a green piece of poster board. In the middle is a printed-out picture of a greenhouse that Ritchie cut out and glued down. Next to it is a stick-figure drawing of me in a skirt and sweater holding a single stick-figure flower. In my other hand is a shovel that's taller than stick-figure me. I'm guessing the flower was a gift from stick-figure Ritchie, who is intruding on my peaceful garden and my peace of mind. Stick-figure Ritchie is telling me to swim like a shark, and stick-figure me is just smiling like the Joker.

"Victor told me you like to garden, and then he told me how he gets Abby doughnuts, and I thought, *Great idea because you need fuel for the day*," he explains.

I want to ask if he would eat sugary carb-loaded dough-nuts on the day of one of the most critical meets of the sea-son, but I stop myself. Over Ritchie's shoulder I see Abby with her back to me pointing her finger in the face of a very confused and defensive Victor. Of all the secrets for Victor to keep, after what happened at the team dinner, this was not one of them.

"Mia," Ritchie says, snapping his fingers in front of my face.

"What are the chances that we would just randomly get paired together?" I say as the thought comes to mind.

"I wanted to apologize," Ritchie begins.

"You already apologized."

"Yeah, but Sloane got in the way—"

"Like, how your girlfriend got in the way?"

"Mia," he says, pleading.

"Don't 'Mia' me, Ritchie. That was humilia—"

"Mia, would you let me talk, *please*?" Ritchie raises his voice. A vein pops out on his forehead, and I freeze. I feel exposed and embarrassed and not sure what to do.

"You don't think that was embarrassing for me, too?" he continues. "You don't think it was hard for me, having an ex-girlfriend, making it impossible for me to move forward, when I just transferred schools in the middle of a semester? Having someone trying to ruin every attempt I'm making at my new life, at making friends? And she succeeded in ruining whatever it was I originally saw in you. And now I barely remember what that was. You've been so wrapped up in your assumptions about that night that you haven't been able to see that someone likes you, Mia! I *liked* you." He sucks in a deep breath, then laughs cynically like he's finally found his voice.

I can tell he's stopping himself from saying more. For a moment we just stare at each other. His eyes staring into mine, not like they're searching but like they're confirming something. He balls his fists at his sides and then lets his fingers uncurl. I feel trapped inside a moment that's repeating itself, only I want to change the outcome. I remember that nervous feeling I had, sitting on the garage steps next to Ritchie that night. But now I don't feel nervous about us getting closer. I feel scared that I've pushed him away. I remember him telling me about his family, about the separation he felt, and I remember how genuine he was. How vulnerable he was. After Amanda showed up, I stopped letting myself see who he was.

"I'm sorry," I say quietly.

"I'm sorry too," he says.

. . .

By the time classes end for the day, my mind is grinding with focus on the meet. This morning feels like a blurry but still tangible memory suspended in a parallel universe. It's like the memory is hanging by my bed, and once I'm done with the competition, I can go home and pick all my feelings back up. But right now, with Abby standing over me braiding my hair, I know what's important.

"Are you excited?" she asks.

"About what?" I ask, thinking that "stressed" or "pumped" would be more accurate descriptions for today's meet.

"Ben? Coming to the meet? Are you really that out of it?" she asks, holding the end of my braid and bending over to see my face.

"No," I say, trying to turn away from her so she won't see the redness in my cheeks. When I feel her still bent over, barely breathing, I clarify, "I mean, yes, I'm excited. No, I'm not that out of it."

"Okay, cool. Because I was about to say . . ."

When Abby finishes braiding my hair, I check my phone one more time. As she crams the rest of her stuff into her locker, I lay my phone on top of my backpack and ignore the twisty feeling in my gut. Ben hasn't responded since I texted him over an hour ago, asking whether or not he's still coming to the meet. I was hoping he'd say yes and maybe I could talk to him about what happened this morning with Ritchie, see if maybe he'd at least listen.

Abby and I follow our teammates out of the locker

room. The humidity around the pool soothes away some of the goose bumps on my skin. I feel both calm and excited again when I see Sloane, Grace, and Grace's kinda-maybe-it's-complicated girlfriend in the bleachers. They met over the weekend at the end of Thanksgiving break when Grace's family went downtown to ice-skate. Grace slipped while racing her dad and knocked Amy over. When Grace told me, I said that sounded like a meet-cute, and she couldn't stop blushing! I smile at them and let my eyes trace over the rest of the stands. I find Ben toward the top. He doesn't notice me because he's showing his friend something on his phone. As they laugh, I feel happy that he's here.

Coach quickly tells us the lineup. Abby and I are paired for the relays at the end of the competition, which is a relief.

With all the noises bouncing around the room, I'm thankful when it's my turn to get into the water. I submerge myself and focus on envisioning each lap, how to maximize each stroke, as my competitors tread. I focus on how the water feels on the surface of my skin, the quick and quiet beat of my heart. I trust in the simplicity of swimming there and back, from one end of the pool to the other. It's just me in the water, competing with myself.

My first three races go well. In the last one I place second, but my time was still one of my personal best. Whenever I get out of the water, my eyes are pulled like magnets back to the stands. Out of the corner of my eye, I see Sloane and Grace waving, though I'm more focused on Ben. I'm curious if he's paying attention, and if not, I wonder what he's doing, what he's talking about, what he's looking at on his phone or his friends' phones. When I finish my laps, I look up to see if he's watching, to see if he's seeing me at my best the way I see him in math club.

Sometimes he is watching, and when I catch his eye on my way out of the pool and he smiles, I think about whether or not we are finally connecting. As I hold my head up high and stride across the slick tile to the diving block, I feel like I'm floating, and there are points when my adrenaline is rushing so much that I almost swear I can float up the bleachers and right into his arms.

I get a short break before the relays, and Abby suggests I invite Ben to come out with us after the meet. We're all going to November Always so that Grace can formally introduce us to Amy. Abby jokes that since it's where things started for Ben and me, maybe that's good luck for Grace and Amy. I wish I had my phone so I could text him and ask him right now. I wish I felt more certain that he would want to hang out with me after the meet, even if he does have other plans.

Abby and I line up for our relay. When I glance up at Ben, I catch him watching me. He's leaning back against the bench behind him. He sees me returning his gaze and flashes me a smile that makes me feel like I can win this whole thing. Like, I have to win.

I'm glad that Abby goes first because she can give us a

strong start, and I can push us over the top with a strong finish. While she's making her way up the lane, I notice the pool doors open, and a familiar figure stumbles and drops a book on the floor in the doorway. When she stands up, I recognize Michelle Zhang from math club. I watch her walk over to the bleachers and scan the rows until she finds whomever she's looking for. I watch curiously, wondering if I completely missed any of the other math club members who decided to come and show support.

As she climbs higher, closer to Ben, I wonder what the chances are . . . but I don't have to wonder for long because when Michelle reaches Ben and his friends, Ben makes one move down so that there's room for her to sit next to him.

Maybe he's being nice. It's not like I know his friends, so if I were her, I would want him to let me sit next to him. I'd also want him to tilt his head toward me so that I could hear him over the loud noises of people thrashing through water. I get lost a little, staring at Ben and Michelle. Instead of wondering about Ben, I wonder about *them*. What are they talking about? What is Michelle doing here?

"Mia," Coach calls from the side of the pool. Eyes wide, she mouths *Focus* to me, and I look down in time to see Abby returning from her lap.

The second her fingers touch the wall, I dive over her, slipping into the water the way a needle would. I push past everyone from the first leg finishing their laps, their limbs kicking and pulling in the quiet around me. When I surface, I take a deep breath and throw myself into the butterfly stroke. Every time I come up, I try to glimpse Ben and Michelle. My stomach twists when I see four figures making their way down the bleacher steps. When I turn over to swim back, I keep watching—glimpse by glimpse—as they all walk to the doors.

I fan out my arms, slipping under the surface. Something catches around my wrist. My reflex is to pull free, but I'm met with resistance. I try to pull through the stroke, yanking my arm toward myself, but I feel plastic twisting and pressing in on my wrist. I push up out of the water and try to free my arm, only to realize I'm caught in the lane divider. It's wrapped around my wrist, and the separated plastic bubbles are squeezing me in place, ensuring my loss of the relay.

I look at Abby, standing behind the diving block. She stops calling my name when our eyes meet, because even though my face is covered in droplets of water, she can probably make out my tears.

I feel guilty when I finally crash on my bed at the end of the night. My parents were fine letting me celebrate with my friends after the meet, under the condition that I go to Sam's bachelorette party on Saturday.

I press my hands against my face, savoring how cold they are from being outside. After the meet, I didn't even wait to see who placed in the top five. I just went to the locker room, changed, and left. I sat in my car outside November Always, waiting until my friends texted me that they were on their way. Without them to distract me, it was impossible not to replay that moment over and over in my head. Michelle sitting down. All of them standing up. My wrist getting caught, me feeling like all of me was tangled in the lane divider right then. Feeling like I was being held in one unbearable place, stuck. It was a nightmare.

Gavin's harsh words managed to seep through while I was sitting in the parking lot. Maybe he's right. I mean, Ben wasn't really interested in me before I started talking about the wedding and all of Sam's plans. And who wouldn't be excited about an invitation to a wedding, especially one as extravagant and detailed as hers?

No matter how much I tried to rationalize Ben's actions, I couldn't completely convince myself that Gavin is wrong. It's especially hard since Ben didn't return any of my calls or texts. I felt bad because as Grace was talking about Amy, a senior at Gavin's school, I barely heard anything she was trying to tell us about her. I gleaned that Amy is nice. She's smart and funny, and she and Grace will go see a lot of Broadway musicals together. I figure Sam's reception isn't the worst place for me to try to make more of an effort to get to know Amy, since Grace decided to bring her to the wedding instead of her cousin.

And that's just it. Sam's reception. Sam's wedding. Where have the past couple of months gone? She and Geoffrey have their bachelorette and bachelor parties this weekend. And then next weekend is it.

And what then? I wonder. The thought is haunting and

awakening. Do I go back to being the girl who gets good grades, swims fast, and knows her way around a polynomial? This whole semester has been about finding a date to Sam's wedding, and it's pushed me to go outside my comfort zone—do more than just study on the weekends and practice after school. But what happens when the wedding happens and all the pressure, the necessity to find someone, goes away? I feel like I do want something more than just a date at the end of this, though I'm beginning to doubt that's going to happen with Ben. Do I ask my friends to continue the meet-cute project? Do I keep trying to put myself out there, and what does that look like without the added pressure of Sam's meddling?

I remember what Ritchie said to me this morning, that I've been so caught up in my own world, I haven't fully seen what's been going on around me. I remember what Grace said about me blaming Sam when everything is really my fault. Maybe they're right. I've been running around trying to find a date for Sam's wedding, when really, I *want* to find a date for *me*.

CHAPTER TWENTY-ONE

Y ou don't really want to go bowling," I prod, slipping down from the sectional armrest and onto the couch cushion next to my cousin Lucas. Geoffrey invited him to the bachelor party, since he's the only young male relative that Sam and I have. We don't get to see him often because he lives with most of Mom's side of the family in Wisconsin.

His lips move as he traces the line he's on in his book. He stops when he reaches the end and pins his finger to the page before looking up at me.

"I *do* want to go bowling, Mia," he says, smiling at me. "It's *you* who doesn't want to take a party bus downtown for ice-skating and a 'girls' dinner.'" He bobs his eyebrows up and down.

I roll my eyes and push myself up off the couch. After sifting through my family's movie collection, I pull out *Chitty Chitty Bang Bang* and hold it with the cover facing Lucas. I do a little dance, but even I know it's not convincing.

"Don't you want to say, *Aunt Beth, please, please don't make Mia go on a stupid party bus. Let her stay home so we can do family bonding and experience the nostalgia of our favorite childhood movie?"*

Lucas watches me over the top edge of his glasses.

"Mia, it's not going to be that bad. Plus, we can do family bonding, nostalgic movie night, once the wedding is over. We could have a sleepover. You could come to the cabin in Wisconsin when the semester ends," he says, getting progressively more excited about his idea.

There's no denying the allure of the Baker—Mom's maiden name—Wisconsin cabin, but it doesn't solve my immediate problem.

I already tried explaining to my mom how unfair it is that I have to go and she doesn't. Her response was a cryptic foretelling of my future wedding and how we will do a special "other" activity then as well. Again, highly unhelpful.

"Plus," Lucas says as I walk around the couch on my way out of the den, "I like bowling, like, a lot."

"Ugh!"

The silver lining is that Sam isn't like other girls. She traded a night out on the town with embarrassing glittery feathery props for a quiet dinner at her favorite restaurant in Little Italy and ice-skating. Part of me wishes she had gone the more traditional route, because then I would for sure be excused from the festivities.

On my way upstairs, admitting defeat, I hear the front door open, and in with the ice queen comes a gust of December chill so strong that I can feel it like a hand on my back.

"Why are you not dressed yet?" Sam asks, passing me on the stairs.

"Because I was busy," I tell her, though I don't explain that I was busy trying to get out of tonight.

"Yeah, right," she huffs, charging down the hall to her room. "Just get dressed," she shouts from behind her closed door.

To my right I hear my parents' door open, and Mom appears in the doorway with a mug in her hand and a book tucked under her arm. While I have to get dressed up, she's dressed down in her snowman-print pajamas and fuzzy slippers.

"If you need my help picking out an outfit, just let me know," she says, winking at me before heading downstairs. Most likely she's going to get another cup of hot chocolate and fold herself into the corner of the sectional in the den. With Dad upstairs watching the national aquarium tour on the nature channel, Mom will practically have the house to herself.

Sam turns her music all the way up. From the hallway the R&B sounds like it's underwater, but once I'm inside my room, someone could easily mistake me for the one with such poor taste in music.

I quickly sift through my closet and decide on thick tights, my green-and-tan floral-print shirtdress, and a pair of calf-high boots. Since my hair has been up in braids for the past week because of swim practice and my lack of interest in doing anything after the meet, I let it down and out. I push and pull my fingers through my hair until it's evenly around my shoulders in waves.

When I open my door to go to the bathroom, I hear voices downstairs. Brooke's stands out, but I can tell that more of Sam's friends have started to arrive. Someone's going on about how they never met Lucas and can't believe he's only a senior in high school. Part of me knows I could go down there and save him. I've been dealing with Sam's friends ever since I was a baby that they all wanted to hold. But a bigger part of me wants to hide for as long as I can.

"Are you almost ready?" Sam whispers from her doorway.

I turn around and whisper back, "Yeah. I just have to use the bathroom."

"Promise not to jump out the window." She tilts her head to the side to put on one of her hoops. I've never been able to put on earrings without a mirror, and it still baffles me how she does it.

"Why are we whispering?" I ask, taking in her navy-blue long-sleeve A-line dress. She's wearing the same kind of tights as me.

"Because I wouldn't put it past Brooke to come drag us down the stairs."

We both hold back laughs.

"You shouldn't wear solid navy-blue tights with a navy-blue dress," I tell her. "Nor should you wear stilettos. You will never forgive yourself when you put them on after ice-skating."

She slips in her other earring and looks down at her feet.

"Good catch," she mumbles, retreating into her room.

In the bathroom I wonder whether or not Sam was joking about the window. She didn't sound like she was trying to be mean or make fun. If anything, it felt like she was telling me not to abandon her.

When I open the bathroom door, Sam is standing in her doorway checking the skirt of her dress for any creases. She's changed into sheer blue tights and a pair of ankle booties. I give her a thumbs-up, and we both grab our jackets and purses before heading downstairs. We suffer through the initial scream and giggle about the upcoming wedding and all of Sam's friends telling her how cute her little sister is, even though I'm standing right here. Then we make our way outside. Thankfully, the party bus is already running, so when the doors close behind me, I'm enveloped in the warmth, scented with black-ice-freshened air.

During the ride, Sam's friends interrogate her.

"What flowers did you choose?"

"How big is the venue?"

"How old is Geoffrey's younger brother?"

"Are they really releasing another new flavor so soon just to commemorate the wedding?"

"What are the boys doing tonight?"

"What does your ring look like?"

"Did you decide how you'll do your hair?"

And on and on.

One by one I answer every question in my head. I'm surprised that Sam's closest friends—her bridesmaids—don't know this information. Yes, I realize that knowing that the venue is approximately 1500 square feet, not including the dance floor, isn't necessarily the kind of thing everyone involved in the wedding has to know. But did none of them hear about the flower emergency a few months ago? That she compromised on the tulips and decided on an arrangement of deep-pink carnations, white roses, and dusty miller? I mean, how was Brooke supposed to coordinate her jewelry with her bouquet if she doesn't even know what's going to be in the bouquet?

"And after a long perilous journey . . . ," Sam says, laughing with her friends. She rests her hand on my knee and glances back at me, as I sink farther into the corner seat of the bus. "Someone finally found a date."

I want to ask why she said it like that, like everything I've gone through to meet her ridiculous demand is some huge amazing joke for her to tell her friends. But I don't, not yet at least.

"OMG, mini-Sam has a boyfriend?" Brooke asks, beaming at me.

Before I can speak, Sam answers for me. "No, not a boyfriend. He's just escorting her to the wedding."

"What's he like?" Armao, Sam's friend from college, asks.

"He's cool. We know each other from math club, and he recently found out that he got into Vanderbilt." I feel a sense of pride when all the girls lean back a little.

"So, a senior boy, huh?" Cheryl, one of Sam's high school field hockey friends asks suggestively.

"Yeah," I say, blushing a little.

"A nerdy romance," Sam says dryly, probably bored that the conversation has drifted so far from her favorite topic, herself.

I answer a few more Ben questions before happily leaning back in my seat and slipping into nonexistence. We go to Valerio's first. It's a cute little *ristorante* tucked under a redbrick building downtown. There are seven of us total. Me, Sam, Brooke, Cheryl, Armao, Stamica, and Colleen. Stamica and Sam met in one of Sam's first design classes, and Colleen is another one of Sam's field hockey teammates from high school. Since there's an odd number of us, and the restaurant primarily specializes in tiny intimate two-person tables, they have to push four tables together, leaving me sitting on the end at a table by myself. But I don't mind. Being in exile minimizes my chances of being roped into a boring conversation about Sam's glory days on the field hockey team or how college was so, *so* fun. I tune in and out of their honeymoon banter, checking my phone under the table and enjoying my linguini alle vongole and blood orange Italian soda in peace.

I do, however, note the second and third bottle of cabernet sauvignon circulating around the table, and Sam's evenly timed—progressively louder—laugh. Everything becomes funny, from the way Geoffrey folds his underwear to the uneven shaping of our server's beard. It's annoying.

Definitely not white-tablecloth behavior, and not the Sam I know.

I wonder how any of them are going to manage ice-skating. Once they stumble off the bus at the rink by the Bean and everybody laces up, I find out. All of them cling to the railing, holding on to each other and giggling like idiots. I take my opportunity and skate away, over to the center of the rink.

Ice-skating alone makes me feel so lonely. On the ice you have your droves of middle schoolers clustered in separate boy and girl groups, pointing to each other across the rink. Then you have couples who hold each other's hands like couple skating is the only way to exist on ice. And then there are families, moms and dads taking their knobby-kneed fawn-like children onto the ice for the first time.

I reach into my coat pockets as my fingers begin to go numb. My gloves are wadded together in my left pocket, but I feel something in my right. I put my gloves on and pull a piece of paper out of my right pocket. When I unfold the faded yellow lined paper, I quickly remember what it is. Gavin and I still haven't talked since our fight, and remembering the awkwardness at the Pie and Leftovers festival makes me want to cringe. This paper is the list Gavin put together of the things to ask my mom to get. More burlap sacks, some seeds for Swiss chard, and a thermometer for the irrigation pipes. I fold the paper and push away the silent wish that Gavin were here, that we could talk about how weird tonight is, how it's making me miss Sam a little, even though she's just across the ice.

I skate around, hiding in the trees, until a couple of boys zipping through nearly knock me over. I figure I should quit while I'm ahead, and I return to the large oval of skaters making their way around the rink. Even though I find Sam and her friends clinging to the railing in a new spot, I skate past them using the layers of skaters between us as a wall.

Skating is like swimming in some ways. Especially when the Zamboni smooths the surface of the ice and there aren't so many scratches making it choppy. In the same way that there's this weightlessness when I'm in water, when I'm skating on ice, it's like I'm flying. And I can skate faster than I can swim. I glide around the rink, savoring the chilled air, the scent of pine trees, maple glazed doughnuts, and freshly roasted walnuts. Maybe I can slip away from the rink for some hot chocolate before we head home.

On my third lap, I skate up alongside Sam and her friends, who are finally getting their footing.

"This wasn't your best idea," Brooke says, laughing a little as she clings to Armao.

"I have no idea what you're talking about," Sam says, laughing. Her eyes look glassy, illuminated by the blinking fairy lights wrapped around the railing lining the rink.

"Well, *I'm* having fun," Cheryl says, confidently pushing herself away from the edge. She tentatively takes a step forward, and her foot hits the ice wrong. Her foot slides out in front of her, dropping her into a split.

I skate forward to help her up, officially exposing myself to the group.

"Mia's back!" Cheryl smiles, grateful for my timely return.

"Where did you disappear to?" Stamica asks, sounding soberer than the others.

I point over to the trees at the center of the rink, where there is a small group of three girls posing for a selfie in front of one of the trees.

"I can barely make it two feet away from the railing, and here you are skating circles around us," Cheryl slurs, amused.

She clings to the railing again, and I skate close by in case she needs me.

"Mia is great at skating," Sam says, a little too loud.

"You are too, with fewer glasses of wine."

Even though I'm just joking, Sam glares at me. No one else sees. What I mean is that Sam is usually a good skater too. We were both forced to get up early every Saturday for lessons. We started going when I was four and Sam was fourteen. I remember thinking it was fun, and being confused as to why Sam always made such a big fuss about getting up early. Nevertheless, once we were there, both of us were focused. Sometimes we'd be competitive, though I think Sam would let me win to make me think we were up against each other. Other times Sam would correct my form and show me the right way to land out of a jump and twist. I liked how when we'd fall over and go to help each other, we'd always pull the other person down. And, no matter how many times we did it, it was always a surprise. That feels like a different universe now, as Sam breathes heavily, holding on to the railing for dear life.

I linger close by, and after another lap I think Sam senses that everyone is beat and ready to hand themselves over to their food comas. It's funny to see how noticeably everyone relaxes when we're back on the bus. I watch the hot chocolate and chestnut stand disappear out the window. A few of the girls close their eyes, and Brooke checks her phone.

"Hey, no phones," Sam whines, tiredly swatting at Brooke's hand.

"What?" she says defensively, pulling away. "Mia was on her phone the whole time we were at Valerio's."

Nice, I think.

"What!" Sam's head snaps around to look at me. "Mia."

"What?"

"You couldn't be away from your precious phone just for one night for me?" she asks, playing victim. A look passes through her eyes, one that makes a nervous knot twist in my stomach. "I really hope you weren't texting any randos, trying to invite some creep to my wedding."

"A creep?" Stamica asks, more curious than horrified.

"Yeah." Sam happily elaborates. "Mia tried to be cute and sneak out to a party for Halloween. She ended up standing on the curb in the middle of the night and needed me to come save her. Turns out, she didn't know the kid she was standing outside with—if he even is a kid." She scoffs, actually scoffs.

A few of the girls look to me, but before they can say anything, Sam adds, "And then she tried to go on a date with God-knows-who, and was mad that she got stood up."

"Oh, Mia," Armao says sympathetically, pouting her lip.

"Don't 'Oh, Mia' her," Sam snaps. "She was out risking her life like some immature twelve-year-old during my bridal shower."

Recognition passes over everyone's faces as they remember the party that I did in fact skip.

"Tell us how you really feel," I mumble.

"What was that?" Sam asks, leaning forward to peer around Brooke at me.

"If you didn't want me to talk, then why did you beg Mom like an immature twelve-year-old to *force* me to come?" I ask, raising my voice to match hers. I don't care if we fight. We're in front of all her friends, not mine.

"Hey now," Brooke says, using her body to shield us from each other.

"I wonder what Geoffrey is doing, anyways," I say, staring right into Sam's eyes. "Probably having more fun than us."

"They're at their party—" Sam starts saying, but Brooke hops to, savoring any excuse to use her phone.

"OMG," she says, tapping away. "We have to check in

with the boys to make sure they're not having more fun than us."

She twists around to take a picture of Sam. Sam smiles, and from my angle—in Brooke's shadow—I can see that the smile doesn't reach her eyes. Sam adjusts her tiara to make sure it's centered. The rest of the girls lean forward a little, curious about the bachelor party.

Brooke sends the photo to Geoffrey's right hand for the night, Bernard. We all wait, a little awkwardly. I can feel desperation, but I can't tell if it's coming from Sam or her friends.

When Brooke's phone dings, Sam peers around her shoulder, her eyes wide and hungry for the response. Everyone leans close, even me. Bernard texted back a wide shot of Geoffrey sitting across from him, a drink in one hand and his other hand reaching out toward a waitress with her back turned. She's looking back over her shoulder at him, and he's turned in his seat smiling up at her. The text says, Just hangin'.

"What!" Sam snatches the phone out of Brooke's hand.

She studies the picture closer, keeping her thoughts to herself.

"What's wrong?" Cheryl asks.

"Do you see how he's looking at her?" Sam asks, her eyes glued to the phone. She quickly texts the picture to herself, and seeing it on her own phone only renews her anger.

"Sam, it's really not that bad," Stamica says.

"I mean, there are plenty of times when I've looked at

my server or waitress like that," Brooke says, slipping her phone out of Sam's hand.

"Yeah, and you're a notorious flirt. So, sorry if that doesn't give me any sense of comfort," Sam mumbles, pulling up Geoffrey's contact on her phone.

Even I'm surprised that Sam would snap at her *best* friend that way. At least when Grace blindsided me, it was more of a rude awakening, not just plain mean.

We all sit silently, listening to the phone ring on speaker. I hope with every ring that Geoffrey won't pick up, that we can comfort Sam instead. Then she'll lose her steam and wake up in the morning with all her marbles. I almost say it, that she's not herself right now, but Geoffrey answers.

I know my sister, so I know that the loud music and Geoffrey's friends talking and laughing in the background don't make things better. Geoffrey finishes a conversation that he's having, and his lack of focus bothers Sam. I know that when he finally does bring his phone back up to his face so that we can hear him clearly, still laughing with his friends, Sam is probably boiling.

Sam asks Geoffrey what he's doing. He says bowling. Sam references the picture that Geoffrey didn't even know existed. He pauses to look at Bernard's phone. He asks if Sam's joking, and Sam starts sobbing. She asks how he could do this to her, so close to the wedding. She says that she doesn't feel like she knows him right now.

"Are you serious?" Geoffrey asks, his voice more stern than anything I've ever heard out of him before.

Sam freezes, listening. Geoffrey goes on and calls her out for her accusation. He says, "After all the unbeliev-able things, the unreasonable requests, and you basically moving into your parents' house—Sam, seriously? This is too far. I can't believe you. How dare you accuse me of being unfaithful? Of even thinking about being unfaith-ful. I mean, really, if a picture—a non-suspect picture—is enough to make you doubt me, are you ready for this? Should we even be getting married?"

Everyone holds their breath. Tears fall from Sam's eyes, but no expression crosses her face. No words, none of her thoughts reveal themselves.

"Brooke," Geoffrey barks, making us all jump.

"Geoffrey, I—" Brooke stops. "She, Sam—I mean—"

"Brooke, just make sure she makes it back to her par-ents' house okay." Then he hangs up, leaving the bus in a tense stillness.

"So, does that mean—" Armao starts to ask.

But Brooke cuts her off with a look.

We ride the rest of the way home in silence. Sam leans against Brooke, keeping her eyes closed even with the steady leak of tears. When we arrive at home, Sam's friends say good-bye, a few hug her, but none of them knows exactly what to say. Even Brooke is quiet, and though I'm always wishing she'd shut her mouth, I feel a little lost without her saying something.

I follow Sam up to the house. Once we're inside, she slips out of her coat and boots and walks over to the stairs.

She sits down on the second step and leans forward to rest her face in her hands. I want to know what's going through her head. I want to know what she's thinking, that she has a plan. I want to tell her I'm sorry.

"Please go, just let me be alone," she whispers through her hands.

So I do just that.

CHAPTER TWENTY-TWO

On Sunday, Abby, Sloane, and Grace FaceTime me into movie night. I listen to them through my headphones talking about the dress Abby got for the wedding. She'd been holding out to find the perfect one because she and Victor haven't had a good excuse to wear more than athletic clothes to school and practice. I'm thankful that my friends still want to include me, but it's hard to focus and be happy for Abby with so much on my mind.

Since this is Abby's weekend, she gets to pick the movie. They set me down on the couch with a view of the TV, and even though I can't see any of them sitting next to me, I can still hear them talking about watching *The Edge of Seventeen* or *To All the Boys I've Loved Before*.

"Guys," I say. I know I'm too quiet, and I don't want to talk loudly because I know there's the chance Sam could hear me through the wall. But when no one hears me, I repeat myself loud enough to get their attention.

Sloane leans into my view, and behind her I see Abby and Grace.

"The bachelorette party," I say, watching as Sloane

leans back so all of them are sitting on the floor in front of the camera.

"Oh, how was it?" Grace asks, smiling.

"Sam and Geoffrey had a fight," I say quietly. "And it was really bad. Like, they aren't talking to each other."

"How did they have a fight when they were at two separate parties?" Sloane asks, popping a Starburst into her mouth.

"Brooke sent a picture of Sam to the best man to see if the boys were having as much fun as us, and he texted back a picture of Geoffrey talking to some waitress—that Sam is definitely blowing out of proportion. But, yeah, then Sam dialed Geoffrey and called him out for it, and it pissed him off."

Sloane raises her eyebrows, looking at Abby and Grace like she's surprised. Abby's jaw drops in shock, but Grace just scrunches her brow—confused.

"Really?" Grace asks. "What?"

"I don't know, maybe the wine got to her a little or she was in a bad mood and was taking it out on him," I say, then pause in my own thoughts. "I kind of feel like it's my fault because Brooke wouldn't have done anything if I hadn't suggested that we weren't having fun."

"Still, you aren't the one who made Sam think Geoffrey was cheating," Grace says. Abby nods in agreement.

"Have you talked to her about it?" Sloane asks, her lips smacking around a new Starburst.

"I mean, it happened last night. I know I'm not her

favorite person right now, and she didn't even want to look at me after we got home." Remembering the way Sam slumped down on the stairs, her face in her hands, makes me feel like it wouldn't be a stretch if she blamed me.

"That's true," Abby says, tapping the remote against her lip. "I think maybe Sam and Geoffrey just have to cool down and give each other space."

"It definitely doesn't sound like Sam," Grace adds, twisting one of her box braids around her finger. "Don't blame yourself, the same way you can't blame her for things."

"Right," I say, remembering my rude awakening at the library. Even though Grace's words caught me off guard, they helped me realize that I'm more in control than I was willing to admit. In the same way, Sam didn't have to jump to the conclusion she did. At the very least, *I* didn't make her see it that way.

Which makes me wonder why that would be her first reaction. She and Geoffrey have been together for almost five years, and neither of them has ever cheated on or questioned the other. So, why now? Where is this coming from?

When I get up to go to school on Monday and see Sam moping back into her bedroom, still wearing her fuzzy robe and silk nightcap, I realize she must have called in sick to work. I try to imagine how her little ArchiTech minions will get along without their micromanager, but I figure—like Abby said—one day off to cool down from the fight shouldn't be cause for worry. I hope that her constant, loud, mucus-filled crying might be over by the time I get home, and she'll be preparing to reenter the world outside her bedroom. Maybe she'll be picking out an outfit for work tomorrow or preparing her lunch, or—even better—packing her bag to go home.

I have no such luck. After school I come upstairs and find Mom and Dad standing outside Sam's door. When I open my mouth to ask what they're doing, they hold their fingers over their mouths. I tiptoe over and lean close to the wall next to her door. Sam is crying on the phone. It's not hard to tell that she's talking to Geoffrey, though "talking" isn't a good way to describe it. It's more like she's pleading—over and over to the point where it's safe to assume Geoffrey hasn't budged yet.

"I don't understand," Dad whispers, stepping away from the door.

We all take a step back, though Sam probably wouldn't hear us if we did talk in front of her door, because of how loud she's crying.

"Understand what?" Mom asks, watching Sam's door like she'll come out any second. I can practically feel Mom itching to give her a hug.

"What happened?" Dad turns to me. "I—I just don't understand how over the course of a few hours everything has changed."

They both watch me expectantly.

"They had a fight," I say, feeling awkward.

"Well, yeah. But about what?"

"Why don't you ask Sam?"

"We did," they say in unison.

"What did she say?"

"She said she hardly knows what happened. She said everything happened so fast, and that's all she gave us," Dad says.

"All I know is, they fought," I say, not wanting to give any more. I don't want to say I suggested we see what the boys were up to, because I'm scared it's my fault that any of this happened in the first place. I'm scared Sam might blame me. . . . I retreat to my room to start on my homework.

I can hear Mom and Dad mumbling outside Sam's door and am relieved when they finally walk away. While Mom is tucked inside their bedroom, and Dad is downstairs feeding his fish, I hear Sam's door open. I pause, my pencil hovering over the derivative I've been solving for the competition tomorrow. I thought she cried herself to sleep earlier, and maybe she did. Or maybe she just stopped crying and stayed in bed for a while.

She passes my door, without looking in my direction, on her way to the bathroom. Instead of wearing her fluffy robe and silk hair wrap, Sam's hair is sticking out. She's wearing one of Geoffrey's concert T-shirts that she stole from him when they first started dating in college.

She looks like the version of herself that usually only slips out during occasional meltdowns and isolated all-nighters, when she's too tired to do her hair in the morning. Only, instead of this being a momentary slipup, she's been consumed by this disorganized Sam. This Sam doesn't oil and twist her hair every night or repaint her nails every Sunday, or work at an architecture app startup. This Sam doesn't boss around anyone, because she can hardly force herself to get out of bed and pour herself a bowl of cereal. She doesn't shower, she doesn't eat, she doesn't remember to turn off the light when she leaves a room.

The last time this Sam came around was sophomore year of high school. Because of Harley, the long-haired drummer who transferred to our district from Pennsylvania farm country. He was her project, bringing him into the folds of city life and of high school. Girls were jealous because Sam just happened to be printing field hockey flyers in the office on his first day. Before he even really passed over the threshold of the school, he was taken. And they were inseparable for nearly three months.

Then Harley fell in with a rock band at school called Bottle Ship and the Sunfish. He started hanging out in the drama-and-music hallway, which—to Sam and her friends—was the source of the bubonic plague. So, without Sam controlling his every thought and move, Harley met Polly—an electric guitarist who needed a drummer and had a soundproof garage attached to a house that was always empty for a few hours after school. No helicopter parents. No little sisters stumbling into the room at the most inopportune times.

Sam was devastated. Our parents were surprised at how affected she was. To them, three months warranted a good cry, buying a deep-dish pizza and ice cream, and waking up the next day a little shaky but ready to go back to school. For Sam, three months meant she would never find love again, that Harley was the One, and now all her life decisions had been brought into question. She started eating French fries from the school cafeteria, drinking soda, and watching TV for a few hours after school instead of starting her homework and snacking on baby carrots or pumpkin seeds. She wasn't herself.

Sam told me the story about Harley when she first started dating in college. Mom thought it was unnecessary for her to put up walls and act like dating was the equivalent of playing defense. But Sam did not want to repeat being vulnerable and genuinely liking someone only to get hurt. Geoffrey was the first guy that I know of who she truly let in, who she felt comfortable being herself with. If she was a wreck after three months with Harley and closed off to the idea of true love for almost six years, I don't even want to think about what she might turn into after five years with Geoffrey, and the threat of her wedding being cancelled.

I hear the bathroom door open. When she doesn't pass my room right away, I picture her standing on the tile floor, her toes nearly touching the hallway carpet. I imagine her looking toward my parents' room, gauging whether or not the coast is truly clear for her to hustle back into her cave. I wait, silently hoping that she might slip into my room and close the door. But even if she does, I don't know what to say. I know she's not okay. I know there's nothing I can do to make her feel better, except build a time machine and go back to not bring up the bachelor party.

Maybe I want her to tell me that she doesn't blame me, to assure me that this distance I've felt between us hasn't grown as big as it feels right now. Maybe I want her to tell me that if the wedding really doesn't happen, she won't hate me forever.

CHAPTER TWENTY-THREE

I try to push Sam out of my mind at school on Tuesday. Today is the last math club competition of the semester. I'm excited because all these endings mean Christmas is getting closer! There is, however, a part of me that wonders what will happen between Ben and me once we lose the main thing we have in common, just before the wedding. I don't know if I want to spend Sam's reception picking out dorm furniture or talking about his acceptance letters. But I'm not sure if I'll have another choice . . . that is, if the wedding is still on.

I push away the jarring thought that there's a possibility the wedding will be cancelled. It has only been a couple of days. Maybe Sam and Geoffrey need a little more time to cool down and they'll find a way to move past it. They'll have the wedding. We will all get to watch her walk down the aisle in her gorgeous dress and dance at the winter-themed reception, under fairy lights, with a fire going and pine-scented candles making us light-headed because they're eating up oxygen from under Sam's heated tent.

All I have to do is get through this competition, and

then I can focus my attention on trying to help Sam and figure out what to do about Ben.

I pass the school Christmas tree on my way into the library for study hall. As I head deeper into the shelves of books, passing the cooking section and the natural history section, I check over my shoulder to make sure no one is following me. I turn right, then left, and walk to the end of a bookshelf that takes you into a dead-end corner where two other bookshelves were pushed together, and then I turn right again and find our secret table.

"There she is," Grace says, staring at me.

I pull out a chair and look down at all my friends and Victor.

"Hi."

"What happened?" Sloane asks, gripping her pen so hard, her knuckles are turning white.

"What?" I ask.

"Your parents texted Grace to let us know that the wedding might NOT be happening!" Sloane clarifies, her eyes wider than a six-lane highway.

"They did what?" I ask, my heart racing. Grace holds her phone out to me, and there is, in fact, a text from my mom saying to be on standby because the wedding might be off.

"Mia!" Abby says, pulling at my attention. But I'm still focused on this text, on the fact that my mom is telling people—that my mom believes there's a real chance the wedding won't happen.

"Oh my gosh," I say, deflating. I sit back in my seat, feeling a weight pressing down on my shoulders. "Oh my gosh."

"Mia, what happened since the other night?" Sloane presses.

"Nothing," I say, feeling like the walls are closing in. "I mean, she still hasn't gone home. They haven't worked it out yet."

I replay the entire ludicrous moment in my head again—as I've done so many times since Saturday night. Sam accused Geoffrey of cheating on her, over a picture where he was clearly trying to get the waitress's attention. *Clearly.* But how could I see that? How could all of her closest friends see that, and she couldn't? And how can he not see that it was a slipup, a moment when Sam went too far, but not a moment that should change *everything*?

Sloane closes her mouth and looks down at the table. Grace watches me for a moment before looking away, processing her own thoughts. Abby and Victor look at each other before looking back at me.

"How is she taking this?" Abby asks.

"Not well at all. I guess if my mom is texting that to people, then things are much worse than Sam's let on to me."

"How are you handling it?" Grace asks.

"It's not my life that's ruined," I say, holding down the lump trying to rise in my throat. I lean forward and pull from my backpack my math notebook and folder, with the practice problems Ben gave all of us.

. . .

By the end of the day, I'm annoyed. The guilt over Sam's bachelorette party is building under my skin, and when you mix in Ben's lack of replies to my texts, and my stress over today's math competition, the combination doesn't bode well for my performance. At this point, I figure Ben and I aren't going to get any closer than we already are. Still, he could at least respond when I ask if he feels ready for today. I check my phone again as I pinch my coat into the crook of my elbow and close my locker. Still, nothing.

It doesn't help that as I'm approaching the math club classroom, I see Ben and Michelle framed in the doorway. He's sitting on top of the desk that she's sitting at. They're laughing about something together. He's showing her something on his phone. At least I know his phone is working.

"Hey, guys," I say, smiling and holding my shoulders back as I walk around Michelle and pull up a chair next to the desk. "Do you feel ready for this?"

"Yeah," Michelle says, fidgeting with her mechanical pencil. "I'm just ready for this semester to be over, to have a break from math and science and—well—everything."

I stop myself from admitting the same, and look to Ben. "How about you?"

"I practiced, studied, did some reverse problems. I'm as ready as I'll ever be," he says, only glancing up at me before looking back at his Instagram feed.

"Oh, and there's this one of her chasing a duck," he

says. Before he tilts his phone so that only Michelle can see, I catch the corner of Carly's face.

"Where is everyone?" I ask.

"They probably already headed to the auditorium," Michelle says, reaching behind her for her backpack. When she stands up, Ben stands up and grabs his bag.

"That's where we're meeting for the competition," Ben adds, all three of us heading to the door, but the two of them pass through together, since I don't fit.

"Oh," I say, swallowing my next question with a little bit of my confidence.

The auditorium is dark save for the stage lights shining down onto the two podiums facing each other. Each one has a mason jar with mechanical pencils and a short stack of block erasers. In between them is a table where the proctor is already sitting, going over the rules with our faculty advisor. Our team has set up on the left side of the stage, and all our coats and bags are strewn over seats in the two rows. We all sit and get clipboards and paper so that we can solve the problem our teammate is working on onstage. It gives us both a chance to practice and a chance to show them what they did wrong if they don't answer the question correctly.

I don't make the effort to try to get a seat next to Ben. He and Michelle sit toward the center, and I sit next to Constance Bowler and Brendon Dockey. We compare our answers to the practice problems Ben gave us and go over how we solved them, what steps we followed. Brendon and I remind Constance to write down the full additions and subtractions when she's solving a problem for the judge. It will take away from her final score if she doesn't show all her math.

When our opponents show up, they don't need time to prepare. They put their stuff down, pick up their clipboards and face forward, ready to begin. We start off with algebra equations. They win the first two questions before Brendon steps up and puts us officially in the game. The judge then moves on to derivatives, and Michelle and our other two Calculus 1 teammates bring us into a leading position. We move on to logs. We only have one person on our team who specializes in those, so she takes all three rounds, and misses only one question.

Then it's time for Ben and me to compete. We decide that I'll go first. I bring my clipboard up to the podium and put a new piece of paper on it. I take one of the mechanical pencils and test it out, writing the date at the top of my paper.

The stage is hot from the lights, and they're so bright that it's hard to make out my individual teammates even though they're sitting in the front row. Someone waves at me, and another person, I think Constance, gives me a thumbs-up.

"Are you ready?" the judge asks, looking back and forth between me and Canterbury's polynomial competitor.

"Yes," both of us say.

The judge taps some button on his computer, and a

graph comes up on the screen. They want us to find the Taylor series for $f(x) = \sin(x)$ about $x = 0$. I start solving for derivatives to identify a pattern. I've already identified that there's a pattern of Ben only texting me, not talking on the phone or really acknowledging me in public. We talk about the wedding and math and nothing else, and there's a pattern where when Michelle is around, it's like I don't even exist, and the wedding doesn't even get him excited. I start plugging numbers into the series and try to solve for a new pattern to generate a new series. So I plug in the fact that the wedding might not happen. I try to evaluate these series of instances for what will become of us. If we only talk about math and the wedding, then without the wedding, we'll only have math. And with math team ending, we won't have that until next semester, so that means after today, after the cancelled wedding, we probably won't talk at all. So, does x equal the wedding? Or is x, what I'm solving for, what happens to Ben and me? And if x is zero, then what's the equation?

The sound of my pencil scraping along the paper feels like it's filling the room. The heat makes me sweat, and I feel an ache in my neck as I bend over to focus on the paper in front of me. Even if both of us get the question right, whoever gets it right first wins the points.

Just as I'm identifying the pattern of odd values for n, I hear, "Sin of x equals . . ." I keep working up until the judge says "Very good" in that quiet yet definitive way of his.

It doesn't feel like a big deal until I turn away from the

podium, with my clipboard against my chest, and catch Ben whispering something to Michelle. He's shaking his head, his eyes following me as I make my way over to the steps.

The equation would be impossible to solve without x, just like Ben and I are impossible if x equals the wedding. But now I don't know if there's really a point to *try* to make it work. Our connection is not happening on its own, not like with Gladys and Harold. And do I really want to spend the reception with Ben, do I really want to walk down the aisle hand in hand with someone who can't focus on something other than himself to listen to me talk about the things going on in *my* life?

Ben finishes his Maclaurin series in record time, leaving us realizing that no one kept track of the score. When he returns to Michelle, she beams up at him, and part of me wonders if she knows about the wedding, that he and I have been talking almost every night until recently. But, then again, does it matter? Have we really been talking about anything worth her worry?

Asking myself these questions makes me realize what I've been trying to suppress. Michelle and Ben are a thing. They're not out about it or that obvious, but to someone who has noticed that Ben's attention has been on one thing in particular recently, it is obvious.

From that night at the diner when Ben started taking an interest in me—or, more accurately, taking an interest in the out-of-this-world wedding—till the moment when Ben told his friend to move over for Michelle at *my* swim meet, the reality was in front of me, nagging at me and daring me to be in denial.

After the competition I grab my stuff and head over to the girls' locker room. Since math competitions run longer than regular math team meetings, I almost always miss swim practice. The girls have already finished practice and conditioning with the boys' team. I say hi to my teammates in the locker room as I pass them on my way to the row of lockers where Abby and I keep our bags.

"How was it?" she asks, rubbing her hair with her towel. I wish I hadn't missed conditioning with the boys' team because of the math competition. In that space of time between when we're done practicing and the boys start competing, we can have fun working out in the pool together. But I care more about missing it because I could really use some time in the water. I just wish I could put on my suit and slip under right now, escape that embarrassing disaster back there in the auditorium.

"We lost," I say, reflexively going to sit down, but remembering I'm not wearing a soaking-wet swimsuit like everyone else.

"Aw, well, we can get ice cream? Or milkshakes?" she offers, pulling her sweatshirt over her head.

"I think I'm still grounded," I remind her, feeling even more defeated.

"When are they going to release you?" she asks.

"I don't know, but my mom is probably sitting at the

kitchen island counting down the minutes until I should be home from that competition," I tell her.

"Okay, well, don't beat yourself up too much. I know you studied your butt off for this, and I mean, what more can you say than, you tried your best?"

"Thanks," I say before giving Abby a loose hug so as to not get too wet. Then I head out through the locker room doors, letting the biting air wake me up.

As I go along the walkway from the school to student parking, I hear another door open and see two entwined figures come out of the building. Our paths intersect on our way to the parking lot, and there's no way for me to hide from Ben and Michelle.

"What happened in there?" he asks, his arm around her shoulders, their fingers interlaced.

"I don't know," I say.

"Didn't you practice? I mean, Mia, you basically lost us the meet," Ben says, laughing a little.

"That's not nice, Benny," Michelle says, twisting out from under his arm to look him in the eye.

"Mia, you're supposed to be one of our best members. I mean, you're on the Calc 2 level. I had such high hopes for you," he says, though I can't tell if he's being sincere or not.

"A lot of people did," I say, not stopping to entertain him.

"Don't take it too hard. Gosh, I know I would be beating myself up."

"Well, I guess it's a good thing we aren't the same

person," I shout over my shoulder, not waiting or watching to see his reaction.

When I close myself in my car, I take a deep breath. Finally alone, I can't pretend I'm not embarrassed and strung-out. I hate that Sam is hurting right now, and I can't believe it might be because of me. And Abby was right. I did try my hardest in the competition, and I still choked. So, what does that say? What does it say that I prepared and gave it my all, in math, in swimming, and in the meet-cute project, and here I am having lost a race, lost a math competition, and failed to find a suitable date to Sam's wedding? I mean, Sam already doesn't want to be in the same room as me, so how much worse will I make things when I tell her I'm disinviting Ben?

My phone buzzes, and I see a text from Mom asking me where I am.

On my way home, I reply.

I drop my phone onto the passenger seat, put my car in reverse, and start moving. I turn around just in time to see someone right outside my back window, and I slam on the brakes. I can't see their face, but I see them shrug and throw their hands up incredulously. Great. I can now add "almost ran over a student" to my list of failures.

I throw open my door, already vomiting apologies, only to look up and see Ritchie.

"So now you're trying to kill me?" he asks. Even though I know he's joking, I feel rotten all over again, and tears come pouring out of my eyes.

"I didn't know it was you—I mean—I'm sorry. I wasn't trying to run you over, I promise. I was just trying to leave—"

"Mia, wait, hold on." Ritchie stops me, stepping closer. He pulls me into a hug. As weird as it feels, it's the most comfort I've gotten from anyone in a long time. I feel like with Sam being annoyed, my parents grounding me, and things with my friends being hot and cold after I settled for Ben, I haven't necessarily been the apple of *anyone's* eye lately. I rest my head against his chest, thankful that his Holloway Charter hoodie is so soft.

"What's wrong?" he asks, taking a step back.

I laugh a little, which might look weird, since my mascara is definitely streaking down my face. "It's kind of a long story," I say, "and I'm actually grounded and was supposed to be home, like, five minutes ago."

"Here," he says, taking his book bag off his shoulder. He unzips one of the pockets and rips the corner of a page out of his notebook. He pulls a pen out, writes down his number, and hands it to me. "If you want to talk about it, call me later. Okay?"

"Thanks," I say, feeling a little confused.

"What?" he asks, closing his bag.

"I thought you didn't like me anymore." I wipe my nose on the sleeve of my sweater, trying to make myself less gross.

"I was more upset that I never got to explain myself to you, that you were walking around thinking I was a cheater and a liar and wouldn't even give me a chance to tell you the truth. But once I got it out, I felt okay again."

"That's good," I say.

"I think part of me thought maybe you'd give me another chance, and then when I was making a fool of myself in the hallway, I realized that wasn't it. I needed to find closure, for me, to admit how hard this move and my parents' divorce has been and how it's been holding me back."

We fall silent, and I feel the urge to hug him again, but I don't know if it would be weird.

"You can talk to me too," I say. I hold up his scribbled phone number. "I'll text you."

"Sounds good." He smiles, and we stand awkwardly in the space between my car and someone else's. Before he leaves, he asks, "Are you sure you're okay?"

And for the first time in weeks, I am.

CHAPTER TWENTY-FOUR

When I get home, I take a shower and continue working on one of my finals essays. My mind keeps drifting back to Ritchie's hug, the way he was still able to be vulnerable with me right after I almost ran him over with my car. I look down at his number. He offered to listen, which is all I've been wanting from Ben. And Ritchie already has listened. That night at the team dinner, I started talking about Sam and how things have changed, and he and I could relate to each other. We were able to talk about something real, more important than theorems and mini fridges.

So I call. I tell him everything, and I figure at this point I have nothing to lose and it's not like I'm trying to win him over, so I even tell him about the meet-cute project and how he factored into it. I catch him up to when I was crying in my car, ready to peel out of the parking lot, and nearly hit him. We actually laugh about some of it, about his ex-girlfriend barging in, and the dog park. He reminds me that all of these instances are just brief moments. It's been rough, but everything always seems bigger in our heads than it is in reality.

We hang up, and I see that it's already midnight. I figure I can put one more hour of work into my paper before calling it a night, but I stop when I hear movement on the other side of my wall. I go out into the hallway and stand in front of Sam's closed door, listening. The only way to find out if she hates me, if she blames me, is to break our stalemate and ask. The more I hide and avoid talking about it, the more time I waste letting the not-knowing eat me up inside.

I knock, listening closely. I think I hear covers being pushed back. Then I hear soft thuds on the floor, and I stand back. When she opens the door, I can't tell from her blank stare if she was expecting it to be me or not. She's not pulling me into a forgiving hug, but at least she's not slamming her door in my face either.

"Can we talk?" I ask.

She moves aside to let me in.

Even though there's more to talk about, Sam and I stick to discussing the bachelorette party. She admits she resented me a little, mainly because I missed the bridal shower and had to be forced to go out with her that weekend. She wishes I would just have more interest, and I admit that she's right. Weddings aren't really my thing, but I should be able to put that aside and be more excited for her. She doesn't blame me for the fight. Her accusation just slipped out, a culmination of unrealistic worry. And once it was out, she couldn't take it back, and she doesn't know how to tell Geoffrey where it came from—which is why they haven't completely made up. He says if it's not a trust issue, then why would she jump to a conclusion like that? And how does she know she'll never do it again if she can't even figure out why she did it in the first place?

"Don't give up, Sam," I say before heading out her door. "There's definitely a way for you guys to make this right. We just have to figure it out."

"You think so?" Sam asks. There's a hesitation and weariness to her voice that I never would have thought possible. I guess we all doubt ourselves sometimes.

"Yes," I say, and I mean it. "That's what sisters are for."

On Wednesday after school, I surprise Mom when I come into the kitchen, ready to go to the garden with her. I figure if Ritchie and I can fix the awkwardness between us, and if Sam and I can start talking again, then hopefully Gavin and I can too.

When I walk into the greenhouse, I find Gavin crouched down inspecting a kale plant that has nearly doubled in size since the last time I was here.

"So, you were right," I say, thrusting my hands into my gardening gloves and grabbing a tiny rake from the back table. I swat the vine that slaps me in the face when I turn around, and I nearly drop the rake on my foot. He's also installed hanging planters. "You were right. Everyone was right about Ben. He thinks I'm an idiot who can't solve Taylor series, and he was only interested in seeing my sister's big fancy wedding, not in getting to know me. He couldn't even stand to talk to me about anything that *wasn't* about him being amazing or good at math or him going to Vanderbilt, or him in general—UGH!"

When Gavin doesn't say anything, I reach into my coat pocket and pull out the list he made, the list that I found in my pocket the night of the bachelorette party when I was skating alone.

"I'm saying I don't want us to tiptoe around each other, because you were right, and I'm admitting it and saying sorry and that I can't handle *this* being weird when everything else in my life is a mess."

Gavin is one of the few people I can talk to, and after chasing Ben, I feel it's important to make things right with him. Why go after someone who doesn't want to be your friend, when you have good friends right in front of you?

He keeps staring at me, so I add, "So say something. Please. I mean, I'm here on a *Wednesday*. If that doesn't show you how much I care, then I don't know what will."

This makes him smile.

"Well, I do know everything," he says, "and I *am* always right."

"Shut up." I laugh.

"I thought you wanted me to talk," he says, quirking his eyebrow, which makes me laugh harder.

I want to say I missed him, but I feel like that would be weird. So I start telling him about the bachelorette party. He beckons me over to the kale, and as I relay every detail

I can recall, he shows me how to check that the vegetables are doing well, and we start going from trough to trough. By the time I finish, the knees of my jeans are freezing from the damp dirt. Gavin also added a temperature control and timer to the irrigation system since I've been gone.

I roll my hands up in the length of my scarf running down my chest, and I take a deep breath.

"Have you thought about any possible way that Sam can fix things?" Gavin asks.

"Yes and no," I say, wringing my hands. "I think the hardest part is that he wants her to tell him why she immediately got so bent out of shape, but she doesn't fully understand it herself."

Gavin considers this, pressing his lips together and running his fingers over his beard. It's coming in fuller. Now it covers his entire jawline up to his ears. The Sherpa collar of his green corduroy jacket is popped up behind his neck and folded down where it would come around to cover his mouth. In a way, it frames his face. And with his brown eyes squinted, his pupils barely discernable, he looks focused.

"Would he talk to you?" he asks, looking at me.

"What do you mean?"

"I mean, if you talk to him about what happened, maybe comment on it from an outside perspective, would he at least listen?"

"I guess. . . . I mean, I don't think he's mad at me." You know, unless Sam has secretly spent the last five years turning him against me in private.

"Maybe it could help for you to be a messenger. Figure out if there's something Sam wants to say or something she's been trying to get him to understand, and maybe you can help him understand. And maybe he'll be more willing to listen because it won't be Sam talking."

"You make it sound simple," I say, mulling over the idea. "Plus, it's not like I can go talk to him. I'm still grounded for that whole Darth Vader fiasco."

Gavin nods. "I think if your parents catch you trying to save your sister's wedding, they'll understand."

I think it over some more, figuring saving the wedding might be the get-out-of-jail-free card I've been looking for to finally fix things with Sam.

"Obviously," Gavin adds, "you will need to tell me how it goes."

"Makes sense. You'd want to know if your idea blows up in my face," I say jokingly.

Gavin rolls his eyes and I unlock my phone and hand it to him. I watch his face as he enters his contact into my phone, his eyes illuminated by the light on my screen. Sloane was definitely onto something when she brought up how attractive he is. I can't help but feel like I missed an opportunity, especially now that we've fixed the tension between us. I like that I can talk to Gavin, that he doesn't judge me for my boy problems and wants me to talk about how I'm feeling. It doesn't matter, though, because he already has a girlfriend.

• • •

Gavin's advice comes to the forefront of my thoughts later when I can't escape the sound of Sam on the phone with Brooke.

"I don't know," she's sobbing.

I tried listening to my music, but Gavin's idea made it hard to fall asleep. That, and Sam's constant shuffling around. The sound of her walking around in her room is easy to confuse with the sound of someone walking in the hallway.

"He still picks up, but he doesn't *talk* to me. He's not giving me clear signals about where his head is at."

I listen. Sam blows her snot into a tissue, probably listening to Brooke responding.

"I tried, Brooke. I don't know. I just don't see it being over because of this." Though, the thought makes Sam cry harder.

More shuffling. I can picture her pacing at the foot of her bed, avoiding looking at herself in her full-length mirror every time she turns around to walk toward her door.

"Well, I don't know, Brooke. At this point I don't care about the wedding. I just want him to talk to me. I miss him!"

I wonder if Geoffrey is still awake. He's the type to go to bed at a reasonable time so that he can get up early, do some yoga stretches, and get in a good five-kilometer run before heading to work. But as I type out Hey, you up? part of me already knows the answer.

Yes, he replies within seconds.

How are you holding up?

I see the typing bubble pop up and go away. I wonder if maybe he won't respond, but then they come back and his message pops up: Honestly, not good.

Are you doing anything tomorrow after 3?

No.

The period at the end seems off, oddly definitive, yet in some ways inviting.

Can I stop by?

As soon as I send it, I realize how weird it might be, to have your maybe-ex-fiancée's little sister want to come over. It's a little suspect, but at the same time I can easily see my dad wanting to go check on Geoffrey. The only reason he hasn't is because he might be afraid that Sam would think he's a traitor.

I watch my screen. Should I make something up like, *Sam gave me some of your things to drop off* or *I found X lying around and realized it was yours*? But then he replies Sure, leaving me in the darkness of my room with the realization that now I have to figure out how I'm going to get them back together.

I've only been to Sam and Geoffrey's place a few times. First was when both families came together to help them move. The second time was when Sam had me over for a movie night, which was really a living-on-her-own-with-her-boyfriend-was-daunting night. After that, I would stop by with Mom if she wanted to pop over with bagels, or if Mom wanted to bring Sam something she'd found while cleaning her room, like a knit hat or a pair of shoes buried in her closet, or if Mom got some of Sam's still-not-routed mail. Nevertheless, every time I came over, their apartment was spotless. Sam and Geoffrey aren't the type to eat junk food or fast food, so when I step over the threshold to follow Geoffrey toward the living room, and see their trash can overflowing with McDonald's wrappers, Chick-fil-A bags, and a Burger King chicken fries box, I know he's having as hard a time as Sam.

When we sit down on the couch in the living room, facing their floor-to-ceiling window with a view of Lake Michigan, I notice Geoffrey's yoga mat rolled up in the corner with a bowl propped on top. Geoffrey pushes a pair of folded socks off the coffee table and folds the blanket that was strewn across the couch, before finally sitting down next to me.

"So," I say, taking in the tornado aftermath that is the rest of the apartment. "How are you?"

I set my book bag down on the floor and before I drop my phone into the front pocket I already see texts. Mom is probably wondering where I am since school ended almost forty minutes ago.

"I don't know," he says, pressing his hands against his face. I notice a few blanket fuzzies among his naps.

"Have you and Sam made any progress? Like, do you think the fight will end soon?"

"She apologized. She said she was sorry." Geoffrey focuses his gaze on the horizon out the window. A cynical smile takes over his lips. "I mean, saying she's sorry doesn't fix everything, and she knows that. It's something we've talked about, how that phrase is meaningless without actions to back it up. Like, what has she done to show that she's sorry?"

I quickly jump to her defense. "She has been a mess all week. She's been crying every night. She didn't mean what she said at all—"

"I don't care if she meant it," Geoffrey admits, looking at me. "Her reflex was to assume the worst about me. After five years, all of a sudden one picture makes her doubt my loyalty. Aren't we farther along than that? Isn't our bond stronger than that?"

I want to say, *No, because Sam has a way of testing the people she loves, usually unintentionally.* But I know that's not what Geoffrey wants to hear.

I look away. I realize that the coasters on their coffee table are pictures of them on different rides at amusement parks.

"Mia, I don't expect you to answer that, by the way. And I'm sorry if I'm putting you in an uncomfortable position by talking about your sister like this."

"Trust me, on any given day at any time, if anybody comes to me and says 'Let's talk smack about Sam,' I'm there. . . . But, I don't know. This isn't one of those times where I think— It's not that I don't think what she did was wrong, I just don't—I guess—understand it either. It's not like her at all, which you know."

We fall silent. Geoffrey offers to get me something to

drink, and I tell him a glass of water will do, because I can see that he just wants to get up, to move instead of sitting in this weird space we've made. While he's over in the kitchen, I check my phone and see one missed call from Mom. I know I can't go home empty-handed, so when Geoffrey returns, I face him and wait for him to sit back down.

"Sam doesn't think you cheated on her," I say. "I keep replaying the bachelorette party over and over in my head, that moment when everything just got out of control. If any one detail had played out differently . . . If Sam hadn't had those last couple glasses of wine, if she hadn't tried to make fun of me in front of her friends, if I hadn't brought up your bachelor party to the girls and gotten them interested—"

"Mia, this isn't your fault," Geoffrey says, bunching his eyebrows together in confusion. "Even if you're the reason the girls got curious about what we were up to, Sam had her reaction all on her own."

"That's not what I'm trying to say." I take a deep breath, collecting my thoughts. I'm thinking about Sam and how, even with all the crazy things she's done, she's still my sister and I love her. I think about us decorating the Christmas tree together every year, when she showed me how to braid my hair, when she made brownies for my second-grade bake sale. "Sam doesn't always process her emotions. When she gets insecure or scared, she starts to push away anything that reminds her of those feelings. Like, when she was freaking out about the flowers. I think both of us know that she couldn't care less what kind of flowers she's holding, as long as she's holding them while walking down the aisle *to you*. It's like the flowers were a token of this wedding, a symbol of this huge unpredictable unstructured change in her life. She freaked out about the venue because the venue is where it's going to happen. She freaked out about me not going to her bridal shower because focusing on me not being there meant she didn't have to focus on being a bride.

"She loves you so, so much, and it's the greatest thing in her life, and simultaneously it terrifies her. So the bachelorette party was another time when she wasn't coping with her emotions and insecurities. She tried to deflect attention by talking about some of my embarrassing moments, and when things caught up to her, for the first time, she put her insecurities on you. She doesn't think you cheated on her. This is her trying to push you, to test if you're really going to hold, the way people test the planks on old bridges so that they know they aren't going to fall through.

"And I know that this close to the wedding, you shouldn't have to prove yourself. But I mean, you aren't. Not really. She loves you. She trusts you. I think the only reason she did it is because she knew it wasn't true and that you would reassure her of that. Which you did, but what she wasn't expecting was for you to also leave. You can't be a broken plank, because if you are, then . . . I don't think you deserve her."

I realize only as I'm saying this that Sam coming after me, getting me grounded, was her weird and twisted way of trying to pull me closer to her. She asked me to help with the wedding, to go to the fitting—just the two of us—to stay up late with her to plot and plan, and I've been pushing her off. I haven't really given her a chance to talk for the past couple of months, and all she's been doing is crying for help. And similarly, I've been talking to everyone but her about the one thing she understands better than my friends—and that's how to begin and hold on to a good relationship. I've been scared that she would either revel in my failures—which I know isn't true—or stress out if I came to her with my meet-cute problems. But I should've given her a chance to be there for me, just like I need to be there for her.

I take a breath and keep going. "You guys were about to—and hopefully still will—make vows to stay together through thick and thin. I think this is one of those thin moments when you have a choice. I think she needs to grow *with you* and know that she can lean on you in times when she's vulnerable. You're her favorite person, and the hardest part about having jitters about this big huge life change is the fact that the change is you—so she hasn't been able to talk to you about any of it. She's feeling vulnerable about you."

"So, she should share that with me. She shouldn't try to push me away—"

"And you're right," I say quickly. "You're absolutely right. So, talk to her. Call her! Just let her know that you're here. Tell her she can't push you away."

I realize that I want someone who wants me the way that Sam and Geoffrey want each other. For who I am, whether or not I answer every math question correctly, whether or not I win every swim meet, and whether or not I have some big lavish thing to give them.

I'd rather go to Sam's wedding by myself or be stuck with Jasper than go with someone like Ben, because even Jasper pays attention to me. Then again, he does have that girlfriend now . . .

"Mia," Geoffrey says.

"Yeah?"

"You don't think it's too late? You don't think *I've* pushed her too far away?"

"No," I say, completely sure. "She still loves you; she still wants to marry you. She just needs to know you want the same—so that I can sleep tonight."

Geoffrey laughs a little, looking over toward the window. His gaze stops short, and I follow it to some more clothes in the other corner of the room. He starts looking around, as if he's waking up from that bad dream he was living in where he didn't clean his apartment for nearly a week and lived like a depressed single man.

"You might want to clean up a little before you call her, so that if she says she's ready to come back today, she won't have to walk into this," I tell him, standing up.

"Right," Geoffrey agrees, looking more stressed, but happier every second.

He walks me to the door and I give him a hug, trying not to breathe too deep, once I realize there's a good chance he hasn't showered either. In my car I check my phone to see that Dad tried texting and both my parents called. I don't want to tell them yet. I want Sam to be the first person to hear from Geoffrey.

CHAPTER TWENTY-FIVE

close the front door behind me as quietly as I can, looking to the den and in the direction of the kitchen. I was expecting Mom or Dad to be waiting by the door, phone in hand, reviewing their texts and missed calls as evidence of my suspect behavior. But I don't even hear anyone talking or moving around.

I take my chances and start walking upstairs, trying to avoid the steps that I know will creak under my weight. As I ascend farther into the house, I hear the dull sound of the shower in the hallway bathroom. I peek through the banister beams and stop before reaching the top few steps, taking advantage of my still-hidden position.

So, someone is showering and my parents are nowhere to be—

"Yes, keep everything as is." Mom's voice scares me so much, I nearly fall back down the stairs. She comes out of her room with her phone pressed to her ear and a huge smile on her face. "Don't cancel a thing. I mean, you shouldn't have cancelled anything in the first place because I said it was only a slight possibility—"

Mom stops at the top of the stairs, and her face contorts. She doesn't know whether to start disciplining me or to share her happiness with me because the wedding is happening for sure.

"Oh, no, I'm still here," she says, waving me the rest of the way upstairs before turning around and pacing to the end of the hallway. "Yes, we will be there next Saturday for the rehearsal, and Sunday will be the wedding."

I go into my room and take off my coat and shoes, then pause when I hear the shower stop and shuffling in the bathroom.

"Mom," Sam says, sounding like her usual authoritative self. "Mom, make sure they know to set up by noon."

Sam stops in my doorway. Her head snaps to the side and she stares at me, bent over trying to wrestle my left boot off.

"Mia," she says, though the word comes out like a deep breath. "Mia, what did you do?" She smiles at me and runs up to me and pulls me to her. "What did you say, how did you do it?"

"Do what?" I ask into the fuzzy shoulder of her robe.

"Geoffrey said you came by and you said some stuff that put things into perspective," Sam explains, leaning away from me so that she can see my face.

I take her in, skin glistening with coconut oil, hair wrapped in a silk bonnet smelling of argan oil and eucalyptus. Her eyebrows are brushed, each hair falling in that weirdly perfect way that makes her face look so put together. Her eyes aren't puffy and her lips aren't dry and her nose is no longer red.

"I feel like if he wanted you to know, he would've told you," I say, laughing a little.

She stares at me for a moment, probably battling inside about whether or not she should push me to talk. "I don't even care," she says. "I mean, thank you. Thank you. Thank you."

"Mia," Mom says, walking into the room and shoving her phone into her back pocket.

"I'm sorry for sneaking off and ignoring your texts," I say.

I feel Sam's grip on me tighten. "Mom, please don't be mad at her for this. She saved my relationship, my wedding."

Mom just smiles, looking between us. "I'm not mad that you went to Geoffrey's. You shouldn't have been sneaky about it, but I'm glad you were able to smooth things over."

"Where's Dad?" Sam asks.

"Geoffrey called him and asked him to come over and help him with something."

I decide to test my luck and ask, "Since I saved the wedding, does that mean I'm un-grounded?"

"Oh yeah," Sam says. "Wait, Mom. Please un-ground her. I feel bad. She wouldn't even be in this mess if it weren't for me."

"Yes, she would," Mom says, frowning a little for having to be the bad guy. "Mia chose to sneak out, and she has to take responsibility for that . . . until your father says otherwise."

"You guys wouldn't have even reacted so dramatically if I hadn't made such a big deal out of it," Sam says defensively.

"Still, Samantha, that doesn't change the fact that it happened. It doesn't change the fact that Mia put herself in a dangerous situation. You keep saying she needs to grow up and be more adult. Part of that is owning up to the wrongs she's committed, and accepting the consequences of her actions." Mom's stern tone lets me know she's serious.

"Do you know when it might be over, though?" I ask before Sam can try to rally for me anymore.

"I can talk to your father," Mom says, sighing. "Just keep up your good behavior. . . . I mean, honestly, he might not even remember you're still grounded. . . ." Mom's phone vibrates, and she pulls it out of her pocket. "Now this is the baker. I have to take this."

When Mom leaves the room, Sam picks up my hands and squeezes them gently.

"I'm sorry."

"It's fine," I say. "Like she said, you didn't *make* me sneak out. I was mad at you . . . for putting me in a position to find a date when I felt like you didn't even think I would be able to. I felt like you were bossing me around with these impossible expectations, and sometimes I felt like you were amused, and I just wanted a break. I wanted to pick something for me instead of feeding into this—this game—"

"Mia," Sam says, but her voice comes out in a whisper.

The way she cuts me off reminds me of how Gavin is definitely right about me being a nervous rambler. "Mia, that's not at all how I felt, how I feel. I mean, I believe in you so much. I didn't think it was funny. I wanted you to step out of your comfort zone, and I really did hope you would find someone you might actually like posing in pictures with, and sitting next to at the head table for most of the night."

She looks down at her hands before mumbling, "But I guess, at times, I did get bitter, too. Sometimes I feel like no one pushes you, and I want you to always be moving forward."

"And I am," I say, surprising myself. "I don't think Mom and Dad have to push me. Growing up, I don't think they necessarily had to push you as hard as they did. I think you would've turned out just fine. But you don't have to worry about me like that. You don't have to try so hard to do things for me. You're my big sister, but I'm not as little as I used to be."

She smiles, a lopsided, bashful but real smile. Not her picture-perfect smile but the Sam smile that used to come out when she got a milkshake brain freeze or when Mom would hand her fresh watermelon at a picnic. The Sam Hubbard smile, not the Davenport ArchiTech Wedding Planner smile.

"I really am sorry that you're grounded, and that I can't fix it. I mean, all the times I snuck out in high school and we ran into each other on the stairs in the middle of the night, you could've told on me. But you didn't."

"I guess we handle things differently," I tell her. "Speaking of which, I'm sorry too. I know you always act a little odd when something is bothering you, and I've been ignoring all your signals and I'm sorry. I want you to be able to come to me and talk about stuff, especially when you can't talk to Geoffrey."

"I love you," she says, wrapping her arm around my shoulders.

I picture her with these same tears in her eyes in just over a week. It feels impossible, how close the wedding is. I feel like it snuck up on us. I imagine Sam with happy tears, only she'll be staring into Geoffrey's eyes. I'll be standing right behind her holding her bouquet and watching as they vow to accept all the crazy and all the love between them.

Which reminds me . . . "Sam, I have to tell you something." She raises her eyebrows, bracing for another potential wedding disaster. "I don't have a date to your wedding after all."

"Wait, what happened to the math guy?"

"He was playing me, made me feel like a complete idiot," I admit, moving over to sit down on my bed. I ended up finally texting Ben my decision on my way home from Geoffrey and Sam's apartment. He just responded with K.

"Mia, you're not an idiot."

"I know, which is why I don't want to spend one of the happiest days of our lives being with someone who thinks that I am."

Sam's shoulders sag. She looks down at her freshly painted toenails, spreading them out in thought.

"If it really does help, I can walk down the aisle with Jasper."

"I'm not going to make you do that," she says, a sly smile spreading across her lips. "I mean, you would rather walk down the aisle with Darth Vader, and that says something."

We both laugh.

"But really, I'll find a way to make it work. I want you to be happy too, Mia. I hope you know that."

"I do," I tell her, feeling the weight lift off my shoulders.

I decide to try my best to be Sam's maid of honor like she originally wanted me to be. I update all the bridesmaids to let them know that the situation from the bachelorette party has blown over, that Sam is tremendously sorry they all had to see her in such a state, but that the wedding is still on. I tell them what time to show up at the venue for the rehearsal dinner, and confirm that Brooke has a date for the wedding. She tells me that it's no longer Josh but a man named Jordan. I tell her I don't care, she just has to make sure he confirms what meal he wants for dinner.

Sam and I review every tabbed page in her wedding binder. She shows me photographs of the final floral arrangements for every table. She brings me home a sample of the final cake she decided on. Unfortunately, it's not the red velvet, but the devil's food chocolate flavor she decided to go with is equally as good.

Tuesday night is the best night because we finally sit in front of the Christmas tree and reminisce about the ornaments. When we get to our spray-painted macaroni picture frames, we call Mom downstairs to take a look. Dad comes into the den to feed his fish, and he ends up sitting with us too. When we finish, Mom and Dad go upstairs and Sam and I heat up apple cider on the stove. We pour it into mugs with whole cinnamon sticks and return to the den to settle in on the couch for a movie.

"Maybe I can see if they'll let your friends come over for a movie night," Sam offers as I click through the different movies on Netflix.

"Yeah, I feel so bad. We haven't been able to have a movie night in weeks," I say. But I know it's my own fault.

Sam takes a sip of her apple cider, and I stop at a movie called *One Day*. Anne Hathaway is one of my favorite actresses.

"Have you seen this one before?" I ask, clicking play after I finish reading the description.

"No," she says, pulling a blanket off the back of the couch. We each use one end to cover our legs, and I sink into the corner cushions of the couch, resting my head to the side.

The movie follows two friends from the day that they meet, and on that same day every year after. We see how through their struggles, growth, and life changes, they stay together. How they return to each other as friends with an undeniable love. At different moments in their lives they contemplate romantic love with each other, but they never seem to be thinking about it—wanting it—at the same time.

I like the movie because it's not funny; it's real. They spend all these years building a foundation of friendship so that when they do finally come together romantically, they're ready. They're better versions of themselves, the best versions, and that makes for a better love. All the work that they put into their friendship, all the patience, makes the end so painful. But, at the same time, that end is true of all great loves. Whether someone dies abruptly or at the end of a long life, every relationship is broken up when one person is no longer alive to be in it.

By the end, Sam's apple cider is cold and unfinished, and her head is tilted back with her mouth wide open. I'm left to watch the credits roll and think about how friendship is such an important foundation to love. I try to think about what guy friends I have that I could possibly build something like this with, and only one face comes to mind. A face with a full beard, dark brown eyes, and an easy smile. The face of someone who already has a girlfriend.

CHAPTER TWENTY-SIX

After I pull the blanket tighter around Sam, I head upstairs and I FaceTime my friends to make a proposition.

"One final go . . . ," Sloane says, chewing her lip.

Her and Abby's faces are pixelated on my phone. Grace's is coming through clearer in her little FaceTime box.

"And you're sure this is a good idea, given that he's already proven to be . . . questionable?" Grace asks, applying rose-hip oil to her face, since she just showered.

"I don't know. After nearly running him over, I think he deserves a second chance," I say, laughing a little.

"She has a point there," Sloane acknowledges.

"So, how do we make this work while you're still grounded?" Abby asks, which is the reason why I called this emergency meet-cute meeting so late at night.

"That's what we have to figure out," I say. I get up from my bed and go over to my desk, where the lighting is better.

"Maybe if your parents won't let you go out, he could come to you?" Grace proposes.

"But how could she have a date at her house?" Sloane asks.

Abby begins to suggest, "Well, maybe it shouldn't be a 'date.' More like—"

"I could invite him over to study?" I figure it makes sense, since finals start tomorrow. Plus, the only way my parents would actually let me hang out with someone is if it's something school related. And this way I have an actual reason to invite Ritchie over, other than, *Oh, I just want to see if I like you enough to invite you to a wedding at the last minute.*

"But your parents won't let any of us come over to study," Abby points out.

"So, tell them he's your partner for a class project. Make it seem like you can't study without him there," Sloane says.

Grace and Abby nod in agreement, and Sloane leans back, feeling proud.

So I text Ritchie to ask if he might want to come over to help me study for my history exam. I tell him that since I'm still grounded, I'd have to tell my parents we're working on a project together or something.

I'm in, he says.

After school on Wednesday, I feel a little nervous but not nearly as much as I did a couple of months ago. My parents agreed that Ritchie could come over right after school for a little while and that we could sit in the dining room to do work. I told Sam about my plan, and she promised to keep Dad busy and told Mom she would come to the house after work, so that Mom could go to the garden and finish up one of her projects before it gets too cold.

So when Ritchie comes into the kitchen after setting out his textbooks, and opens the fridge, making himself at home, I feel excited and a little self-conscious. He told me that he's never tried a matcha latte, so I put ice into two glasses and start brewing some hot water from the Keurig to make the matcha paste.

"Are these apples up for grabs?" he asks, reaching for a bottle of water.

"Definitely. Almost anything in there is free game," I say. "Just don't eat Sam's super salad. She's very territorial over that."

"Noted."

I pour some milk over the ice and feel Ritchie watching as I pour the matcha. The way the green descends over the white, mixing in slowly, is kind of mesmerizing.

"That looks cool," he says when I hand him his glass. He takes a sip and adds, "Thank you."

We go back into the dining room, and I sit down in front of my computer with my digital study guide, open textbook beside me, ready to focus. Ritchie starts crunching on his apple, and I realize how quiet the house is. I know Sam is up in her room, and after Dad said hi to Ritchie, he went into the den to check on his fish. Even so, it feels like we are completely alone.

Before, it was so easy to talk to him about—well—

anything. Now that I have something specific that I want to say, I don't know how to start a conversation. I can't just jump in and ask him to the wedding, at least not without context. Then again, he already knows about the meet-cute stuff and that I'm not going with Ben anymore.

I sneak glances at him, hoping he doesn't notice. He's wearing jeans and a blue-and-green flannel. He got a haircut, so now it's almost a buzz. It makes him look older. The more I picture him walking me down the aisle, the more my brain keeps switching up the image with Gavin. Ritchie is taller than Gavin, so I'd have to tilt my head really far back if we slow-dance. Gavin is also more attractive, with his full lips and his curly beard. But Ritchie is single and Gavin has a girlfriend. So I need to get Gavin out of my head and focus.

"Ritchie," I say, but it comes out at the same time that he says my name.

I blush, wondering if it's at all possible that he was reading my mind just then.

"What's up?" I ask, pulling my latte closer to take a long sip.

"There's something that I've been wanting to talk to you about," he admits. He looks down at his book and starts fidgeting with his pencil. His nerves begin to make me nervous.

"What is it?"

"Well, I know that when we first met, there was something there. And since then I feel like we've become more like friends."

He pauses, watching for my reaction.

"Yeah?" I say, agreeing. "Yeah, I feel like we are better as friends."

He lets out a deep breath, relieved. Then he smiles and looks at me the same way he looked at me when he talked about his family. He's comfortable again, and I feel the same sense of familiarity that brought us close so fast.

"There's this girl that I've kind of been talking to. She's in my biology class, and I've been trying to figure out how to talk to her, and—well—she's on the swim team. And I was wondering if maybe you knew anything about her that could help me out—like, if she's single, if she likes going to the movies, or what she likes to eat."

His leg bounces under the table and he rubs his palms on his jeans. He's cute when he's nervous—not cute in an *I like you* way, but cute in a *My friend likes a girl* kind of way. That initial spark between us has completely faded, but it's been replaced with ease. Boyfriends, you have to win over. It should never be a lot of work, but you might have to trade in your jeans and hoodies for a cute dress. You might have to hold back all your baggage on the first few dates before it's okay to open up. But boy *friends* don't take that much. You can be yourself, all the good and bad parts—the insecurities—up front. And if you vibe together, then you vibe. Then you can talk about your sister's wedding and plotting meet-cutes, or your parents' divorce and how you miss your brothers who are right in front of you.

"You, my friend," I say, smiling, "are a nervous rambler."

CHAPTER TWENTY-SEVEN

S ince I finished all my papers in advance, when the bell rings after history on Thursday, I am officially done with the first semester of my junior year. Grace meets me at my locker after school and follows me out to my car in the student parking lot. I hand her my phone to pick what music we listen to while I drive, feeling a little self-conscious about the fact that Gavin and I have been texting since I thanked him for the advice about going to Geoffrey. We've been talking about everything and nothing.

The first time I texted him after he gave me his number was after I got home from Geoffrey's and Sam and I stayed up strategizing how to make up for lost time and get all the bridesmaids back on the same page. I was excited to tell him the plan worked, but sad to say I wouldn't be going to the garden on Friday since I would be going home from school to do more wedding stuff with Sam.

Since then, we've mainly talked about studying for finals. Today, I've already told him that I think I did well on my history exam, bad on my biology final. He thinks he did average in calculus and maybe better than he thought he would in chemistry, but both of us are aching for our grades to come in. I sent him pictures of the candy Sloane snuck into study hall for all of us, since we didn't have any work to do.

His name pops up on my screen whenever I receive a text, and I can tell Grace definitely notices.

"So," she says, drawing out the O.

"Yes?"

"What ever happened to Darth Vader?" She turns the music down and looks at me.

"I honestly forgot that he even existed. I have no idea."

"He never texted you after the night at the diner?"

"No," I say, glad that I don't feel sad about it like I used to. I deleted our conversation after Sam used it as the butt of her joke at the bachelorette party. I figured since Darth was old news anyways, he deserved to be out of sight and out of mind.

"I kinda wanna know who he was."

"You were acting like he was some child predator!" I laugh in disbelief.

"Okay, okay," she relents. "But what if he wasn't? What if he *is* someone we know? What if he goes to our school and we see him every day—"

"What if it's Victor?"

"Mia, don't be ridiculous."

"Why not? You sound ridiculous."

Grace shakes her head and goes back to picking the music. I ask if she can play "Heart" by RKS. She moans and groans, but when the guitar starts strumming through my speakers, she gets quiet and I relax.

"Gavin is that guy from the garden, right?" she asks when the song ends.

I glance down and notice a text notification sliding off my screen.

"Yeah," I say, sounding more casual than self-conscious.

"Sloane said he seems pretty cool."

I let the statement hang in the air between us, not sure where she's going.

"He's been texting you," she says, flipping my phone over in her hand. "I haven't read anything, so don't worry."

I'm glad that she drops it, since I'm not really in the mood to talk about how I kind of like Gavin even though he has a girlfriend. No reason to speak problems into existence. Grace picks a few songs by Lauren Sanderson before turning down the music again.

"Are you okay?" she asks.

"Yeah, why?"

"I don't know. You just seem different," she says, watching the people crossing the street in front of us. They're coming from the one ice cream stand that stays open year-round. How anyone would want to walk around in the cold with freezing-cold ice cream in their freezing-cold hand is beyond me.

"Like, you haven't been busy after school with swim practice, and you haven't really talked much about Sam— which I guess is a good thing. . . ."

I can feel her watching me now.

"Swim season is over," I say.

"Yeah, but you always go to the boys' conditioning," she says awkwardly. "Like, you never let the season end when it's actually over."

"Well, it's time to try something different with my free time," I say, though I can tell it's not that convincing.

"Did you hit your head or something?" she asks, laughing a little.

"No," I say, smiling. "I guess I realized that there's more to life than hiding underwater. I've spent so much time doing homework after school and watching movies about adventure and romance. If I go outside, I could *have* an adventure. I might fall in love."

Grace stares at me for a second, frowning.

"I'm gonna have to dig my Mia manual out of my closet, because clearly you're malfunctioning."

"Or maybe I'm just changing," I offer, slowing my car to a stop in front of her house.

"Again, super weird. Super *not* Mia," she says, gathering her backpack from between her feet. When she closes the door behind her, I roll down the window, and she bends over to say, "Call me when you've rebooted, okay?"

"Go inside," I tell her, laughing. I watch her disappear down her driveway before I head home.

On Friday, before I leave school, I stop by Shannon's locker and give her a note. When she asks who it's from, I tell her that I was given specific instructions not to reveal any information, that I'm just the messenger. I add that between us, the guy who wrote the note is one of the good ones. I walk away feeling excited for both Ritchie and Shannon.

Gavin and I have another productive day at the garden, sanding down the table in the back of the greenhouse and brainstorming different uses for it. We could set it up as a stand where we could sell vegetables in this summer. Or, if there's enough money, we could get an electric stove top and some cooking supplies and have a kind of chef's table where people can pay to come and pick veggies and make their own meal. He mentions that my mom came through the greenhouse earlier this week to check on our progress and said it would be a great place to have a wedding, which I find ironic. Maybe if the greenhouse had been up and running a few months ago, Sam might have thought to have her wedding here. She and Geoffrey did fall in love designing a greenhouse.

We've been sitting on an extra burlap sack on the floor of the greenhouse, with hot chocolates from Starbucks. Gavin turns to me, his expression serious. Without a word he pulls two tickets out of the breast pocket of his jacket and hands them to me. They're for the Rainbow Kitten Surprise concert tonight at the Riviera Theatre, a beautiful old-fashioned gem with red velvet seats and gold detailing along the ceiling and walls of the concert hall. He explains that they're a gift from Gloria, for him finishing a couple of his final essays early.

"Oh my gosh," I gush. "Gavin, this is awesome. You are so lucky. Rainbow Kitten Surprise?"

He smiles at me, his eyes twinkling. I wouldn't be able to stop smiling either if I had the opportunity of a lifetime tucked into my pocket.

"Gavin, do you even *know*?" I ask. "Like, this is so cool."

"Come with me," he says, setting his cup down on the ground.

"I'm grounded," I remind him, realizing Mom never got back to me after she spoke with Dad. I feel a hole pierce through my chest. Of course I have to be grounded on the night of an RKS concert, right here in Chicago.

"Why don't you just ask?" he pleads.

"Why don't you take your girlfriend?" I ask. "I know I love RKS, but whether or not they're her thing, she'd probably love to just go with you."

"She—uh—has a family thing tonight . . . ," he says, picking up a twig. He starts twisting it into the ground, and I realize that without her, he might not have anyone else to go with. RKS is amazing, but none of my friends listen to—or like—their music either.

"Gavin, I really wish I could. But my parents have already said no to so many other things. I doubt they're going to let me go to a concert."

I turn the tickets over in my hands, savoring the fact that this is how close I'll get to an RKS concert for right now.

"Mia, if you don't even try, then of course the answer is

going to be no," he says, raising his eyebrows because he knows he's right.

"Gavin, I just don't want to be told no again. Plus, I feel like if I keep bugging her with it, she might tell my dad and make my grounding longer."

"Your mom doesn't strike me as the type," he says, sipping his hot chocolate. He's the kind of person who takes the lid off instead of drinking it through the lid hole.

"And what kind of person do you think she is?" I ask, watching the warm steam waft against his face.

"The kind of person who can be swayed."

He's definitely not wrong about that, but when it comes to the decisions she and my dad make together, there's usually no budging.

"What are you going to do?" I ask, realizing that if I were him, I would be torn between not wanting to go alone and not wanting to waste the chance to see RKS.

When I hand the tickets back to Gavin, he looks at them, shuffling them in his hands like cards. Without a word he hops up, forgetting the lid to his Starbucks. I grab it and stumble after him out of the greenhouse into the evening winter darkness. We make our way to the floodlights at the other end of the garden grounds, and Gavin squints until he finds Gloria and my mom gathering supplies that were left out.

"Mrs. Hubbard," Gavin says, holding the tickets in his hand.

"Yes, Gavin?" Mom looks up, surprised to see us both

standing here. She brushes her hands off on her jeans.

"I have a request. You see, since I finished all of my finals, my grandma got me these tickets to see my favorite band, Rainbow Kitten Surprise, tonight. And none of my friends like them. My friends think their music is weird and don't value the lyrics like I do. But Mia knows the band. She's proven to me that she really listens to them and understands them on the kind of level of a fan who would deserve the concertgoing experience.

"And I know that she's grounded for making some poor choices that even I myself tried to talk her out of. However, she is also finished with her finals, and my understanding is that she's gotten good grades this semester like myself. I think, in spite of her mistake, that both of us are responsible, good kids, and—well—I'm wondering if there's any way she could come to the concert with me so that my gift won't go to waste, because not only would I waste the one ticket if I go alone, but I don't know if I really feel comfortable going alone. Because—"

"Gavin," Gloria cuts him off. "You're going to talk Beth's ear off with all that."

We watch my mom, and she starts to laugh, her breath disappearing into the air in front of her face. Gavin turns to look at me for any clue as to whether this is a good sign, but I don't know. She doesn't usually laugh like this.

"What do you think, Gloria?" Mom asks, leaning her weight against a pitchfork stuck in the ground.

"I mean, Gavin has worked really hard in school and

with the greenhouse, and that's why I gave him the tickets. And without Mia we wouldn't have finished everything that fast."

"What time is this concert?" Mom asks.

"At seven," Gavin says, hopeful.

Mom looks at me, and with Gavin's back to me, I bring my hands together and mouth *Please* over and over.

"Home by eleven," she says, staring into Gavin's soul. "Any later, and both of you will have us to answer to."

"What? So I can go?" I ask. "Should I record this in case Dad tries to say otherwise? Like, oh my gosh!" I turn to Gavin, and his jaw is already dropped. "I have to go get ready!" I say, looking at my watch. It's already 5:06.

We help Mom and Gloria put the supplies away, and then all four of us walk to our cars in the parking lot. By six fifteen he has texted me that he's on his way, and Sam is helping me do my hair. She's pulled my hair apart so that it's half-up, half-down. The top half is six cornrows going back into a loose ponytail. The bottom is out and natural, crunchy and soft from her thorough argan oiling.

By the time I hear the front door open, Sam is touching my eyelashes up with mascara and I'm clasping a necklace. I'm wearing a black T-shirt dress with an equally long gray sweater and a pair of brown Chelsea boots with a slight heel. Sam is lending me her tiny elephant pendant necklace and a pair of gold hoops.

"He came up to the door," Sam notes, giving me a suggestive side-eye as she puts her makeup away.

"He knows Mom," I tell her, running to put away my hot air brush.

Sam follows me downstairs, and in the entryway are our parents and Gavin. Gavin is wearing a pair of black jeans, a turquoise T-shirt, and his corduroy jacket. On his feet are the same pair of mustard-yellow Vans that I have.

"That's interesting because Mia's sister and her fiancé are working on an agricultural project. I'm surprised Beth hasn't mentioned it to you," Dad is saying as I put my coat on.

Even though Dad is talking to Gavin, Gavin is staring at me.

"Hey," I say, taking him in, taking in the fact that we are about to go see our favorite band in concert.

"Hey," he says, shrugging a little.

"Remember, by eleven," Mom says.

"Of course," Gavin says, returning his attention to my parents.

"And no funny business," Sam adds.

I turn to her, both to glare and to hide the blush rising to my cheeks. "Sam," I hiss.

We say good-bye to everyone and duck out the door. Even though my family is just a couple of inches of wood away, I feel relieved once we're outside. I wave Gavin over to follow me when he starts down the walkway to the driveway. I remember running down the front lawn on my way to meet Darth Vader, and now I can take my time. I'm not doing anything wrong, and as I look back at the grass glistening with frozen water droplets and see Gavin's familiar Vans, tonight feels right too. Right, but too late for me to try to make it something more.

"You have your own car?" I ask when we arrive at an old blue Ford pickup truck.

"Yes?" he says, like he's surprised I didn't know.

"I've only seen you getting into Gloria's little car," I remind him, stepping past him when he holds open the passenger door for me.

Once he's in the car, he hooks his phone up to the FM transmitter for his radio and starts scrolling through his Spotify.

"I don't know what music we should listen to," he admits, still looking down at his phone. "I mean, my reflex is to start with some Rainbow Kitten Surprise, but we're about to go see them and I don't want to spoil it. I want the concert to be the first time I listen to them today."

"True, good point," I say.

We decide to listen to Fickle Friends and COIN. When "Growing Pains" comes on, I have to restrain myself from belting along to the lyrics, both so that I don't embarrass myself and so that I'll still have a voice for the concert. I ask Gavin if he's seen RKS live before, and he says no. He's seen some heavy metal concerts with his friends, and he went to a Yanni concert with Gloria a couple of years ago. But he's never gone to a concert for his music.

"Nicest fans you'll ever meet," he tells me about the heavy metal. "Just not really my kind of scene."

We fall silent for some time, listening to the music. I

watch Lake Michigan flying by as Gavin looks for our exit off 41. When we rejoin local traffic, I'm surprised by the amount of people and cars moving throughout the neighborhoods and side streets.

Gavin decides to park in a neighborhood a couple of blocks away from the theater so that we won't have to pay any jacked-up fees. When he turns off the car, we look at each other and take a deep breath. Then we're out of the car and walking.

"Thanks, by the way," I say as I loop my wrist through his elbow so we don't lose each other in the crowd of people pushing their way toward the theater.

"For what?" he asks, shouldering our way toward the Riviera neon lights.

"For thinking of me when you got the tickets, and for getting me a much needed night of freedom."

Gavin laughs a little, his smile stretching so that his eyes squint.

"I figured your mom wouldn't be able to say no to me."

"Oh really? That's a pretty bold assumption."

"I feel like you underestimate her," he says, holding the door open for me.

I savor the warm air as I feel blood return to my face and fingers. Gavin takes a second to shove his gloves into his pockets and then pulls out our tickets.

"Maybe you're right," I tell him after we're directed to our seats.

"Plus, let's face it, your mom loves me."

"What could possibly make you think that?" I ask as Gavin points to a couple of seats on the end of a row. I'm relieved that we get to sit on the end. Part of me wonders if Gloria planned it that way. She seems like an end-of-the-row kind of person. All my friends like to sit in the middle, but if we sit on the end, then we don't have to step over a bunch of people when we have to go to the bathroom, and we don't have to wait for anyone to move if there's an emergency.

We're in the middle section of the balcony, third row from the front. I think, in a theater like this, with high ceilings, that balcony seats are the best. We can see perfectly, and we'll hear the music right as it bounces off the wall.

When I peel my eyes away from the ceiling, I find Gavin staring at me, smiling.

"Good seats?" he asks, even though I think he already knows the answer. When I nod, he goes back to my previous question. "Well, there's the fact that she brings me coffee on days when you're not there. She always asks me about school, and I ask her about retired life. Honestly? I think she's in love with me."

We both can't help but laugh at the thought.

"What does she say, though? About being retired."

"I feel like I'd be breaking girl code if I tell you Beth's inner thoughts," Gavin admits.

"Well, it's a good thing you're not a girl."

"Touché," he says, having to yell a little as the theater fills up. "But she asks about you. She asks if you mention what's going on in your life. She's worried she isn't connecting with you."

Not what I was expecting.

"And what do you tell her?" I try to sound like I'm not panicking on the inside about the possibility that my mom has been getting fed crumbs about my ongoing boy crisis.

"I tell her that school is a normal continuous pressure, and that you're excited and nervous about the wedding."

I let out a sigh. "Good."

"She told me about Sam making you find a date to the wedding, and how she overheard you and your friends making a plan where they set you up on dates," he says as the lights go down.

I turn to him, probably looking like he just told me his dad is the Zodiac Killer, but as the openers take the stage, I lose my chance to respond. The theater erupts into cheers and applause. Even though I have a million questions, one being to ask when—exactly—my mom clued him in about my embarrassing quest, I stay calm. Gavin stands and starts clapping and shouting into the chaos, so I do too. Instead of being stressed and freaked out, I release everything I can into the abyss of noise. When RKS finally takes the stage, I fold myself into the familiar drumbeat and bass guitar that have put me to sleep, carried me to the community pool at dawn, given me a lifted heart, or held me when I was down.

I can't believe I'm in the same room as Rainbow Kitten Surprise. I can't believe they sing my favorite songs better live than on the recordings. When they play "First Class," Gavin and I turn to each other, our voices lost in the chorus, but our mouths clearly capturing each word. It's unreal, too fairy-tale-like, to get to have this experience.

By the time we reach Gavin's truck a couple of hours later, the ringing is fading and my hearing starts to come back. I look up at the sky from the street where we parked and can see the stars, a rarity in the city. He opens the passenger door for me and then runs around to the driver's side. We sit in silence for a few minutes to let the car warm up. I close my eyes and imagine myself back inside the concert hall. The memory is so fresh, and it's still a memory I can't believe I get to have.

"Safe to say that was amazing," Gavin huffs, pulling out of the parking space. "Do you want to pick the music on the way back?"

"Sure," I say, connecting my phone to his transmitter.

I can't help myself. I ask Gavin if we can listen to more RKS, as long as he isn't tired of them yet. He says that would be impossible, so I line up some of their best songs from tonight, some of which were songs I'd forgotten they had. At a low volume, I replay our amazing night, and let my eyes trace the cityscape out my passenger window. With the dashboard vents blowing hot air at me, it's hard not to let my eyes drift closed.

Time enters this warped state, and I feel like maybe I black out for part of the ride home, because suddenly I see the familiar shape of my house come into view. I look at the windows lit up in the kitchen and in my parents' room. Sam's car is still parked behind mine in the driveway. I turn back to look at the clock and see that it's only 10:37 p.m.

"Is it okay if we keep listening to music for a bit?" I ask, feeling a little nervous. "I just don't want tonight to end. I know that once I get out of the car, I go back to being a grounded girl whose sister is getting married in a couple days."

"And inside the car, you're a girl who just saw her favorite band in concert," Gavin says, understanding me.

We slip back into a comfortable silence as "Lady Lie" oozes from the speakers.

After a couple of songs, Gavin turns the music back down and asks, "So, after everything—like, Ben, Darth Vader . . . and Ben—did you end up finding someone to go to the wedding with?"

I laugh a little. "No," I say. "There were more guys than just them. I mean, my friends came up with this plan where they would set me up to meet guys—which, I almost forgot, my mom told you about. But, yeah, the whole point was for my friends to orchestrate the moment when I would meet the guy—you know, the 'meet-cute' moment—so that it was like the meet-cutes in their favorite movies." I watch for his reaction. He's surprised, maybe a little confused. "It was a nice idea, but I think it failed, because when it came to the stuff that mattered, I didn't really have anything in common with them."

"And, what stuff matters?" he asks, looking at me in a

way that makes me feel exposed, like he can see the parts of me he's been wanting to see.

I try to think, remembering what Harold said about allowing yourself to see more than what you think you need to see. "The ability to hold a good conversation, honesty, attention to detail, good taste in music, a good sense of self, some common interest that isn't forced."

"Forced?"

"Like, math, flirting with guys I barely know, pretending to understand anything about dogs—"

"Gardening?"

"No," I say quickly.

"But didn't your mom make you volunteer?"

"Yes," I say, trying to choose my words carefully. "But I didn't feel like I was being forced into it, not after we really started fixing the greenhouse."

Gavin nods but doesn't say anything. I wonder what he's thinking. I wonder if I made my feelings obvious or if I made things weird, or maybe if everything is in my head. The silence makes me feel awkward.

"First Class" comes on, so I reach for the volume knob, and accidentally bump Gavin's hand. I look up at him, ready to apologize, but when I find his eyes already staring into mine, I freeze. The air between us feels like strings being pulled tighter. It's like his face has its own force of gravity, or maybe my face has its own gravity. I just feel close to him, and I feel myself being pulled closer to him. His mouth opens slightly, and I find myself anticipating the words I hope come out. I want him to say he wants what I want—

"Mia!"

My muffled name startles me. I turn around in my seat to see Sam tapping on my window. She's wearing gingerbread-men pajamas and has a Sherpa blanket pulled tight around her shoulders. She points at the ground, her breath beginning to fog up the glass. Gavin presses the button to open the passenger window, letting a gust of cold air prickle my face.

"Hi," I say, trying not to sound too obviously annoyed.

"It's almost curfew," she huffs. "You don't want to get in more trouble. Come on."

I look at the clock, and she's right. I have two minutes to be inside the house.

"Thanks for tonight," I say, looking back at Gavin. I feel guilty and sorry knowing that he has a girlfriend even though nothing happened.

Sam pulls the door open for me, and when she shuts it after I've gotten out, she leans through the window and asks, "So, are you taking Mia to my wedding?"

Every hair on the back of my neck stands up. The urge to run up the front lawn and disappear into the house is strong, so strong, but I resist. When I turn around and see Gavin looking like he just saw a ghost, I have to interfere.

"Sam, no," I hiss. "He has a girlfriend."

"Oh?" She looks back and forth between us.

"Bye, Gavin," I say, pulling Sam up the lawn before she can say something else.

I drag her by her Sherpa blanket and wait until we are inside with the door locked and the porch light off. Then I turn to her and say, "That was totally on purpose."

"I swear it wasn't," she says, holding her hands up in surrender.

"I don't need you asking boys out for me, Sam."

"Mia, I'm sorry. I didn't think I was. I thought you were on a date."

"And what could possibly make you think that?"

"Oh, I don't know, Mia," she says sarcastically. "Maybe because the last time you asked me to do your hair and makeup, and you cared what I thought about your outfits, was when you were into—what's his name, Billy Sorg?"

She watches me, waiting for my comeback. I don't have one, though, because she's right. After Billy, I swore off boys, romance, and the entire notion of making yourself vulnerable to the mere possibility of heartbreak. Billy Sorg was my Harley, only Billy didn't just leave me for someone else. He kept me hidden. I was the shameful dirt-colored smudge on his otherwise-perfect white life. We "dated" in secret, though I don't know if that's what I would really call it. Starting in seventh grade, Valentine's Day became a big deal. Some of the older people in our grade were thirteen, and being an official teenager meant their parents thought it was more okay for them to date. So relationships started popping up here and there, and Valentine's Day was a day to go public with gifts, cards, and flowers. It was almost a month into—what I thought was—our relationship. He said he didn't want to tell anyone right away because his parents weren't okay with him dating until he was thirteen.

Since he turned thirteen at the beginning of February, I thought Valentine's Day was the perfect time to finally go public. I brought a card that I'd made myself, and a baseball cap that I'd gotten from the mall with the Bears logo on it. He was sitting at a lunch table before school with his friends, and when I gave him the gift, ready for everyone to finally know about us, he laughed at me. He wrapped his arm around Camille Ford's shoulders, twirling a piece of her blond hair around his finger, and said I was delusional. That my crush on him was cute.

After all this time, I've finally found a good—nice—guy who I don't think would ever do something like that. He has good hair, good taste in shoes and music, and the rare ability to hold an interesting conversation. So Sam is right to think I was on a date, because deep down I wanted it to be one. Only, Gavin is taken.

"Oh, goodie," Mom says, coming downstairs. "I thought I heard you both down here."

"She was home on time," Sam says, holding my gaze before looking at Mom.

"How was it?"

"Amazing," I say, because it was, and because I wish I could have more nights like this with Gavin.

CHAPTER TWENTY-EIGHT

On Saturday, the eve of the wedding, I watch Lake Michigan under the setting sun as we drive to the Butterfly Bed & Breakfast for the rehearsal dinner. Sitting in the back seat of Mom's car while she and Dad talk quietly in the front feels weird because I've gotten so used to Sam being around and ushering us to tastings and selection meetings. Heading to the rehearsal without her reviewing every step along the way feels off. I feel like a piece is missing. I always felt that way when she left for college and I had to get used to family time meaning three people instead of four. But I started getting used to her being around again, nagging in that familiar way that isn't always annoying. Sometimes it's just a reminder that she's there, with us.

The music playing from the speakers covers my parents' conversation like a light dusting of snow. Through the window, I see the houseboat lights, their colors twinkling on the water. I try to take a video to send to Gavin, but it comes out too blurry. Instead I text him that "Gypsy" by Fleetwood Mac is playing on the radio. He replies, calling it a classic.

I wonder what our song would be. What would it be like if "First Class" played at prom and I rested my arms over Gavin's shoulders, stood with my chest against his chest, my forehead tilted up to meet his tilted down. Sam told me that she and Geoffrey have a playlist of songs from different moments in their lives. She said that *their song* is "Jupiter Love" by Trey Songz, but that's inappropriate to play for their first dance at a wedding. I was surprised when she told me they'd chosen "I'll Be Seeing You" by Billie Holiday. That's a true classic, tasteful. That's probably the only detail of Sam's wedding that I'm jealous of.

The rehearsal itself is small. Mom and Dad sit off to the side while Sam directs me and her bridesmaids with Geoffrey and his groomsmen about how to walk down the aisle. We practice until we get it perfectly timed to the orchestral music she chose for her procession.

When Abby and Victor show up, they wave to me from the back of the heated tent and unfold some of the chairs waiting to be set up tomorrow. Soon Sloane and Grace trickle in, and I feel more excited with them there. Originally Sam didn't invite them to the rehearsal, but she changed her mind after deciding to let me go to the wedding without a date.

Even though the reception is going to be inside the precious temperature-controlled tent, Sam arranged for the rehearsal dinner to be inside the dining room of the inn. I sit at a table with my friends that ends up pushed close to the table my parents, Sam, Geoffrey, and his parents are all sitting at. Cheryl, Armao, and a few groomsmen push another table up against ours, and we end up with a long banquet-style-feast setting. It feels cozy and close as conversations float up and down the table the way a ripple flows through a slinky.

Eventually I tell my friends about how embarrassing it was when Sam asked Gavin if he was taking me to the wedding.

"I thought they were on a date," she says defensively. "I really wasn't trying to cause trouble."

"He probably didn't care, to be honest," I say, secretly wondering what he thought. Does the idea of him taking me to the wedding resonate at all in his imagination the way it does in mine?

"You guys have been talking a lot, though," Grace says before eating another spoonful of cake.

"What do you talk about?" Sloane asks.

"Music, mostly. We talk about the garden, school, the wedding—you know, normal stuff."

Sam sits back in her chair and looks between me and my friends. When she just stares, it makes me feel uncomfortable.

"What?"

"Nothing," she says, flashing me a familiar mischievous smile.

I roll my eyes, wondering what price I would have to pay to know her thoughts right now.

Sam reviews the plans for tomorrow with everyone,

pointedly telling my friends to arrive early with the wedding party to help out, before we all head our separate ways for the night. Sam follows us home in her car because she and Geoffrey want the first time they see each other tomorrow to be when Sam comes down the aisle.

Once we're all back at the house, Sam kicks off her stilettos in the entryway and leans against the wall. Mom tells us to change into our pajamas and meet her in the den. Mom comes down sometimes in the middle of the night when Dad snores too loud. Sam used to crash on the sofa when she'd sneak midnight snacks after staying up doing homework or reading. Sometimes they'd run into each other, and when I'd hear them talking, I would sneak to the bottom of the stairs and listen. One time, when I was eight, I fell asleep and Mom carried me back to my room and told me that the only person not invited to the secret girls' club is Dad and that I should come to the next secret meeting.

So sometimes we'd all end up in the den at one or two in the morning. Mom would make us hot milk and get Oreos out of the cabinet, and as I got older, I realized it was a twilight time of the night when Sam and I felt safe confiding in Mom the things we couldn't say during the day. Sam would mostly talk about boys; I would talk about my friends. After Sam moved away to college, whenever she was home for break, I wouldn't sleep at night. I would lie awake, specifically waiting to hear a door open or a floorboard creak. I didn't want to miss a chance to hear about her life far away from here, to know what she was doing.

Now by the time I get down there, Mom and Sam are tucked under blankets on opposite sides of the couch. They're each holding a mug of cocoa with whipped cream, marshmallows, and chocolate syrup. I grab my mug off the coffee table before sitting down in the middle and pulling the ends of their blankets over my legs.

"By the time we got to the wedding, your father and I couldn't have cared less. We wanted it to just be over so we could get to the part where we could spend our lives together. All we could think about was falling asleep together and being able to wake up and the first thing we saw be each other."

"Aww," Sam says, looking down at her cocoa, somewhere in her own thoughts.

"How did you know that Dad was the one?" I ask.

Mom smiles a big goofy smile, the kind of smile you can't control. You can't help yourself when you feel so happy that you smile like that.

"Oh, Mia," she says, though something in her voice makes it seem like she's saying it more to herself or to her memory. "Out of everyone I had ever dated, he just . . . I felt like I was returning to a place that I had once been a long time ago. Like everything I was missing was all there in him. And for him, all those missing pieces were with me. And together we created a whole that felt like home."

"I feel like that's how Geoffrey and I are," Sam says, chewing on a marshmallow. "He balances out my special brand of crazy."

"That's a godsend," Mom confirms, making Sam gasp and me laugh.

Part of me wants to text Gavin and ask him how he and his girlfriend met. I want to ask him what her name is, what she looks like, what school she goes to. I realize that my curiosity is something I've been burying, and it's been easy, since Gavin and I don't see each other every day. But if we're going to be friends, I know she's a part of him that I'll have to accept and like.

Still, I want to ask if he thinks she's the one. I hope that he would say she's not, and that maybe I could ask him what he thinks about finding the one person you're meant to be with the same way you find your way back to some familiar place.

CHAPTER TWENTY-NINE

Sunlight slants through my window, casting a pink hue around my room as the light bounces off my white walls. It looks peaceful, and in the rays of light tumbling to the floor, I can see little dust particles floating around. I can see all the little tiny bits of nothing that exist all the time even though we can't always see them. In the quiet I wonder if Sam is awake on the other side of our wall. I wonder if she got up and did yoga, or if she made a smoothie for breakfast, or if she went for a quick run, or if she's redoing her nails because she decided at the last minute that a darker shade of green would be perfect.

I expect to open my door to the familiar color-coded tornado of wedding planner Sam, but instead I find an empty hallway. Still, there's excitement in the air. It's the same as when I would wake up first on Christmas, ready for presents even though everyone else was still sleeping.

I knock lightly on Sam's door. Nothing. I twist the knob silently and open the door just a crack to find her still in bed. She's lying on her stomach, a drool stain starting to widen on her pillow.

"Aw—"

"AH!" I shriek.

"GRAPES!" Sam yells.

"What?" Mom and I ask, opening Sam's door wider.

"Sorry," Mom says, rubbing my shoulder.

"Good morning?" I say, smiling at Sam, who now has no choice but to rub the sleep out of her eyes and get out of bed.

"I was having a dream about the grocery store," Sam explains through her yawn.

"Makes sense," Mom says. "I'll go wash off some grapes."

"It's prime wedding time!" I say, jumping up and down. "You're about to be Sam Hubbard Davenport, prin*cess* of jam."

"Ha ha, you're so funny," Sam says, her voice hoarse and monotone.

"I'll go make coffee in addition to those grapes," I say, leaving her be.

With all of us up, the house comes to life. Sam and Dad shower first while Mom and I get coffee and breakfast figured out. Then we eat together. Mom and I leave the table early to go shower and get dressed in our sweatpants and tennis shoes. Dad just puts on his suit because he doesn't see the point in changing at the inn when he can just be ready. Mom mumbles something about him needing to be more helpful, while she pours another cup of coffee into a travel mug.

We pile into the car and I text my friends to make sure

they're on the way. Before I put my phone away, I text Gavin an excited emoji saying, Today is the day. Brooke is already at the inn, dressed and standing out front when we arrive. She's holding a tablet in the crook of her elbow and has on tennis shoes that—interestingly enough—work with the bridesmaid's dress.

She's in charge of directing people about where and how to park and where to go once they've gotten out of their cars. Since the inn is only meant for a small number of guests, we had to get approval to park in the driveways and on the lawn. Sam and I hustle inside to the dressing room, where Sam's hair gets pressed and curled; her eyes are painted with powder to become an earthy-tone-with-green smokey eye; and her lips are shaped, moistened, and polished to look like a rich-burgundy-colored berry.

My hair gets separated into two parts. The back is pulled into a knot bun and the front is braided into five braids, all laid over the rest of my hair and tied into the bun. Barrettes with little pearls on the end are fastened into the bun to hold the braids in place. The woman who does my makeup gives me browns, bronzes, and desert reds; and for my lip color she goes with a slightly-darker-than-nude brown. When she holds the mirror in front of my face, I honestly can't believe I even had the potential to look this good. I feel a little funny when I realize that the one thing I want to do the most is take a selfie with natural lighting and send it to Gavin, just to put myself on his radar and see what he thinks.

"Sam, we have a situation—"

I look up to see Grace, Sloane, and Abby frozen in the doorway to the dressing room, staring at me, not Sam. They all look beautiful in their dresses. Sloane has on an indigo floor-length chiffon dress with silver leaf detailing around the neckline. Abby is wearing a pink dress with sequin embroidery and scallop sleeves. And Grace's dress reminds me of Halloween because it makes her look like a princess. It's a pale shade of blue with a pleated skirt and floral-print top.

"What?" Sam asks, making weird wide eyes at them.

Sloane makes different eyes at Sam, and I realize they're doing that thing where they have a conversation that no one can hear.

"The eagle hasn't landed," Abby says, winking.

"What?" Sam asks again.

"The eagle hasn't even left the nest," Grace adds, pushing a few tendrils behind her ear.

"The eagle is having car trouble—" Abby says, biting her lip.

"His car broke down," Grace corrects.

"What are you talking about?" Sam asks impatiently, picking up the front of her dress so that she can stand up.

Sloane tries to make eyes at Sam again, which looks weird, especially with Armao and Cheryl trying to mimic her facial expression.

"Ugh, just say it," Sam says.

"Gavin's car broke down, so he can't make it," Abby says, and she immediately steps back so that she's hidden behind Sloane, who is even taller than normal in her glossy black pumps.

"WHAT!" Sam screams. "NO."

"What?" I ask, looking down at my phone. Gavin still hasn't texted me since I sent him that emoji.

"Mia," Sam says, a lot quieter. "I was trying to do something, and . . . um."

"We could try picking him up?" Grace offers.

Sam's head jolts right back up. She checks her phone for the time and then turns to me. "Mia, Gavin doesn't have a girlfriend."

"What?"

"And we called him last night to see if he was doing anything today that would be better than spending a whole day with you," she explains.

"What? Wait, what?" I look down at my phone and text, Hey????

"We could try to go pick him up," Sloane says, tapping on her phone. "He texted me his address. It's not that far from here at all."

"Do you think you'll be back in time?" Sam asks, biting her lip.

"Would you be willing to stall for a little bit if we're not?" Sloane asks.

Sam looks from them to me, raising her eyebrows.

"I'm still stuck on you somehow figuring out that Gavin doesn't have a girlfriend, and *you*," I say, pointing at Sloane, "are *texting* him?"

"We can catch her up on the way," Grace says, taking my hand and pulling me toward the door.

"This will work. Everything will be fine," Sloane is saying. I hear her tell someone not to let Sam cry, and then I hear the door to the dressing room close. I don't see it, though, because Abby and Grace are ushering me down the hallway at the fastest pace we can move in high heels.

"What's going on? Can someone please tell me?" I plead.

"Sam asked me about Gavin's girlfriend," Abby explains. "She said she didn't believe you when you said he had one. So I said I didn't know anything about him. She asked your mom if she had his number, which your mom was able to get from Gloria, and your sister worked some magic—aka asking him direct questions over FaceTime—and found out that he doesn't have a girlfriend and he likes you."

"When?" I ask as we burst outside, none of us wearing coats.

"Last night, while I was helping her 'set up' the dressing room," Grace says, smiling.

Sloane catches up to us and holds her phone down so that we can all lean forward and look. I'm familiar with the street that his house is on. I've actually probably passed it before.

"Whose car are we taking?" I ask, looking around.

Right outside the entrance to the Butterfly Bed & Breakfast is a cobblestone walkway that winds down three steps flanked by winter aconite and two low-cut hedges. We follow the path around to the parking lot, which is full of Sam and Geoffrey's guests' cars. I can already see that my and Grace's cars are blocked in. Sloane runs across the wraparound driveway to where people have started double-parking, and when her shoulders sink, I can tell her car must be blocked too. Abby got a ride from Victor, but she doesn't even know where he is right now, to get his keys.

"What do we do?" I ask. I check my watch. It's 10:36. The wedding starts at eleven. The house is a little more than a mile away, which is nothing if we have a car.

"Let me see the map again," I say, looking down at Sloane's phone. "Why won't he respond to me?"

"He said his phone didn't charge last night, so it might be dead," Sloane says. "He hasn't replied to me for a bit."

"So, we can't even tell him to try walking here," Grace realizes.

I look around as more of the Davenports and Hubbards roll toward the inn. We're running out of time.

"*The Wedding Date*," Abby shouts, clapping her hands together.

"What?"

"*The Wedding Date*. It's a movie. At the end Nick is about to leave to go back to America after he and Kat have this big fight, and Kat realizes that he's the one for her, so she runs off to find him. It's, like, the end of your rom-com. All these meet-cutes, and now you have to go get your man, Mia! Now that we know who he is," Abby explains.

I think. The streets around here aren't that tricky, and I can use my phone to get to Gavin's house . . .

"Okay. I'll run to Gavin's house and we'll start walking back toward the inn. You guys go find Victor and get his truck and start driving on the path on Sloane's phone until you find us, okay?"

"Okay," Grace says. "So, should we—"

I don't hear the rest of what she says because I kick off my heels, take up the hem of my dress, and start running. All of my swim practices, drills, and out-of-water conditioning have made me ready for this. I run down the driveway, past my very confused-looking grandparents, and turn onto the residential street that the inn is on. I run to the end of the block, take a right, and start down my nearly-a-mile stretch. With every step my heart beats faster, my blood throbs through my head, and my arms grow tired from holding the dress. Instead of thinking about the pebbles I feel biting into the soles of my feet, I focus on everything else. I focus on Sam's wedding starting in less than fifteen minutes. I think about Gavin, liking me. I think about Gavin and me drinking Starbucks in the garden, about us sitting in his truck listening to music, about us hanging pipes in the greenhouse, about us texting about everything and nothing, about us awkwardly seeing each other outside the community garden for the first time . . . at the diner, when he came in and I was sitting with Ben on the night I was supposed to meet Darth Vader. I think about when I told Gavin that Ben was the guy I'd had a crush on, how excited I was that he'd showed up and saved the day, just minutes before Gavin came through the doors of November Always. I think about Gavin saying how much he doubted that Darth Vader was someone I didn't know, and Darth Vader telling me he wasn't a complete stranger. Suddenly it all clicks.

So when I turn my last corner and see a small figure dressed in black standing next to a pickup truck stuck at the end of a driveway, I run faster.

"Gavin!" I shout, my voice breaking without any breath.

His head snaps around and he starts running toward me.

"Mia!" he calls out when I'm just two houses down from his.

Then I crash into his arms, dropping my dress around my feet and leaning into him, wrapping my arms around him, feeling confident in knowing that he has feelings for me.

"Gavin," I huff, placing my hands on his chest and feeling how soft he is. I feel his hands sneak around my waist until his arms are basically the only things holding me up.

"Breathe, Mia," he tells me.

I force my head back so that I can look up at him, and wheeze a few more times. "Gavin, it was you. You are Darth Vader." He nods. "The lie? Your girlfriend?"

"When I saw you with Ben—" He stops, searching my eyes. "I thought you'd finally gotten the guy you wanted, without even giving me a chance."

"I didn't know," I tell him, feeling a little overwhelmed just thinking about it all. "When I stopped receiving mes-

sages from Darth Vader and we started texting I just figured he'd forgotten about me. Did you—"

"Smooth swap, huh?" Gavin smirks.

"Yes," I say, and laugh. He swapped his name into
Darth Vader's contact. I look right into his eyes. "Gavin,
I've been wanting the guy to be you."

"I like you Mia," he says, resting his forehead against
my sweaty forehead. "So much."

I snake my arms around the back of his neck, letting his
hair fill the space between my fingers. "I like you too," I
whisper into the small space between our lips.

Without hesitation, his lips find mine. They consume me
completely; the soft warmth makes me feel more alive than
I've felt in a long time. It feels like everything, but it feels
effortless too. Even though he's never held me in his arms,
it's like I've been here before. It feels like the place I belong.

"Nice kiss and all," Sloane shouts. "But I was really
hoping to see your sister get some action today, you know,
at the altar and stuff."

I turn around and see Victor's truck. Sloane is standing
in the truck's bed, wearing her winter coat and holding
mine. Abby and Grace wave from inside. Victor honks the
horn and gives a thumbs-up, though I can't tell if it's to me
or Gavin.

"Ready for a wedding?" I ask, looking up into Gavin's
eyes, their familiar darkness.

"And everything after that too," he says.

ACKNOWLEDGMENTS

First, I would like to thank my mentor and friend, Siobhan Vivian. Without you, my writing would not be where it is today and this project would not have been possible. I also would not have found my amazing agent, John Cusick, whom I am so excited to have by my side for this debut and for works to come.

Next, I want to express my gratitude to the editorial team at Simon & Schuster Books for Young Readers. You all have been so patient with me and made this experience brilliant and memorable. I remember reading the proof and still not believing that this is real! Krista Vitola and Dainese Santos, you both have been my rocks and pushed me to make this novel more than what I even imagined. Furthermore, I am grateful to copyeditors Jenica Nasworthy and Bara MacNeill for catching all the holes and saving characters from suddenly wearing glasses or spontaneously sprouting beards!

Thank you to Mel Cerri and Chloë Foglia for bringing Mia and the personality of these pages to life on the cover. Thank you to everyone at Simon & Schuster who helped make this book possible and helped get it into the hands of readers.

I must also thank my parents for always believing in me, and my brother, Thomas, for hyping me up.

Lastly, I want to thank my friend, roommate, and partner in crime, Brittany, for keeping me going and keeping me positive even when it has been hard to do so.